TANE'S WAR

TANE'S WAR

BRENDANIEL WEIR

First published in 2018 by Cloud Ink Press

www.cloudink.co.nz

Cover design: Suzanne Day
Book design: Greg Simpson

ISBN: 978-0-473-41564-8

Brendaniel Weir was born in Auckland and has
been an LGBT community activist since he took
part in the Homosexual Law Reform marches as
a schoolboy. He has written educational television,
worked in various roles in the film industry and
is a lecturer in English language.

In 2002, he won the Portal Magazine of Speculative
Fiction short story prize and in 2012 his Acrostic
Poem artwork *Super* exhibited at Auckland Council's
Nathan Homestead gallery. In 2013, he graduated
with a Master of Creative Writing (Hons.) from AUT,
also winning the post-graduate writing prize.
Tane's War is his first novel.

*To those who sacrificed for a society that wanted to forget them
and to those who still have to fight every day.*

PROLOGUE

DAVENTRY · 1899

THE **Y**OUNG **B**OY **C**LAPPED **H**IS **H**ANDS **IN** **G**LEE. 'Tell me the rest, Papa.'

'It's getting late, Zach. Perhaps you should sleep now.'

'Please!' Zach peeled back the blankets and jumped onto his father's lap. 'I want to hear the rest.'

The man ran his hand through Zach's blond hair. 'Well, alright, but after that it's straight to sleep.' Zach snuggled back against his father's chest and listened.

'Onward they whirled him, Those immortal steeds,
With joy that pair,
Bore battleward their lord,
Drawn by the immortal horses...'

Zach's hands shot into the air. 'Xanthos and Balios!' he finished.

The father laughed. 'I think you know it better than I do.'

Leaning forward, Zach grasped his father's shirt sleeves. He poked at the cufflinks that secured the stiff white linen around his father's wrists; silver links each displaying an enamelled horse head, one black, one white. 'Which one is Xanthos?' Zach asked.

The father placed his wrists side by side so the two horse heads were together. 'Xanthos means white,' he said. 'So he's the light one.' He picked up Zach and lay him back on the bed. 'Time for you to sleep.' He pulled the blankets up to cover the boy's shoulders.

'I want a chariot when I grow up,' said Zach, 'and two horses to pull me just like Xanthos and Balios.'

'Tell you what, when I get back from the war, we'll build you a trolley. We can yoke one of the ponies to it.'

Zach's face scrunched up. He rolled onto his side, away from his father. 'I don't want you to go to the war.' His voice was muffled by the pillow.

'No crying, Zach. You need to be grown-up about this.' The man placed his hand on the boy's shoulder. 'I'll be back from South Africa before you know it, and we'll build that chariot together.' Zach didn't reply; he just buried his face deeper in the pillow.

The father looked down at his son for a moment then undid his cufflinks and placed them beneath the lamp on the bedside table. 'I'll leave Xanthos and Balios here. Then you'll know I'm thinking of you.'

Zach rolled over and looked at the cufflinks. The two horses' heads were outlined with a bead of polished silver and, as they faced one another, the warm light flickered off the shiny metal. 'Do you promise to come back?'

'No soldier can make that promise, son,' he kissed the boy on the forehead, 'but don't you worry about me.' He turned the oil lamp key to extinguish the flame and the long glass shade, etched with a spiralling pattern of fern leaves, dimmed. The orange colour bled away until the ferns were silver and their shadows danced on the bedroom walls. The man turned to the door and with a final sputter, the flame died. 'Sweet dreams, son,' he whispered into the darkness.

CHAPTER 1

Pukekohe · 1953

IT WAS THE LONGEST SUMMER OF BRIAR'S LIFE. Winter seemed to end in the middle of the year when Edmund Hillary returned home. The picture of the tall Kiwi mountaineer, with the sun reflecting off the peaks behind him, filled the front pages and, for months, the whole of New Zealand celebrated the return of their favourite son. For Briar, it was all sunshine after that.

And 1953 just continued to get brighter. The new Queen of England announced she would visit Auckland in December. Briar's heart raced when he read that the royal tour would come right through Pukekohe. He dashed to his father's room, waving the article, and begged his father to take him to see the new monarch. He was given a terse *no* but the morning of the parade, his father reneged and they took the bus into the town centre, pushed themselves to the front of the crowd and, when the Royals passed, the whole world seemed to glisten.

'Mum would have loved that,' Briar said as they walked home. His father nodded then grew silent. Briar knew the silence was his father's way of crying. So Briar talked. He talked to fill the quiet left by his father's sadness. He talked because he felt guilty for bringing up his mother. He talked so he didn't have to think about her or be told for the thousandth time that he was just like her. When he got home, Briar smiled at his dad as though nothing was wrong then slipped into his room, took the photograph of his mother from the bookshelf and wrapped his arms around it. He lay on his bed, holding her, and didn't move until his father called him for dinner.

The next day they celebrated New Year's Eve. In the afternoon, Briar went with his father to the RSA and they sat at a table in the garden bar underneath a crisscross of crepe paper streamers and coloured light bulbs. His father went inside and when he returned, he was carrying two glasses of beer.

'You're almost sixteen,' he said. 'It's time you started being a man.'

They sat and sipped and Briar chatted about the new game of solitaire he was learning. His father was quiet, staring at his beer glass as though drinking was a serious business. When they had both finished, Briar's father slipped a couple of half-crowns onto the table.

'I'm going to be late tonight, son. After midnight I reckon.' He tapped the coins. 'Go have some fun. See a movie or something. I know you love the flicks.' Without waiting for Briar to respond, he stood up, took his glass and disappeared inside.

A few minutes later, Briar was walking the five blocks from the RSA to Alistair's house. He felt guilty because he knew his father wouldn't approve.

'I don't want you seeing that boy anymore,' his father had told him two weeks earlier.

'Why?'

'I've heard things about him.'

Briar had felt his cheeks redden. 'What do you mean? Alistair's my best friend.'

'Not any more. That's got to stop, right now,' his father had said. 'People are talking about him. You're to stop bringing him around here and you're not to go to his house either.'

'But his mum's...'

'That boy's mother is the problem,' his father had yelled. He'd calmed himself with a deep breath. 'She's been too soft on him. He's turning into a...' He'd stopped and just glared at Briar.

'A what?'

The palm of his father's hand had smacked the kitchen table making Briar flinch. 'You know what I'm talking about. We don't mention those sorts of people in this house. It's disgusting.'

So, for two weeks, Briar had only seen Alistair at school. They would sit together in classes they shared and, as soon as the bell rang to signal interval or lunch, they'd run to the library and find a quiet corner to huddle and chat about the movies. After school they'd walk home together, going as slow as they could to stretch out the time.

Now it was New Year and Briar couldn't bear to spend the evening alone. So he hurried up the path to Alistair's house and, when his friend answered the door, Briar held up the two half-crowns with a mischievous grin. Leaving the RSA, Briar felt the coins weighing heavily in his pocket, a consolation prize to pay for his father's absence. Now they were two gleaming possibilities.

Alistair went and spoke to his mother and came back with coins of his own. The two boys ran down the street, high on one another's company, with the rest of the year ahead of them.

They bought ice cream cones three scoops high and had to lick them as fast as they could so the drips of sticky yellow didn't fall on their legs. They swung on the swings at the park, pushing each other higher and higher until Briar flew out of the seat and rolled across the grass in fits of laughter. As the sun set for the last time in 1953, they bought tickets to an eight o'clock screening of *King Solomon's Mines*.

In the dark, they leaned their heads together and whispered, deciding which scenes they loved the most and which actors would win awards. At half time they rushed to the confectionary counter and lined up to buy Fanta and Jaffas, and when they saw a boy from their English class waiting ahead of them, Briar couldn't help laughing at the way he was wearing socks over the hems of his trousers. Alistair elbowed Briar to shut him up and they both closed their mouths tight, but the more they tried not to giggle, the more snorts of laughter escaped. The boy turned and scowled at them and when they went back to their seats, they saw him sitting stiffly between his parents so they sank down, trying to stay out of sight.

In the second half of the movie, Alistair and Briar found themselves swept up in the story. When the cannibals attacked, Briar jumped in fright and grabbed Alistair's arm. Alistair smiled and put his head against Briar's. As they leaned on one another, Briar became intensely aware of Alistair's presence, his long legs on the seat beside him, the slow movement of his Adam's apple as he breathed and the muscle in his shoulder that was brushing Briar's cheek. When Allan Quatermain gathered the heroine in his arms, Briar's heart was pounding and he looked up to find Alistair staring into his eyes. He craned his neck up, Alistair's lips pressed against his and they sat there in the darkness with their lips locked together and the movie soundtrack echoing their every feeling.

For three days, Briar couldn't get the smile off his face. He smiled to himself each morning as he made breakfast for his father. He grinned at the neighbours when they stopped by to deliver a batch of freshly baked scones and wish them a happy New Year. Every time he heard a love song on the radio, his eyes lit up and it seemed that the lyrics had been written just for him.

His happiness couldn't last. 1953 was over. The neighbour knocked on the door and told his father there was a phone call on the party-line. His father slipped on his shoes and went next door to take the call. He was gone for almost an hour and when he returned, he wouldn't look Briar in the eyes. He marched straight to the hall cupboard, pulled out a large leather satchel and passed it to Briar.

'Go to your room and pack your things,' he said.

'But...'

His father silenced him with a raised hand. 'This is not up for discussion. It's decided.' Briar's mouth hung open. He stared at the empty satchel. 'It's my fault,' his father muttered. 'After your mother was gone, I got soft.'

'What are you talking about? I don't understand.' Briar's whole face screwed up and a vein at the side of his head pulsed. 'Where am I going?'

'Just go pack your things. Now!'

There was a knock at the door and when his father answered it, a policeman was standing on the porch. He came inside, frowned at Briar and disappeared into the kitchen with Briar's father. Briar stood, rooted to the spot, staring after them. When they emerged a few minutes later, his father finally looked at him. It was a look of pure disgust.

'I told you not to have anything to do with that boy,' his father said.

Briar's eyes were filling with tears. 'Dad, please. We were just mucking around.'

'I don't want to hear it.'

'But we didn't do anything,' wailed Briar. 'He's my friend. Please don't do this.'

'This is what's best for you.' His father looked away, 'It's what you need.'

'But this is my home. I live here.' Briar's eyes flicked to the policeman. 'I don't want to go.'

The policeman stepped between Briar and his father. 'Just do what you're told, boy. It's time for you to become a man.'

CHAPTER 2

Hunua · 1954

BRIAR WAS DELIVERED TO THE FARM in an old truck. It bumped and twisted its way up the long driveway, trailing a plume of dust. The truck's body was tired, rusted and patched but the engine purred and sounded just like an Austin should. A reliable motor, oiled and cared for by men who knew, at least, how to love a machine.

Summoned by the squeal of brakes and the crunch of gravel, Tane emerged from the woolshed, wiping his hands on his faded black singlet. A tall man in his mid fifties, Tane's arms and shoulders revealed the sinewy muscles built by a lifetime of physical work. A faded anchor tattoo decorated his right arm and he walked with a slight limp. Behind him came a crew of teenage boys. They too were dressed in faded black singlets but, where Tane wore resignation, they wore smiles. The boys laughed and pushed one another—old enough to be learning a trade yet young enough to find fun in the work.

Stopping near the truck, Tane took a cigarette that had been tucked behind his ear and rolled it in his calloused fingers. From nowhere, he conjured a match, struck it to light the fag then with a lazy flick, sent it spiralling into a beaten tin that was nailed to the side of the shed. The spent match traced a line through the stifling air; an arc of tiny smoke rings marking its way to its target. It was the most mundane of magics, the sort of thing men learned in barracks and trenches where life's little pleasures helped pass the day. A subconscious trick for Tane but the boys noticed.

An older man climbed from the truck's cab. George Dwyte was in his sixties and pounds had started gathering at his waist. His linen shirt was pasted with sweat to his neckline. Arching his back, he sighed, removed his hat and ran fingers through hair that had long lost any hint of colour but retained a regimented military cut.

George nodded to the boys. 'Afternoon lads.'

'Afternoon Major Dwyte,' they replied in a ragged chorus.

Tane beckoned to one of the older boys, 'Aussie, get that truck unloaded, eh?'

With a quick nod, Aussie rounded up two of the younger lads. Leaping onto the deck of the truck, he started passing down groceries and farm supplies.

George left them to it. He turned to Tane, 'I got most of what you needed but I had to borrow some money from Dan Miller,' he said. 'So on the weekend, I'll need you to do the Millers sheep.'

'But he's way over in Ararimu. I need the boys here,' replied Tane. 'There's a lot of work piling up.' He frowned. 'Can't keep ignoring it or we gonna be short for grazing this winter.'

A pained expression crept across George's face. 'Tane, I trust you to manage things with the boys but I made a promise to the Millers.'

Tane scratched his head and shrugged. 'Well, I guess we could put off cutting the hay for another two or three days. No sign of bad weather.' His voice grew thoughtful, 'The boys would have to work Sunday...'

George cut him off with a pat on the shoulder. 'Good man, Tane. I knew you'd sort it out.'

From inside the Austin, Briar watched the two men talking. He felt like he had arrived in another country. The shock of being dragged from his life in the city had not been dulled by the long wordless drive across Franklin and up the twisting gorge road into the Hunua hills. He gathered up his framed photograph, his leather satchel and his fears and slipped out the passenger door of the truck. The farm boys stared at him, sizing him up. Some were older than Briar but most were around his age or a little younger. Yet, Briar knew he was skinnier and weaker than any of them. His flop of dark hair and clean shirt stood out amongst their short-back-and-sides and grimy singlets. He clutched his possessions like a shield.

George put a hand on the newcomer's shoulder. 'This is Briar,' he announced. 'The superintendent has asked me to put him to work on the farm.'

Tane grunted and looked Briar up and down. After a moment he shrugged. 'Well, I guess we can do with the extra hand.'

'Trust you to see the positive,' said George. He sounded relieved, glad to be passing Briar on. 'We were military men, if we can't sort him out, nobody can. Get Victor to show him the ropes.'

'I'm not sure Victor's the right person for that job...'

'Of course he is,' George interjected. 'He's the senior boy around here. I think of him as their sergeant.'

The sound of feet jumping to the ground made them glance back at the truck. It was now unloaded. George checked his watch then winked at Tane. 'Better get to my wireless. I've got a small fortune riding on that filly from Rotorua. She's a sure thing.'

'The four year old? ' said Tane. 'I thought she was lame.'

As the two men talked racehorses the farm boys gathered around Briar, throwing questions at him.

'How come you been sent to the farm?'

'Where you from?'

'Did you get in trouble?'

'Are you an orphan too?'

Briar felt like he was being shot at. He opened his mouth. Closed it. Opened it again. The farm boys stared and Briar felt his throat constricting. Everything was happening so fast. He tried to push out answers. *I shouldn't be here. It's all a mistake. They're going to take me back to my dad's.* No words would leave his throat. A blush spread across his cheeks and he hung his head, letting his hair cover his eyes.

George stepped around the front of the Austin and frowned when he saw the knot of farm boys. His voice rang out, silencing their questions. 'He got involved with some unsavoury people in the city. He's here to stay on the right path.' George scanned their faces until all eyes were lowered in submission. 'That's all you need to know and I don't want to hear any more about it! Understood?'

There was a muttered chorus from the boys, 'Yes, Sir.'

George spoke to Briar. 'The past is the past.' He nodded in the direction of the farm gate and the Hunua gorge beyond. 'We left your past at the bottom of that road. Do we understand one another?'

From the way George emphasised the word *past*, Briar knew the man had been told everything. He felt shame reddening his cheeks as he nodded in obedience.

George turned once more to the boys. 'I expect you all to make him welcome and show him what we do around here.' He glanced at Tane. 'All yours,' he muttered, then climbed back behind the wheel of the truck. The motor coughed to life, wheels turned on gravel and the old truck puttered up the driveway towards the large white farmhouse on the hill.

Tane watched George drive off then motioned towards the woolshed. 'Alright boys, back to work. Lessons start again at four and I want this flock finished.'

As the farm boys drifted into the shed, Tane called one of them back. 'Victor, come here.'

Victor jogged over. He had a pained expression on his face.

'What?'

'Since you're the oldest, you can show Briar the ropes. Start him on sweeping.'

'But I got the Young Shearer competition coming up. I can't look after some...' Victor scowled at Briar, 'some city kid.' He shrugged at Tane. 'Gotta concentrate on my training.'

'You'll do what I ask of you.'

'That's not fair. Get one of the younger guys to babysit,' moaned Victor.

'Enough of your lip.'

'But Mrs Dwyte wants me to...'

Tane cut him off. 'I'm well aware that Mrs Dwyte wants to show you off.' Tane took a breath, calming himself. 'You've got free time Friday afternoon. Do your training then. In the meantime, *Major* Dwyte needs this farm to pay its way and so long as you live here, you'll do as you're told.' Without giving Victor time to respond, Tane turned and walked away.

Victor muttered at Tane's retreating back, 'Stupid Māori shit.' He turned and glared his resentment at Briar. The silence stretched and Briar found himself holding his breath. Then, without a word, Victor turned and walked towards the woolshed. Briar just stood, clutching his photo and satchel, unsure whether he should follow.

Halfway to the shed, Victor called over his shoulder, 'Well, hurry up.'

The breath poured out of Briar. He began to follow Victor but was stopped immediately by the older boy's sneer.

Victor pointed at Briar's possessions. 'And you can leave that crap out here.'

CHAPTER 3

Hunua · 1954

BRIAR'S FIRST NIGHT AT THE FARM WAS A CONFUSION of rules, duties and timetables. He was shown through the dormitory, the kitchen-hall, the schoolroom and given schedules of work that had to be done. He felt numb as he muddled his way through it. The enormity of the change in his life finally registered as he lay on a narrow cot after lights out. In the dormitory around him he could hear other boys in their cubicles, the rustle of bedclothes and the shallow breath of sleep. In his own narrow cell, he curled into a ball and sobbed into his pillow.

'Check out the city kid,' laughed Victor when Briar stepped out of the dorms early the next morning. Briar was bleary-eyed and still half asleep. Victor stood in the yard, surrounded by several younger boys. 'You look like a sheep that's overdue for a good shearing.' Briar winced as Victor grabbed a handful of his hair and pretended to clip it from his head. A few of the boys sniggered.

'Why's ya hair so long?' asked a boy who was a couple of years younger than Briar. 'Makes ya look like a girl.'

'CityGirl! That's perfect,' said Victor. 'Maybe we should find him a dress.'

After breakfast, Briar was given work clothes; a uniform in truth, although nobody called it that but it defined them all as effectively as any prep school garb. Rough cotton shorts, a black singlet and a pair of oilskin chaps belted together with a hand-cut thong. The second-hand clothes hung awkwardly on Briar's skinny frame as though they knew he wasn't ready to fill them. The exception was the boots—black leather, scuffed from age and use, a deep crease across the upper from years of flex. They slipped easily over Briar's feet and fitted like they were made for him. Their soles were thick and serious, and when he laced them on he felt their weight swinging at the end of his legs like hammers. A feeling of power. Working men's footwear.

Tane appeared and led them to the woolshed. He told Briar to wait by the door while he set the boys to work. Briar was just beginning to think he'd been forgotten when Tane reappeared.

'Come with me, boy.' He took Briar by the shoulder and led him to where Victor was already oiling a complex looking handset. 'I just want you to watch today. From here you can see the whole gang. Try and get a feel for how the shed works. And don't be scared to ask Victor questions. You've got some catching up to do. Even the youngest boys are already clipping.'

Tane walked off and Victor scowled at Briar. 'I might have to put up with you standing there but if you get in my way, you're just another sheep.' He brandished the handset menacingly, a plated grey cylinder with an aggressive looking set of steel teeth at one end. 'These shears could hurt a soft little CityGirl.'

Briar stepped back, pressing against the wall. 'Ah sure. Don't worry, I'll stay back here.'

'Yeah, you do that.' Victor went back to adjusting the shearing handset. 'Anyway, dunno why you're watching me, you won't be using the Wolseley for years. Gotta master hand clipping first.' He nodded down the row of workstations where other boys were arming themselves with what looked like oversized pairs of scissors. 'Only me and Aussie are good enough to use the electric.

And I'm better than him—if anyone tells you otherwise, they're a liar.'

'So how long have you been using the electric machine? I mean, how long have you been here at the farm? I mean...' Briar's voice petered out as Victor glared at him.

'I'm twenty. *I'm* the oldest.'

Briar nodded.

Victor continued, 'I've been on the electric for almost three years.'

'Bet you're good with it then.'

'Good enough that I'm gonna be running this farm one day.'

From the far end of the shed there was the sound of a banging door followed by Tane's voice hollering 'first sheep'. Victor reached out and flicked a large switch high on the wall and Briar jumped as the shed around him sprang to life. A machine whirred; boys' voices called out and the sound of sheep's hooves on wooden slats echoed around the walls. The smell of animal urine and lanolin and dung, which Briar had noticed the moment he entered the woolshed, suddenly intensified, filling his nostrils. He screwed his face up and tried to breathe through his mouth.

A young boy appeared dragging a sheep on its back. To Briar, the poor animal looked limp, half dead with its eyes rolling and its head hanging back. As the boy pushed the animal into Victor's holding pen it suddenly kicked to life, springing into the air as though jumping some invisible barrier. Almost without looking, Victor stepped into his pen and grabbed the animal, hauling it to the centre of his station. With a deft sweep of his left leg, he clamped the animal between his calves and pressed his knees over its hips. In a single fluid motion his left arm swept the fore-legs back, exposing the belly and he bought the handset down to clip a clean stroke across the abdomen. Dirty wool fell away leaving a stripe of white so clean and dazzling that Briar found himself staring at it until Victor's voice yelled over the noise.

'This is how an expert does it.' He completed another perfect stroke. 'If you're not as useless as you look, you might be able to do this in about ten years.'

Briar watched, half horrified, half fascinated, as Victor worked the rest of the fleece from the sheep. He made the final cuts, shoved the naked animal down a chute at the back of his station, then hooked another from his pen. Moments later he was repeating the same rhythmic movements: press, sweep, flick, press, sweep, flick. To Briar, Victor was part of the machine.

For hours Briar watched the gang work. There were ten shearing stations and in eight of them, boys were shearing with handshears. Others delivered sheep or gathered up the fleeces. In the middle of the shed, more boys processed the wool on large tables or packed it into huge bags. The shearing machine was the beating heart of the woolshed. The motor, housed in the power room beyond a dirty plywood wall, spun a set of grooved wheels. Snaked around them, a series of serpentine belts transferred momentum above the boys' heads and across the shed, then, via the overhead gearwheel, down shafts that flexed like long skeletal fingers into each shearing station. The belts whirred and flapped and emitted a swarm of sounds that Briar could feel in his bones.

By the time Tane called lunch, Briar had developed a begrudging respect for Victor; his bragging seemed well justified. To Briar's unpractised eye, he could shear like a master.

The young boy who had been delivering sheep to the holding pens appeared at the opposite rail of Victor's station. 'How many did you do?' he asked Victor excitedly.

'Dunno. Wasn't counting. Clippers kept jamming so I was a bit slow.'

'I lost count,' Briar said to the boy.

'Oh, you still there?' Victor replied without looking at Briar. 'Thought you might of wandered off when you saw the hard work begin.'

The young boy looked over at Briar. 'He sure is fast, eh? It's so crap that we have to use hand shears when *we're* on shearing.'

'What's wrong with hand shears?' Briar asked.

'They're so old fashioned! Ancient technology. We should all be learning on the electric.'

Tane appeared behind the complaining lad. 'You need to learn first things first, Tommy.'

Tommy flicked around to face Tane, 'Oh sorry, Sir. Was just telling the new guy that most of the woolsheds around have electrics in them now.'

'Which is no reason to ignore traditions. The old way teaches you to respect the fleece.'

'But when we go out working we'll all be using electric shears.'

'If you can't master a pair of hand-shears, you will always be sloppy on the machine.'

'But why...'

'I don't need your opinion, boy. Get your arse up to the dining hall.' Tane waved his hand dismissively. 'All of you.'

CHAPTER 4

Hunua · 1954

BRIAR DUCKED AS ANOTHER FLEECE WAS THROWN. This time it was from the other side of the table. 'Sorry,' he muttered, whipping his broom out of the way.

Four boys, in two teams of two, were gathering up the freshly shorn fleeces and hurling them onto the trimming table. They moved around the shed, gathering each clipped fleece as soon as it was off the animal, and Briar seemed to always be in just the wrong place.

After a week at the farm, he still felt as awkward as the day he'd arrived. While younger boys sheared and dagged and skirted and packed, he had been assigned to sweeping and clearing the tables after the edging and rolling of each fleece. It seemed a simple task. Yet it eluded him. The secret was in the timing. There is a rhythm to a shearing gang, one based on common understanding; a knowledge of the underlying structure of the work—its bars and phrases and rests. He had been told what he should be doing but he was constantly offbeat.

At the top end of the shed, Victor was setting the pace. As he turned a sheep to finish the tail end, he cast his eye to the slim boy working with hand-shears in the station alongside him.

'You're not trimming a bloody rosebush, Reggie. Clip lower!

You're leaving half the damn fleece on.'

'It's not that much,' Reggie replied.

'It's half a bloody inch.'

Reggie grunted and pushed his clippers deeper into the wool. Victor flicked the last tuft off his own ewe and pushed her into the chute. Turning to his holding pen, he found no replacement waiting for him.

'Sheep!' he yelled just as a boy appeared dragging an animal. Victor stepped out and grabbed the boy by the collar. 'Get a bloody move on. Nobody slows *me* down.'

Briar looked around at the sound of Victor yelling for a sheep. He watched the twenty year old berating the younger boy, and was quietly relieved that, for once, it wasn't aimed at him.

'Watch out!' a voice called from behind Briar. Distracted by Victor's outburst, Briar was moving too slowly and a falling fleece trapped the head of his broom against the table. He jerked the broom to free it but the freshly cut fleece was not as light as it looked. The wool lifted and packed, snaring the broom's head and, instead of retrieving his tool, Briar fell and rolled backwards into the ewe being shorn in the bottom station. As he turned around to apologise, the sheep kicked, one hoof bashing him hard in the forehead. He yelled and crunched forwards, clutching his head in pain.

Victor's howl of laughter echoed down the woolshed. He pointed at Briar with his handset. 'Man, that's the funniest thing ever. What a dork!'

The whole shed turned to look at Briar. Within seconds, the rhythm of labour was replaced by a chorus of jeers.

Victor called out to Briar, speaking slowly, one syllable at a time as though he was addressing an idiot, 'You sweep the table when it's empty. Not when it's full, CityGirl.' This elicited another round of laughs.

Watching from the work station opposite, Aussie frowned, 'Leave him alone, Victor. Can't you see he's hurt?'

'Sod off, Aussie. What's it to you?' The two older boys glared at one another as Briar knelt on the floor, clutching his forehead.

Another boy pointed at Briar's broom, still trapped under the fleece.

'Look, he doesn't even know how to lift a pile.'

Seeing the broom trapped in the fleece, Victor's eyes narrowed. 'That was a perfect fleece. If you marked it, I'm gonna mark you.'

Briar felt his cheeks turning red. He stumbled to his feet. 'I gotta use the loo,' he muttered and bolted from the shed.

Outside, Briar sat on a hay bale, head in hand, his shoulder hunched against the dirty green iron of the woolshed. At the sound of approaching footsteps, he glanced up to find Aussie looking down at him.

'Hey, are you okay?'

'Don't worry about me. I'm just the stupid kid from the city.'

Aussie shrugged. 'Look, forget about Victor. He just wants to look cool.'

Briar could feel the bruise already spreading across his forehead. He dropped his hand from his face and Aussie winced as he caught sight of the discoloured bump. 'He hates me,' said Briar. 'They all hate me.' His voice was on the edge of tears.

Aussie tilted his head and smiled gently. 'Not all of them'.

Briar looked at him for a moment, not understanding. Then, as he recognised the gesture of friendship, he felt ashamed of his self-pity. He muttered a reply, 'I keep trying so hard, but I'm really bad at this. I can't even lift a full fleece.'

'It takes a while to get the knack. Give it some time, alright?'

'I'm just getting in their way. It's no wonder they don't want me in there.'

'They always rag someone new.' He reached a finger out and touched Briar's bruise. 'You've gotta have a thick skin.' Briar still looked unsure. Aussie put a hand on his shoulder. 'I'll look out for ya. But you've gotta stand up for yourself. Especially with Victor.'

Aussie raised an eyebrow. 'He's a bit of a coward under all that bluster.'

'He's angry at me all the time.'

'I think he can tell that you're smart.'

'What do you mean?'

'He was crap at school. He couldn't finish third form. He even had a fight with the teacher. Tried to hit her.'

'Why?'

'Cos she used to make him read out loud. Or try to. He wouldn't do it. Just sat there every time and scowled at her.'

'Maybe he just hates reading.'

Aussie shook his head. 'One day when Major Dwyte came by, she dragged Victor up the front and told him to read a poem. Victor went bright red then started yelling at her. Kept saying that the letters looked backwards. He threw the book at her and she called him a lazy idiot. Major Dwyte had to get between them. Hold Victor back.'

'That's mad.'

'Yeah well, he never came back to the schoolroom after that. When we had lessons he'd get work around the farm.'

'Why does he have to take it out on me?'

'He's testing you. To see if you're scared.'

'He is scary.'

Aussie shrugged. 'Some of the other boys think so too. Especially the younger ones. But they all call him "dunce" behind his back.' He tapped Briar's chest with his finger. 'Just do yourself a favour. Stand up for yourself. Sooner you do that, the sooner he'll leave you alone.'

Briar took a deep breath. 'Okay, I'll try,' he said.

Aussie smiled. 'Good. Come on then, back to work, eh?' He slid his arm over Briar's shoulder and guided him back into the woolshed.

CHAPTER 5

Hunua · 1954

FROM THE HIGHEST RIDGE ON THE DWYTE FARM, Briar squinted westwards. In the hazy distance, across the Karaka flats, he could just make out the smudge of Pukekohe. He closed one eye and reached out his hand to hold the town between thumb and forefinger. How could the place that had been his whole world appear so small? He laid his head against his sleeve and sighted down his arm. Bang! He screwed both his eyes shut and his mind was a bullet flying through the air. Away from Hunua, over Karaka, over the railway and past the school. He landed outside his father's house and his old life filled his mind; the white letterbox and chain link fence, the textured wallpaper that smelled of stale pipe smoke, his bed which he had made the morning he left and the blue weatherboards, dirty and peeling under the eaves where the rain never washed. And the front door. A heavy timber frame with a sailing ship etched into the glass panel; a picture he had traced with his finger a thousand times as a child. It all seemed so near and for a moment he imagined he was back there but the soundtrack of cicadas and bleating sheep filling his ears was at odds with the picture in his mind, and he couldn't hold on to the daydream.

Briar opened his eyes again and farmland surrounded him.

The dark green hills on either side seemed like the walls of a prison. A prison he'd been incarcerated in for two weeks. He turned and ran down the hill, slipping into the woolshed just as Tane appeared from his office to call 'first sheep.'

Briar reached for a broom then winced as a hand grabbed his shoulder. The grip was like a vice. He turned to find Victor scowling at him. The older boy pushed him down the shed. 'You're still useless at sweeping but Tane says you have to learn something new.' He rolled his eyes at the suggestion Briar could learn anything then stopped at the bottom of the shed in front of the main pen. He pointed at the boy who was stepping through the gate. 'Take over from Ty. Push the sheep in from outside and bring 'em to the shearers.' Without any further instruction, he walked away.

Briar looked into the main pen. Two sheep cowered in the far corner. He looked up at Ty. 'Um, how do I get them on their backs?' he asked.

Ty closed the gate and mopped his forehead with his singlet. 'You just twist their front legs. But there's only a couple left. We should get some more in here first.'

Victor's voice hollered down the shed. 'Get up here, Ty!' Ty winced and they both turned to find Victor glaring in their direction.

'Could you just tell me how?' Briar asked hastily.

Ty wouldn't look Briar in the eye. 'Um, you'll work it out.' Without another word, he walked away.

Briar scratched his head, trying to work out how to get more sheep inside. He'd spent all his time at the other end of the shed and he'd never seen it done. He noticed a framework that looked like a chute in the back wall. The last two sheep were cowering against it and he figured that was where they came in but the corrugated iron of the wall seemed to continue down to the ground and, from where he stood, there didn't appear to be an opening.

'Hey, mate.'

Briar jumped. He flicked around to find Aussie standing beside him.

'So much for Victor showing you the ropes. Come on, I'll get you started. It's pretty simple.'

'Won't Victor be mad at you for helping me?'

'I don't care and anyway, he can't tell me how to do my job. I've been here almost as long as he has.' He motioned for Briar to follow him outside.

Briar swallowed with relief and hastened after Aussie.

Outside, the stockyard was packed with hundreds of sheep that the boys had driven in from the lower paddocks the night before. The enclosure was twenty feet from the woolshed and a narrow race connected it to the woolshed wall. The sheep in the yard looked wary.

'How come they were in there all night?' Briar asked.

'Helps them empty out,' said Aussie. He raised his eyebrows. 'Believe me, you don't want 'em pissing and crapping all over your station. Gets impossible to work. Besides, it's bad for them to be on their backs with a gut full.'

He led Briar to the race and showed him how the trap-gates at either end of the race slid upwards to open a passage through into the woolshed. The gate in the shed wall was a sheet of corrugated iron with a handle riveted to it. Briar slid the contraption up and down, marvelling at how perfectly the two sheets fitted together. It was no wonder he hadn't been able to see it from inside.

They circled around to the back of the stockyard and Aussie clapped his hands and kicked the lower rail to harry the sheep forwards. The animals pushed away from the noise, pressing even tighter. Then, like a valve opening, one sheep stumbled into the race, followed by a surge of others. Aussie dashed back to the gate, waited until a few dozen sheep had passed through, then pushed it down.

'There. That'll keep you going for a while,' said Aussie. He led

Briar back inside and took him into the main pen.

'Hooking them can be a bit of a runaround,' said Aussie.

'Hooking?'

'Catching them. We call it hooking.' Aussie frowned in thought for a moment then shrugged. 'Dunno why.' He eyed the sheep. 'Anyway, the trick is to use their flocking instinct.' He chose his target then advanced quietly towards the tightly gathered animals. 'Just press 'em gently until one runs. They'll all follow the leader and you can grab the back one.' A nervous energy surged through the sheep and they leapt away. He darted forward and plucked one from the back of the bunch as they rattled past. In a single fluid movement, he reached over its shoulder and grabbed its foreleg, lifting the front of the animal and sweeping its back legs off the floor. He backed out of the swing gate dragging it towards his shearing station. Aussie winked at Briar, 'I'll leave you too it. You'll get the hang of it.'

Over in the shearing stations Briar could see a couple of empty side pens. He realised he didn't have long. He looked at the animals in the main pen with him. They suddenly seemed larger. He took a deep breath, inhaling the musky stink of wool, and wondered who was more nervous.

Aussie had made hooking look easy but Briar had never been a physical child. He was city born and bred and, while his father had always given him chores to complete, he had encountered very little hard labour. At school there had been sport to develop their constitution but his skinny frame and wistful nature had marked him as a liability on most sports fields. In a world where school pride was measured through rugby, cricket and athletics, the tall and powerful had relegated the short and skinny to the benches. Books and imagination had been Briar's exercise.

He had no choice. The time had come to get physical. He took a deep breath and stepped forward. As one, the sheep's heads turned towards him. He crouched a little and pushed towards the rearmost animal with his arms held ready in front of him. They bunched up even tighter and their heads began flicking from side to side, looking for an escape route. Briar stepped again, a slow tiny step. Another. Then another. He could almost reach out and grab one. Suddenly they were moving, with a sound like a flock of startled birds. He sprang forward knowing, even as he did, that it was too late. His hands clutched at empty air and he back-peddled awkwardly, slipping over and crashing into the side of the pen. The sound of laughter echoed along the shed and, as he picked himself up, he noticed several farm boys pointing, enjoying the entertainment.

Three more times Briar tried, and each failed attempt increased his embarrassment. Picking himself up for the fourth time he noticed Aussie watching from the far end of the shed. Deep down, he felt something change. A spark of determination flashed through his mind. He needed to prove that Aussie's faith in him was not misplaced.

Briar squared his shoulders, crouched down and advanced once again on the flock. This time he didn't wait for the sheep to move. Instead, he lunged out a moment before he thought they were about to run. It worked. He felt his hands closing around fistfuls of warm wool. It was not graceful. The momentum of the animal pulled Briar off his feet and the reek of sheep shit filled his nostrils as his face hit the floor. But he didn't let go. He pushed himself onto his knees and got his arms around the animal's chest then, slipping and sliding, clambered to his feet. As he dragged the sheep across the pen, his teeth gritted and his face smeared with muck, the boys who had been watching turned back to their work.

Briar used his elbow to unlatch the swing gate just as he had seen Aussie do. He flicked the gate inward with his boot, pushed his hip into the opening and dragged the sheep out. Glancing over his shoulder he noticed Aussie watching him. A smile spread across the older boy's face and he gave Briar a thumbs-up. Briar felt a surge of pride that was completely out of proportion with the mundane nature of his accomplishment.

Mastering that small task and catching his first sheep, in its own way, altered Briar's world. The small boost in self-confidence changed his perspective. As he delivered sheep to the shearer's holding pens, he felt, for the first time that he could be useful. As he let go of the fear of failure, he began to sense things in the woolshed he hadn't noticed before. He was not the only target. Others, too, received their share of teasing. The banter was light-hearted, a mild sort of mocking that reinforced the connection between the workers. To his genuine surprise, it was a connection he yearned to be a part of.

After lunch they returned to the shed and work resumed, Victor and Aussie in the top two work stations using the electrics and eight other boys shearing by hand. Briar was still finding it difficult to catch the sheep but once he had one, he had mastered the art of twisting them onto their backs. He would drag them up the shed to fill Aussie or Victor's side pens or deliver them directly to the younger boys who were shearing by hand.

An hour later, Victor paused, clutching a half-shorn animal between his legs. He frowned at the wall behind him. Putting down his handset but still holding his sheep with one arm, he leaned awkwardly and pressed his eye up to the wall. There was a gap between the wallboards at the back of his station offering a narrow peep into Tane's office. He smiled then shoved his half-shorn animal back into his holding pen. He waved to the two boys gathering fleeces.

'Davey. Roy. Come check this out!' The two younger boys dropped what they were doing and dashed over to have a look. As Roy peered through the gap, Victor nudged him. 'See, I told you! She's back. That's the slut that was here before.'

Roy turned and frowned at Victor. 'How d'ya know she's a slut?'

Victor sneered at the younger boy's naivety. 'Didn't see her come from the house, did ya? She must be sneaking onto the farm. Why else do you think she'd do that?'

'Oh, right.' said Roy.

Davey shoved Roy out of the way and peered through into Tane's office. 'Is she sexy?' he asked Victor without looking up.

Victor grimaced in disgust. 'Don't be gross, she's a Māori.'

Davey wasn't really listening. He wiggled his hips excitedly. 'I'd sleep with her.' He glanced up. 'Are they gonna do it?'

'Probably,' said Victor.

Half way down the shed, Briar had just handed a sheep to Col when he heard the sound of hooves on wood. He flicked around to find a half-shorn sheep running towards him. He acted instinctively, reaching out and grabbing it as it leapt past. He looked the animal over. The clipped lines were tidy and cut very close to the skin. This had been shorn on the Wolseley. He looked towards the two electric stations. Aussie was head down, busy with a sheep but Victor along with two boys was peering through the wall and his holding pen was open, the gate wedged on the loose floorboard.

Briar called up the shed. 'Victor, this one isn't finished. Where should I put it?'

Victor and Aussie looked up at the same time. Aussie frowned when he saw Victor crouched by the wall. 'Damn, Victor. You're slowing us down.' He waved his handset at Roy and Davey. 'You two, get back to work.'

The boys dashed off, looking guilty.

Victor balled his fists. 'Piss off, Aussie. You're not the boss.'

'No one's the boss. We're all meant to be working.'

'Don't tell me what to do. I'm the best *shearer* here and I'm the one who gives the orders.'

'I don't care if you can shear in your sleep,' Aussie said. 'I just wanna finish up quick. We have free time tonight.'

By now, all the boys had stopped and were looking. Several muttered agreement. Victor glowered. 'Stuff you, Aussie!' He stormed over and snatched the half-shorn ewe from Briar. He leaned close to Briar's ear, 'I'm gonna get you later, you prick.'

Briar stiffened at the threat. He glanced past Victor at Aussie who gave him a little nod, encouraging him to stand up for himself.

Taking a deep breath, Briar straightened up. 'Stuff you, Victor. I didn't do anything wrong.'

For a second Victor looked shocked. Then he exploded. He let go of the sheep and grabbed Briar, one hand seizing his shirt and the other closing around his throat. He shoved Briar backwards, slamming him into a wooden post. Briar dangled, feet off the floor, and Victor spat his words.

'Little shit. Think you're smart?'

Before Briar could choke a reply, there was a yell from the top of the shed. Aussie vaulted over the side of his station and in six flying strides, he crashed between them, breaking Victor's grip.

CHAPTER 6

Hunua · 1954

THE INSIDE OF TANE'S OFFICE WAS DIM. Bronze sunshine, filtered through a cobwebbed window, bathed everything in aged light. A line of harder daylight snuck around the edges of the door, highlighting a fine layer of dust on the floor. Against one wall sat an old timber desk with a mismatching chair and above it an ink drawing pinned to the wall—a lone cavalryman on a horse. Apart from a mug holding a handful of pencils, the desk was empty, its surface scarred with dents and gouges. Beside it, a sturdy shelf held dozens of wool ledgers, a few old books and a large valve radio.

Opposite the desk a doorway led into the woolshed. This internal door was closed but the noises of the shed washed through the wall, muted by the layer of thick wallboards.

A tall Māori woman stood face to face with Tane. She had short hair and wore flowing black slacks. Her grey shirt, sleeves rolled up, was covered by a threadbare tailored vest, its embroidered silver lilies worn to a grey swirl.

Tane looked down at a photograph in his hands, a faded black and white picture showing a statue of two rearing horses. He brushed his thumb along the bottom of the frame to rub away the dirt and peer at the lettering beneath. It read 'Xanthos and Balios'.

'Where'd you find this?' Tane asked the woman.

'I went back to the house in Awhitu. It's deserted now. Just birds and rats.'

His nod was almost imperceptible. 'That's sad.'

'The picture was in the fireplace, in the ashes. The light caught it…' She paused, tilted her head, 'I think it wanted to be found.'

Tane smiled at the idea of the picture finding her. 'I haven't seen this for years. I thought it was lost,' he said.

The woman smiled. 'I knew it was yours, Dad. You told me that story a hundred times. Xanthos and Balios, Achilles' horses. They couldn't be beaten so long as they stayed together, eh?'

'That's right, my girl.' His fingers momentarily touched his chest where a shape was hidden beneath his singlet. 'That picture was given to me after the war.'

'You never told me *that* before.'

Tane's eyes glazed as he became lost in whatever memory he was recalling. His brow creased slightly. 'It was from a friend's mother.'

The woman opened her mouth to ask more about the picture but seeing the conflict on her father's face, she changed her mind. Remembering the reason for her visit, she straightened herself up. 'Dad, I came to tell you something. Something important.'

He nodded, waiting for her.

'I've met someone. His name's Paul. He's from Wairarapa. We're going down to live on his farm.' She held her breath as she waited for his response.

Tane reached out and took her hand, a smile lighting up his face. 'Ano te pai, my girl. I'm happy for you.' He paused for a moment. 'Have you told your mother?'

She pulled her hand away. 'Why should I tell her?'

'Mere cares about you. You should talk to her.'

'But we always end up fighting.'

'That's because you and Mere are so similar.'

'I'm *not* like her,' she snapped.

'She'd want to know. She's your mother.'

'I doubt she'd give a damn.' She put her hands on her hips. '*You* raised me. Not her. You're my family so I'm telling *you*.'

He held up his hand. 'Okay, okay. I know better than to argue with my little storm.'

'Not so little any more, eh?' She straightened her back to show off her full height. 'I think I'm officially a big girl now.'

He shook his head at her antics. 'I wish you'd visit more often'.

'I don't really like it here. You know that. The Dwytes are creepy. So many secrets.'

'Don't judge the Major. The last war changed him.' Tane frowned. 'Can't even imagine the choices he had to make.'

'It's not him, it's his wife. When she looks at me, it's like she's looking at dirt.' She put her hands on her hips. 'She looks at you that way too. Why do you stay here?'

Tane stopped her by holding up a hand. 'I don't expect you to understand. The Major and I went through a war together. He's part of my life—of my past. I can't just leave him—he needs me.'

The woman scowled, but after a moment she nodded. The two of them just looked at one another. Eventually she broke the silence, 'Dad, I've been wanting to ask you something.'

Tane just waited.

'How come *you* never lived with anyone? Was it because of me?'

Tane's face darkened and he looked away. 'Girl, it's complicated.' He stared out the dirty window beside his desk. 'When Wiremu didn't come back from the war, your mother, well, she couldn't cope.' He looked at her and his expression softened. 'It doesn't matter. *You* were the most important thing. Looking after you brought love into my life again.'

'Again?' His daughter raised an eyebrow. 'So there was someone?'

He shook his head. 'It doesn't matter. It's a long time ago.'

'It does matter. I want to know.'

'It's the past. I don't want to talk about the past anymore.

You're here to tell me about your future.'

The woman wasn't listening. Her eyes were creased in thought. 'Was it before the war?'

'Enough. I've forgotten the bloody war.' His voice was a little louder than he had intended and he raised his hands in apology. 'It wasn't like people think.'

She stepped forward, took the picture from him and put it on the desk. Then she took both his hands in hers. 'Dad, don't be angry. You don't have to talk about the war. I just want to know about her.' She shrugged. 'Did she live in New Zealand? Was she Māori? Is she still alive?'

He struggled to find words. 'You wouldn't understand. It was a mad time. We were so young...' He was silent as he wrestled with his thoughts. Finally he shook his head. 'No. That was another life. It's gone now.' He drew in a long breath and stepped back to look at his daughter. 'You've come with good news. I really am happy for you.'

'Thanks Dad. I was worried you might be upset because I'm going away.'

'Well, it makes me think I should've seen you more these past few years.'

A loud knock sounded at the inside door and they both glanced towards it. 'Damn. I better check on the boys.' He waved at his chair. 'Have a seat. I'll just be...'

The knock sounded again, more urgent this time, accompanied by the muffled sound of raised voices through the internal wall.

The woman glanced towards the outside door. 'My ride will be here any minute. Sounds like you're busy so I'll leave you to it.' She threw her arms around him. 'I'll visit again soon,' she whispered.

'Good to see you, girl.' He sighed. 'I'm gonna miss you when you're gone.'

She pulled away, tugged at her waistcoat then slipped outside, throwing a last smile over her shoulder as she went.

He stared at the door as it closed behind her.

The knock sounded again on the internal door, breaking his reverie. 'Wait a damn minute!' he called.

He reached inside his shirt and pulled out a military-issue chain from around his neck. Hanging from it was a pendant. He looked at it fondly for a second then, touching it to his lips, he placed it back inside his shirt.

Straightening his shoulders, he turned and crossed his office. Opening the internal door, he was confronted by the sound of raised voices cutting through the noise of the woolshed.

A worried looking young boy stuttered, 'Sir... Sir, Victor and Aussie is fighting in...'

Before the boy could finish, Tane stormed through the doorway.

In the woolshed, Victor threw another punch at Briar but Aussie shoved Victor's shoulder fending off the blow. Victor growled in frustration and redirected his attack at Aussie. Briar started yelling at Victor to stop and, around the shed, all work halted as the farm boys watched the escalating fight.

Tane appeared from his office doorway and his voice cut through the shed. 'Stop that right now!' The boys paused, just long enough for Tane to cover the distance. He grabbed Victor's collar and hauled him back, spinning him around and towering over him.

'What do you think you're doing?' Tane yelled.

Victor pointed at Briar. 'That little CityGirl let my sheep loose. He's useless!'

'The boy's only been here two weeks! You're meant to be training him. Not bullying.'

Aussie piped in. He was bristling. 'Victor's had it in for Briar from the first day...'

'Enough!' snapped Tane. He glared at Aussie and Victor. 'You two are here to help on the farm, not act like a couple of delinquents.'

Aussie looked aggrieved to be sharing the blame. 'But I was just...'

Tane was not interested in hearing anybody's excuses. 'Shut it, boy!'

Apart from the whirr of the Wolseley, the woolshed had grown silent. Tane turned around and glared at all of the farm boys. 'I've taught you better than this.' He shook his head. 'On this farm we're a family. We help each other. We don't fight.' He turned back to Aussie and Victor and with a quick glance at Briar, reached a decision. 'All three of you can come back after dinner and do scrubbing.' He nodded dismissively to Aussie and Victor. 'You two, get back to work.'

As the woolshed pulsed back into action, Tane scowled at Briar. 'Come with me, boy.'

Moments later, Briar stood nervously beside Tane's desk. The internal door was still open and he could hear the sounds of work restarting in the woolshed behind him. Words tumbled through his mind as he tried to construct an explanation for what had happened. *I didn't start it. He was picking on me. His sheep was loose.* The phrases lined up on his tongue like ammunition waiting to shoot down Tane's anger.

'I know this is hard for you,' Tane said quietly, and his fingers drummed lightly on the desk.

Briar hesitated, caught out by Tane's unexpected tone.

Tane continued. 'I've known the superintendent a long time. He's a wise man. Strict but fair. If he sent you here, then this is the right place for you to be.'

Briar's shoulders dropped and his eyes teared up. 'But I don't want to be a farmer.'

Tane frowned. 'You need to accept your new life. It might seem hard for now, but the past will fade.'

Briar shook his head. 'No. I'm going to get back to my life.

Back to my friends and my dad and my school.' He swallowed and squeaked. 'One day.'

Tane stood up and placed a hand on the boy's shoulder. 'Briar, life doesn't always give us what we want.' He nodded towards the open door. 'This is your home now. In time, the boys will accept you. They'll become your friends. Your family.'

Briar looked at Tane's face. At the concern he could see behind the weathered features. He wanted to scream his defiance. To tell Tane he was *not* going to stay, *not* learn to shear, *not* be part of the farm but when he opened his mouth, his father's face appeared, frozen in a permanent expression of disappointment and disgust. Briar's mouth closed and he remained silent.

'Cheer up, boy. I hear you're improving.' He nodded at Briar's skinny arms. 'And with more work, you'll grow stronger. Now smile and get back to work, eh?'

Dismissed, Briar headed for the door. He looked down at his feet passing across the floorboards of Tane's office and for a moment he didn't see boots. He saw sandals crossing the pedestrian bridge at the Pukekohe railway station each morning, he saw bare feet racing down the timber hallway of his father's house when he got home each afternoon. He saw the polished shoes he'd borrowed from Alistair for the prize giving last year.

He spun around. 'I was good at school!'

Tane just looked at him.

Briar's fists clenched at his sides. 'I was the best in my class! I always got good marks. And my teachers liked me.' He stopped. His shoulders slumped and the tears that had been welling finally forced their way out. 'It's not fair!' his voice cracked. Tears rolled down his face and he sobbed for a full minute as Tane watched.

Finally the tears stopped. Briar sucked a wet breath. 'You don't know what it's like!' He looked up into Tane's eyes. 'To be ripped out of your life. To be told you can't go to school anymore!' For a moment he glared at the man standing silently watching him. Then he spun around and disappeared into the woolshed.

Tane looked at the empty doorway as Briar's angry words echoed in his office. He slumped back in his chair and his head nodded almost imperceptibly. 'Oh I know what it's like, boy,' he muttered. 'I remember all too well.'

CHAPTER 7

AUCKLAND · 1912

THE VIEW FROM THE CROW'S NEST MADE TANE'S heart beat faster. It wasn't just the breathless climb, hand over hand halfway up the mizzenmast or the dizzying height once he was in the tiny crow's nest. Or even the way the steamship's gentle sway was magnified into an exhilarating swing. The real reward was the feeling of freedom that surged through him as he looked down at the wharves beneath. The piers reached into the harbour like wooden fingers snaring ships that sailed up the Waitemata.

Tane stretched himself up so the crow's nest rail was pressed against his abdomen then, grasping the rail, he tensed his body, closed his eyes and slowly tilted his chest forward until his feet lifted into the air. His head and shoulders sank and his legs rose until he reached the balancing point. For a moment he lay there, his rigid body horizontal. The only thing holding him was the hard steel rail clenched in his fists and pressing a line across his stomach. Then, one finger at a time, he released his hands, first his left, then his right. He stretched his arms out, stopping every few inches, aware of each tiny movement. Finally his arms were wings. He teetered there as the ship swung back and forth and gusts of wind whistled through wires. He was flying. He snapped his eyes open and looked straight down. Barges and ferries churned white water around the pilings. Wharfies scurried across the deck unloading nets of cargo onto carts and trucks. He was a bird, soaring above them all, above the docks, above the harbour. If he lifted his head and flapped his wings he could catch the wind and fly off to any place in the world.

'Down you come, Tane!' yelled Mr Gilbert, hands cupped around his mouth.

The world rushed up and seized Tane as he grabbed the railing again. His heart was pounding. 'Coming!' he hollered as he tilted his feet back onto the floor of the crow's nest. He took one final glance at the view then, holding the railing with both hands, vaulted out of the nest and onto the mast ladder. He swung from side to side as he descended, his hands jumping every second rung until he leapt the last six feet to the deck.

Mr Gilbert shook his head. 'You're a damned sea monkey.' The towering stevedore smiled indulgently down at Tane. 'If your mother knew I was letting you climb up there, she'd probably kill me. So don't you go telling her.'

'Don't worry, I won't say nothing.' Tane looked back up to the crow's nest, 'Can I climb it again? Before they sail?'

'Dunno about that, lad. We'll have her loaded soon.' He frowned in thought. 'I imagine the captain will be away on the ten o'clock tide.' He looked out towards North Head and the channel beyond. 'Don't worry, there's always another ship. If not, I'd be out of a job!'

'I guess.' Tane sounded disappointed.

Mr Gilbert patted him on the shoulder then tapped his boot on the ship's deck. 'Can you remember her vital statistics?'

Tane's mood brightened. He straightened up and started reeling off figures. 'Yep. The *Lady Trident*. She's a converted corvette. Built in '89. Two hundred and sixty-four feet stem to stern. Forty-two foot beam.' He paused and his brow furrowed in concentration. 'Um, thirty-four hundred register ton, I think.'

'Well, lad, you should know that last one. You helped load

a heap of it today.' Mr Gilbert stretched his back and his spine cracked. He let out a long sigh. 'You worked hard helping us today, boy. Your dad would have been proud.'

'Thanks Mr Gilbert,' said Tane. 'I wish I could come tomorrow. The *Otaki*'s docking isn't she?'

'She is indeed. We'll be loading carcasses until after dark.' He crouched down to Tane's level. 'But you've got more important things to be doin' tomorrow. It's your first day at the comprehensive.'

'Yeah!' Tane's eyes widened. 'We went up to the school for the interview. Me and Mum. They have twelve classrooms. And they do science. Experiments and everything. And they have a footy field. Mum says I can be on a team. And...' Tane's excitement suddenly dulled. 'But I don't know anyone else who goes there.'

'I'm sure you'll make lots of new friends.' The sound of a steam whistle made Mr Gilbert glance towards the customs house. He stood back up. 'Well, that's the Harbour Master. I better go tally my counts.' He reached into his pocket and flipped the boy a coin. 'There you are, lad. Now run along or your mother'll have me guts for garters.' Pulling a notebook from his back pocket, Mr Gilbert headed for the customs house.

Tane examined the coin. A 1910 thruppence. Only two years old. He wondered how many hands it had passed through on its journey from England to New Zealand. Maybe someone famous had touched it or perhaps it had been used to pay for something exotic. He sighed to himself, the coin had seen more of the world than he had, that was for sure. Rubbing the shiny thruppence between his fingers, Tane muttered a wish three times.

'I want to see the world. I want to see the world. I want to see the world.' A sailor had told him that anything small and valuable could be a touch piece. So maybe it would work. Maybe it would grant him his wish. He flipped the coin with his thumb then plucked it from the air and tucked it into his back pocket. Whistling to himself, he strode down the gangplank.

The quickest way home was to climb the fence and sneak across the passenger wharf but the waterfront was busy and with so many people around he might be seen. He'd been caught once before and he wasn't keen to repeat that episode; he'd had to scrape barnacles for an entire weekend. So before he reached the graving dock, he ducked between the trucks and carts that were bouncing their way along the street and headed down Sailors Alley.

The buildings on either side blocked the fading evening light. Even though it was barely wide enough for two carts to pass, the alley somehow felt huge, like the doorway to another world. There was colour everywhere. Playbills, plastered to walls, proclaimed wonders to be witnessed; marvels of modern medicine or performances of breathtaking beauty. The people were colourful too, an assortment of faces and accents from lands near and far.

As he walked he ran his finger along the wall. The irregular brickwork at the back of Paragon Outfitters eventually gave way to the grimy plastered finish of Stone and Company followed by the painted timber gates that enclosed the rear of the fish shop. "Fischer's Fish is Fresher" is what the signage on Queen Street claimed but at the back of the fish market there was always a lingering tangy smell of rotten fish, despite the efforts of the old man who could be seen at the end of every business day with a mop and pail, swabbing the tiled courtyard behind the gates.

Halfway down the alley he came to the Crown and Rooster. He glanced up fondly at a tiny window on the second floor. For many years his mother had worked here. During the holidays, when the Māori school was closed, she had brought him to the tavern. For hours on end, he would play in the keg room where his mum, or one of the working girls, could check on him. They were magical days. Making huts from empty sacks and broken chairs or inventing clever traps to try and snare the rats that would scurry from time to time along the beams or across the floor. Each evening, when Sailors Alley came alive, he would climb on a barrel to peer out the window, watching all the hustle and bustle. To a young boy, it had been the theatre of life seen through a pane of glass. Now he was older he was no longer in the audience, he was on stage. He looked around him. The dusk chorus filled his ears; sailors laughing, street vendors hawking, wharfies fighting, prostitutes flirting. In his body he could feel it like a pulse.

Of late, Tane's mother had begun warning him to stay away from the alley.

'You shouldn't be going there,' she would say. 'It's not healthy for a boy of your age. Besides, it can be dangerous.' Tane would nod his head in agreement then roll his eyes when she wasn't looking. He was grown now. Fourteen. He wasn't a child any more.

A man walked past stuffing a pie into his mouth and Tane was suddenly aware of how hungry he was. He took a deep breath and his nostrils were filled with the mouth watering smells of busy kitchens. He picked up his pace, jogging down the alley. Hopefully his mother would be making dinner now. He smiled to himself as he stepped around two drunk sailors holding one another up as they urinated against a wall.

'Oi, look out, Tane.' Tane was so busy watching the sailors that he almost knocked Marcy over. He spun around to find her clutching a parcel to her breast. 'Slow down, lad. You'll be the death of me.' Marcy was one of the girls who had worked at the tavern. Although "girl" was rather a polite term since Marcy might have been older than his mum. It was hard to tell with her face painted in makeup.

'Sorry Miss Marcy.' Tane smiled and straightened to his full height. 'I've been helping Mr Gilbert unload the *Lady Trident*.'

'The *Lady Trident*? Hmm, that's one of the big steamers, ain't it?' she asked.

Tane was always pleased to talk about ships. 'Yeah, she docked on Tuesday. In from Paradip, India. Third biggest to dock this year.'

Marcy looked impressed. 'You sound like a seasoned wharf master. I hear you're starting at the state school tomorrow.'

Tane smiled. 'Yep. I get to learn Geography and Machining!'

Marcy laughed. 'Well, listen to you. You'll be running this whole wharf one day and the likes of me'll have to call you "Sir."'

From the opposite direction, a tall young man pushing a broom cart trundled across the cobbles. Veering at the last minute, the driver leaned on the handles, pushing the side of the cart into Tane.

'Look out ya little shite, this thing's heavy,' the young man growled. Tane stepped back hurriedly, rubbing his hip where the passing cart had clipped him.

Marcy shook a finger after the young man. 'Now, you watch where you're going, Joey Farrell. Young Tane here has a real future, and I won't see the likes of you pushing him around'.

Joey stopped his cart and looked over his shoulder. 'A real future? A little wog like him! He's just gonna be another wharf-rat.' Joey's glance slid across to Marcy and his expression turned into a leer. 'Tell you what Marcy, I'll give *you* a real future if you gimme an hour o' your time'.

'You wouldn't know what to do with it,' Marcy scoffed.

Joey pushed the cart and trundled off, sneering over his shoulder, 'Who'd wanna touch you, anyway.'

Shaking her head, Marcy looked at Tane. 'I hope you know what an opportunity that school is,' she said. 'That Joey's sour because he ain't got no prospects but you, you really do have a chance.' She looked around the alley. 'A chance to climb above all this.' Her face suddenly showed its age. 'Some of us never got that opportunity. Life's harsh, boy. We all do what we have to do.' She grew silent. After a moment, she patted his shoulder again. 'You'll do good, Tane. I know you'll do yourself proud.'

'Of course, Miss Marcy.'

The old prostitute gestured towards the Crown and Rooster. 'Why don't you come in and I'll get you some lemonade. To celebrate your first day at high school.'

'No thanks. Mum will be waiting for me.' He turned to leave.

'I really think you should stop in for a little while. Old Frankie's got a new puppy. It's ever so cute.'

Tane frowned at her, not wanting to be rude. 'I gotta go. Have to get my stuff ready for school tomorrow.'

Marcy put a hand on his shoulder. 'Tane, your mum's... entertaining.'

His body tensed. He tried to pull away from her grip but her fingers held his shirt. 'I really think you should stop in. Just for a while.'

'She's not entertaining! I know what she's doing!' His words came out a little louder than he'd intended. He looked down, scowling at the ground.

For a moment Marcy tried to look sympathetic but then her face hardened. 'Don't you be judgin' your mum! She's had to make some hard choices bringing up a boy all alone. She's fed you and clothed you.' Her voice softened a little. 'Look Tane, she's gotta earn a living just like the rest of us. She's worked real hard to get you into that school.'

With a flick of his shoulder, Tane broke her grip. 'I don't care, I'm going home!' He spun around and dashed off.

Marcy stood, shaking her head, watching him disappear down the alley, weaving his way through the crowd.

The run along Shortland Crescent and across the beach towards Resolution Point calmed Tane down. He slowed to a walk and matched his pace to the pulse of blood in the side of his head. Off the gravel, through the sand, onto the grass. Finally his breathing slowed as he stepped onto the hard-baked dusty clay.

This was the industrial sector, Mechanic's Bay and it had its own rhythms; scrapes and beats that were harsher than the freighting docks. The calls of workmen were drowned by the hiss and pound of steam hammers and the screech of wheels grinding on tracks. It wasn't just the noise that set Mechanic's Bay apart. The smells here were different too. They permeated everything. Coal smoke and creosote and tar mingled with the stagnant tang of mangroves from the inlet. Beneath it all, rust—the metallic scent of iron and blood. Of ships' hulls and rail wagons. The smell of men conquering their world. Tane could taste it on the back of his tongue. He closed his eyes and breathed it in. This was home.

The shack he shared with his mother was a timber lean-to erected against the long wall of a boat building shed. A railway line passed only twenty yards from the door and, as he stepped onto the tracks, Tane instinctively glanced west to check for wagons. The lines receded across dusty ground before they disappeared into a tall rail shed. There was nothing rolling. Heat shimmer was the only movement. He hesitated as he approached the shack; Marcy's words still in his head. After a moment, he quietly opened the door and slipped inside.

He stood still, allowing his eyes to adjust to the dim light. His mother was not in the main room but he noticed the new picture. A white rose on a green background. She had been working on it for days and now it hung with a dozen other needlework designs pinned to the scrim of the far wall. She called this her "orphans' gallery." Pictures that refused to sell and would come back with her again and again from the weekend market where she hawked her art along with other bric-a-brac. He cocked his head and considered the new rose. It was better than the other orphans. Lifelike. With nicely graduated colours. Someone would buy it.

A rustling emerged from beyond the scrim wall. His mother was in her bedroom. Tane's body tensed at the sound of a muffled voice. A man's voice. He scowled and turned to leave but it came again. A quiet chuckle this time followed by the sound of his mother's voice. Tane strained to make out her words. He took a deep breath and crept into the main room, placing his feet carefully so as to make no noise.

From the walls on either side, painted figures watched him; old playbills torn edges carefully re-pasted. Sarah Bernhardt smiled, urging him on but Alexander the Crystal Seer was less sure, hypnotic eyes scowling from beneath his turban.

Tane crossed the room then stepped carefully up onto the sofa, a cushioned bench in the corner that doubled as his bed. It had a tendency to squeak when he put his full weight on it so he reached up, above the scrim, and hooked his fingers over the wall boards. He could feel the oiliness of the soot under his fingers. To his left, a heavy curtain covered the doorway between the two rooms. He leaned out and peeped through the gap at the top of the curtain. He could see a narrow slice of his mother's bedroom; a low dressing table and beside it, a tall mirror, the silver backing faded to brown around the edges.

His mother spoke again. He could hear her clearly now. 'In future, don't go to the Crown and Rooster, just come direct to me,' she said. She was on the bed.

A naked man stepped into view. Tane's frown deepened and he felt both his fists clenching. He wanted to yell at the man, to drive him from his mother's bedroom. But he also felt something else. A pang of excitement and he couldn't stop himself from staring. The man was tall and lightly muscled. He seemed awkward without clothes. He dressed himself slowly, slipping on bleached pants then stepping into trousers. He seemed to take forever to button the fly. His shirt and braces went on together and he adjusted each cuff with fussy movements, constantly checking himself in the mirror. He brushed his moustache with his fingers then responded to Tane's mother in a thick British accent. 'Yes. I might just do that but our arrangement must stay strictly confidential.'

'Don't worry,' Tane's mother reassured him. 'I'm not like the other girls at the tavern. I understand discretion.'

The man glanced over his shoulder towards her. 'Well you certainly seem a cut above the usual... entertainer,' he finished.

As Tane watched, the man checked the mirror again then reached for a jacket and cane. 'Well, I have important matters to attend to,' he said. 'I'm sure we'll do business again.' Without waiting for a response, he pushed through the curtain into the main room.

Caught by surprise, Tane shoved himself away from the doorway. The fingers of his right hand slipped on the sooty wallboard and he found himself stepping heavily off the sofa. He staggered backwards, knocking over a chair.

The man halted, a shocked look on his face and without warning he whipped his cane at Tane. The tip of the stick caught Tane's cheek and he gasped at the sharp sting.

His mother's alarmed voice called from the bedroom, 'Tane? Is that you?'

The man growled through clenched teeth, his voice low enough for only Tane to hear. 'You little devil.' The man glanced over his shoulder at the bedroom then, with a menacing grimace at Tane, he dashed across the main room and disappeared out the front door.

Tane's mother appeared in the bedroom doorway clutching a blanket around her naked body. 'Darling, what happened?'

Stunned, Tane reached up and touched his cheek. He winced as his fingers found a nasty welt. A drop of blood seeped down his face.

Tane's mother rushed forwards, then, remembering she was naked, stopped. 'Pour some water. I'll be right out to tend that.' She disappeared into her bedroom to dress.

CHAPTER 8

AUCKLAND · 1912

'**DON'T FORGET TO LISTEN.** You get distracted too easily'. Tane's mother brushed his fringe away from his eyes.

He pushed her hand away. 'Mum! I'm fourteen, I'll be fine.' He glanced sideways to see if anyone else was looking. It must have been the twentieth time he had heard the same lecture from her that morning and he quietly wished she would just go home and leave him to it. He bit his lip and said nothing because he knew she was as excited for him as he was nervous.

A hundred new students were gathered on the school field, each flanked by beaming parents. Families mingled, sharing greetings. Courteous questions about others' children brought the opportunity to espouse the virtues of their own.

Tane and his mother stood on the edge of the crowd, watching. The students were all of a similar age. Tane stood out, not only for being accompanied by a single parent but because of the colour of his skin. Only a handful of non-European students could be seen and most of those were Chinese.

On the steps of the main building, an elderly man came forward and lifted a megaphone to address the crowd. 'Good morning to you all.' Everyone focused on him. 'I'm Headmaster Pearson. It's wonderful to see you all here on a day that is an important stepping stone in the lives of your sons and daughters.' His tone grew solemn. 'We are charged with the most important of tasks; educating the next generation. We take that responsibility very seriously and we expect the same from our pupils.' He hunched forward, speaking down to the new students. 'You all have the potential to succeed and if you remain focussed, you will achieve. Those that fail do so because they lack discipline.' He straightened up. 'I hope my message will be taken on board by each and every parent here. Your children will succeed only with your help. They require discipline at home as well as at school.' He turned to a pastor standing behind him. 'In a moment, I will assign classes. Now I will ask Pastor Williams to lead us in a prayer.'

A little later the parents were dismissed. Mothers and fathers gave their children a final pat on the shoulder or kiss on the cheek and drifted away towards the school gates. Tane's mother pulled him into a hug. He stiffly returned her embrace.

'Thanks for coming, Mum.'

'I'm so proud of you,' she whispered.

The headmaster's voice boomed again from the steps, 'All students please assemble in front of me.'

Taking a deep breath, Tane pulled away from his mother. 'I'll be fine. See you tonight.' He turned to follow the throng of excited students.

The headmaster launched into another longwinded address. Students shuffled their feet as they listened to an endless list of rules and regulations. Finally the lecture drew to a close and the headmaster turned to the group of staff behind him.

'Let me introduce your teachers.' He pointed to a large man standing at the front of the group. 'This is the middle school dean, Mr Proust. His son graduated as one of our top students in the sixth form last year.' The enormous gentleman stepped forwards. He beamed proudly. Tane joined in with the polite applause.

The headmaster continued, introducing an older couple. 'Your English master, Mr Nelson, who will see to your grammar and his wife, Mrs Nelson, who will be teaching our young ladies the art of bookkeeping.' Mr and Mrs Nelson stepped forward and smiled. To Tane they seemed ancient.

The headmaster spoke once more. 'Your mathematics master, Mr Ryan. He has two daughters here at the school, one of whom is Auckland regional typing champion.' As the students applauded, a familiar face came forward. Tane's jaw dropped open. It was the customer his mother had been entertaining the night before.

Mr Ryan moved to the front of the steps. He smiled as his eyes scanned the assembled pupils. Tane's hand instinctively reached up to touch the welt on his cheek and he shrunk down, desperate to blend in. Mr Ryan's gaze rolled over him and for a second he thought the man hadn't recognised him but the teacher's eyes flicked back, peering straight at him. The smile disappeared from Mr Ryan's face. Tane lowered his eyes. He could feel his heart beating faster.

Rolls were called and pupils were lined up and marched off in class groups. Badge-wearing prefects led each column up the steps and through the towering doors. Tane found himself waiting in a corridor, last in a line of thirty. Large black and white tiles covered the floor and continued up the wall to where a row of leather satchels hung from pegs. Against the opposite wall, paired shoes, which they had freshly removed, peeped from polished wooden cubbyholes. The whisper of soft woollen socks on the cool floor was the only sound. Tane slipped his hands into his pockets and rubbed his knees together. It was cold inside the tall brick building even though it was a warm morning outside.

The classroom door opened and a man's voice commanded. 'Enter.' The pupils filed slowly into the classroom.

As Tane approached the open door he could see rows of wooden desks, each with its worktop hinged open against the pencil groove and inkwell. Each pupil claimed a desk, removed the exercise books from inside, closed the lid and sat down.

The boy in front of him stepped through the door but before Tane could follow, Mr Ryan stepped out into the hallway and stopped him.

The teacher barked instructions at the pupils seated inside the classroom. 'Get out your maths exercise book and write your name and room number on the front. I will return shortly. There is to be no talking.' With that he closed the classroom door then scanned up and down the corridor. Confident there were no witnesses, he grabbed Tane by the ear and started marching him towards the rear of the building. 'Come with me, boy. You and I have something to discuss.'

Tane was dragged through a swinging door that led out onto the backfield. As soon as they were outside, Mr Ryan twisted Tane around and shoved him against the wall, his black gown billowing. He leaned down, close to Tane's face.

'I don't know how a wharf rat like you got into this school, but you're not welcome! Understand me?'

Tane reached up to cover his welt. 'I don't care. I won't tell...'

'Shut up! If I see you at this school again, I'll see to it your whore of a mother goes to prison. You hear me?'

Tane stared at Mr Ryan, terrified.

The teacher slammed him harder against the wall. 'Do you hear me!'

All Tane could manage was a wide-eyed nod.

With both hands, Mr Ryan spun him around and shoved him onto the playing field. 'Now get out of here!'

Tane backed away.

The teacher narrowed his eyes. 'If you mention any of this to anyone, I'll see that you both suffer! You *and* your mother.' He turned and disappeared into the school building, his gown snaking into the corridor behind him.

Tane stumbled backwards, his steps slowly turning into a run, then a sprint. His heart thumped in his chest and he felt the hopes and dreams of that morning slipping away. Reaching the far side of the field he threw himself behind a fence. With his back against the palings he pulled his knees up to his chest, trying to suppress sobs that shook his body.

CHAPTER 9

———

Hunua · 1954

IF THE DOUGLAS SKYROCKET SUCCEEDS and reaches twice the speed of sound, then the Navy will have beaten the Air Force to the finish line.

The crackling voice came from a radio sitting on the fleecing table. It was mid-afternoon when Tane had emerged from his office carrying his wireless and motioned for the boys to gather around. They had put down their tools and rushed to listen to the broadcast and now they were huddled around the radio.

Tane adjusted the tuning knob again and tweaked the bent wire aerial. The excited voice of the American announcer emerged from the static.

In the distance we can see the P2 patrol bomber with the sleek, swept wing shape of the Skyrocket beneath.

Tane jabbed a finger at the wireless. 'The P2. That's the drop plane. They strap the rocket to its belly and take it up to twenty thousand feet. Listen.'

And now you can see it folks. The rocket has detached and is flying on its own power. The turbojet engine will be producing over 6000 lbs of thrust. Wait... we're receiving a signal...

The commentary paused and the boys pressed forward, straining to hear.

Yes! We've just had confirmation of the first sonic boom. The aircraft has broken the sound barrier. If all goes well, it should reach Mach two right over the airfield.

Tane smiled. 'Half way there. Imagine being the pilot in that, eh?' He tried cranking the radio's volume knob but it was already at full.

And here it comes, streaking across the sky. There was a boom in the background like a compressed clap of thunder, and the American voice grew even more animated. *That's it folks! You heard it. The second sonic boom! The D-558 Skyrocket, piloted by Scott Crossfield, is the first manned aircraft to reach Mach two.*

The announcer's excitement spilled out of the wireless. The boys cheered and clapped each other's backs. Even Tane's eyes were wide with the thrill of the moment. 'Yep, those Yanks know how to do it,' he said. 'They showed the Japs that they owned the Pacific and now they're showing the Russians they own the skies.'

Briar was at the front of the crush, elbows resting on the fleecing table and for once he felt like one of the farm boys, a feeling aided by the fact that Victor was away at a competition. It had been a week since the incident with the loose sheep and Briar had mixed emotions about what had happened. The image of Aussie flying to his rescue was etched in his mind and every time he thought about it he felt grateful. He also felt embarrassed about the way he had blurted out his feelings to Tane, and because of this, he had spent the week avoiding the man.

Tane turned off the radio, smiling at the boys' excitement. 'Pretty cool, eh?' He folded the aerial back behind the set. 'Okay. Come on, back to work. If you finish the main pen, I've got some chocolate left over from the church fair.' With a cheer, and a renewed sense of vigour, the boys returned to their stations.

With Victor away, Aussie was the only one using the Wolseley. He would shear three sheep in the time it took the other boys to clip a single animal. Working as the passer, Briar was constantly filling Aussie's holding pen and the two of them began to develop their own banter.

'Heck, aren't you finished yet?' Briar teased as he dragged another ewe towards Aussie's side pen.

'Just dawdling so your poor muscles can cope,' Aussie responded without looking up. His tone was dead serious but the little smile at the corner of his mouth gave him away. Then, stealing a glance to check Briar was watching, he threw the clippers in the air and flicked his leg over the sheep's head, turning the animal onto its feet. His left hand whipped out and caught the handset and at the same time, his right hand delivered a whack to the sheep's rump, sending it skittering into the release chute. Briar laughed at the display of agility then had to step out of the way as two boys appeared and gathered up the fleece lying around Aussie's feet. They disappeared with the freshly shorn wool and Aussie nodded his head at the ewe Briar was holding.

'Batter up, boyo.'

Briar looked at him quizzically.

'Don't put her in the pen,' said Aussie. 'Bring her over here, I'll shear her next.'

Briar nodded in understanding. 'Well, since you're *finally* finished.' He rolled his eyes in mock exasperation and Aussie chuckled.

Briar dragged the animal into the work station then used his shoulders and a flick of his left foot to shunt the sheep's weight from his own legs to Aussie's. Aussie slid his left arm through Briar's and grabbed a fistful of wool. For a second their heads were almost touching and they both froze, looking one another in the eye. They both smiled.

Briar released the animal and stepped away. 'I could slow down. Let you catch your breath,' he said.

Aussie leaned over the sheep and began the first clip across its groin. 'If you slow down any more, you'll be standing still,' he replied with a smirk.

Behind Briar a voice called for a sheep. Aussie looked up. 'Go get 'em, Speedy.' As Briar headed off towards the holding pen, Aussie's voice called after him, 'See ya soon.'

An hour later a car horn honked outside the woolshed. The farm boys took the sound as a cue to down tools. Wiping muck off their hands, they hurried outside and Tane emerged from his office to follow them. Briar joined Aussie, leaning against the hot painted iron of the shed.

'I guess Victor's back,' said Briar.

Aussie nudged him playfully. 'Don't worry about it. So long as I'm around I reckon he'll ignore you.'

Briar shaded his eyes from the bright sunshine and squinted at the green Morris Minor car. A short man got out of the passenger seat and walked around to open the door for the woman who was driving. Briar recognised him—Father Patrick, the parish priest who he had seen each Sunday at the chapel in Hunua village. He didn't look like a priest today. He wasn't wearing his collar, just a plain shirt, open at the neck. As Father Patrick opened the door, Mrs Edna Dwyte emerged.

Aussie pointed at her. 'Have you met the Major's wife yet?' he asked.

'Not really,' said Briar. 'I've seen her at church and up by the farmhouse but she's never spoken to me.' He watched as a wide floral sunhat emerged from the car. 'Does she always dress like a movie star?'

'Yeah,' Aussie replied. 'Sorta the opposite to her husband.'

Briar remembered Major Dwyte collecting him from the police station and their long silent drive back to Hunua. Try as he might, he couldn't remember what the man had been wearing. All he could picture was the way the Major's hat seemed a size too small, pulled down hard onto his head, and a bead of sweat slowly dripping from behind his ear as he hunched over the steering wheel. 'Does Major Dwyte dress badly?' he asked Aussie.

'He dresses fine but like a working man. Not like a rich cat. Only time I ever see him dress up is for the races at Ellerslie.' He smiled. 'Or funerals. For those he always wears his old uniform.'

'He was in the war then?'

'He fought for the Pommies in the Great War but he was some sort of liaison in the last war. Secret documents and stuff, I heard. Don't try asking him about it, he gets real grumpy.'

'Oh, right.'

Victor was sitting in the front seat of the Morris Minor holding a large trophy and chatting to the two girls in the back. One of the girls was the Dwytes' daughter, Rosemary. She was seventeen and occasionally wandered around the farm. All the farm boys noticed her.

'Who's the other girl with Rosemary?' Briar asked Aussie.

'That's the neighbour's daughter. Diana Colton. Their farm's on the other side of the river.' He pointed towards the row of tall macrocarpa trees at the bottom of the hill. 'Serious money.'

Tane strode past them, heading for the car. 'Alright, take a breather,' he announced to the farm boys. 'Go stretch your legs but don't go too far, we'll be back to work soon.' There was a chorus of assents and a couple of boys took off. Most of them stayed where they were, eager to see Victor's trophy.

Mrs Edna Dwyte emerged from the vehicle. She brushed the creases from her harlequin-print dress and adjusted her sunhat. Seeing Tane approaching, she leaned forward and muttered to Father Patrick.

'For heaven's sake, be careful what you say around that damn Māori,' she said.

'Edna, we've talked about this before. I can't say I'm fond of the man but he *is* one of my parishioners.'

'He has far too much influence on this farm.'

'George needs him to help train the boys.'

Edna scoffed. 'Victor is almost twenty now. He's perfectly capable of training them.'

A concerned look crossed the priest's face. 'Edna, I don't think either of us should interfere. The boys seem to like Tane...'

Edna cut him off, 'Boys of this age need discipline. Not friendship.'

By now, Tane was only yards away and Patrick's voice dropped to a whisper. 'Please don't ask me to take this up with your husband again.'

A glare momentarily darkened her features. 'Fine. Ill take care of it myself,' she hissed. Then she turned and her face transformed into a smile, 'Oh, hello Tane.'

'Hello Mrs Dwyte. How was the competition?'

'It was wonderful. Victor won, of course. He made the other shearers look like a bunch of school boys.'

'Well, I'm glad it's done with. Now he can concentrate on his work.'

'Victor is the best worker on this farm.' Edna looked meaningfully at Tane. 'He's ready for greater challenges.'

'There's plenty of challenges to keep him busy around here.'

'His win shows he's a born leader. Perhaps it's time for him to take more responsibility.'

Tane nodded. 'His win is good for the farm.'

Edna raised an eyebrow. 'Victor won. Not the farm.'

'His win shows we're doing good training,'

Edna's smile vanished. 'It certainly shows that *Victor* knows what he's doing.'

Father Patrick frowned then leapt into the conversation. 'Yes. Well. Victor has been invited to demonstrate his skills at the Auckland Industry Show next month. I think that's wonderful. Don't you?'

Inside the car, Victor listened for a moment as Mrs Dwyte sang his praises. He smiled at the girls in the back seat but only Diana was paying him any attention.

'Mrs Dwyte really thinks you're the bee's knees, doesn't she?' said Diana.

Victor shrugged. 'I guess.' His eyes slid towards Rosemary.

Diana nudged her friend who flicked around to find him staring at her.

Rosemary sniffed and straightened herself up. 'It seems you're well named.'

'Huh?' blurted Victor.

She reached out and touched the trophy in his hands. 'You're Victor and you're victorious.'

His eyes lit up as her fingers lightly stroked his prize. 'I *always* win.'

'Is that so?' She sat back and turned her head to look out the window. 'Well, it's good that someone is getting what they want,' she muttered. Her forehead creased in a frown. 'Do you actually *know* what you want, Victor?'

'Yeah. Of course,' his reply was immediate. Then he looked uncertain. 'Um, what do you mean?'

'There's a whole world out there.' She looked back at his trophy and grimaced. 'And horrifying as this thought is, you might just be holding a ticket out.'

Victor frowned. He pulled the trophy back into his lap. 'Yeah, this *is* my ticket. I'm gonna show them all that *I* should be calling the shots around here. You'll see.'

The shake of Rosemary's head was almost imperceptible. Her eyes flicked towards Diana and a smile slowly formed at the corner of her lips. She leaned towards Victor and lowered her voice a little. 'I'll tell you a secret, Victor. I know what I want too.'

'What, what do you want?'

'I want something impossible.' She shrugged her shoulders and sighed. 'A magic stead that could fly me away from here. Like Pegasus. Heck, I'd even settle for a pumpkin carriage, so long as I could go find a new life. One that wasn't boring.'

'I don't understand...' Before Victor could finish, Mrs Dwyte's voice summoned him from outside. 'Victor!'

He glanced over his shoulder at Mrs Dwyte then back at Rosemary. 'I reckon I could fly Pegasus.' He slipped out of the car.

Diana listened to the adults conversing. 'Your mother can talk up a storm,' she said to Rosemary.

Rosemary wouldn't be distracted. She was staring out towards the woolshed, focused on something. 'There he is. Aussie,' she sighed. 'Damn, even his name sounds sexy.'

Diana screwed her face up. 'Jeepers Rosemary, you really are smitten, aren't you?'

'I can't stop thinking about him,' Rosemary's tone grew serious. 'You don't know what it's like. Every day I see him but I can't even talk to him because my mother would never approve.' She paused and a smile crept onto her face. She licked her lips. 'Sometimes he works shirtless and I think about kissing his...'

Diana cuffed her before she could finish. Suppressing a giggle, she looked out the window at the object of Rosemary's affections. 'Well, Aussie is damn good looking. I'll give you that. But Victor has nicer eyes.'

'Yuck! Victor's horrid,' said Rosemary.

'Then why do you encourage him?'

'I suppose I shouldn't but...' Rosemary's fingers played with the door handle. 'I'm sick of the way everyone gets to tell me what to do. Sometimes I hate being a girl. It's like being at the bottom of the ladder. Older people are more important. Boys are more important. At least with Victor, I can be the boss for a change.'

'He has a crush on you?'

'To be honest, I used to like him. He's kind of sweet in a dumb way but then I realised something. He *wants* to be here. He actually thinks Hunua is a good place to live. Can you imagine it? Spending your whole life in this tiny, boring place. Surrounded by the same people doing the same damn things every day of your life.'

'You really hate this place so much?'

'Don't you?'

Diana contemplated Rosemary's words. 'My older brother was like you. He couldn't wait to leave.'

'You could go to London. Live with him.'

'I don't mind Hunua. It's home. It can be slow sometimes, that's for sure but it's not *so* bad.' Diana shrugged. 'I've got my horses. I'd hate it if I had to leave them behind.' She peered out the window again. 'Who's that?' she asked, pointing her finger. 'The one beside Aussie?'

'I don't know his name.' Rosemary sounded disinterested. 'Some new boy they sent from town.'

'He looks a bit...soft. Doesn't seem like the farming type.'

They were both silent for a moment then Diana spoke. 'I heard what you said to Father Patrick today.'

Rosemary flicked around. 'What are you talking about?'

'You shouldn't flirt with him. He's a priest. It's sort of... disgusting.'

'I wasn't flirting. Not really.' She leaned a bit closer, lowering her voice. 'He's still a *man*, you know. Besides, if I stay on the right side of him, it keeps mother happy.' Rosemary looked back out the window. 'And so long as mother thinks I'm still her little angel, I get a bit of freedom.'

'You're going to give him the wrong idea too.'

'He's a priest. He can't have *ideas*.'

'Like you said, he's still a man,' said Diana.

Rosemary giggled. 'Do you think they get frustrated? Priests?'

'Let's not find out.'

Rosemary straightened her back, pushed up her cleavage then nudged Diana. 'Come on, let's make a grand entrance and stir up the boys!' Without waiting for a reply, she pushed the door open and hopped out of the car.

Diana's exasperated sigh went unheard. She slid across the seat and followed Rosemary. The two girls walked along the driveway in the direction of the farm house. After a moment, Rosemary leaned against her friend's shoulder, steering them towards the front of the woolshed where the boys were gathered.

'Hello boys,' said Rosemary as she stopped by the woolshed.

'Hi Miss Dwyte,' came a chorus of enthusiastic replies.

She turned to where Aussie and Briar were leaning against the side of the shed. 'Hello Aussie.'

Aussie muttered a polite response. 'Hello Miss Dwyte.'

'Have you been working hard today?'

'Yeah. Of course.'

Diana piped in. 'So who's your friend?'

Aussie clapped Briar's shoulder. 'This is Briar. He's new.'

'Briar. That's an unusual name...' Diana stopped herself before she could finish.

'For a boy?' Briar finished for her. 'Yes. So I'm constantly told.'

Rosemary brushed a lock of her hair away from her eyes, tucking it behind her ear. 'In a few weeks we're going to the Auckland Industry Show. Aussie, you should come along.'

Victor appeared behind Rosemary. 'He can't come,' Victor blurted. 'I'm the one that's been asked to shear.'

Rosemary jumped in surprise. She flicked around and glared at him. 'Yes he can. I'm sure Mother will let him.' She looked back to Aussie. 'You want to come, don't you? It'll be fun.'

'Um, dunno,' Aussie shrugged, 'Guess it would be fun, but...'

'Nah! He can't come,' Victor's voice cut him off. He suddenly found both girls looking at him. 'He just can't. It's impossible.'

'What do you mean, impossible?' said Rosemary.

Victor was silent for a moment, his lips working up and down. Then his eyes lit. 'There won't be room.'

Rosemary scoffed, 'Of course there's room.' She turned and gave Diana a wink. 'He can sit in the back with us.'

'No!' Victor stepped between Rosemary and Aussie. 'He'll need to stay here to help Tane.' He turned and sneered at Aussie, 'Besides, he'd rather stay and look after his little sissy friend.' Aussie tensed and straightened his shoulders.

Seeing the tension mounting, Briar spoke up. 'Um, so what did you win, Victor?'

Victor sneered and jabbed his trophy at Briar. 'You don't even know what this is, do ya?'

'It's a trophy, I guess.'

'This is damn important, you little pussy. I'm the best young shearer in the district. The only junior who's mastered the Bowen technique. And don't you forget it.'

The farm boys were now gathering around Victor. With a dismissive scoff, he turned away from Briar and held his trophy up. 'This is what you can win if you ever get as good as me,' he said to the boys. 'Who wants to hold it?'

Aussie gestured to Briar and the two of them moved a few yards away from the throng. Aussie shook his head. 'Victor's such a nosebleed,' he muttered.

'Don't worry, I'm getting used to it,' replied Briar.

Aussie slouched back against the shed. 'I wish he hadn't won. Now he's gonna be full of himself for weeks.'

'Why didn't you compete?' Briar asked. 'You're a better shearer than him.'

'Actually, he's pretty fast.'

'But I've been passing just as many sheep to your station.'

'Competitions ain't my thing. Besides,' he put on a stupid voice, mocking Victor's tone, 'I don't use the Bowen technique'. They both suppressed a laugh.

Briar continued the mocking. 'Bowing technique huh? Shooting down the competition was he? He doesn't look like William Tell to me.'

Aussie glanced over Briar's shoulder to where Victor was still trying to impress everyone. 'No, he's definitely cupid. Or something that rhymes with cupid.'

The image of Victor as a winged baby struck Briar as particularly comical and he laughed out loud. Aussie's face took on a look of warning, but before Briar could register this change, he continued.

'Well, if Victor's mastered the Bowing technique I guess he'll be tying his own shoelaces now.' He chuckled at his own joke then froze as he registered the silence around him. He turned slowly to find everyone staring at him, Victor's eyes wide with anger.

Rosemary looked at Briar then at Victor. Her voice broke the silence with a peal of laughter. Victor looked mortified. She quickly covered her mouth, but the smile remained in her eyes. She took Diana by the elbow and left, heading up the driveway towards the farmhouse.

Victor's entire head went red. He spun on Briar. 'You... You... I'm....' His words couldn't work their way past his rage. He shoved his trophy into the hands of the nearest boy and clenched his fists. As he barged at Briar, Tane's voice called out.

'Briar! Get over here and meet Mrs Dwyte.'

Victor froze, his wrath reined in by Tane's command but as Briar ducked past him, Victor's words finally spat themselves out. 'Gonna kill you.'

CHAPTER 10

Hunua · 1954

IT WAS EVENING AND GEORGE AND TANE were in the stables, a long barn fifty yards down the driveway from the woolshed. The two men sat on hay bales in the open doorway and looked out at the sun setting over the Hunua hills. The crickets chirped in the warm twilight and above the paddocks, the first stars emerged in the evening sky.

George got up and dug amongst a pile of horse tack to produce a bottle of scotch and two glasses. Kicking a third bale between them to use as a table, he set the bottle down and uncorked it.

Tane nodded towards the woolshed. 'I should be finishing the tallies.' His objection was half-hearted.

'Don't be dour,' George replied as he filled the tumblers. 'The wool ledgers will wait for tomorrow but a good single malt is like a willing woman, it should never be stood up.' Passing a glass to Tane, he settled back against one of the large open doors. 'Edna tells me Victor won the trophy today.'

'He knows his way around a shearing machine. I'll give him that.'

George lifted his glass to eye level and peered at the amber liquid then downed half of it in a single gulp. A contented sigh escaped his lips. 'I get the impression you don't like the boy.'

Tane sucked down a slug of his own whisky before answering. 'He's an able young man. Best we've got on the electric but...'

'But what?'

Tane shuffled his feet.

'Come on, spit it out, man.'

'He's changed a lot in the last few years. He's not good with the other boys. Pushes them around.'

'Once they go out into the workforce they'll have to deal with worse than Victor. Maybe he'll toughen them up.'

Tane swirled the whiskey in his glass. 'They need guidance, not bullying.'

'In the army, the only guidance a soldier needs comes from their commander. It's the same in a work shed.'

'Even soldiers need to think for themselves and who knows *what* these boys will do with their lives.'

'We know exactly what they will do. We aren't training leaders here, Tane. Putting ideas in their heads, ideas above their station, is doing them a disservice.' George drained his glass. 'Discipline! That's the key.'

Outside the stables, a round pen enclosed a rough circle of sandy dirt. Tane looked across the pen where a horse stood with its head over the railing. The animal's eyes were fixed on the lower paddocks where other horses were grazing by the river. 'As orphans these boys have no family to help them. Their road will be harder than most.' He finished his drink and put down his glass. 'That doesn't mean they can't have tōnui.'

George frowned at the Māori word.

'Prosperity,' Tane corrected.

George scoffed. He poured them both another measure. 'You're good with those boys Tane but let's just concentrate on turning them into shearers. They need discipline and that's why Victor's good to have around. Edna thinks so too.'

'She doesn't know any of the boys except Victor. Aussie has a better feel for the land. And the animals.'

'Victor's win shows he's good at what he does. It will motivate the other boys,' said George. 'Besides, it will keep the Bishop happy. Without the church support we wouldn't be training the boys here.' He leaned forward, shaking his glass. 'And we need those boys. Times are tough. Wool might be up but the bottom's fallen out of mutton.'

The chorus of crickets grew louder and George poured himself another drink. Leaning back, he rubbed his shoulders on the rough timber behind him. 'I'm not getting any younger and life's not getting any easier.' He shook his head. 'I don't know how much longer I can run things around here. The damn politics of it all is doing my head in. Between the bank and the bishop and the wife, it's worse than bloody wartime.' He drained his whisky in two slugs then stared at the empty glass. 'When I first bought this land, I figured I'd be retired by now. I planned to pass the farm on down my family line. To a son. A boy who could take on the property and continue my family name but after Rosemary was born, Edna refused to have any more kids. So here I am still slaving away at my age.'

Tane took a sip from his tumbler. 'You've got a family. You've got respect. How would a son make that different?'

'Knowing the farm would be looked after once I'm gone. Somehow I'd feel better.'

Tane frowned. 'We all want to protect our whenua. There's others who can tend the farm.'

'Who?' snapped George. 'My wife might be younger than me, but she has no interest in the land. With no son to take over, my only hope is that Rosemary will marry a man who wants the farm.' George's voice had risen in frustration and the horse looked around and stamped its foreleg in the dust. George poured himself yet another glass. His hand was unsteady as the whisky took effect. 'I love my daughter of course, but I dreamed it would be different.'

Tane contemplated the gathering darkness. 'I dreamed it

would be different.' He turned the glass backwards and forwards in his hand watching the liquid swirl. It compressed the wan light from outside into a hollow reflection. 'I dreamed I'd come back from the war and get treated the same as everyone else. That I'd get respect. I learned different. People never change.'

'Let it rest, Tane. You're talking mumbo jumbo now.'

The evening had cooled. The two men sat for a while in silence on opposite sides of the doorway. The crickets stopped chirping and the last of the colour faded from the sky.

George grumbled something indistinguishable into his glass then cleared his throat. 'So, are you coming to the races tomorrow night? What do you think of Henry Grafton's new horse?'

CHAPTER 11

HUNUA · 1954

THE FOLLOWING MORNING TANE STOOD LEANING on a chunky gatepost at the farm entranceway. Behind him the driveway wound past the woolshed and up to the large farmhouse. The morning was young but already it was hot.

'That's it, Red. Turn it as you walk,' Tane called instructions to a young farm boy who was struggling with a roll of shiny barbed wire. Further down the fence line other boys were nailing strands to newly set posts. The old fence had been dug out and its twisted coils of runners, rusty with age, lay like abandoned sculptures along the road edge; each section of dead fence encasing a skeleton of lichen covered batons.

The farm stretched over more than twelve hundred acres and maintaining the fencing was a task that ate into every summer. Lambs would find any loose wire or sagging strainer or rotting post and wiggle their small bodies through the gap. Lost in the excitement of their new world they would forget the location of their secret door. The mournful bleats of separated lambs and the accompanying cries of distressed ewes were just another part of the summer soundtrack.

The green Morris Minor pulled into the farm entranceway and behind the wheel, Mrs Edna Dwyte was peering up towards the house. At the last moment she noticed Tane and the car came to a lurching stop.

She backed up a few yards until she was beside him then wound down the window, 'Hello, Tane. I need to speak to Victor.' She glanced past Tane to see if she could spot Victor amongst the boys nearby.

'Victor's gone down to the shed to collect pliers.' Tane raised an eyebrow, 'Is there something wrong?'

'Of course not. I just want to congratulate him for winning his trophy.'

'He has the trophy. His head is big enough already.'

There was an awkward pause as they both stared at each other. Tane glanced over his shoulder to check the boys weren't within earshot then stepped closer to the car window, 'I know why you're doing this.'

'You know nothing!' Her voice made the nearest boys look up from their work. Edna sunk back into her car seat and she spoke through gritted teeth, 'Just send him up to the house as soon as he's back.' She wound the window closed and drove up the driveway.

Edna parked her car on the gravel yard in front of the farmhouse; an imposing gabled villa with tall sash windows. Flower boxes, planted with chrysanthemums, lined each end of the front porch and a carefully measured garden of white roses and hydrangeas led to the front door.

She climbed out of the car just as Rosemary appeared on the porch, 'Mother, did you get it?'

Edna reached into a white carrybag and pulled out a sunhat covered in blue feathers and lined with gold braid.

Rosemary clapped, 'Can I wear it to the party at Ellerslie? Please, Mother. It's so perfect.'

As she crossed the gravel Edna frowned, 'We talked about that. I don't really think the Ellerslie ball is an appropriate social outing for you. Those girls in the city are a bad influence.'

'You said you'd ask Father!'

'I haven't had time. Anyway, I know exactly what he'll say.'

'You mean he'll say exactly what you tell him to say.'

'Don't you take that tone with me. You should be thankful that I bought you the hat.' Edna climbed the stairs to the porch. 'The Country Women's Institute is putting on a tea dance at Drury next weekend. You can wear your new hat there. Victor can accompany you.'

'I don't want to go to another CWI social. It's all the same people. All your friends.'

Edna pushed Rosemary into the house ahead of her. 'I'm not going to argue with you. If you can't be civil, get up to your room and stay there. I've got a visitor coming.'

Twenty minutes later Victor jogged up the steps, across the veranda and knocked on the front door.

'Come in, Victor,' called Edna.

Victor cautiously tried the handle and finding the door unlocked, let himself in. Closing the door behind him he stood in the wide hallway looking around at the coloured glass door panels and the framed paintings on the walls. He jumped when he heard Edna's voice again.

'Don't be shy. I'm in the sitting room.'

He walked down the hall and peered into the room. A small table was set for two; a bone china tea set accompanied by a large plate crammed with a selection of cakes and biscuits.

Edna appeared carrying a teapot. She nodded at the food and sat down. 'There's fresh cream to go with the cake if you'd like some.'

Victor hesitated by the door.

Edna frowned at him, 'What is it? Don't just stand there. Sit down.' She poured two cups from the pot.

He approached the table. 'Um, are you sure, Mrs Dwyte? I'm still in my work clothes.'

'That's fine, Victor. This is a farmhouse. The furniture has seen plenty of sweat and dirt.' She peered at his hands. 'Tell you what though, why don't you pop down the hall to the bathroom and wash your hands.' He nodded and, with an enthusiastic glance at the cakes, disappeared down the hall. As he passed the stairway he looked up to find Rosemary looking down at him. He smiled up at her.

'Um hi,' he stammered, 'Are you...? Will you...?' He looked over his shoulder. 'We're having cakes in there. Your mum and me. Why don't you...' But Rosemary was already gone.

'Wait,' Victor grabbed the handrail to follow her, taking the first three stairs in a single leap. The sound of a door closing stopped him. He hovered but the sound of movement in the sitting room made him turn back down the stairs.

When Victor reappeared in the sitting room Edna was sipping tea.

'Nothing is more important than a good cup of tea,' she said. 'Now sit down and have something to eat.'

'Thanks, Mrs Dwyte.' He crossed the room, pulled out a chair and sat down.

She handed him a cup of tea on a saucer. 'There's milk in the jug and there's honey or sugar.' She took a dainty sip from her cup, 'You know, you and I haven't had much of a chance to really get to know one another but I've been watching you for a long time.'

'Um, sure Mrs Dwyte.' He was sitting stiffly in the chair and his eyes were swivelling around the room taking in the polished wooden furniture and expensive decorations.

'You should try to feel more comfortable, get used to being here. I plan to have you up here more often.'

'Really?' He smiled, picked up his cup and took a slurp of tea.

Edna nodded. 'Now, do you know why you're here, Victor?'

'Um, because I won?'

'That's one reason. I want to reward you for winning the competition. For all your hard work. But it's more than that.' She placed her cup and saucer back on the table and used a teaspoon to stir the milky tea, 'You know, Victor, you've been living here a long time. Almost half of your life. I think of you differently to the other boys. I think of you more as... family.' She looked up, 'I want to talk to you about the future.'

Victor reached out and shoved a cake in his mouth. At the last minute he realised she was watching and he tried instead to take a more delicate bite. The cake broke in half, falling from his mouth. He snatched at it and caught a few crumbs as the rest dropped into his cup, sloshing tea onto the saucer and table. For a second Edna looked horrified.

Victor froze, 'Damn. I'm sorry. I dunno what...'

She raised a palm to calm him and shook her head slowly, 'You haven't had the advantages of a decent upbringing. I know this is all new for you.'

He pushed his chair back and stood awkwardly. 'I should go.'

'Don't be silly. Sit down. We need to talk about some things.' Victor sank back into his chair. 'Look, Victor, it's about the farm. Major Dwyte and I only have one child, our daughter.'

'Rosemary,' he blurted sitting upright, 'I know. She's... I... We're friends.'

'That's good. You should be friends. It's time the two of you really got to know one another. You should think of her as family too.'

Victors eyes widened, 'Really. You think so? She and I would make a good family?'

'The important thing, Victor, is that I've been doing a lot of thinking about the future. The future of the farm. My husband can't run things around here forever. One day he'll need to rely on someone else. Someone who will respect him. Respect his wishes. Respect the way things have always been done.'

He beamed, 'I'm your man! I can do that.'

Edna smiled, 'We will still be around of course. We won't be leaving our home but the day to day things will need to be handled by someone talented and hardworking.'

'I can. I really can. I always do what the Major wants.'

'Of course you do, Victor. You're trustworthy. You have good blood,' she leaned forward and lowered her voice a little, 'but you need to make sure that my husband sees you working hard. Sees you taking on responsibility. He needs to realise just how capable you are.'

'Don't worry, I will. That's what I always try to do.'

'Good. That's what I wanted to hear,' she stood up and wiped the spilled tea from the table. She took his cup away and brought him another from the sideboard. 'There's one more thing,' she stood over him and put the cup on the table then lifted his chin with her finger so he was looking up into her eyes, 'this conversation needs to stay between us. Major Dwyte is a busy man and doesn't need the distraction. Can I rely on you to keep this little talk to yourself?' Victor nodded and Edna smiled. 'Lovely,' she let go of his chin and sat back in her chair. Picking up the cake plate, she offered it to him, 'Help yourself. I know young men are always hungry.'

The sound of the front door opening was followed by Tane's voice calling out, 'Victor? Where are you?'

Victor froze, 'Damn,' he scowled through a mouthful of crumbs, 'I better get back to work.'

'You stay right there. It's good for that man to see you're different from the other boys.' She got up and disappeared into the hallway. Victor watched her leave then grabbed a couple of biscuits and slipped them into his pocket.

A moment later Edna reappeared with Tane in tow.' We've been celebrating his win,' she said to Tane. She crossed the sitting room and placed a hand on Victor's shoulder, 'He won that trophy with skill and hard work and he deserves a reward. He's the hardest working man on this farm.'

Tane's eyes narrowed. He ignored her. 'Are you just gonna sit there stuffing your face, boy?'

Victor jumped up and his chair almost toppled over, 'You *told* me to come up here.'

'I told you to go find out what Mrs Dwyte needed, not to abandon your work.'

'She... I was just...' Victor glared at Tane who held his gaze. Eventually Victor looked away. 'I better go,' he mumbled then bolted out of the room. A second later the front door slammed shut as he exited the house.

'Now listen here... ' Edna started.

Tane didn't let her finish. He spun around to face her and his eyes narrowed. 'You and I need to talk.'

'You will not use that tone in my house. I'll be speaking to my husband.'

'You do that, and while you're at it, explain to him why you dragged Victor away from important work.'

'Victor was my guest. You have no right to barge in here and treat him that way.'

'Your husband holds me responsible for those boys. The only reason Victor's still here is to help train them.'

'He's here because he's the best.'

'I don't need someone who thinks he's the best. I need someone who will do what he's told.'

Her voice grew angry, 'He's good enough to be *running* this farm.'

Tane's volume rose to match hers. 'That's not your decision. Aussie is much better suited than Victor.'

'Victor's staying on this farm!'

He shook his head, 'When you treat him different like this it drives him and the other boys apart. It's bad for morale.'

'Then stop treating him like he is just one of the boys.'

'He *is* just one of the boys.'

'No he's not!' Her voice was like a slap.

Tane said nothing and there was a long silence. Finally he spoke, 'Edna, I know about Victor.'

She froze, 'What do you mean?'

'I know what you're trying to do.'

Edna looked down at the table where Victor's cup was balanced precariously near the edge. She pushed it back onto the table and there was a tiny chime as it rattled on its saucer. 'What are you talking about?'

He looked her in the eye, 'This farm has been my life for a long time. I care about it. Putting Victor in charge would be a disaster.'

For a moment she tried to maintain her composure then stabbed a finger at him, 'That's none of your concern! You'd say anything to discredit him and I'm sick of it.' She pointed at the door, 'Get out of my house. Just leave!'

He glared at her for a moment then walked out. Stepping into the hallway he collided with Rosemary as she tried to duck away. 'What the...?' he muttered.

Rosemary backed away from Tane. 'Sorry, I was just going to the bathroom.' Tane shook his head and left.

Rosemary glanced at her mother in the sitting room then started to walk away.

'Wait,' said Edna. 'You were eavesdropping!

Rosemary spun around. 'What did you mean about Victor being family?'

'Why is everyone poking their nose in today? That's none of your business.'

'I'm not stupid, you know.'

'What's that meant to mean?'

'Ever since I can remember you've always protected him. You pushed father to keep him on the farm and now you want him to be part of the family.'

'He deserves our help. He's a decent young man and he's missed out on so much...'

Rosemary pointed at the front door. 'All those boys missed out! Red and Aussie, the lot of them.'

'You watch your words, young lady.'

Rosemary stepped into the sitting room and stared intently into her mother's eyes. 'Just because Tane can't work it out doesn't mean I can't. You're trying to get me to marry Victor, aren't you?'

For a second, Edna's jaw dropped open. She looked at the crumbs of cake and said nothing.

Rosemary pressed on, 'You want him to take me to the dance, you say you want him to be family, you tell him not to tell Father about your little chat, you even give him Father's shirts after a couple of washes!'

'Since when was being charitable a sin? How dare you talk to your mother this way!'

Rosemary stepped closer, shoving her nose right in her mother's face. 'It's true. I can see it in your eyes. That's why you keep trying to force me and Victor together. You'd marry me off to him so he can look after your precious farm. You want to trap me in a miserable marriage with a halfwit farm boy, you want me to rot here for the rest of my life!'

'I won't listen to this. Not from you. Not from anyone.' Edna's lip quivered and a tear rolled down her cheek. 'I've poured my life into you, done everything I can to be a good mother. And you have no idea what the world out there is like. What men can be like.'

Rosemary stepped back, shocked by her mother's tears. 'What is it then? Why are you crying? Over Victor?' She shook her head in disbelief. 'Why would you cry over him... do you, oh God, you fancy him for yourself, don't you?'

Edna flinched as though she had been physically struck. 'Don't ever say that again. Are you out of your mind?'

Rosemary leaned closer and softly whispered, 'If you don't tell me, I'll tell Father about your little tête-à-tête with Victor.' She raised her eyebrows suggestively. 'Maybe I'll even go to the dance with Victor and let him kiss me. Would that make you happy Mother? Jealous maybe?'

'How did you ever get to be so cruel? You don't understand.'

She slumped into a chair and broke into an agonised cry, her mascara running across her pink cheeks. 'He's like a son to me, he's the son... I never had.'

Rosemary grimaced, 'It's not my fault I was born a girl. God, you're so unfair!'

'Stop it, I've had enough, just stop it,' Edna wailed but Rosemary was unmoved. Edna pulled out a handkerchief and blew her nose. 'I forbid you from talking to Victor without my permission.'

'You're mad! One minute you want me to marry him and the next you forbid me from even talking to him.'

'I never said I want you to marry him. That can never happen, you hear me, never!'

'Or else?'

'I said stop it! That's enough. He's like a son to me, and a brother to you.'

Rosemary smiled. 'How sweet, like brother and sister. Well he's not my brother and I'm never going to treat him like one. Neither will he. All he wants is to get under my skirt.'

'Jesus Christ! You are evil... you can't talk like this about Victor!'

Rosemary's eyes narrowed, 'Why?' she demanded. Edna covered her face and tried to turn away from her daughter. Rosemary exploded in frustration, 'Why, why, why?'

As Rosemary kept chanting, Edna covered her ears to shut the sound out, but it wouldn't stop. Edna's teeth gritted and her face screwed up until finally she yelled, 'Because he *is* your brother, that's why!'

Then there was nothing but silence and the chirping of birds.

Rosemary glared down at her mother. 'You've been lying to me. My whole life.'

Edna sniffed and wiped her face. 'I will not discuss this with you.'

Rosemary wasn't listening. 'It all makes sense. You've always tried to control me. Make me just like you. This perfect young lady,' she shook her head, 'but it's all a lie!'

Edna suddenly stood back up, her fists clenched at her sides, 'Don't you judge me! I was seventeen. Just a child. Do you think I wanted to give my son away? My family gave me no choice!'

'And now you've got him back and he's far more important than the rest of us.'

'Don't say that. You're more important to me than anything. It was a terrible time of my life. You can't imagine what it was like. Falling pregnant out of wedlock means losing everything. Everything! Society would have called me a whore and men would have yelled the loudest. The same bloody men who will gladly do the deed.'

Edna was interrupted by a loud knock on the front door and both women froze. The knock sounded again.

'Don't you say a word!'

'Can I go to the Ellerslie races?'

Edna looked at her daughter and shook her head in disbelief. 'Fine, you can go but not a word of this to anyone!'

'Not as long as I get what I want,' said Rosemary.

There was a third knock and drawing a breath, Edna stepped past Rosemary and into the hall to answer it. A postman stood on the porch his arm raised to knock yet again.

'Special delivery, Ma'am,' he peered at the envelope in his left hand, reading the address, 'it's for a Private Chapman.'

'I don't know anyone named Chapman. You must have the wrong address,' Edna, still sniffing, looked him up and down. 'You're not our regular postman.'

'It's an army letter, Ma'am. Defence force business. There is a note saying it can be given to a Major Dwyte.'

'I am Mrs Edna Dwyte. Major Dwyte is my husband.'

'I see. Well, if you're the Major's wife, you can sign for it. Just sign this form here.'

Edna's eyes narrowed. '*If* I am the Major's wife?' She snatched the form from the postman's hand then glanced down the hallway. Rosemary was glaring at her.

'Get me a pen from your father's study would you, dear,' Edna said softly, her voice offered no hint of the tension in the air.

Rosemary rolled her eyes. 'I guess nobody knows who you really are,' she muttered. She turned and headed for George's office to reappear moments later with a pen.

Edna hastily filled out the form then shoved the paperwork at the postman and grabbed the letter from the startled man. 'Thank you, I'll see that my husband gets it.' Before the postman could reply, she closed the door.

'Does Father know?'

Edna spun around, shocked by the question. She stammered, 'What business is that of yours?'

'Does he know?'

'It doesn't affect him. I won't have him judging me and I forbid you from mentioning it.'

'He's your husband. He has a right to know.'

Edna's eyes narrowed. 'What is this? Haven't you done enough, now you're going to blackmail your own mother?'

For several seconds, Rosemary stared at Edna in silence. 'I don't know. But I do know things are going to change around here.' She stepped forward and plucked the letter from her mother's hand, 'I'll put this on Father's desk. It might be something he needs to know.' She turned and stalked down the hall towards the Major's office.

Victor picked his way down the gully where several boys were pulling out lengths of old fence. At the bottom of the hill Dennis and Nate were digging a fresh post hole. Dennis looked up and saw Victor.

'So, what was that about?'

'Mrs Dwyte gave me morning tea. Special stuff. Cakes and everything.'

Dennis looked sceptical. 'What, just you?'

Victor reached into his pocket and pulled out the biscuits

which were now crumbling at the edges.

'Wow, for real!' said Dennis. 'Did you go inside the house?'

Victor nodded. 'Yep. It's real posh.'

Nate was now standing beside Dennis, listening. 'Far out. You're so lucky.'

'Oh, that's nothing,' said Victor, 'we talked about Rosemary. Mrs D said we would make a good family—me and Rosemary.'

Both Dennis and Nate's eyes widened. 'You lucky thing,' sighed Nate, 'Rosemary's such a honey.'

'You two will be a great couple,' said Dennis.

'Yep. We sure will.' Victor chewed on a biscuit. 'I gotta make my move soon. I think I'll get Rosemary a present.'

CHAPTER 12

Hᴜɴᴜᴀ · 1954

'GO YOU BEAUTY!' GEORGE YELLED FROM THE RAIL. His voice was drowned by the thunder of hooves as eighteen sweating thoroughbreds galloped across the finish line. Jeers erupted from the stands behind him and as he lifted his hat to mop his brow, a confetti of torn totaliser tickets drifted past.

'So the outsider won then?'

George turned to find Tane approaching him with two glasses of frothy beer. He waved his winning ticket at Tane. 'A late run and a whopper of a finish! Just like I predicted.' George's eyes were alight. 'Should have seen it. Magnificent!'

Tane handed him one of the drinks. 'Lady Luck's been with you today.'

'Pah! Luck has nothing to do with it. Picking a winner is a science. You've got to understand what makes a good horse.'

He turned and leaned on the rail and Tane did the same. The white painted balustrade ran around the outside of the racetrack, stretching past the stands and curving elegantly into the distance. In the middle of the field, large gaily coloured letters spelled out the words "Franklin Racing Club". The two men sipped their drinks as the P.A. crackled with a barely comprehensible announcement. Tane frowned as he noticed the ticket in George's hand. 'That's a big bet.'

George stiffened slightly and tucked the ticket into his fist. 'Not really. Not when it's a sure thing.' He took another swig of his beer. 'Anyway, that's two wins and a place I've picked today. Not a bad Sunday by anyone's standards, eh?'

'That's worth toasting.' Tane raised his glass. 'To horses.'

George's response was almost a reflex. 'Hear hear. To King and country.'

'Queen and country,' Tane corrected him.

'Of course.' George shook his head. 'Goddamn that's going to take some getting used to!' He tapped his glass against Tane's. 'As you say, to our new Queen.' They both lifted their glasses and drank a toast. 'Something came up today,' said George.

'Oh yeah?'

'Something from the past. Made me think about the first time we met.'

Tane frowned. 'It's been a long time since France,' he mumbled.

George fiddled with his glass. 'I know we've never really talked about it. Guess we didn't need to. But... well...' He cleared his throat. 'I still remember *that* day. In the training camp. The day you saved my commission.' George stopped and waited for a reply.

Tane just stared at the ground, the muscle beneath his temple twitching minutely.

'I remember that you held your tongue,' George continued, 'and I haven't forgotten what they did to you.'

Both men drank in silence. In the distance fresh horses emerged to warm up on the track.

Finally, George drained the last of his beer. 'When I discovered your name wasn't Chapman, I didn't know *what* to think. But your actions were enough for me. Didn't matter what your name was.' George glanced around to ensure nobody was within earshot. 'In all these years, you've never told me why. Why Johnny Chapman?'

Silence stretched as Tane stared at the ground. Eventually

George shrugged. 'Forget it. I guess every man is entitled to his secrets.'

At last Tane spoke. 'I've never been one for talking, Major. I'm more of a listener.'

George grunted in acknowledgement then reached into his jacket and pulled out the letter. He held it out to Tane. 'Well, this came yesterday, and I thought you might want to talk.'

Tane took the envelope from George's hand. He examined the name on the front, reading it again and again.

George watched his reaction. 'I've known you for almost forty years and for the last fifteen, you've lived on the farm. Seeing that name reminds me that there are still secrets between us.' He nodded at the letter. 'It's your business, I won't pry but let me know what to do with it. Do I send it back? Or does it belong to the only Johnny Chapman I've ever known?' He glanced up at the public address system as it announced the next race. George tapped the empty beer glass in his hand. 'Might get me another. Got to spend some of these winnings. Meet me back at the truck in an hour or so.' George walked off.

Tane limped across the path to the grandstand and dropped heavily into one of the front row seats. He rested the letter on his lap and just looked at it. After a while he shook his head. 'Johnny Chapman. I thought you were gone forever.'

CHAPTER 13

AUCKLAND · 1914

TANE WAS SIXTEEN AND MOVED WITH TIRELESS ENERGY. He wove his way through Sailor's Alley, left and right, never slowing. Carts and trestles, smells and whistles, skirts and faces, foreign sailors. The energy of this street never changed. Britain's declaration of war had gripped New Zealand and for the last two weeks, everywhere he went, it was all that anyone talked about. But not here. In Sailors Alley it was business as usual. These people already knew that life was dangerous.

With a running leap, Tane grabbed an overhead lamppost, swung himself onto the top of a tall brick wall then settled down to watch the human tide below. He looked back through the evening market stalls, past the traders, the punters, the lounging prostitutes. All the way to the parlour where he had spent the afternoon in pain. He lifted his sleeve and touched his arm where the flesh was still raw. Burning skin puffed around the edges of the dark ink. An anchor. To tie him to the sea.

That morning he had been told he wasn't good enough. He had lined up at the enlistment office, given his name to the Corporal, even explained how he knew his way around a ship. They had rejected him. Too young they said. As he walked away he knew he had to do something to prove them wrong. Something to show he was a man. So he had gone straight to find Billy.

Billy was nineteen and already had five tattoos—or "inks" as he called them. He loved to show them off.

'Here,' he said, pointing to an anchor high on his left bicep. 'This was my first. Got it when I was younger than you.' He moved his finger down to a skull and crossbones. 'This one I got a couple of years ago after my dad died.' He grimaced. 'He was a vicious bastard, but hell, he *was* my dad and he was all the family I had.' He rolled up the sleeve on his other arm. 'These two I got last year,' he said. 'That one is my initials and the shamrock is to remind me where the family came from.'

'That's four. I thought you said you had five.'

'Well, the last one's a bit raunchy.'

'Come on. Show me.'

'Dunno, Tane. You might be shocked.'

'I'm not a kid any more. Show me. Please.'

Billy smiled and cocked his head. He checked to ensure nobody was around then unbuckled his trousers and slid them down. His private tattoo was on his right hip. A mermaid sucking on the cock of a smiling sailor. As Tane examined it, he felt the blood rushing through his whole body. He knew that he wanted a tattoo. That he wanted to be just like Billy. That he could deal with pain and was old enough to make his own decisions.

Billy laughed at Tane's expression and reached out and mussed his hair. 'You should do it, boyo.' He pulled his pants up, reached into the pocket then handed Tane some coins. 'Go get inked. You can pay me back later.'

Tane had done it. He gently touched his fresh anchor with the tip of his finger. The sharp pain made him wince. He did feel older. He knew what his mother was going to say but it was worth it. Rolling his sleeve back down he decided he would stay out late. That way his mother might be asleep when he got home.

As he looked over the alley, his shoes started tapping a sub-conscious rhythm against the dirty brickwork. The wall opposite him was plastered with posters, most of them depicting a mus-cled lion on a rock and calling for New Zealand men to *Enlist in Britain's War With Germany*. It was a new poster of the quar-tered red and white of the Saint George cross that grabbed his attention. He instantly recognised it—the flag of the New Zealand Shipping Company. Below the picture of the flag was a recruit-ment notice and Tane leaned forwards to peer at it. *New Zealand's merchant navy needs you! Work for New Zealand's truest shipping line. Able bodied men wanted now. Eighteen years and older. No experience required.* A smaller notice had been glued carefully to the bottom of the poster. In narrow black letters it announced, *Join This Sat-urday! Queen Street wharf. 8 am.* Tane's mind wandered as he imag-ined himself sailing the world on a ship. Visiting exotic ports. Meeting new people. His shoulders slumped as he thought about how far away his eighteenth birthday was—a year and a half; it seemed like a lifetime.

An argument rose above the evening hubbub. Fifty yards up the alley, a fruit vendor was shaking his arms and pushing away a drunk who had knocked some produce to the ground. Tane jumped down from the wall and made a beeline for the tem-porarily unattended table. As he passed the stall, he plucked an apple from a basket and ducked around a corner. Before he got five yards, a large calloused pair of hands grabbed him by the shoulders and thrust him against a wall. Tane found himself staring up at Mr Gilbert.

'Mr Gilbert. What! Let me go.'

'I saw you pinch that apple, boy.'

'I didn't pinch nothing.'

The old stevedore shook his head in disapproval. 'What hap-pened to you, Tane? You were growing up to be a good kid. Now look at you. Stealing.'

'I was gonna pay.' Tane felt ashamed. 'I just have to get some pennies from my mum.'

'Your mum! You've got a cheek using her as an excuse. That

poor woman has given up her dignity so you could have a decent life. She even got you into the state school but you refused to go.'

Tane's face darkened. 'I couldn't go to school!'

'Don't give me that, boy! You were too lazy,' Mr Gilbert nodded at the apple in Tane's hand, 'and here you are still thinking of yourself.'

Tane's voice rose in frustration. 'I was pinching it *for* my mum if you wanna know! She's drunk all the time. Can't even feed herself. Spends most of her time yelling at me.' He hurled the apple down the alleyway then scowled at Mr Gilbert. 'She doesn't yell at the men she's *entertaining*. She's always got a nice word for them!'

Mr Gilbert pushed him away, shaking his head. 'Your father would have been ashamed of you.'

'You don't know anything about my father!'

'Your father was a hardworking man. He could drink, mind you, but he was honest. He wouldn't approve of your thievery.'

Tane's fists clenched. 'My father was a hero!'

'Who told you that?'

'He died in the Dog Tax War.'

Mr Gilbert laughed out loud at his assertion. 'Now, that's what comes of not going to school. Nobody died in the Dog Tax War. It was just a bunch of upstarts trying to scare people.'

'You're lying!' screamed Tane. He dove past Mr Gilbert and sprinted down the alleyway.

Twenty minutes later, Tane ducked through the front door of his home. He'd been growing and it felt like the shack was shrinking. His mother's voice whined at him before he'd even shut the door.

'Where have you been all day? I told Mr Smith you'd get his workshop cleaned out. Since you won't go to school you can damn well work.'

He grimaced at the slur in her voice. He turned to find her seated at the table, a needle paused over her sewing and an open bottle beside her. She looked tired. Her hair was matted and her clothes grimy. 'I'll do the workshop tomorrow,' he said.

'You haven't been with that boy Billy, have you?'

'Leave Billy alone.'

'He's trouble, that boy,' her eyes narrowed.

'He's my friend. He... he looks out for me.'

'I won't have you spending time with him.' She frowned, peering at Tane whose eyes were now fixed on the floor. 'I don't like the influence that boy has on you. It's unhealthy.'

'What do you mean unhealthy?'

'You talk about him like you worship him.'

'What are you talking about? We're just good friends.' He turned away from her and tugged his sleeve down a little lower, wincing slightly as the fabric brushed the fresh tattoo. 'You can't tell me who my friends are. That's my business.'

'Your business is it?' she snapped. 'Well, I'm your damn mother, so it's my business too.'

'You don't even know him. You've only met him once.'

'Yeah well, once was enough. I know a bad apple when I meet one.'

'Stop talking about him. You can't stop me being his friend.'

His mother's hand banged down on the table. 'So long as you're living here, you will do as you're told!'

Tane whipped around and they glared at each other. Finally Tane spoke, anger in his voice. 'You're a liar.'

'What?'

'Mr Gilbert said nobody died in that war up north.' He crossed his arms. 'You lied to me about my father.'

For a second, she froze. Then she looked down at her sewing. 'Don't change the subject.'

Tane took a step towards her. His throat was constricting and he had to try to get the words out twice. 'Tell me it's not true.'

Her hands scrunched the fabric in front of her. She was silent for several seconds then her words came in a rush. 'Your father loved you, that's all that matters.'

'You said he was a hero.'

'It doesn't matter. He died up north.'

Suddenly Tane was yelling. 'But he was killed fighting in a war!'

'Why are you talking about your father? He's gone and nothing can bring him back.'

'You told me he was a hero!'

'He got killed breaking up a fight between two strangers!' she yelled back. The truth echoed into silence.

His mouth opened then closed. His words, when they came, were almost a plea. 'No, that's not right. You said...' His voice cracked and he just stood staring at his mother.

She threw her sewing onto the table in front of her and took a drink straight from the bottle. 'You want to know about your father? The truth? He went up north to support his *family*!' The word was bitter. 'The family who never did a bloody thing to help us!' Anger crept into her voice. 'I begged him not to go. We were his real family. Not *them*! But your father could never say no to his brothers. Thanks to them, we were left with nothing!'

'You lied! You lied to me!'

'I was protecting you.'

'You're a liar. A damn liar!'

'How dare you.' She leapt unsteadily to her feet and her sewing box clattered to the floor spilling its contents of silver needles. They scattered like a whisper of tiny chimes, laying a minefield between her and her son. 'I've done things no woman should have to do just to support you and you keep defying me. Well, I've had it! You can get out! You're old enough to look after yourself. Just get out!' She pointed wildly at the door, staggered drunkenly and had to prop herself on the table. 'See if your friend Billy will look after you because I'm done with it!'

It was early evening by the time Tane got back to Sailors Alley. He wiped the tears from his face as he walked between the stalls.

Each time he saw a familiar face, he forced his features into a smile and casually asked the same question.

'Don't suppose you've seen Billy around?'

Finally, a woman struggling with a crate of rags, pointed towards the customs house. 'As a matter of fact, I passed him a few minutes back.'

Tane muttered thanks and hurried in that direction. A moment later he recognised Billy's blond hair. Billy was deep in conversation with a middle aged woman.

He jogged up to them. 'Evening Billy.' Billy and the woman both turned to look at him.

'Hey, Tane. How's tricks? Didn't see you at the beach this morning.'

Tane opened his mouth to reply then, glancing at the woman, he changed his mind and clammed up.

Billy smiled. 'Cat got your tongue? Spit it out, boyo.'

Tane's eye's flicked again towards the woman before he took off his cap and mumbled a reply. 'Um, Mum threw me out.'

Billy sniggered. 'Yep, business as usual when dealin' with the female o' the species. Crazy as bedbugs.' The woman cleared her throat and Billy offered her a placating smile. 'Sorry, Betts. Didn't mean you.' He looked back at Tane. 'Guess you'll have to wait 'till your mum cools down.'

Tane wrung his cap in his hands. 'You don't understand. I can't go back there.'

Billy frowned as he finally registered the look on Tane's face. He dropped his streetwise accent. 'That's harsh, Tane.' There was an awkward pause as Billy seemed unsure what to do. A little embarrassed, he turned back to the woman. 'I'll be there in a shake. Tell him to deal me in.'

With a nod, she hurried off.

'So what are you gonna do?'

'Dunno.' Tane stepped a little closer to him. 'Guess I need somewhere to stay.'

'I guess you do.' Billy scratched his head. 'You gonna go to the Crown and Rooster?'

'Nah. The girls will tell me to go back home and old Frankie doesn't like me now. Says I'm getting old enough to pay for the girls' company.'

'Then where you gonna go? Can't just wander around all night.'

Tane looked him in the eyes. 'You're my family now, the only one I've got left.'

For a moment Billy looked confused. Then with a nod of his head he wrapped his arm around Tane's shoulder. His streetwise voice was back. 'Don't worry, me young cocker, I know what it's like to have ya back against the wall. Billy'll take care of ya. Tell you what, meet me here at eleven.'

The tension on Tane's face melted into a smile of relief. 'Alright.'

'And don't you go starting any trouble.' With a smile and a muss of Tane's hair, Billy hurried off after the woman.

As Tane watched his disappearing figure, he couldn't help but sigh.

Across the street, a door opened and Marcy stepped out in time to see the expression on Tane's face. She broke into a beaming smile and her voice cut into the evening. 'I know that look. I've seen it a hundred times.' She sailed across the street and grabbed Tane's arm. 'You're in love! Awww, who's the lucky girl?'

Marcy looked along the street to find the object of his affection. There were no young women to be seen; just vendors, sailors and Billy disappearing around a corner.

Tane looked at the ground.

'Don't be ashamed, Tane. It's normal to have a crush at your age.'

Tane couldn't look Marcy in the eye. 'I don't think you'd understand.'

'Don't be daft, boy. You think I'm not a romantic? Think I've never been in love?'

'I'm sure you have, Miss Marcy. But...'

'But what?'

'This is different.'

She smiled indulgently at him and used her forefinger to brush his fringe away from his eyes. 'Tane. Being in love is being in love.'

For several seconds, Tane was silent, struggling with something.

'What?' She leaned close. 'What's wrong?'

'Marcy... it's... he's...'

'It's what?'

He glanced back up the street but Billy was gone. Losing his nerve, he mumbled at the pavement, 'She's nobody.'

Marcy shook her head. 'Well, this nobody, she's sure got your heart racing.' She leaned close and whispered. 'Love is rare, my boy. Don't be afraid of it. Tell her. Whoever she is, tell her how you feel.'

Tane looked into her eyes. 'But what if...'

Marcy put her finger to his lips, silencing him. 'The best thing you can do is to just tell her. Be honest about your feelings lad, or you'll end up with a lifetime of regrets.' She sighed, 'Trust me.'

Straightening up, she threw her faded red shawl over her shoulder. 'Anyway, enough of all that.' She pulled him along the street with her. 'Come on up the tavern and say hello to the girls. We ain't seen ya for months.'

'I don't know if I should. I've gotta meet someone at eleven.'

'That's hours away. You're not worried about Old Frankie are ya?'

'I don't think he likes me anymore.'

'He's just sour he ain't young and handsome like you.'

They wandered down the street, he wearing a resigned smile, she chatting happily.

CHAPTER 14

AUCKLAND · 1914

TANE PULLED HIS KNEES UP TO HIS CHEST. He was starting to worry because it was well after eleven and there was no sign of Billy. Tane had spent an hour visiting Marcy and the girls at the Crown and Rooster before making his excuses and slipping away. Since then he'd been waiting in the alley. The marketplace which had felt so crowded and exhilarating was now deserted and everything was wrapped in gloom. The music of early evening had vanished, replaced by a muted bass-line of creaks and thuds and the occasional flare of an angry voice. A snoring drunk, draped around the base of a street lamp, provided the only steady rhythm.

From the doorway where he huddled, Tane watched the foot traffic. People, in ones and twos, hastened past wrapped in their shadows. Tane shivered. Perhaps Billy had forgotten. He hugged his knees even tighter and lifted his collar to cover his neck.

'You miss the boat?'

Tane woke with a start. He must have dozed off. He looked up to find Billy standing over him. With a sigh of relief, he got to his feet and dusted himself off. 'I thought you'd forgotten.'

Billy's face broke into a tipsy smile and he slid his arm around Tane's shoulder. 'When the cards are falling in your favour, never walk away.'

'Of course. Figured it must have been something important.'

'Always respect Lady Luck. She comes to those who woo her.' Billy waved a finger in Tane's face. 'With her on your side, you will always win the game.'

Tane looked confused. 'What game?'

Billy reached into his breast pocket and, with a little flourish, produced an ace of clubs.

'Oh. Yeah. The game.' Tane took the card from him. He turned it over and examined the reverse. 'Do you think you could teach me to play cards one day?'

'Well, why not. About time you learned how to take care of yourself. Nothing to it really. It's all about mastering the bluff.' Billy swept around with his arm, taking in the whole of Sailors Alley. 'All of this... our whole life... it's a bluff. Understand that and you will always be one step ahead.'

Tane nodded enthusiastically. 'A bluff. I'll remember that.'

A door slammed across the street and they both looked around. Billy frowned, suddenly more sober. 'Come on, time for the foxes to retire to their den.' With Tane in tow, he started down the lane towards the old wharves. 'You ain't seen my room at the Ritz, have ya?'

'Nope. You told me it was on a ship?'

'Oh yeah. On the Titanic.'

'Long swim then?'

'Just remember to go *around* the icebergs.'

They both laughed as they broke into a jog.

An hour later, they lay sprawled side by side on a tattered mattress in Billy's den; an improvised squat in an abandoned ship's hull. Sacking, which was hung from a driftwood frame, covered rusty walls. Two upturned crates harboured a random assortment of bric-a-brac; coloured bottles, cracked plates, tattered playing cards. Items of clothing seeped from a broken wooden chest and three candles sputtered in a holder, throwing ripples of yellow light against the walls.

'So she reached under the table and started rubbing his thigh,' snorted Billy. 'You shoulda seen the look on his face. His eyes grew big as eggs. I thought he was gonna pop.'

Tane smiled. 'So what did you do?'

'Just kept dealing like I was none the wiser. Completely straight faced. I sped the game up though, dealt faster, played my cards quicker. Pretty soon he was making bad calls; betting on bad runs, folding before he should.' He leaned forward and gave Tane a wink. 'I could tell when she started moving her hand up further. He almost dropped his cards.' He laughed again at the memory of the poor man's face. 'I tell ya what, it's the ultimate distraction for any bloke. A little rub in the right place and suddenly they're thinking with the wrong head.'

'You're jazz, Billy,' Tane breathed. 'I wish I could do all the crazy stuff you do.'

Billy cupped his own face with both of his hands, raising the pitch of his voice like a girl, 'Aw shucks... thanks for the compliment, Mister'

Tane laughed. He shoved Billy's shoulder. 'Don't be a louse.'

Billy stretched himself out on the mattress again. 'You know what, Tane? I really trust you. I think we could both help each other out. Partner up.'

Tane swallowed. 'I'd love to help you out. I'd do anything you want.'

'Cool, because I'm planning something. Something big and I want you to be part of it.'

'Sure. What is it?'

'Can't tell you yet. It's still in the planning stage. Before I make any decisions I have to ask you something.'

'Of course. I got no secrets from you.'

'What do you plan to do about your mum?'

'What do you mean?'

'Are you gonna go back and live with her? Maybe tell her stuff?'

'Don't be stupid, I never tell her a thing and anyhow, I ain't going back to live with her. She doesn't understand me.'

Billy reached over and rubbed Tane's head. 'Poor boy. Just starting to learn that life ain't all duck soup. Well don't worry, I got your back.' He knelt up, leaned across Tane and blew out the candles. The warm flickering glow was replaced by a trickle of blue light leaking in around open bulkheads. He paused, arms either side of Tane's shoulders. 'It's fun having you here. I get a bit sick of me own company.' He broke into a toothy smile then pushed himself back onto his side of the mattress. 'We should try and get some kip. We've been chewing the fat for an hour.'

In the semi-darkness, Tane watched him snuggle down into the blankets. 'Billy, I have to tell you something.'

'What?'

Tane opened his mouth to continue but couldn't bring himself to speak. Several seconds passed in silence before he finally worked up the courage. 'It's just that...'

Billy rolled over to look at him in the dimness. 'It's just what?'

Tane took a deep breath. 'I think I'm in love.'

'Wow. That's killer, boyo. Who with?'

Tane looked down at his own hands. They were nervously entwining one another. 'I...' He shook his head. 'It's hard to say it.'

'Just tell me.' Billy sounded amused. 'Can't be that bad.'

Tane breathed out in frustration. Then in a single fluid movement, he pushed himself up, leaned across and touched his lips to Billy's. For the merest second the two boys were suspended, lips together. Then Billy shoved him away, sitting bolt upright. They stared at each other in the gloom, Billy's face screwed up into a deep frown.

Tane's eyes widened in fear. He swallowed and his eyes flicked towards the doorway.

'Ha!' Billy's teeth flashed as he suddenly grinned. 'You're such a bonehead. Wrestling is it? I'll show you!' Throwing off his blanket, he dived across the bed, grabbing both of Tane's wrists. Tane struggled half heartedly, a sigh that might have been a laugh pushed out of him. With a twist and a triumphant whoop, Billy was on top, pinning him to the mattress. Breathing hard, they looked into each other's eyes.

A moment later, Billy frowned and looked down at Tane's crotch. Tane gasped with excitement and shame.

Billy shook his head and rolled off. Tane hastily grabbed the blankets to hide the swelling in his trousers.

'Shit. Tane. You've been spending too much time with ya mum. You need to meet some girls.'

'I know lots of girls. It's not...'

Billy raised his voice, cutting him off. 'You're not listening to what I'm saying.' He stood up, pointing a finger down at Tane's crotch. 'You need to get yourself some time under the skirts.'

Tane pulled the blanket further up and began to tremble.

Billy noticed Tane's reaction and his anger melted. He sat back down. 'Look, don't wick out on me. We all get steamed up sometimes. Especially at your age.' Tane relaxed a little.

Billy scratched his chin. 'We've just gotta find you some female company. Maybe tomorrow I can ask Betts if she knows someone.' His eyes lit up. 'Actually, that's the ticket! You know them girls at the Crown and Rooster real well.' He sat up straight. 'I'm sure they'd do a favour for *you*.' He nudged Tane. 'If ya know what I mean.' His face grew more excited as he formulated a plan. 'And while you're getting some for yourself, you could help out your mate Billy. Since I'm taking care of you and everything.'

'I don't know,' muttered Tane.

Billy wasn't listening. His eyes had glazed over as a vision slid into his mind, 'If you could get Sal to do me a freebie, I'd show her such a good time!' He wriggled his hips. 'I mean she must get sick of all them old sailors. I been dreaming of that Sal. Every night. She's got nice tits, that girl.' He lay back down, propping himself on his elbow. 'So what do ya reckon? Could you talk to her for me?'

Tane looked a little dazed. 'Yeah, sure. I'll talk to her.'

'Thanks, boyo. That'd be humdinger!'

Billy lay down and pulled the blanket over him. 'Anyway, get some sleep. We need to be out of here before anyone's around. Gotta keep the den secret.'

'Yeah, of course.' Tane let out a long slow breath. 'Night, Billy.'

In the semi-darkness Tane turned over and wiped away the moisture at the corner of his eye.

CHAPTER 15

AUCKLAND · 1914

IN THE SHADOWY INTERIOR OF AN EMPTY WAREHOUSE, five young men were gathered around Billy.

'I got the lowdown from the lorry boys,' he said. 'The crates have been sitting in the customhouse for a month and they're right at the back of the storehouse. The owner is some toff from England and he's stuck on a ship They won't be missed, or not for a while anyway.' Billy shrugged. 'By then we'll be long gone.'

Four of the boys laughed, but the oldest one frowned and spat a gob from the side of his mouth. 'Dunno, Billy, if we get caught it'll do us in.'

'Quit moaning, Rex.' Billy flashed a confident smile at the other boys. 'It'll be a walk in the park. Once we extract them and get them back to my den, we'll split up the loot.'

Rex wrinkled his nose and stared up at the long corrugated steel roof. He took his time to stretch his neck, first left then right. The staccato drumbeat of pigeon wings broke the hush before he replied. 'You better be right.'

'Don't worry, I got it all planned.' Billy crouched down and grabbed a lump of coal. He pointed to the youngest boy, a skinny teenager with buck teeth. 'Scotty here can slip between the bars that cover the dunny window but we need a bigger opening to get the crates out.' He scraped two black lines on the ground. 'So, this is the alley behind the customs shed.' He drew a large rectangle. 'And this is the customs shed. The windows are in this back wall. They run along the top.'

Another boy spoke up. 'That's twenty feet high. How do we get them down? We ain't got wings.'

'I been boning up on the customs shed.' Billy added some detail to the diagram on the floor. 'The fire escape's here. It runs above the storeroom.' His lecture was interrupted by an insistent banging on the warehouse door. He leapt up and hastily rubbed out the diagram with his boot. The boys melted away into the shadowy corners of the building and he snuck to the door and squinted at a tiny window, to see through the soot-covered glass. Then a smile spread across his face and he hauled open the door.

'Tane! You made it. I thought maybe you'd changed your mind.'

Tane slipped through the door and Billy closed it behind him, sliding the lock bolt closed.

Tane removed his cap. 'Sorry, Billy. Took me ages to find it.' He reached under his shirt and handed Billy a page that had been torn from a book. On it was a plan view of a building.

'Perfect.' Billy put his arm over Tane's shoulders. 'Now, you sure you wanna do this? I'm happy to have you as part of the gang but it ain't been long since you were tossed outta home and I need to know you're a man now. That you're not gonna go back and blabber to ya mum.'

Tane nodded. 'I want to help you. I want to be part of the team.'

Billy guided him into the warehouse. 'Good lad. You're my lucky charm.' The other boys materialised and gathered around again. Billy scratched his head for a second then tapped Tane on the chest. 'So, you'll be our lookout.'

Billy held up the page for the others to see. 'Tane's gotten us a proper map of Customs House. Now, where was I...'

It was three in the morning and the moonlight was painting everything in shades of blue-grey. Tane was leaning against a brick wall at the end of the alley, trying to seem nonchalant. He looked nervous and for the umpteenth time he checked down the street. There was no movement, just long walls and inky shadows; Friday night revellers had long since found beds.

Sixty yards down the alley, Billy and Rex stood beneath the fire escape. Tane gave them a thumbs-up and, at the signal, Billy climbed onto Rex's shoulders then stretched up to reach the lowest runner. With a swing of his legs, he hoisted himself onto the lower fire escape, unlatched the drop ladder and lowered it quietly. Rex scurried up to join him. They crept along the runner to the next ladder then zigzagged their way to the top level where a line of windows ran the length of the building.

From inside his shirt, Billy produced a flattened length of iron. 'Pry bar,' he whispered, the moonlight turning his toothy smile blue.

'Give it here,' Rex's reply was terse. 'You keep watch.'

'Relax would ya. Tane's our eyes.'

'I don't trust him. Looks like a pantywaist to me.'

'Watch ya mouth. He's my friend and if I tell you he's tight, he's tight.' Billy handed him the tool. Rex scowled but set to work prying the window open.

Billy leaned over the metal railing and checked up and down the alley. At one end Tane was flattened against a wall, otherwise it was all clear. A sharp rasping sound made Billy jump. It seemed deafening in the late night hush. 'Shit Rex, do it quietly, you'll wake the whole damn town!'

'I am being quiet! It was stuck.' He pulled the window slowly upwards.

Billy hastily scanned the alley again. 'I coulda been quieter than that.'

'No ya bloody couldn't...'

A muted whistle from inside the building cut Rex off. The

signal repeated and Billy stuck his head in the window and whistled back. A moment later two hands gripped the lower edge of the window frame and a face appeared as a boy pulled himself up. 'Found 'em.' The boy was breathless as he hung by his fingers. 'They're real heavy. You ready?'

'Yep, ready.'

The boy's hands let go and there was a dull thud as he landed back on the mezzanine floor inside. A series of muffled grunts was followed by the appearance of a long crate.

'Shit, that's big,' said Rex as he and Billy both grabbed for it. 'You think it'll go through?'

'Quit whining, I checked it all out. It'll fit.' Billy briefly crossed his fingers then placed a foot against the wall to get more leverage. They both tried to get their hands on the crate but it was exactly the same width as the window frame and there was nowhere for them to get a firm grip.

'Shit,' muttered Billy. He pushed the crate back inside and hissed down to the boys below. 'You're gonna have to get your end higher and push harder.' A muted reply came from inside and the end of the crate disappeared for a few seconds before reappearing, this time at a better angle. The first ten inches of the crate slipped through, and Billy and Rex finally got a hold and pulled. As the long crate slid outwards, it became wedged. The two of them strained and, for a second, the box was jammed. Then with a squeal of timber against metal, the box slid free. They both winced at the noise and froze, holding their breaths and listening to the echo disappearing down the alley. As second after second of silence ticked by, they gently put the crate down on the fire escape. They smiled at one another.

'Wonder what we got?' Rex whispered.

'It's damn heavy,' Billy replied.

'Here's the other one,' the muted voice called from inside. A second crate appeared. This time Billy and Rex knew the drill and they eased it through the window without a sound, placing it on the fire escape beside the first.

Rex ran his hand over the top of the second crate then pulled the pry bar from his back pocket. 'Let's see what we got.'

Billy frowned. 'No. Get it back to the den first.'

Ignoring Billy, Rex dropped to one knee and began prying the lid off the crate. Billy grabbed his forearm. 'That's stupid. We need to get these outta here quick.'

Rex elbowed Billy's hand away. 'What if we got the wrong ones? Just gonna lift the corner, not take the whole lid off.'

'No!' hissed Billy. 'Gimme the pry bar.'

Rex scowled. 'Leave off! I can look if I want. You said we're all equals.'

'Don't be a bloody loony!' Billy lunged for the pry bar, trying to grab it out of Rex's hand. Rex tightened his grip and they both wrestled for the tool. Billy's superior strength started winning the tug of war so Rex sprung to his feet, shoving Billy's hands away. Off balance, Billy stepped back but instead of the flat runner, his foot caught the edge of the crate.

He gasped. Grabbed for the rail. His hand flailed at empty air.

He fell, twisting, head first, his brief scream silenced by the sickening wet thud as he hit the ground. The pry bar clattered musically beside his prone body.

'No!' Tane screamed from the end of the alley.

A light went on.

Standing, staring, mouth open, Rex took several seconds to register what had happened. His eyes flicked to the crates then down the alley. He looked again to where Billy lay crumpled. Then he bolted. Scrambling down the fire escape he leapt to the ground and sprinted off.

Tane dashed down the alley and threw himself to his knees beside Billy. His friend's head lay on a strange angle and blood was beginning to pool like a halo beneath it, slowly staining his blonde hair. Tane placed one hand each side of Billy's head and pulled his face forwards.

'Billy! Wake up. Get up!'

From the distance came an alarmed shout and, down the alley, another light flicked on. Tane looked towards the sound and staggered uncertainly to his feet but his eyes were drawn back to Billy. As though registering the sight for the first time, he gasped and fell back to his knees. 'We have to go!' he hissed at Billy's prone form. He pawed Billy's chest and grabbed his shirt. 'Get up. You can't...' he sobbed.

Another shout from the distance was accompanied by the sound of running feet.

'Don't leave me. Billy, please don't leave me.'

The night burst with the shrill of a whistle. Lights sprang on in the customs shed, washing the alley in pale colour. Tane's body reacted, his legs lifting him like springs, ready to flee. His hand held onto Billy's. Two policemen appeared at the end of the alleyway and Tane's whole body tensed. Still he hovered.

'Get him!' yelled one of them, pointing his truncheon at Tane. 'Get that little hori bastard.'

With one final glance at Billy's corpse, Tane sprinted down the alleyway. Behind him came long piercing whistle bursts and a policeman in pursuit.

Two hours later, Tane skidded to a halt, chest heaving. He was trapped. The policeman was only yards behind and Tane had just dashed into a blind alley. Tall brick walls towered either side and ahead. Blocking his escape was a wide culvert with a timber fence on the far bank. It felt like he had been running forever. He turned around but the policeman appeared, blocking his retreat. Hauling down another gulp of air, Tane sprinted towards the culvert, launching himself across the gap. For a second he thought he would reach the top of the fence but it was too high and his hands and face slammed against the rough palings. His feet scrambled as his body slid sideways, ribs impacting on the culvert's stone edging, knocking the breath out of him. For a second he sprawled there, dazed, blood seeping from the fresh graze on his cheek. The policeman yelled and Tane was suddenly focussed again. He climbed to his feet, struggling for purchase on the narrow ledge. Pushing himself flat against the palings, he stretched one arm up until his fingers found the top rail. Then he hauled himself over, groaning as his chest scraped the timber.

He landed with a thud and slumped back against the fence. He'd been running on ever-reducing bursts of adrenalin; his movements now felt weary and his vision was blurry. It was dawn and he couldn't continue. He found himself in a stock yard; brick buildings on two sides, enclosed by the fence and a long gate at the far end leading to the street. Canvas tarpaulins were stretched on ropes where they had been washed down and empty crates were stacked along one wall. To his left, parked against the fence, a loading cart with a coat draped over the wheel. His eyes darted around, searching the shadows for the coat's owner. There was nobody to be seen. The sound of footfalls through the fence told him the policeman was looking for another way around. He didn't have long.

He grabbed the coat and slipped it on. It was many sizes too big for him. The police knew his face so he needed to cover himself. His breathing slowed a little and he felt the exhaustion in every joint of his body. He couldn't keep running. He needed to hide.

He eyed the tarpaulins, wondering if they might offer a hide-out but it was too obvious. He crossed the yard to make a hasty inspection of the stacked crates, peering into them, calculating whether he might fit inside. He froze as a motor coughed to life nearby and panic seized him again. A squawk made him flinch then look up: a line of gulls on the building parapet watched him. For a moment he stared at them, frowning. He stepped back and scanned the side of the building. A flue pipe emerged from the wall near the street and extended straight up, terminating above the roof line. It was thin, probably from a small forge but it was anchored by metal straps every yard or so. Abandoning the crates, he went to the flue pipe and hauled on it with both hands. It only moved a fraction of an inch. He forced down three deep breaths.

'Don't break, please don't break,' he muttered then swung his legs onto the wall and laid his entire weight back against the pipe. It creaked a metallic complaint, but held. He started climbing, his newly acquired coat dangling beneath him like a pair of broken wings.

A workman hurried by and Tane lowered his head. It was full morning now and he found himself back on Customs Lane. He had lain on the roof for what seemed an eternity as the sun inched its way into the sky and when he had finally climbed down he hoped the police would be gone. Almost immediately he had run into them, and now it was cat and mouse again.

Hunching over, face down, he picked his way towards the docks, heading for Billy's den. He couldn't think where else to go. He crossed Custom Street and followed the red iron fence eastwards. As he neared the shipyard, a motorised car carrying four policemen emerged from the wharf, bumping its way across the rails that ran up the middle of the street. Tane turned away and buried his face in his collar but he was exhausted and his reactions were too slow. One of the coppers squinted in recognition. Tane ran. Behind him someone shouted, a motor revved and the chase began again.

He dived across the road, into the crowd of morning workers and turned up the first alleyway. It was narrow, just a pathway giving access to doors in the side of a building but it turned right at the end, and Tane was deposited out onto lower Shortland Street. There were people moving here too, though fewer than on the waterfront. He melted into the crowd, trudging along, matching their pace. As he turned onto Queen Street, a whistle blew from behind him, followed by a voice calling. 'I saw him! This way!'

He walked faster. Almost immediately, he saw a policeman

coming straight at him. He shrunk back against the wall with a whimper of resignation. At least the endless exhaustion of the chase would be over now. But the copper stormed right past focussed on the shouts coming from Shortland. Tane staggered forwards thanking his blind luck and forcing himself not to run. A tram trundled past and he seized the opportunity, ducking behind it to sneak across the street. As it continued up the street, he slipped out to head along the waterfront but there was a crowd blocking his way and he was brought to an abrupt halt. A throng of men, both young and middle-aged were gathered at the barricade beneath the New Zealand Steam Ship Company sign. As he watched, a uniformed guard opened a gate and the men poured through to line up in front of a recruiting desk. Tane stepped onto the street to go around the crowd when a voice made him turn. A woman at the bottom of Queen Street was pointing at him. Panic gripped him and he braced himself to make a run for the den. A motor truck growled its way past momentarily blocking the woman from sight, and he realised there was another option. He spun around and leapt into the crowd pouring through the gate.

A tall young Māori man staggered backwards as Tane pushed his way deep into the queue. 'Hey, take it easy. There's plenty of time.'

'Sorry.' Tane looked apologetic but he stayed where he was.

The man shook his head. He looked Tane up and down. 'Nice coat, e hoa. Bit big don't you think?'

Tane looked down at the coat then peeled it off and tucked it under his arm.

The man smiled at his reaction. 'Guess it doesn't matter. If we get hired they'll give us a new uniform.' He nodded at the graze on Tane's cheek. 'You had a hard night?'

Tane reached up and touched his face. 'Oh, yeah. I sorta... um...'

'Well, I hope the other guy looks worse.' The man leaned

forward and winked at him. 'Don't worry, I hear there's plenty of fighting in some of the ports we'll be going.'

As the man talked, Tane looked back through the gate. Beyond the haphazard line of men he could see a policeman talking to the woman. As Tane watched, the constable looked around peering suspiciously at the line of men. Tane shrunk down trying to remain hidden.

The young Māori man turned to see what Tane was looking at. He raised his eyebrows. 'You weren't kidding when you said you had a hard night, eh?'

Tane's eyes widened and he braced himself to run again but the man just offered him a conspiratorial smile. 'Hey, don't fret. We've all had our run-ins with the coppers.' He looked more closely at Tane. 'So where you from? You Ngati Tai?'

'Huh?'

'You're Māori. What tribe you from? What iwi?'

'My dad was Māori. But I don't really know what iwi.'

The man looked horrified. 'Didn't your dad teach you? Tell you about your hapu? Your ancestors?'

'He died when I was little. He had some brothers, but they were up north somewhere.'

'What about your mum?'

'She doesn't want me around,' he mumbled. 'I've got no family anymore.'

The man was quiet for a moment. He frowned and scratched his chin. Finally he straightened up and nodded. 'Tell you what, you stick with me, eh? I'll teach you about whānau.' He held his hand out. 'I'm Wiremu, Wiremu Toa. What's your name?'

Tane took Wiremu's hand and shook it. He opened his mouth to introduce himself then hesitated.

Wiremu laughed. 'Don't tell me. You ain't got no name either?'

'Ah... Johnny.'

Wiremu raised an eyebrow. 'Just *Johnny*?'

Tane looked down. Over his arm, he noticed a laundry tag

hanging in the jacket. He squinted at the tiny letters that spelled out *Sam Chapman*. 'Chapman,' he blurted. 'Yeah. Johnny. Johnny Chapman.'

Wiremu leaned close lowering his voice, 'Brother, you better know your name better than that by the time you get to the desk.' He stood back, reached into his coat and pulled out a letter. 'You got papers?'

'Nah.'

Wiremu shrugged. 'But you gotta show them your name. And where you live.'

'Um, I lost them.'

Wiremu shook his head in disbelief. After a moment he put his arm on Tane's shoulder.

'Hey don't worry... *Johnny Chapman*. I'll say you're my cousin. I got a letter from the vicar so I reckon they'll believe us, eh?'

They smiled and shuffled forward in line as the clerk called *next*.

CHAPTER 16

———

HUNUA · 1954

FROM HIS DESK IN THE WOOLSHED OFFICE TANE could hear the farm boys beginning their workday. The pitch of the electric shearing machine rose until it was producing a steady tenor drone. For once Tane didn't get up. The boys knew the drill. Instead, he opened the desk drawer and looked at the letter inside. It remained unopened. *Johnny Chapman.* He mouthed the name that he hadn't heard in decades then reached to pick the letter up. Before his fingers touched the envelope, he hesitated. He shut the drawer, got up and walked around his office. He checked the spare handsets. He picked up a couple of loose wool tufts that had drifted in from the work area. He tidied the books on his shelf. Eventually he found himself back at his desk, staring at the framed picture that his daughter had returned to him.

He grunted in frustration, reached into the drawer, scooped up the letter and tore it open. Unfolding the leaf of paper it contained, he flattened it on the desk and leaned forwards to read in the dim light. His finger followed the words as he read. He frowned after the first few lines then muttered the words out loud.

In line with this directive, the War Office is paying out all monies accrued from deferred payment at discharge. At the withdrawal date of 12 August 1919, your deferred payments were invested on your behalf in approved government bonds. These bonds have been cashed resulting in a payment, less administration fee. Please find a bearer cheque enclosed. It can be cashed by the named bearer or transferred to another payee once endorsed by a Royal Postmaster or Registered Solicitor.

Tane sat up straight. He turned the letter over to find a bank cheque attached to the reverse. His eyes widened as he read the amount printed on the authority; *one thousand, nine hundred and ninety-seven pounds.* He stared at it for a full minute. Then with a shake of his head, he folded it up, slipped it back into the envelope and returned it to the drawer.

A few moments later, he stepped through his office doorway. The woolshed was humming as the boys buckled down and got on with the morning's work. He nodded and even allowed himself a small smile.

Walking up the shed he spoke to Aussie. 'What was your count for yesterday?'

Aussie had just finished a ewe. He flipped it onto its feet and sent it down the chute then pushed his shoulders back to stretch his spine. 'I made it a hundred and eight. But Victor seems to think it was one ten.'

'I need an accurate count. These are straight to the works and they'll be checked through the gate at the other end. The counts need to match.'

They both looked around at the sound of a door banging. From the far end of the shed Victor emerged carrying a toolbox hoisted on one shoulder. As he walked up the shed, he passed Briar who had just delivered a sheep to one of the hand shearers. Victor twisted his shoulders and the back of the toolbox smacked Briar in the head. Briar pulled away clutching his ear.

Aussie grunted in anger. He put down his handset but before he could rush to Briar's aid, Tane's hand was on his shoulder.

'Leave it,' said Tane.

'Let me go. I'm sick of Victor bullying Briar.'

'You shouldn't get involved. Not this time.'

'But Victor's being really cruel. All Briar did was make a joke in front of Rosemary.'

Tane shook his head. 'You've been here a long time. Have you learnt nothing?' He nodded down the shed to where Briar was still clutching his ear. 'You can't fight his battles for him.'

'But I can't do nothing. He's...' Aussie's fists were clenched. He breathed out and slowly opened his hands. 'I just don't want him to get hurt.'

Tane said nothing. He let go of Aussie's shoulder.

Aussie frowned. 'I just want to protect him.' He glanced towards Briar again. 'He's so... I don't know. Vulnerable.'

Tane nodded slowly. 'You're right to stand up for your friend but you must let him make the first step. Otherwise he'll never stand up for himself.'

'Yes, Sir. I guess.'

Tane walked off. Aussie took a deep breath, retrieved his handset then called for a new sheep.

Victor headed for the power room. Tane wanted his help changing the gaskets on the Ferguson, a backup motor for the Wolseley they had salvaged from an old tractor. He saw Tane enter the power room ahead of him and he smiled to himself. Stopping in his tracks he turned and beckoned to one of the boys.

'Dennis, get over here.'

Dennis picked up his broom and jogged over to him. 'Good job on Briar's head,' he said.

Victor scowled. 'That's just the beginning. We're gonna show him.' He nodded at the power room door. 'Tane's gonna be in there all morning. You remember what we talked about last night?'

Dennis nodded enthusiastically.

'Could you do it now?'

Dennis glanced across at Briar and smiled. 'Yeah, I reckon I can.'

'Good. Go do it now,' said Victor. 'If anyone says anything, just say you were at the toilet.'

'You sure I ain't gonna get in trouble about it?'

'Nah. If he snitches we'll say he does it all the time. That he's like a baby and still has a problem. I spread the word to Nate and some of the others. They'll all play along.'

Dennis nodded and headed for the exit.

At the end of the day when work finished Briar made a bee line for Aussie's station. Aussie was cleaning his handset.

'You playing cricket?' Briar asked.

'Yep, it's Wednesday.' The large end-door of the shed had been thrown open and groups of boys were heading straight up to the house lawn. Aussie hung the handset up. 'You should come and play on my team.'

'Do I look like a wampaging wabbit?'

Aussie huffed, 'We're just the *Rampagers*. Not Rabbits.'

'Weally? You weren't wampaging wast week.'

'Hey, don't mock my team,' Aussie aimed a playful flick at the side of Briar's head. Briar winced as Aussie's fingers brushed his fresh bruise. 'Oh shit. Sorry, Briar, I didn't...'

'Don't worry. It's nothing. Victor bumped me this morning.'

'Yeah I know.'

Briar brushed the hair away from his ear to show the lump.

Aussie reached out and touched the bruise gently with his fingers. He opened his mouth to speak then hastily looked away. He grabbed his shirt and stepped out of his station. 'I mean it. You should come and play.'

'Trust me, you don't want me on your team. I'm rubbish at sports.'

'Doesn't matter. So long as you're having fun. And anyway, we've got some good players.'

'Victor's got all the good players.'

'Nah. We got some. Tim's good. Always gets us double figures and Buzz can catch a shooting star if he can concentrate on the damn game.'

'And Victor's got Victor.'

'He's not superman, you know.' said Aussie. 'He's got his weaknesses. I always bowl him eventually because he's predictable. I pitch him the same ball for two overs. Then I suddenly change it. Gets him every time.' Aussie leaned towards him and looked him in the eye. 'If you stand up to him, he eventually goes down. Just takes some time.'

The smile disappeared from Briar's face. 'I already tried standing up to him It didn't work.'

'Hey, I'm just trying to help.'

Briar turned away and muttered a reply, 'Don't think I'll play today.' He headed towards the open door.

Aussie ran to catch up with him. He grabbed Briar's arm. 'Please come and watch at least. I always do better when you're there.'

Briar was silent for a few seconds. 'Maybe. Are you batting first?'

'Dunno. We'll toss for it.'

Briar shrugged. 'Okay. But I'm gonna go get my book.'

Aussie broke into a smile. 'Great.' He slipped his shirt on and headed off after the other boys. He called over his shoulder, 'Don't read too hard. I read somewhere it's bad for you.'

Five minutes later, Briar climbed the five steps to the dormitory, a long narrow prefab that stood on piled foundations. The front end of the dorms housed a common room where boys could hang out in their spare time. It boasted two large tables, several tatty couches and shelves piled with board games and sports equipment. The weekly dormitory inspection was on Saturday and that meant the common room was a mess for the other six days of the week and Briar had to step around bats and balls and comics. Heading down the corridor he glanced into each boy's partition, a narrow space with identical furniture; a bed, a wooden school desk and a tall locker to stow their clothing. There was a broken model plane on the floor of one and, in another, a collection of bottle tops was spread across the bed covers. Walls were decorated with haphazardly pinned magazine pages, leggy fashion models competing for space with gun slinging movie stars.

Briar stepped into his cubicle. It was almost bare. He had arrived with nearly nothing and until only a few days ago, it had felt like a temporary stop—a place he was waiting to leave. Things had changed. With a smile he realised he no longer spent each day wondering when he would be gone. He was starting to feel like he belonged here. It was all because of Aussie. His smile broadened at the thought of Aussie and he suddenly remembered the cricket game. He grabbed a book from his desk when he noticed something amiss. The photo of him and his mother was gone. It was the only decoration in the room and it usually stood on the small windowsill.

He froze and looked slowly around the room. The bed, which he had made that morning, was messy, the blankets twisted and crumpled. Briar felt a chill run up his spine. He reached down and pulled the covers back. In the middle of his sheet the picture of Briar and his mother lay in a puddle of urine. A strangled sound escaped from his throat, part gasp, part scream as he grabbed the photo. Lifting the frame he saw his mother's face had been distorted by the human waste. He gagged as yellow liquid seeped from the picture and he let go of it and covered his nose.

He stood beside his bed and stared at the swollen photo and the stained sheet. Feelings of belonging vanished and once again all he could see was a bleak future in a place where he would never be accepted. He sank to his knees and sobbed.

There was nobody to comfort him. Eventually his tears stopped. He was left crouching in silence with the tightness of dried tears on his face. A shudder shot through his chest and he felt a cold hardness form inside him. He clamped his jaw to stop it quivering and climbed back to his feet. His eyes narrowed, his fists clenched and he kicked the bed. Spinning around, he seized his satchel from its peg and swept his few possessions into it. As he ran back down the corridor, he spat at the empty cubicles. 'I hate you all!'

It took him three hours to reach the head of the Hunua gorge. He ran until the breath wheezed from his lungs and his body burned. Then he walked. Despite the steel in his heart, his eyes were wet again and his mind was filled with the image of his mother growing blurrier with every mile. He couldn't stop. He was terrified that if his feet stopped shuffling forwards, if the pain stopped drumming in his chest, if the pulse stopped throbbing in his ear, he would lose her. The image would be gone. His mother. Her laughter. The feeling of family. They would all fade away and he would be left alone with nothing to tell him who he was.

The sun hung low in the sky as he passed the last farm and approached the bush clad cliffs of the gorge. The road crested a rise then dropped away into the steep ravine. Ahead of him, through his blurred vision, Briar saw a figure emerge from the trees. It was a centaur, half horse, half man. The creature stepped onto the road and turned towards him, quickly growing larger and darker. Briar squinted into the setting sun but the dark figure swayed from side to side and his eyes couldn't bring it into focus. Fear rose in him and he backed away, raising his satchel in defence.

'Briar, running away won't help.'

'Tane!' Briar's whole body slumped in relief as he saw Tane on a horse. 'How did you find me? I thought you were... How did you know?'

'I came to guide you home.'

Briar scowled defiantly. 'I *am* going home. I'm going to my dad's.'

'You're looking for your past.'

'It's where I belong.'

'It's where you came from but it's not where you belong. Not anymore.'

Briar glanced over his shoulder at the road he had walked down. 'I can't go back to the farm. I just can't.'

Tane dismounted. He lifted the reins over the horse's head. 'The farm *can* be your home. If that's what you choose.'

Briar was suddenly spitting words. 'I hate the farm. I'm crap at farm work and I slow everyone down. They hate me. And they don't even *know* me.'

Tane said nothing and Briar's tirade faded into the stilling air as he mumbled, 'I won't go back.'

'You can't run from your fears.'

'I'll never belong there. I'm not like the other boys.'

'We are all different.'

'You don't know me either!'

The light behind Tane faded and the lines on his face grew deeper. 'Nobody will ever know you if you keep running,' he said. He turned away and checked his horse's tack. 'You're growing up, Briar. You need to accept that.' He slipped two fingers under the girth strap and tested the tension. 'I won't stop you. *You* must choose. Stay and be part of our family. Or go. I'll tell them I couldn't find you.'

Briar looked past him and down the Hunua gorge. The winding road was no longer clear, a hundred yards into the gorge it disappeared into the gathering darkness. 'But if I come back, Victor won't stop.'

'If you stand up to your fears, you'll find you have friends.'

Briar pressed his lips together but couldn't stop them from quivering. He looked beyond the gorge to where the sun was perched on the horizon. Its horizontal light was throwing everything into sharp relief. 'I used to have friends...' His voice cracked. He couldn't finish his sentence.

The sun sank below the hills.

'Your old life is gone, boy.'

The shadows of the hills reached out and folded their cloak around Briar and the hardness inside him melted as quickly as it had formed.

'Why does everything always have to change?' he said.

There was no answer.

'I don't really have a choice, do I?'

'We always have a choice.'

Briar breathed out a long sigh. 'Okay. I guess I'll give it another try.'

Tane nodded. He lifted a foot into the stirrup and swung himself into the saddle. 'She can carry two if we walk.' He leaned down and reached an arm out.

Briar looked around one final time. Darkness had finally erased the landscape. With a deep breath he took Tane's arm and hauled himself up onto the horse's back.

Tane clicked his tongue and goaded the horse forwards. 'Try and relax, son. We've got a long road ahead of us.'

CHAPTER 17

BRIAR FLINCHED UPRIGHT. His heart was pounding. It was still dark. Before dawn. It took him a second to realise that something was grasping his shoulder. A hand. His eyes followed the arm upwards to find the dim outline of Tane standing over his bed.

'What...'

'Shhh, come. Quietly.' He beckoned for Briar to follow then exited the dorms.

Briar slipped out from under the covers, fumbled for his shirt and shoes in the darkness then tiptoed after Tane, wondering how a man so big could move without sound.

Light began to colour the dawn sky as Tane led him to the stables, a building Briar had been in for the first time the night before when they returned on horseback. The went into a round pen which adjoined the building. On the far side of the pen, a large open doorway led into the stables. Hay bales were scattered near the entrance but the space beyond was dim.

'Come right in, boy. There's someone I want you to meet.'

Briar stepped inside to find a horse tied to a railing.

'This is Wairua.' Tane placed his hand on the animal's forehead. 'She's new on the farm. You and her should spend some time together.' He scratched the horse under the chin. 'Horses are honest creatures. They don't lie. Don't judge.' Tane patted Wairua on the shoulder and walked away.

For a second, Briar just stared at the horse and Tane was almost out the door before Briar blurted out, 'But what should I do?'

Tane stopped. 'Get to know her.' He pointed to the far corner of the stables. 'There's some brushes over there, start by brushing her down.' With that Tane was gone.

Briar found himself alone with a horse. He looked closely at the animal; most of Wairua's body was coloured brown and a hint of red reflected from her mane but her hooves and the lower part of each leg were dark, an earthy tone that was almost black. The horse turned its head to look at him and Briar couldn't help smiling. He went and fished around in the corner and eventually found some brushes.

'Okay girl, I'm just going to give you a little brushing.' He approached with a brush in hand. The horse whickered, its nostrils flaring. Her head turned to peer suspiciously at his outstretched hand.

Briar froze, wondering if she might react badly to the brush. The horse suddenly seemed very large. After a moment, Wairua looked away so Briar inched forwards and gently pressed the brush into her shoulder. She flinched. Her front legs stomped the ground and her shoulders and neck flicked upwards. Briar jumped back, his heart racing. With a sharp twang, the twine attaching Wairua to the rail snapped. She took three awkward steps backwards until her rump pressed against a barrier then she flicked around and trotted out of the stables into the round pen.

Briar breathed to calm himself. With a shake of his head he followed the horse outside and climbed onto the rails of the round pen to look for Tane. The driveway beyond was empty.

Briar frowned, climbed down from the fence and contemplated Wairua standing on the far side of the pen. 'Come on, girl.

Let me brush you. You'll like it.' He inched his way towards the horse, his movements reduced to slow motion. A second before he could touch Wairua, the horse flicked her tail and trotted out of reach. She seemed less distressed this time so Briar crept after her trying to calm her with words. 'Wairua, hey girl, don't be afraid. Let me brush you. We can be friends. Just give me a chance.'

The horse's nervousness kept winning. Again and again she trotted away before Briar could touch her, moving around the edge of the pen with him circling behind.

Finally, Briar stopped. He threw the brush down. 'I'm tired of this game!' He slumped back against the railings and looked at Wairua in the full morning light. The horse was slim and somehow her head seemed a little too big for her body. Briar wanted to brush her, pat her, show her he liked her and even more, he wanted to succeed, show Tane he was worthy of this favour. He frowned and looked around. The pen was large, maybe thirty paces across. A bit like a sheep pen. Just like a sheep pen, Briar realised, the more empty space there was, the harder the animals were to catch. He needed to get Wairua back into the stables where she couldn't escape so easily.

He stood up. 'Alright girl, you're going back inside now.' Briar moved around so he could push her towards the stable door. This time he didn't try to make himself small and unthreatening. Instead he stood tall and stretched his arms out, hoping to block the space behind him and force the horse to back up. 'Back you go. Go on. Inside.' Wairua's eyes looked at the open space beyond Briar but he waved his arms over his head to pre-empt her movement. 'Don't even think about it. Just go back into the stables, there's a good girl.' He pushed closer but the horse's legs didn't move. Instead Wairua lifted her neck higher and higher, straining it back to keep an eye focused on the approaching boy. Briar got to within a yard of Wairua and stopped. The horse's chest was quivering and he knew she was about to move. She snorted, stomped again and rose up on her hind legs. He lunged for the short length of twine that was hanging from the bridle but Wairua leapt past him and his hand closed on empty air. He ended up on his hands and knees.

He dusted himself off and glared at the horse. This just wasn't working. He needed longer arms, or something to push the horse around with. He went into the stables to search for a tool. In one of the stalls there was an assortment of old ropes, bottles and, against the wall, a few lengths of wood. As he reached for the longest of these he noticed a barrel with the lid ajar. A warm earthy smell arose from it, strangely appetising, like molasses and freshly dug soil. He lifted the lid and the smell intensified. His stomach rumbled, reminding him he had not eaten dinner the night before. He dug his fingers into the moist mix of grains and chaff; it was horse feed. Briar dropped the stick, armed himself with a handful of feed and wandered back out to Wairua.

He approached the horse with the feed on the flat of his hand. Wairua eyed the offering. Her neck lowered gently and she sniffed the handful of food, nudging it gently with her upper lip. Briar reached up with his other hand and for the briefest moment, he touched Wairua's quivering neck. It was warm and sinuous; tense with contained power but Wairua's nerves took over once again and she crow-hopped forwards, pushing his hand away as she ran to the opposite side of the pen.

Briar cast the last of the feed into the dirt. 'Damn you. I give up! I can't do anything right.'

He stomped into the stables and slumped down on a hay bale, his head in his hands. He was hungry and tired and frustrated and his failure with Wairua was bringing back all the emotions of the day before. Why did he come back with Tane? He should have kept going. He could have been in town by now, walking into his old classroom, seeing Alistair again, the two of them reaching out and holding hands. His teacher's face filled his mind. And the headmaster's. And his father's. Every adult had the same look on their face—disgust. His daydream collapsed and Briar felt he had nothing. All the doors to life seemed closed except for one narrow path, one he had never wanted to travel.

He flinched at the tease of warm breath on his neck. Slowly turning his head, he found Wairua sniffing his shoulder. He reached up gently and touched her muzzle. She didn't retreat. Cautiously he rose to his feet, turning to face her. Wairua let out one final resigned whicker but she remained where she was and they stood there, two timid creatures.

Briar smiled. He gently ran his fingers through Wairua's mane and the muscle beneath twitched as she stretched her neck sideways, enjoying the sensation.

Outside, obscured by a clump of flax, Tane nodded to himself then turned and headed off towards the woolshed, rolling a cigarette as he walked.

CHAPTER 18

Hunua · 1954

TWO WEEKS WENT BY AND FOR THE FIRST TIME since arriving on the farm, Briar had a spring in his step. There were four horses on the property and Tane had made him responsible for grooming them. Each day he would get up before dawn, collect them from the paddock, brush their coats and clean out their hooves. Afternoons were the best. Between work and study, he would go and spend time with Wairua. A whistle would bring her trotting up to him looking for a scratch or a handful of the feed Briar had taken to carrying in his pocket. There was a bond forming between them. Wairua was more than a pet. She was a friend.

It was Friday and that afternoon they had no lessons, just free time until dinner. Briar was already out of the woolshed door, heading for the lower paddocks when Aussie grabbed him by the wrist.

'Hey, aren't you ever coming to cricket? I miss having you there.'

Briar felt a twinge of guilt. He really hadn't spent time with anyone since meeting Wairua. 'I will come but I can't just now. I have this other thing. It's taking up a lot of time.' He shrugged at Aussie. 'Besides, I only played on your team twice and I was pretty crap.'

Aussie smiled. 'Well, you're never gonna be an A-grade cricketer but I miss having you there. Always felt like we had a fan.'

'Actually, I sort of miss watching you play,' Briar gave him a cheeky smile, 'and it was great research. I'm planning to write a book on how to lose gracefully.'

Aussie laughed. 'Surely you mean disgracefully.'

'The disgraceful game. Hmmm, has a certain ring to it,' Briar scratched his head, 'and come to think of it, you *do* play disgracefully. I heard about the full toss that smacked Dennis in the nuts. That wasn't very graceful.'

'He deserved it after what he did on your bed.' Aussie scowled. 'Can't believe he didn't get punished.'

The smile disappeared from Briar's face. 'Yeah well.'

Aussie stepped closer to him. 'They claimed it was you pissing yourself. Why didn't you speak up?'

'Forget it. I don't care anymore.'

Aussie opened his mouth to object but Briar raised his hand to stop him. 'It's in the past. I honestly don't care.'

Aussie's frown softened. 'You've changed.'

'Have I? Yeah. Maybe I have.'

'I like it. You seem... happier.'

Aussie's expression was tender and Briar realised how much he had missed him. 'You should come and meet Wairua. She's the most amazing horse.'

'Wairua eh? I'd love to,' Aussie gestured up towards the house lawn, 'but right now, the team needs me.'

Briar glanced towards the lower paddocks. 'Wish you could come now. I wouldn't mind having someone else around.' He lowered his voice, 'I didn't ask permission but I'm going to try to get on her today. Tane says she hasn't been ridden since she failed as a racehorse but I reckon she'll let *me* sit on her.'

'That's cool. Sounds a bit scary though.'

'Wairua's not scary. She's just... I dunno. Nervous, I guess.'

Aussie glanced around at the sound of raised voices drifting down from the lawn. The cricket game was beginning. He put a hand on Briar's shoulder. 'I have to go play but I'd love to come and meet your horse sometime.'

'That'd be nice,' Briar smiled.

Aussie let his hand rest on his shoulder for another second then turned and jogged up the hill.

Briar headed for the lower paddocks and, as he walked, he could feel the touch of Aussie's hand every step of the way.

After dinner that night, Briar ran to the stables to find Tane. He rushed through the gate into the round pen, almost colliding with Major Dwyte.

'Sorry, Sir. I'm looking for Tane.'

The Major frowned at him. 'You're the new boy, er...'

'Briar, Sir.'

'Yes, of course. How are things going? Are you settling in?'

Briar looked at the ground. 'Um. Yes, Sir.' He shuffled his feet. 'It's all good.'

'Pleased to hear it. The most important lesson you'll learn here is that making your way in life takes hard work.' The Major reached for the gate latch. 'Tane's in the stables.' He let himself out.

Inside, Briar found Tane putting away a bottle. Tane must have seen the excitement on his face.

'What is it, Briar?' he asked.

'Sir. I can sit on Wairua now.' Tane's eyebrows raised. 'I know you didn't say I could but she trusts me. I knew she would let me.'

Tane nodded slowly. 'That's good. It does show she trusts you. You need to take your time. She failed on the track because she was too jittery.'

'Would you teach me to ride? I mean, to ride properly?'

'I'll show you the basics but I'm not the best teacher, Wairua is. If you listen to the animal, you'll learn from each other.' Tane checked his watch. 'You better move, boy. You've got evening chores.'

Briar's shoulders slumped a little. 'I'm only on rubbish tonight and there's still lots of light. I could get Wairua now...'

Tane held up his hand. 'Tell you what, I'll meet you here in the morning and we'll see what we can do. Now, vamoose.'

At dawn the following morning, Tane stood holding Wairua's halter while Briar tended to the horse. Briar released a fetlock as he finished picking a hoof and Tane nodded his approval.

'Alright, let's get you mounted.' Tane led the horse up to one of the slatted stalls and turned her side-on. 'Up you get, lad.'

Briar frowned. 'What about equipment? Shouldn't I have reins and saddle and things if I'm going to learn proper riding?'

Tane laughed. 'This is Hunua, boy, not Huntingdon.' He thought for a moment. 'It's good for the horse to get used to being tacked. Especially since she hasn't had it for a long time.' He leaned into the stall behind him, grabbed an empty sack and flicked it over Wairua's back. 'Here, this can be your saddle blanket. Put it on her whenever you ride.'

Briar glanced at the pile of leather horse tack in the far corner of the stables. 'But you use a real saddle.'

'You need to *learn*. And to do that you need to feel what's happening. The horse will speak to you,' he touched different parts of the horse, 'through her back, her flanks, her neck. A saddle will just make you deaf.'

Briar looked sceptical.

Tane took a deep breath then rummaged in the stall again. He produced an old length of rope. 'Here's a trick for you, boy.' He showed Briar how to twist and unthread two figure-eight knots, one at each end of the rope. Then he tied the rope into either side of Wairua's halter to form reins. He waved the rope at Briar. 'First lesson. You must never pull on this. Keep it short but soft so you can feel each other's movement.' He demonstrated by pulling the reins back, just to a point where there was no sag in the rope. 'Alright, enough talk. Up you get,' said Tane.

Briar climbed onto the slatted timber of the stall and threw his leg over Wairua's back. He froze for a moment but the horse stood calmly so he wriggled forward.

Tane handed Briar the reins and led the horse out into the round pen. 'I'll teach you how to use your legs. The rest will be up to you.'

Twenty minutes later, Briar had Wairua walking around the pen unassisted. He stopped the horse in front of Tane, beaming from ear to ear. 'It feels amazing up here. Makes me feel free. Like I could ride off forever and go anywhere I wanted.'

Tane smiled at his enthusiasm. 'Oh, I remember that feeling,' he said. 'I remember it well.'

CHAPTER 19

Pacific Ocean · 1914

THE NEW ZEALAND SHIPPING COMPANY had set up their recruiting desk in an open-sided tent. Three men wearing matching woollen shirts sat at the desk and behind them a tall steamship was berthed against the dock. Tane and Wiremu approached the head of the line. Tane took one last glance back towards Queen Street, but there was no sign of the police.

One of the recruitment officers finished scribbling in a notebook. 'Next,' he called. Wiremu stepped forward, pulling Tane with him and handed the man his documents. The officer gave the paperwork a thorough inspection. 'What about you?' he glanced at Tane.

Before Tane could respond, Wiremu answered. 'This is my cousin Johnny Chapman. I can vouch for him. He got a letter from our vicar too but we lost it.'

The man frowned. 'You're required to have at least one letter of introduction.'

'He had it this morning but when he put his jacket down it disappeared. Someone must have swiped it.'

The man looked them both up and down. 'I don't suppose you have a scrap of experience between the two of you?'

Wiremu shrugged. 'I been shearing for five years. Just like it says there.' He pointed to one of the letters lying in front of the officer. 'I ain't scared of hard work.'

Tane straightened his shoulders. 'I've helped unload plenty of ships. I know my way around deck cargo and holds,' he said.

The officer raised an eyebrow at him. 'I've never seen you before. Who you been working with?'

Tane opened his mouth to mention Mr Gilbert then hesitated as he realised it might give away his identity.

'Look, there's men waiting. I haven't got time for tale spinners.' The officer looked at Wiremu. 'We'll take *you*. But your young friend...'

Before the man could finish, Tane pointed at the ship docked behind him. 'That's the *Tongariro*. Four hundred and fifty-seven foot stem to stern, fifty-eight foot beam. Forty-nine hundred net register ton and seven hundred and sixty gross. She usually berths in Wellington but I guess she's in Auckland loading butter. Before she was berthed, the *Coptic* was alongside taking on mutton. She's four hundred and thirty foot long with a forty-two foot beam. And she's famous for being in the moving pictures.'

The recruiting officer seemed impressed. He looked Tane up and down again. 'How old did you say you were?'

'Eighteen, Sir,' Tane replied straightening his shoulders again.

The officer thought for a moment then scribbled their names on two cardboard tags. He handed them to Wiremu along with his papers. 'Alright Toa and Chapman, we'll give you a try. Get yourselves to the pier office to register. They'll assign you.'

Eight hours later they were on a train headed for Wellington along with two officers and a dozen young recruits. They travelled through the night and the next morning when they arrived they were assembled on the rail siding and escorted to the company's Wellington office. One of the officers explained that the company was investing in more ships to take advantage of a new route that was opening. Tane guessed immediately that he was talking about the Panama Canal. For years, the Auckland wharves had been full of talk about the Americans completing the "cursed crossing". The French had originally tried to build it but failed. Tens of thousands of men had died from disease and disaster as the French engineers attempted to link the Pacific and Atlantic oceans. An old wharf hand had sworn to Tane it was Neptune rising to punish humans for tinkering with his domain. Now the Americans had finished what the French had started and there was a new route open, one that cut weeks off the passage between the Pacific and Atlantic oceans.

In the office, a clerk entered Tane and Wiremu into the seamen's manifest of the New Zealand Shipping Company. Tane watched as the clerk dipped his pen in black ink then wrote *Ordinary Seaman (O.S), Johnny Chapman* along one line of the huge green book. He and Wiremu exited the office with huge smiles, filled with a spirit of adventure. As *Ordinary Seamen*, they would each be earning seventeen pounds a year, a sum that seemed like a prince's ransom to Tane. They had only one night to celebrate their newfound careers in Wellington because they were both assigned as deck crew on *HMS Antebellum*, bound for London the following day.

Like all New Zealand Shipping company vessels, *HMS Antebellum* was painted in the company livery; black hull, white superstructure and a yellow funnel. When Tane and Wiremu boarded the boat, it was already a hive of activity. A team of deckhands was loosening both the forward and aft lines so they could be unhitched by dockhands on the wharf below. The thrum of the deck and the occasional hiss of venting steam told Tane that the boat had a full head and was ready to sail. Sure enough, minutes later the forward lines were released and they drifted astern, swinging the ship's bow away from the dock. The aft lines were dropped a moment later and the whole ship shuddered as the screws began to turn. They pulled away from Wellington dock, and to Tane, it felt like the fulfilment of a dream. He lifted his face to the overcast sky, closed his eyes and felt the wind blowing through his hair as they steamed west. At Ward Island they turned south and as they passed Pencarrow Head, the narrow passage gave way to the broad expanse of open water. Tane couldn't help but cheer. Wiremu laughed along with him and their excitement drew a smile from some of the able seamen. The boatswain was not so forgiving. He glared at the smiling crew and barked at Tane.

'Save your wind, boy. You'll be doin' men's work as soon as we set a heading,' he looked Tane up and down, 'and stay out of the way if you don't know what you're about.'

Tane nodded at the men coiling the mooring lines amidships. 'I can fake a rope,' he said.

'Can you now?' replied the boatswain dubiously. 'You look like another landlubber to me.' He nodded to the crewman who was working closest to them, a tall man with a shock of wiry red hair. 'Take a breather, Creighton. Let's watch this lubber make a fool of himself.' He raised an eyebrow at Tane. 'Well, hop to it then.'

Tane stepped up and braced himself over the low coil of heavy rope. He spat on his palms and rubbed them together then gave a nod to the line handlers. They began feeding the rope towards him. He grabbed the rope and, twisting it with his left hand, laid it down in a circle, using his weight to keep downward pressure and ensure the growing coil remained tight.

The boatswain watched Tane's performance. After a while, he pulled a pipe from his jacket and tucked it into his mouth. 'You'll do,' he muttered and with no further comment, he headed off towards the stern.

The nearest rope passer patted Tane on the back. 'Nice job, lad. That's high praise from the boaty.' Tane smiled. The red haired man stepped forwards and held out his hand. 'You must be Chapman. We ain't been introduced but you've been assigned to my detail.'

For a fraction of a second, Tane hesitated. He still wasn't

accustomed to his new name. Then he grabbed and shook the man's hand. 'Yep, that's me, Johnny Chapman.'

'I'm Creighton,' the man pointed to his own hair. 'Always easy to find, just look for the fire top.'

The rope passer piped in. 'This is where he claims to be a Viking.'

'Shut up, Brakovich, what would you know? Your ancestors were a bunch of goat lovers.' Creighton turned back to Tane. 'It's true enough though. I inherited this hair from Eric the Red himself. One of my ancient ancestors.'

'Well, the Vikings were great sailors,' said Tane.

Creighton slapped his own chest. 'It's in the blood.' He took the rope from Tane. 'I'll take over here. You best stay with the other lubbers. The old man has called for an all-hands as soon as we're set. He's going to address the crew.'

Tane rejoined the new recruits and as the boat turned and set a north-westerly heading into the Southern Pacific, the whole crew assembled on the rear deck. Standing against the rail, Tane watched the dark green shores of New Zealand slip away behind them and his head filled with memories; grief as he pictured Billy's broken body, relief at escaping the police, and a pang of guilt as he imagined his mother, sitting at the table with her needlework, unaware that he was sailing away. New Zealand had been his home. His life. The only place he had ever known. But it was time to go. As the land faded to a thin green line on the horizon, he took a deep breath and turned his attention to the Captain who stood above them on the bridge castle deck.

'You've undoubtedly heard the rumours that we are bound for the new ocean canal in Panama. Now we are underway, I can confirm that is the case.' There was a mutter of response from the crew and, glancing around, Tane noticed smiles and frowns. The Captain ignored the crew's reaction and continued. 'Each and every man should feel proud that this boat will be the first of the New Zealand Shipping Company fleet to make this voyage. We hope to make London in thirty-four days.' There was surprise on some of the men's faces as they realised how speedy the voyage would be. 'More than half of you are new to the boat and I expect the same dedication that you gave to your previous captains. We also have new recruits onboard and you will all be expected to help bring them up to speed.' He stopped for a moment and scanned the crowd. 'I have always run a tight ship. I will not accept laziness or poor behaviour on my boat. I expect professionalism and good seamanship from every one of you.' He nodded to the third mate to take over then disappeared towards the bridge.

Like all of the crew, the third officer was wearing a thick navy-blue jumper with the NZSC logo emblazoned on the breast, but his also carried white epaulettes showing a single gold stripe, designating his position. He dismissed the crew to their stations, instructing the new recruits to stay.

'Welcome onboard the *HMS Antebellum*,' he said. 'She's been my boat for ten years. She's not the largest in the fleet but she's quick in a fair sea and sturdy in the weather.' He reached behind him and patted a bulkhead. 'She'll take care of you if you take care of her.' He looked at each of the recruits in turn. 'The Captain expects all of you to follow orders without question. You are ordinary seamen. Unqualified. Everyone else working on this boat has earned his ticket and you will pay them the proper respect. Your own training will begin soon and if you work hard, you can earn your rating within a year.' He lifted a clipboard to read from it. 'I'll start by giving you your crew assignments.'

They were bound for London via Panama Canal but their first call would be at Pitcairn Island, a port they expected to make on the sixth day. They cut through light seas, making good time. Tane and Wiremu were assigned to Creighton's work detail and the huge red-haired mariner put them straight to work. For days they mopped and swabbed until it felt like they had washed every square inch of the boat. Then they were taught to scale rust and buff the freshly scraped iron before painting it with a thick oily paint that stuck to everything it touched. They learned their way around the cargo holds and the correct ways to fasten down the winch knots as the cargo moved. Work was gruelling, physical and often boring. Tane learned to appreciate Creighton's patient guidance. Creighton was tireless and never complained about the work. In fact, his broad sense of humour made each watch pass more quickly. Working alongside him, as part of a team, Tane developed a sense of comradeship he had never felt before.

On the fifth day out, the new recruits, or "lubbers" as the experienced crew liked to call them, were released from their details and introduced to the skills of marlinspike seamanship; proficiencies they would have to master in order to qualify as able seamen. Under the watchful eye of the boatswain, a gruff man with a beard as grey as the overcast sky, they practiced splicing and knotting rope and using the large lipped pliers to trim the heavy strands—a job made more complex by the thick sheep hide gloves that needed to be worn.

That night, in the mess, one of the senior deck crew had called for volunteers to stand the mail buoy watch. Tane smiled to himself. He'd spent most of his life on the docks and knew the tradition of playing a joke on a gullible new recruit.

'It's one of the most important duties onboard,' explained the man to the eager listeners. 'Any urgent mail being delivered to the ship is stowed on the mail buoy and we pick it up mid passage. Someone has to stand watch for the buoy and hook it onboard as we pass.' The experienced crew all nodded and muttered their agreement, some of them barely able to hide their smiles.

'But what about the radio room?' asked one of the lubbers. 'If it's urgent, won't they transmit it?'

'Morse code is just for short messages, lad. Anything complex has to be written down.'

In front of him, Tane noticed Wiremu's back straighten as he went to raise his hand. Tane shoved Wiremu in the back then whispered in his ear, 'Just keep quiet.'

A moment later, a lubber called Biggs jumped to his feet. 'I'll do it!' He was one of the youngest recruits, not much older than Tane.

'Good on ya, lad,' said the senior crewman. 'You'll be perfect. Those young eyes of yours will spot the buoy no trouble at all.' From nowhere, the man produced a box. 'Now there's a couple of things you gotta wear. It's tradition. And of course so we can distinguish ya from the other crew.' From the box he produced a huge red rain cloak and a yellow pointed hat. 'This is the mail buoy uniform. Let's get it on ya.' He lifted the cloak over Biggs' head, slipping it over his shoulders.

'Gosh, it's rather big.' said Biggs, frowning at the bright covering.

'Don't be worrying about that. You've got an important job to be doing.' He tightened the cape around Biggs' neck. 'They make 'em so one size fits all.' Around the room a few of the crew were stifling laughs. 'Now, let's get the hat on ya.' He tried pushing the yellow hat onto Biggs' head but it was too small and wouldn't fit so the crewman used the cord to tie it tightly under Biggs' chin. He stepped back and surveyed his handiwork. Around the mess, a chorus of affirmation went up.

'Right and proper.'

'He's the mail man.'

'Important work.'

By now Biggs had a dubious expression on his face. But at the chorus of support he straightened his shoulders and nodded enthusiastically.

'Come on then,' said the crewman, 'I'll give ya the special mail hook and show you where to stand. Captain says we should be passing the buoy in the next hour or two.' He placed his hand on Biggs' shoulder. 'You may be missing out on a few hours of free time, but you'll earn the respect of your shipmates.' He led

Biggs out of the mess, winking over his shoulder at the rest of the men. As the door shut behind them, the whole room went up in a peel of laughter.

Wiremu frowned at Tane, 'That's mean-spirited.'

Creighton, sitting nearby, heard him. 'It's just a bit of fun, besides, it's teaching you all a valuable lesson. You can't afford to be gullible. Just wait until you visit some of the foreign ports. There's people there who would sell you your own dreams and fleece you for every penny.' He nodded in the direction Biggs had left. 'They'll tell him the truth in a couple of hours and he'll be none the worse and a little smarter in future.'

That night when they went to bed, Biggs' hammock was empty. A little later, he entered the bunkroom looking sheepish. There was a round of applause as he came in and Biggs looked like he wanted to die from shame. Several of the able seamen got up and shook his hand or patted his back and explained that they had undergone the same ragging. Eventually Biggs was laughing along with the rest of them.

The next morning everything changed. In the early hours, while they slept through the twelve-to-four watch, the wind had veered and risen to gale force. They woke to the groaning of iron as the riveted seams of the hull were stretched and compressed by the movement of the ship. Their hammocks, strung bow to stern, soaked up most of the ship's roll, the side-to-side movement of the vessel but each time the boat crested a wave and pitched down into a trough, the head end of the hammocks would jerk, jarring the occupants.

Tane woke with a start. He glanced around the sleeping quarters to find all of the new recruits wide awake. The rest of the deck crew, experienced seamen, remained asleep, one or two still snoring as the ship shuddered its way through the heavy sea. It was the look on Wiremu's face that made Tane roll out of his hammock. His new friend was as pale as a ghost, his eyes wide, his mouth hanging open, struggling for breath. As Tane watched, Wiremu's body convulsed and he gagged. His mouth snapped shut but not before a mouthful of vomit had shot onto his chest.

Tane grabbed Wiremu's swaying hammock and pulled the side down, urging Wiremu to roll out. 'Come on. You need air. Let's get you up on deck.' As Wiremu struggled to sit up, the ship pitched again and he was ejected from his hammock landing on his knees on the deck. Tane helped him up and they staggered across to the portside hatchway. Before they could climb the steep stairs, the hatch swung open and a shrouded crewman stepped through in a gust of wet sea air. He leaned hard on the heavy iron door and closed it before stripping himself out of a long oilskin jacket that was dripping seawater onto the painted iron deck. As the hood was peeled back, Tane saw it was Creighton.

'Boss, I need to get Wiremu outside.'

Creighton shook his head, 'Third mate says he wants everyone to stay below decks.' He descended the stairs and looked more closely at Wiremu, frowning sympathetically. 'I was like that my first time out.' He looked back up the stairs then handed Tane the coat. 'Alright, get him to the quarterdeck, aft of the bridge castle. It's fairly sheltered there. The fresh air will help.' He stepped aside to let them pass. 'Just avoid the mate or he'll make you go below.'

It took almost ten minutes to get Wiremu to the stern of the ship. They stayed hard against the bulkheads as they moved, trying vainly to avoid the shower of spray that would descend on the ship every time she pitched forwards. When they got to the rear deck, Tane grabbed a cleat attached to a rear-facing bulkhead. The *HMS Antebellum* pitched steeply up and seemed to hang there forever before plunging down into the next trough. As the ship righted herself and her bow sucked itself free of the inky sea, a rush of churning water surged across the decks washing across Tane's boots. Wiremu doubled over and retched again, his shoulders and back shaking.

Tane grabbed the oilskin hood that was flapping from

Wiremu's shoulders. 'That's it!' he yelled over the sound of the wind. 'Get it all out, mate!'

The only answer from Wiremu was a long rasp as he cleared his throat. His body swayed as the ship moved under him and his right arm reached back, flailing until he found Tane's arm which he clung to with a vice-like grip. Tane grabbed the cleat harder and braced one shoulder against the bulkhead, providing a steady support for his friend.

This was their first real experience of a heavy sea and Tane was relieved to find that he already "had his sea legs". He didn't think he would be able to sleep through a storm like this, well not yet anyway, but he was unaffected by the seasickness that was giving Wiremu so much trouble. As he stood there with the gale blowing around him and the seas raging, he was filled with a weird energy. Like a waking dream. He felt as though he was riding the storm with the winds and the seas of the Pacific at his control, carrying him towards his destiny. He couldn't help but laugh out loud.

By the following morning the seas had abated and they sighted Pitcairn Island. The northerly gales had slowed their passage and they were behind schedule. The *HMS Antebellum* approached Pitcairn at full steam passing Nancy's Stone and rounding the south-eastern point of the island. Only as they approached Bounty Bay did the captain finally allow the ship to wash off speed. The third mate once again addressed them on the rear deck.

'We'll be taking on deck-cargo, mostly wool bales. I want it all secure and lashed by midday. There's to be no idle chatter with the locals. They're strict Adventists here and they've got their own ways.'

Clouds disappeared as they hove-to at the long wooden wharf below the scattered buildings of Adamstown.

'Get those camels overboard,' ordered the third mate and Tane and his detail were put to work deploying a chained series of wooden logs that provided a barrier between the iron of the ship's hull and the unfendered wooden pier. The work of loading began almost before they had stopped moving and breakfast was forgotten. Instead, the galley mate brought them biscuits and hunks of bread and cheese that they scoffed at their posts.

Tane was surprised to see that almost half the people working on the island's wharf were women. Many of them looked Polynesian—although with light skins. They lifted and hauled the freight alongside the men and none of the *Antebellum* crew seemed to think it odd. When Tane asked Creighton about it, the big man frowned.

'It's the way they do things here,' he said. 'Technically, this is an English colony but the locals have their own rules.' He shrugged. 'The population's pretty small. So I guess they've all got to work.'

'Is it true? About the *Bounty*?' Wiremu had heard the crew talking in hushed tones about the residents of Pitcairn.

'It's true enough that they are the descendants of the mutineers.' He nodded towards the harbour. 'On a calm day, you can see the wreck sitting on the bottom, just off the starboard there. Some say it's bad luck to sail these waters.' He glanced back at the wharf where the locals were loading wool bales onto a chain hoist. 'Any talk you've heard about devil worship is just scuttlebutt and you shouldn't pay it any mind.' He leaned closer to Tane and Wiremu. 'I hear the captain is related to one of them,' he whispered. 'Not the mutineers, but a preacher who came here to bring the word of God.'

'The third mate mentioned they're all Adventists,' said Wiremu.

'Well, I guess the butter-bar should know. He's been sailing with the captain for ten years,' Creighton chuckled, 'but I heard it different. I heard the preacher was chased out of England for getting a very young member of his flock pregnant.'

The last of the bales was lifted from the dock, hoisted up to the gantry arm then swung onto the deck where it was manhandled into place by a detail of deck crew. The ship's whistle blew and there was a scurry of new activity as the boat was made ready to depart.

'The cook said we usually stop here. Maybe even get ashore,' said Tane.

Creighton glanced around to check they were out of earshot of any other crew. 'We're in a hurry, that's for sure. There's word that more merchant ships have gone missing in the North Atlantic. I think the captain wants to make Panama as quickly as possible and join a convoy for the Atlantic crossing.'

Men, fore and aft of them, released mooring lines and the camels creaked as the pressure of the hull was released. An inch gap opened between the boat and the wharf. Then another and another and to Tane it felt like the wharf was moving away from them.

Creighton stuck his head over the side to gauge the distance. After a moment he called to the detail. 'Okay. Let's haul it.' The five of them leaned over and pulled the camels up the side of the boat. When the tops of the poles emerged over the bulwarks, Creighton called for them to hold and he looped a length of rope around the head of each pole. Once the rig was secure, the detail flipped each wooden pole onto the deck, until all of them were lying in a row, secured by the chain that held them together.

Creighton stepped back and removed his gloves. 'You four get that stowed. I need to break out deck straps.' As he turned to head fore, he patted Tane on the back. 'Don't worry, Chapman. I hear we're going to be stopping here on most crossings. You'll get to bathe in Botany Bay soon enough.'

The rest of the Pacific crossing was plain sailing. Apart from a couple of brief showers, the sky remained clear and the sea mild. It grew hotter and Tane and Wiremu eventually found themselves working in singlets and short pants, scraping iron under the baking sun and breathing air so humid that it felt like sucking down liquid. The only break had come as they crossed the Equator on the evening of their nineteenth day at sea. Most of the seamen ate quickly and left the mess, leaving the new recruits along with a few others to finish their meal. Eventually, the third mate appeared and instructed all of the lubbers to assemble on the rear deck. When the young men got to the stern, they found a part of the deck enclosed by a circle of rope. Facing the circle sat a small bench. The third mate ordered them all to stand inside the circle and not to move even if their lives depended on it.

'Seafaring is one of the greatest traditions of mankind,' he intoned, 'but the sea can be a harsh master.' He raised his voice, 'You have been called to stand trial to see if you are worthy to serve Neptune. I call upon the ancient god of the sea and his bride to oversee the ceremony.'

Two crewmen emerged. "Neptune" wore a cloak with an assortment of shells sewn to it. His "bride" wore a torn dress with two large objects inserted at chest level to create an enormous bosom. His head was adorned with a wig of seaweed and both of them wore crowns made of driftwood. A peel of laughter went up from the recruits as Neptune and his bride hammed their way across the deck to sit regally on the bench.

'Shellbacks, come forward and test your brothers!' called the third mate. From all around, crewmen emerged dressed in an odd assortment of torn clothing decorated with shells and driftwood. One of them stepped forward with a small keg and a wooden cup. The rest formed two lines making a passageway of bodies between circle and bench. Standing in the rope circle, Tane found himself at the end of the two lines of men peering along the human corridor at the seated "gods".

The keg holder stepped up to Tane. 'Are you willing to be tested?' he called in a loud voice. Tane looked around at his fellow lubbers. They were all smiling and urging him on.

'I am,' he called out, nodding his assent.

The man poured a full cup of rum. 'Drink this spirit of the sea.' He held the full cup up and everyone cheered. Tane took the cup and with a deep breath he threw his head back and drank down the rum. It burned his throat and he almost gagged but he got it down and held the cup out, upturning it to show it was empty. The crew cheered again.

'Approach Neptune, the king of the sea. But only if you can weather the storm!' cried the third mate.

Tane stepped between the lines of men, heading for Neptune. There was a rustle along the lines and suddenly the crewmen had things in their hands. A bucket of water was thrown at Tane's head. Then another. As he staggered forward, flails made of seaweed whipped his back and short lengths of rope beat his legs. He crunched over, hands covering his head, and dashed down the corridor of sailors. Finally, he staggered up to Neptune and his bride and the "weather" from the crewmen ceased.

'Kneel!' commanded Neptune. Tane fell to his knees. His head was starting to swim as the rum took hold. Neptune stood and placed a hand on Tane's head. 'You have crossed the line and passed the test. You are now a shellback. Arise and join your brothers.' The bride gave Tane a seaweed flail and pushed him into the line of crewmen.

Each of the new recruits drank the rum and passed through the ever-growing passage of shellbacks. Once they were all done, the rest of the crew welcomed them as brothers with a chant of "shellbacks, shellbacks, shellbacks" and the mug was passed around the rest of the crew. One man played a harmonica, others clapped or sang along and they celebrated until the keg was finished. Two hours later, Creighton gathered up Tane and Wiremu, both of whom were sprawled on the deck, and helped them to the bunkroom.

The following morning felt like the worst day of Tane's life. His head throbbed with pain and the bright sun seemed to burn its way right through his brain as he struggled to focus on painting the inner bulwarks. He vowed to himself that he would never drink rum again.

CHAPTER 20

PANAMA · 1914

THEY APPROACHED THE PACIFIC COAST OF PANAMA in perfect weather. Several other steamers stood off the port of Balboa, awaiting their turn to pass through the canal. The captain ordered them to lay anchor. An hour later a harbour tender came alongside and a port master wearing a red jacket boarded the *HMS Antebellum* to transact their passage. The boatswain announced that they would be at anchor for a day and many of the engineering crew appeared on decks having been granted a watch or two of recreation time. There was no rest for the deck crew. The third mate had them run out ladder hoists and scrub down the hull.

Tane and Wiremu worked together, sitting on a plank suspended above the deep green waters of the Gulf of Panama.

'Do you miss home?' asked Tane.

'Well yeah. I want to be with my girl Mere,' said Wiremu, 'but it's like I told you. We've got a baby coming and we need money.' He stopped scrubbing for a moment and shrugged. 'She's gotta have somewhere to live. Her and the baby I mean.'

'Why can't you live with your parents?'

'You don't understand what it's like between some of the tribes. My people won't accept her and her people won't accept me. They don't think we should be together.'

'That's harsh, Wiremu.'

'My father is the worst. He's so stuck in the past. Stupid grievances from when he was young.' Wiremu's tone grew agitated. 'Why should I care? That's his life, not mine.'

'Maybe he doesn't want you to get hurt.'

Wiremu laughed. 'Ha, Mere would never hurt me. She's... she's... well, she's just not like that.' He glanced around at Tane and a smile crept onto his face. 'Mind you, she can have a temper.' He winked and nudged Tane with his elbow. 'All the good ones do, eh boy?'

It was Tane's turn to laugh. 'I'll take your word for it,' he said. He wiped the sweat from his forehead. 'I hope I can meet her someday.'

'Of course you will.'

Wiremu was cut off by a stern voice from above. 'Oi! You're not being paid to gossip. You should have finished that plate by now.'

'Sorry, Sir,' Wiremu called up. 'We're nearly done.'

They both set their brooms back to scrubbing. 'I miss my mum even though she was always yelling at me,' Tane said quietly. 'I've decided I'm gonna put some money aside for her.' He paused. 'I wish she could just do her needlework.'

'You're a good boy and you're lucky to have a mum.'

Tane perked up. 'Oi, stop calling me a boy. I know my way around this boat better than you.'

Wiremu used his legs to push them away from the hull so he could check the whole plate. After a moment he nodded and called up to the man above. 'Done! Move us to the next one.' With a slight jerk, the ropes and plank began moving aft. 'Tane the sailor *man*, eh? Well, Mr Sailor Man, we better get to scrubbing or they won't hoist us up for lunch.'

The third mate woke them early the following morning.

'Show a leg!' he yelled, as he came into the bunkroom. 'Captain wants us moving in an hour.'

As Tane turned out, he realised that the boat was already thrumming. The engineers must have been stoking and running up the boiler for an hour or more. He realised he no longer woke to the sounds of the ship's operations. He touched the tattoo on his arm and smiled sadly. It was a gift from Billy, and now it seemed particularly appropriate.

They were underway within the hour and as he watched the landscape slip by, Tane was thankful that he was deck crew. They steamed past the Pacific entrance and navigated Balboa Reach. The curved bay narrowed and eventually funnelled them into a broad river whose waters grew dirtier each mile they steamed. Land slid by on either side—swathes of farmland dotted with a chaotic sprawl of ramshackle buildings and smoking fires. Every so often the farmland was punctuated by pockets of dark green bush with lush palm trees leaning over the water. They slowed as they approached a wall of grey concrete set between scarred clay banks. Tane realised it was the Miraflores locks. In the mess the previous evening, he listened in fascination as the third mate explained the workings of the canal—three different systems of locks lifting the ship ninety feet up to the level of Gatun Lake and then back down and into the Caribbean.

The *Antebellum* lined up to enter the left lane of the first lock, and Tane leaned over the rail to watch a steam tug helping to push the bow around. They slid into the narrow slip of water, their starboard hull almost touching the centre wall. Tane's detail were tasked with manning the front mooring cleats, attaching and detaching the ropes from the mules which ran on tracks along either side of the locks and guided the boat through. To Tane, these machines looked like large square rail engines but they ran almost silently and he could only hear the squeak of wheels on rails as they floated along beside the ship, one fore and one aft on either side. He was surprised to feel the vibrations of the ship's screw turning as they entered the lock.

'We'll be under our own steam,' explained Creighton. 'The

mules just keep us pointed in the right direction. They don't pull us.'

They crept past the first open gate and into the lock. Tane watched the huge double-skinned barrier pass beneath them and the wall of the second gate draw closer. Suspended in front of the closed gates was a huge fender chain.

'What's the chain for?' he asked Creighton.

'It's to stop us if anything goes wrong. Don't want anyone ramming the gates.'

The boat slowed and came to a stop and they waited for a good ten minutes before they could see anything happening.

'They've gotta close the gate behind us,' explained Creighton. 'So they can fill the lock. It's exactly the same as a river lock.' Tane looked confused and Creighton laughed. 'Plenty of those in England. I've spent a few holidays there with my grandfolks.' Tane nodded then they all crowded to the bow rail to watch the front lock gate open.

Water behind the double set of gates was many yards higher. As the gates cracked open, seawater came jetting out from around the edges and quickly grew to a cascading waterfall. Tane felt the ship lifting beneath him and the mules either side spooled out more rope. Shortly the giant fender chain was lowered to the lock floor and he felt their screw engage. They moved slowly into the second lock and the entire process was repeated again. The final set of gates opened and Tane's crew unhitched the mule lines. The *HMS Antebellum* sailed out onto Miraflores Lake, striking a straight course for the Pedro Miguel locks. These would lift them up to the Gaillard Cut, an artificial valley almost eight miles long that would, in turn, lead them into Gatun Lake.

Several hours later, when they passed the township of Gamboa and sailed into the broad waters of Gatun Lake, the deck crew were dismissed to the mess for lunch. The excitement of the canal trip had fired Tane's imagination and he stayed glued to the bow rail. After a while Wiremu reappeared with a kerchief full of food.

'Here, can't have ya starving away to nothing.' He handed Tane several slices of bread, some cold lamb and a fresh apple.

'Thanks. I'm famished.' Tane's reply was half lost as he tore into the food.

The two leaned side by side on the railing and watched the landscape of Panama sliding past. In the distance the slipway for the Gatun locks appeared, the final part of the canal's lifting system. It would lower them ninety feet, back down to sea level.

'It sure is different from home,' said Wiremu. Tane grunted his agreement; he was still engrossed in his food. Wiremu stripped his singlet off so he was bare-chested. 'The damn heat's the real problem.' He used his singlet to wipe his brow. 'I wonder what it will be like in England.'

'Well, we get three days shore leave to find out.' Tane took the last bite of apple and threw the core into the waters of the lake. 'Creighton said he'll show us the sights of London if we want.'

'That'd be great. I just wish Mere was here to see it too.'

'You really do miss her, eh?'

'Yep. Sure do.'

He reached into the pocket of his trousers and pulled out a photograph. The picture was torn and frayed around the edges but Tane could see a line of young men and women in front of a corrugated iron shed. At one end of the line, Wiremu stood with his arm around a girl.

'That's Mere there. With my baby inside her.'

Tane leaned forward to inspect the image. The girl had her hand on her belly but she didn't look pregnant. 'She looks really nice.'

'Yep. She was always kind to me.' Wiremu looked at the picture for a few seconds then slipped it back into his pocket. He turned around so his elbows were leaning on the rail and tipped his head back so his face was bathed in sunshine. 'You'll understand one day, Tane. You'll find the right woman.'

Tane looked away. 'Yeah, I guess.' There was a moment of

silence between them before he continued. 'At least I've got my best friend with me.'

Wiremu turned to look at him and broke into a smile. 'Yeah. That's exactly what we are, eh? Best mates.' He slipped an arm over Tane's shoulder. 'And we're gonna stick together no matter what.'

Three hours later they exited the canal and steamed into the Caribbean Sea. Tane and Wiremu saw the first signs of the war raging in Europe. A huge battleship was anchored off the port of Colón, protecting Cristóbel Harbour. Many of the deck crew swarmed to the port side to get a look at the warship as they slipped past.

'It's huge. Look at the size of those guns,' said Wiremu.

'She's massive alright. One of Roosevelt's "Great White Fleet",' said Creighton. 'I guess they don't want Europe's war coming here.'

They lay anchor again to take on fuel and the coaling ship that tended them was also a U.S. naval vessel. It flew the naval jack, a blue flag displaying the forty-eight stars of the Union. All of its crew wore uniforms, even the coalmen. The *Antebellum*'s deck crew were drafted to help with loading and it took several hours to fill and trim the coal bunkers. When they finished, Tane burst into laughter at the sight of Wiremu. They were both black from head to toe with coal dust. The third mate ordered the ladder hoists deployed and men were given sponges and lowered on the planks, three at a time, to wash themselves down in the seawater. The crewmen stripped off their clothes and grabbed the opportunity to laugh and dive and splash.

Tane launched himself from the plank before it reached the water, hitting the surface with a joyful whoop. He plunged into the sea and the warm tropical waters closed over him. Propelling himself back to the surface, he stripped off his soot covered pants, scrunching them in his hands to remove the dirt. A sponge hit the side of his head and he looked around to find himself surrounded by happy crewmen flinging articles of clothing or wrestling one another under. He smiled then laughed out loud as a sense of freedom and adventure washed over him. He had found a family. Life was perfect.

CHAPTER 21

Hunua · 1954

IT WAS EVENING FREE-TIME. Briar lay on one of the old couches in the dormitory common area and looked out the window at the deep green hills of Hunua. For the last two weeks, he had spent every spare second practising his horse riding but today was an exception. When he gathered up Wairua first thing in the morning, she was moody and didn't want to take the bridle. When Tane checked her, he discovered that she was in season.

'She'll be restless coming into heat,' explained Tane. 'She will have been fighting with the other horses.' He shrugged. 'It's nothing major but don't ride her for a couple of days.'

When evening came, Briar suddenly found himself at a loss. Aussie had gone to town with Major Dwyte to find tractor parts and they still hadn't returned. After an early dinner, Briar retired to the dormitory to read. At this time of day, the dorms were usually deserted, most of the other boys preferring to spend the long summer evenings outside. Not tonight. At the far end of the bunkhouse, a huddle of boys whispered and laughed. An undercurrent of excitement filled the room. Something was being planned.

The front door opened and Aussie walked in with a duffel bag over his shoulder. The group of boys beckoned to him and he put his bag down and joined them. They absorbed him into their group and talked at him with animated hands and faces. Eventually Aussie threw his head back and laughed then nodded his agreement to whatever they were discussing. He detached himself from the group and walked across the room to where Briar was reading.

'What you up to?' Aussie asked.

Briar lifted his book to hide his face.

Aussie smiled. 'Oh, playing dumb are we?'

Briar dropped his book an inch just in time to catch a glimpse of something flying through the air. A fraction of a second later, Aussie crashed onto the couch beside him and Briar almost bounced onto the floor. His book went flying and his hands dug into the couch.

'Boy, you must weigh nothing,' laughed Aussie.

Briar scrambled to retrieve his book. 'And you must be a flying elephant.' He flipped the pages to find his way back to the story.

Aussie grabbed his arm and pulled him off the bed. He nodded his head in the direction of the farm boys. 'Come on. You have to come too.'

'Come where?' Briar glanced at the knot of boys across the room. Red was performing some sort of dance, gyrating his hips and clutching his chest as though he had D-cup breasts. 'Where exactly are they planning on going?'

'Col found out the Marist girls are staying at the church camp ground. Apparently they've been out hiking today. They should get back late and take a shower.' He shrugged. 'Red reckons there's a hole in their shower block wall. The guys wanna sneak down and take a peep.'

'Oh.' Briar looked at the book in his hands. 'I see.'

Aussie snatched his book and closed it. 'Well?'

'Well, I'm sure you'll enjoy your walk.'

'Man, you gotta come.'

Briar looked again at the huddle of laughing boys. A part of him wanted to distance himself but a stronger part wanted to belong. He nodded slowly. 'Alright, I'll go. So long as you're going.'

Aussie threw a mock punch into his shoulder. 'That's the spirit. Go with the flow.'

The door opened again and Victor walked in and gave the boys a thumbs-up. 'Let's go,' he turned and left and the boys rushed after him.

'I didn't realise Victor was going,' said Briar.

'Don't worry about him. We're not at work now.' Aussie put his arm across his shoulders and pulled him towards the door. 'Anyway, just stick with me. He won't take any notice of us.'

It was almost dusk and a dozen boys were crouched behind a low paling fence enclosing the back of the camp ground. Twenty yards away Briar could see the long narrow prefab that housed the ablution block. Steam and giggles escaped from the showers. Light flickered around the cluster of copper pipes that emerged at floor level and emptied into a concrete drain. Several boys were daring one another to risk a closer look.

'You go first,' Red whispered to Dennis.

'Nah.' Dennis pushed him. 'You go.'

'You're the quietest.'

'But you've been here before.' The two boys tried shoving one another towards the fence.

'Oi!' Victor yanked them both back. 'Stop acting like little sissies.' He thrust Red forward. 'Red, you go. Show us where this hole is. Then we'll come over one at a time.'

Red looked like he was having second thoughts. 'What if Tane finds out?'

'Stuff Tane. He'll never know we were here.' Victor pointed towards the shower block. 'Go.'

Red scrambled over the fence. He dropped to the ground and snuck slowly up to the wall. He froze for a second, listening, then pointed his finger down to the hole where the pipes emerged from the building. He had to crouch and twist his head sideways to peer through the gap. After a moment he glanced back, wide-eyed with a huge smile on his face. He signalled his triumph with a thumbs-up.

Dennis jumped over the fence and crossed the open space in a crouched run. He stood impatiently beside Red for a moment then grabbed him and hauled him out of the way. Red squawked in protest before covering his mouth and shrinking back against the wall. Dennis glued his eye to the gap.

Another boy reached to clamber over the fence but before he could go, Victor hauled him back. 'I'm next!' He glared at the boys around him. 'Oldest first and you only get a minute each.'

'But...' several boys started to protest.

'That's the rules!' Victor hissed. He disappeared over the fence. The rest of the boys pressed forward, arguing in harsh whispers about who was the oldest.

Briar and Aussie quietly sunk to the back of the group.

'Not in a rush to take a look?' asked Aussie.

Briar's face reddened. 'Um. Dunno. It's... I'm...'. Behind Aussie, the excited farm boys were peering over the fence. Red reappeared and another boy climbed over, headed for the shower block. Briar's shoulders slumped. 'I guess... yeah, I suppose I should.' He turned around to go back to the fence when, for no reason at all, a picture of Wairua appeared in his mind. He remembered the first time he had patted her, the horse's head over his shoulder, her nostrils flared, cautiously testing Briar's scent. Something inside Briar let go.

He turned back to Aussie. 'You know what? I don't really want to look at naked girls.' He held his breath waiting for Aussie's response. Aussie just looked at him with an expression that was half frown, half smile. The silence stretched and Briar tipped his head back and watched the last fingers of daylight withdraw from the sky leaving a transparent atmosphere. 'But you go have a look.'

Aussie's reply was almost a whisper. 'Nah, I don't wanna look either, I'd rather stay here and talk to you.'

'You were the one that wanted to come along. Don't miss out because of me.'

'Honestly. I don't really care if I look.'

'Why?' Briar cocked his head. 'Is it against your religion or something?'

'Um, I didn't really think about that. I guess it is sort of bad.'

'Do you believe in God then?'

'Yeah. Don't you?'

Briar shrugged. 'My mum went to church. But not my dad.'

The sound of a scuffle made them turn towards the fence. The boys were still jostling over their pecking order. Aussie put his hand on Briar's shoulder and guided him to a clearing a dozen yards back. 'We can watch them from here.' They plonked themselves down on the grass. Aussie raised an eyebrow. 'You really aren't like the other guys, are you?'

'I'm trying to be.'

Aussie nodded slowly. 'Why were you sent here by the cops?'

The question caught Briar off guard. 'Um... I'm not supposed to talk about it.'

'I won't tell anyone.'

Briar tilted his head in thought. Then he closed his eyes and lay back on the grass.

'Hey, don't sweat it,' said Aussie. 'If you don't wanna tell me, that's cool.'

A tiny sigh escaped Briar's throat. 'You've gotta swear not to tell.'

'Of course I won't. Don't you trust me?'

Briar opened his eyes. 'Yeah. I think I do trust you.' He propped himself up on an elbow. 'My dad threw me out and now he doesn't want me back.'

'That's tough but why did you get sent here?'

'It was because of this boy from my English class. It was at New Year's. At the movies. Well, it was because of what happened at New Year's.' He stopped as he realised his words weren't making any sense. He could feel his pulse racing. He took a deep breath and started again, more slowly this time. 'This boy saw us kissing. At the movies. Me and...' He felt his chest tighten and a familiar sense of shame crawling over him. He struggled to push the next words out. 'Me and my friend.' He wanted to say his friend's name but couldn't get his tongue to do it.

Aussie didn't react. He just watched Briar, waiting for more detail.

Briar sat up, pulled his knees up to his chin and wrapped his arms around them.

Aussie put a hand on his arm. 'Tell me about your friend.'

Briar's breath caught in his throat as Aussie touched him. The tiny hairs on his arm stood up like they were reacting to a static charge. 'We went to school together,' he whispered. 'We were...' Before he could finish his sentence, a shriek pierced the evening and they both jumped to their feet. It was a girl's voice. It was followed immediately by the clunk of a window swinging open and a stern, matronly voice.

'Who's that? Is somebody out there?'

All the boys sprinted down the dirt road, fleeing from the scene of their mischief. Gravel crunched beneath their feet and whoops of laughter wrapped them in a shared sense of conquest. Briar was amongst them, his heart pounding so fast he felt giddy. His lungs burned, wind pushed the hair from his face and he too smiled as Aussie flew through the twilight beside him.

They eventually slowed and the smell of ferns and lemonwood and the cooling earth filled the air. Boys puffed hard, peeling off sweaty shirts.

The bragging started as soon as they caught their breath.

'Oh man! Two girls showering together!' Red tucked his shirt into his belt excitedly.

Dennis trumped him. 'I saw three, and you could see everything!'

'There were two when I looked,' said Hunter, a tall skinny boy usually as quiet as a mouse. 'One of them had bush and one didn't. I almost split my pants!' He used his forearm to make an erection gesture and the boys hooted and sniggered.

A younger boy moaned, a scowl on his face. 'You buggers, I didn't get a look because you made so much damn noise.'

'Tough luck, suck it up,' Victor's reply was echoed by several others.

'Did the old cow see us?' asked Van, a chunky fourteen year old. 'I only saw the girls' backsides. Then the window opened.'

'Nah,' scoffed Victor, 'we were too quick and anyway that old matron's as blind as a bat.' He scrunched up his eyes, bared his teeth and flapped his arms. His bat impression earned another round of laughter.

'Damn nuns!' moaned Van.

Red spoke up proudly, 'Don't worry about the matron. I made a possum noise as we were taking off. To fool her.' He demonstrated a possum call that sounded like he was being strangled.

'That doesn't sound like a bloody possum,' said Victor, as he turned off the road and onto a bush track, motioning for the rest of the boys to follow.

'Maybe a dying possum!' laughed Aussie.

'Or a choking possum.' Dennis threw his hands around Red's neck and pretended to strangle him.

'Nah, that's the sound of you choking your chicken!' sniggered Hunter.

Briar was the last to turn off the road and as he walked down the track, he looked up. The stars were out and the silver night sky flickered through the spindly manuka that towered either side of him, slicing the world into frames. It felt like being in a cinema, like being part of the projection and he suddenly imagined himself in British East Africa, jogging along a winding jungle path. Ahead of him, Aussie's bare back was the muscled torso of Tarzan. The theme music played in his head and his feet paced along the dirt track, keeping time with the music. The path narrowed and gorse bushes reached out and brushed him but he didn't flinch. He just lifted his head and watched the silver light flickering on Aussie's skin.

CHAPTER 22

Hunua · 1954

THAT NIGHT, AFTER THE BOYS RETURNED to the farm, Briar couldn't get the cinematic images out of his head. When he fell asleep, they continued to play in his dreams and along with them came memories of New Year's Eve. Lights dimmed and when the movie started, he and Alistair floated off their seats and were transported into the screen. Alistair became Allan Quatermain leading Briar on a search for King Solomon's mines. Endless stone stairways led them to a steamy, humid cave where young shirtless men shore the fleece from golden sheep. A drum beat hypnotically and a skeleton appeared pointing its bony finger. 'Pack your things!' screamed the wight. 'Time to become a man!' Briar turned away in terror and threw himself into Alistair's arms. But it was no longer Alistair. It was Aussie.

Briar sat bolt upright, wide awake in the darkness. He was covered with sweat. Throwing off the bed covers, he collapsed back on the mattress, tossing and turning for what seemed like hours before he finally found sleep again.

The next morning was Saturday and Briar woke tired. After breakfast he trudged his way down to the woolshed in a daze. The shed was hot and stuffy and he found it hard to concentrate on the morning's work but the boys managed to finish the flock and after lunch they were dismissed on free time.

Briar wandered down to the paddocks and rounded up Wairua. As soon as he climbed on her back, his energy returned and half an hour later he was riding along the western ridge. With a small twist in his seat he redirected the horse between two kahikatea trees where a track ran into the ranges. He closed his eyes and tipped his head back, looking up into the crowns of ancient ponga trees. The muscles of the horse's back massaged him from side to side; a sinuous rhythm that rose through his back and shoulders and left his upturned head swaying from side to side.

The trail widened and started to descend as he pushed Wairua into a trot. The horse steered around roots and stumps, sure footed and as keen as her rider to enjoy the freedom. At the bottom of the hill, they slowed to a walk again as the path dropped down into a stony riverbed but before Wairua could wade through the water, a voice made Briar jump.

'I thought I was the only one who knew this trail.'

He twisted around to see a boy riding up behind him. He was trimly dressed in slacks, shirtsleeves and a buttoned waistcoat. A cheesecutter was pulled down hard on his head.

'Ah, sorry,' Briar stammered.

The boy pulled his horse to a stop, staying in the shadows of the manuka trees. Briar squinted trying to see him clearly. He couldn't be sure of the boy's age. His voice sounded young but his upper lip was darkening with a moustache so Briar assumed he was older.

The boy raised an eyebrow. 'Why are you sorry? It isn't *my* trail. It's a national park, after all.'

'Oh yeah,' Briar muttered. He examined the boy's horse; a grey, probably seventeen hands tall. It was kitted out in polished leather tack. 'Nice saddle.'

'Did you forget yours?' The boy looked at the piece of sacking Briar was perched on.

Briar glanced down and felt the sting of humiliation burning his cheeks. Wairua snorted and it felt to him like she was laughing. He puffed himself up. 'Actually, I prefer to ride bareback.'

'Looks like a good way to get hurt.' The boy leaned forward and gave Wairua a frank looking over. 'Wanna have a race?'

Briar's newfound confidence wavered. He'd only tried cantering a few times and that was on a flat field. 'I dunno if I should.'

'Don't be a coward!' The boy nodded up the trail. 'Come on, just to the top of that next hill.'

The word coward sat in the air. 'Well, I suppose...'

Before Briar could finish, the boy whipped his grey and took off, fans of water flying from his horse's legs as he splashed through the shallow river. For a second Briar froze, startled, then he kicked Wairau into a canter dashing, after the other rider. His ears were instantly filled with the rush of wind and the drumbeat of hooves. Woven through came the sound of the boy bellowing *go go go* and Briar's own voice leapt from his throat shouting his excitement and terror. They flew across the riverbed, up another trail and through a long winding ditch. Briar clung and bounced on the edge of control and finally they tore up a steep incline towards the crest. As they approached the ridgeline fence, the boy glanced back to find Briar hard on his heels, Wairua's flattened head only a length from the grey's thrashing tail. The boy adjusted his posture; leaning forwards and raising himself off the saddle. The grey sailed over the fence.

Wairua adjusted her pace to follow and Briar panicked, throwing his body back, away from the approaching obstacle. His legs clamped like a vice to his horse's sides. Wairua threw her head up, side checking and bucking to a halt but the devil of momentum would not be denied and Briar was flung like a fleece into the air, across the fence, arms and legs flailing. He landed on his back, the hard ground ramming the breath from his chest as he slid into a chute of ferns.

He lay there dazed and winded. Then sound and sight returned to him. Air rushed back into his lungs. For a moment he lay there coughing and spluttering. Concern for Wairua filled his mind and he jerked upright to look for her, his flailing hand hitting something warm.

'Ouch!' The boy was crouched over him and he clutched his face where Briar had just hit him.

Briar stared, in suprise.

'Are you alright?'

Briar didn't answer. He just twisted his head around searching for Wairua. She was standing on the other side of the fence, head down, grazing as though nothing had happened. Briar's shoulders slumped in relief and a small sigh escaped his throat.

'Are you alright?' the boy repeated. 'Have you broken something?'

Briar frowned and turned his head back to look at the stranger.

The boy leaned closer and raised his voice. 'Can you speak?'

Now his face was close, Briar saw that half the boy's moustache was missing, a line of dark makeup smeared across his lip where Briar's hand had touched him.

'What! You're not a boy. You're Rosemary's friend.'

Diana bounced to her feet. 'Damn.' She hovered indecisively for a moment then turned towards her horse standing a few yards away.

'Hang on. Don't go.' Briar rubbed the back of his head which was ringing with every word he spoke. 'I don't care.'

Diana stopped and looked back at him.

'Honestly. I won't tell anyone,' said Briar.

Diana wiped the rest of her moustache off with her shirt sleeve.

He smiled at her. 'I'm Briar, by the way.'

'I already know that.' Her voice was flat.

'You're a great rider. I've never seen a horse jump like that. How do you do it?'

'You do exactly the opposite of what you did.'

For a second Briar scowled at her insensitivity. Then he realised that a smile was playing at the edge of her mouth and he couldn't help laughing, and this brought more throbbing to his head. He winced and tried to swallow the laugh but it escaped in little explosions, nasal hiccups that started Diana laughing too. She giggled cautiously then more openly as each of their outbursts ignited the other until finally Diana plonked down beside Briar and held out her hand.

'Dee. Well, actually my real name's Diana but I hate it. So I'm Dee.'

Briar shook her hand. It felt odd; he'd never shaken a girl's hand before. Girls didn't do that. It felt like they were breaking some rule.

Dee leaned around to peer at the back of his head. 'Are you okay? You hit pretty hard.'

'Yes, I noticed.'

She winced. 'Is it painful?'

'It'll be fine,' he shrugged. 'I'd like to say it's the first time I've fallen but that would be a big lie.' He arched his back and groaned. 'The rest of me seems to have escaped unharmed. Well, mostly.' Briar looked more closely at Dee's attire and couldn't help frowning. 'So... how come you're dressed like that? Like a boy, I mean.'

'Because I'm sick of being told to act like a *young lady*.' She rolled her eyes and started counting things off on her fingers. 'Always keeping my clothes clean. Not speaking until I'm spoken to. Putting on makeup if I go out of the house.'

Briar glanced at the black smear on his hand. 'Well you definitely put on makeup.'

She touched her upper lip. 'Easy for you to laugh about it. You're a boy. You're allowed to have fun.' She crossed her legs, tucked them under her and leaned forwards waving a finger for emphasis. '*And* you get to decide what to do with your life. Good grief, my mum's already inviting every young man in Franklin for dinner. She's desperate to get me married off and if she has her way, I won't have any part in choosing.'

'At least your mum cares about you.'

Dee covered her mouth in embarrassment. 'I'm so sorry. That was really insensitive…'

Briar waved her to stop. 'No, it's okay. I'm not an orphan like the other farm boys. I mean, my mum died when I was young but I have a dad.' He frowned. 'Had a dad.'

She still looked uncomfortable.

He changed the subject. 'So anyway, where'd you get those clothes?'

'They were my brother's.' She nodded at her horse. 'So was Star.'

'Star, huh? That's a good name. He's a tall horse.'

'Yep. Well, my brother is six-foot two so he likes a tall horse. He taught me to ride. To ride *properly*, anyway.'

'Properly?'

She snorted derisively, 'My mother says nice girls don't gallop or jump. How stupid is that?'

'Don't you ride with your brother anymore?'

'He's gone away. Went to London to become a lawyer.' She looked down at the clothes she was wearing. 'They fit well, eh?' She squashed her breasts with the palms of her hands. 'Well, apart from these, that is.'

Her comment set them laughing again. Eventually Dee glanced around at Wairua who was grazing along the fence line.

'You did well keeping up. Especially riding bareback.'

'Thanks.'

'Your balance needs work though.'

'No kidding.' Briar had meant his tone to be ironic, but there must have been a little hurt pride showing because Dee frowned at him.

'Don't be offended. Seriously, you just need to put your heels down. It'll lower your seat.' She noticed Briar's baffled expression. 'Oh. Guess you haven't had many lessons then?'

'Nah. Well one, I guess.'

Dee contemplated Briar for a moment. 'I could teach you if you want?'

'Really? Would you?' His momentary excitement was dulled as he thought it through. 'I don't have any money to pay you.'

'Don't be daft. I just mean we can ride together and I can help you. Show you what you're doing wrong.' She stood and brushed the dust off her trousers then she reached out a hand. Briar took it and she helped him to his feet. 'That way I get someone to ride with.'

'That'd be swell.'

She collected her horse, taking it by the reins and Briar climbed over the fence to Wairua who was grazing peacefully, muzzling at the tufts around the base of a tree.

Dee pointed in the direction of the farm. 'Bring her this way. There's a gate just over the hill.'

CHAPTER 23

HUNUA · 1954

LIFTING THE BRACE WITH HIS ELBOW, Briar dragged another ewe into Aussie's side pen. It was late afternoon and they had been shearing all day but for once Briar wasn't feeling exhausted. Along with his farm skills, his fitness was improving.

He looked around at the sound of the grinding wheel and watched a cascade of sparks as Tane sharpened a pair of hand shears at the work bench at the top end of the shed. Tane tested the end of the blade with his thumb then, satisfied, he uncoupled the spinning sharpening stone. He pulled a rag from his pocket, mopped his brow then yelled over the din.

'Last sheep!' A jolt of energy flowed around the shed as the boys realised the end of the workday was within reach. Tane strode over to Aussie and Briar. 'Aussie, when you're done with that ewe, teach Briar the basics with hand-shears. I want him to start on crutching and dagging tomorrow.' He turned to Briar, gave him the slightest of nods then handed him the shears he'd just sharpened. Briar took the tool and examined it. A smile slowly spread across his face. He had just graduated. Although there was no choir, no speech from the headmaster and only Aussie to witness the ceremony, it felt more meaningful than any certificate he had earned in school.

As Tane walked off, Aussie flicked a quick smile up at Briar. 'See. Told ya you were doing well.' He set back to shearing. 'Go get me some water while I finish this one. Then it's your turn.'

From his own station, Victor looked up when he heard the grinding wheel. He frowned as he watched Tane approach Aussie and Briar. Although he hadn't finished with the sheep he was holding, he switched off his handset so he could listen. When he heard Tane's instructions, Victor scowled. He spat on the floor then waved Dennis over.

'Aussie's such a suck-up,' he growled to the younger boy. 'It's meant to be *me* doing the training round here.'

'Yeah, ain't nobody faster than you.'

'This is an insult. Aussie's trying to prove he's better than me.' Victor flicked the Wolseley back on and finished the last few clips on his sheep. He shoved his finished ewe at the chute and dealt it a frustrated kick to send it out. The animal's hip slammed against the wall and it scurried away, limping down the chute. 'I been on this farm since I was ten. Longer than anyone.'

'You always do the training,' said Dennis. 'Tane should respect that.'

'That bloody Māori's doing it on purpose. He's trying to put Aussie above me.'

'But he knows you're the best. You even won the trophy.'

Victor spat again on the floor. 'I've busted my ass working in this shed. Mrs Dwyte wants me to run this farm one day.' He flipped two fingers down the shed where Tane was disappearing out the side door. 'Tane's holding me back but I'm not gonna stand for it.'

'What ya gonna do?'

Victor's eyes narrowed as he thought for a moment. Then he grinned. 'I know how to deal with this.' He nodded towards his own side pen where a large irritated ram was butting its horns against the gate. 'Let's see how quickly CityGirl's lesson fails if we add a bit of fight.'

Dennis looked at the ram then back at Victor. He frowned in confusion.

Victor rolled his eyes. 'Briar won't be able to shear the ram. It's too strong for him.'

'Oh right,' smiled Dennis.

'Go distract Aussie for a minute.' Dennis nodded and headed across the shed. Victor slipped into his pen and wrestled the ram onto its back. He strained to hoist the ram over the fence at the back of the pen, hauling it up by its ring of horns. With a grunt he got it over the fence then dragged it behind the posts at the top end of the shed and reappeared on Aussie's side of the building. He checked to see that nobody was looking then heaved the animal into Aussie's pen. The ram fell on its side and its horns whacked into the floorboards with a solid crack but between the noise of the electric handset he was wielding and the questions Dennis was throwing at him, Aussie failed to notice. Victor grabbed the ewe from Aussie's pen and hauled it out. It was much lighter and he had it back on his own side of the shed in moments.

Briar returned with a mug full of water just as Aussie pushed his sheep into the chute. Dennis was hanging on the divider nattering and watching Aussie work. As soon as he saw Briar, he climbed down and disappeared.

'Here. It's not very cold,' Briar handed the mug to Aussie.

'So long as it's wet, I don't care.' Aussie gulped down the water then beckoned for Briar to join him in his station. He took the hand shears from Briar and held them out to demonstrate. 'So these are pretty simple. Just squeeze 'em.' He slid his hand up the grip. 'The secret is to hold the top end. That way you don't get blisters so quickly.' He passed the shears back and Briar squeezed them together a few times. 'That's it,' Aussie said, 'but you gotta learn to close them slow and steady.' He nodded at Briar's next attempt. 'Good, that's it. Alright, let's get you a sheep.'

He stepped into his holding pen but hesitated when he saw

the big ram. He looked back at Briar. 'You know, maybe we should start you on something smaller.' He stepped out of his pen, heading down the shed to fetch a ewe.

'Where you going?' Victor called from the other side of the shed.

Aussie stopped. 'I'm getting a ewe to train Briar.'

'Tane put that ram in there. He wants Briar to start with that.'

'But I thought...'

Victor cut him off. 'Don't you know anything? We always start with a ram. Pointless if it ain't a real test.'

'It's Briar's first time...' he glanced towards the door where Tane had left the shed.

Victor put his fists on his hips. 'This is why I should be doing the training. You can't hack it.' He started across the shed towards Briar. 'I'll train him. I'll show him how a *real* shearer handles a pussy little ram.'

Aussie jumped back to his station and lifted a hand to halt Victor. 'Leave off. If Tane wants the ram done, we'll do it,' he said.

Victor snorted and turned back to his own station.

Aussie looked at Briar. 'Don't worry. A ram's really no different. Just need to hold it harder.' He slipped into his side pen and stood facing the ram for a few moments, sizing the animal up. Then he lunged forwards with both arms and grabbed the animal by the horns twisting them one hundred and eighty degrees. The ram's body was flipped by the neck and Aussie immediately hauled it backwards, dragging it out of the pen and into his station. Unlike the ewes it continued to struggle, kicking out with its hind legs and flexing its spine.

The ram's fighting didn't slow Aussie. He backed into his station to stand beside Briar. 'Here, you know how to hold him. Same as if you were dragging him.' Briar grabbed the ram with both hands and on the count of three, they lifted it across so it was pinned against Briar's legs. Aussie kept his grip on the animal. 'Yeah that's it. Now pull it in harder against you.'

Briar followed Aussie's instructions and once he had the ram clamped hard against his shins and his left arm around its neck, it stopped struggling.

Aussie slowly let go and when he was sure the ram was secure he reached up, collected the hand shears and passed them to Briar. Then he moved to the front of the station and crouched down to hold the ram's hind legs. 'Alright. Off you go. Start with a clip under its right foreleg.'

Briar took a deep breath and pressed the blades into the wool on the animal's chest. The fibres didn't part easily, they clumped and compressed beneath the tool. So he tried again, pushing into the fleece with the points of the blades, wriggling the shears deeper until there was a long tuft of wool standing between the cutting edges.

'Good. Yeah that's better,' Aussie said. 'Don't be scared to push it right in. Doesn't matter if ya nick them. It's part of life.'

Briar squeezed the shears, expecting to see a line of wool fall away from the ram's chest but the tool turned in his hand, the blades forced sideways by the thick oily fleece, clamping the wool rather than cutting it.

'Don't worry, that happens,' Aussie smiled, 'to everyone.' He reached a hand up and forced the shears open again. The ram kicked at the air with its free hoof.

'Bloody animal!' he muttered, grabbed the thrusting leg and held it still. 'Now try again. Once you get the shears into the fleece, push down to lay them against the hide.'

Briar tried again but once more the blades turned and grabbed the wool. 'It's really hard,' he grunted, through clenched teeth.

'Don't worry, you'll get it. You need to turn your hand more.' Aussie cautiously let go of the ram's legs and this time the animal didn't kick. 'Like this.' He reached up and tried to guide Briar's hand. Briar winced as his wrist was twisted to an awkward angle. 'Hang on, you're not holding them right.' Aussie stood up and stepped back into the station. He slipped behind Briar and reached his arm around him, placing his hand over Briar's on the grip of the shears.

Briar breathed in sharply and his body tensed. His eyes flicked up to see if anyone else was watching but the boys were all busy, heads down as they rushed to finish up for the day.

Aussie pushed Briar's hand into the fleece, 'Like this.' The tips dug down until they reached the hide and at the last minute Aussie rolled his wrist to lift the tips of the blades clear of the skin. His hand squeezed Briar's with even, powerful pressure. The heel of the blades bit into the wool then there was a long grainy cinch as the shears sliced through the fibres of the fleece. 'Just like that,' breathed Aussie into Briar's ear, 'then you follow the line you made.' He let go of Briar, slipped out of the station and crouched down to hold the ram's legs again.

Briar breathed out, 'Okay.' He pushed the shears forward into the wool. It was much easier now there was on open patch to work from; he didn't need to wriggle the points down to the skin. He squeezed the shears slowly with all the power he could wring from his grip. He was rewarded with the sound of a clean cut, the whisper of the shears slicing and the click as they closed flat.

'Nice,' Aussie praised his success as two other boys, finished with their work for the day, wandered up the shed and leaned on the divider to watch. 'Now follow the line you've started.' He ran his finger over the ram's chest. 'Along here.'

Briar followed Aussie's directions and, a minute later, a fresh line of fleece hung from the animal's chest.

'That's pretty good,' smiled Aussie and the two boys who were leaning on the divider nodded in agreement. Red appeared and jumped up beside the others to watch.

From across the shed, Victor scowled at Briar's success. He hissed at Dennis, 'If he wants a bloody audience, let's give them a show.' Victor crouched down and pressed on one of the three-inch floorboards. The boards ran horizontally across the shed. Each one was stained and worn and there was an inch gap either side to allow discharge from the animals to drain away. The floorboard that Victor leaned on moved a little. 'This one runs right under him,' he said. 'It was catching my gate so I climbed under there last week and wedged it. It still shakes sometimes when Aussie's working. I bet Briar is standing right on it.'

Dennis smiled. 'You reckon we can move it?'

'Yeah, I'm pretty sure but we need to remove the wedge first.' He pulled a flick blade from his pocket and handed it to Dennis. 'Go under the shed and pry out the wedge. Let's see how he goes on one leg.'

A minute later Victor could see Dennis through the gaps between the floorboards. The boy was beneath the floor, lying on his back and pushing his way through the thick layer of sheep pellets. Victor motioned for him to hurry and a moment later Dennis' upturned thumb poked through one of the slots signalling success.

Victor tested the board again with his hand. The movement was much freer. He stood up and balanced his full weight on the end of the board. Then he jumped down hard on it.

Briar's second line across the ram's chest was better than the first, the stubble left behind was shorter and more even. Just as he began a third line, his right foot was flicked sideways. It felt like the floor had moved. Briar's right arm instinctively swung upwards to counterbalance himself.

Aussie dodged back as the waving blades whooshed past his face. 'Hey, easy!' Briar froze as he realised he had almost stabbed Aussie. One of the boys watching started laughing. The animal sensed it's foreleg was free and began to thrash wildly. Aussie clamped down harder on the ram's hind legs. 'Grab it,' he yelled through clenched teeth. 'Careful with them shears.'

Briar regained his footing and without taking his arm from around the animal's neck, he passed the shears to his left hand.

He swung his right arm out like a club. With a dull thud, it connected with the ram's hoof and Briar grunted in pain. He didn't flinch. He flicked his elbow closed, trapping the foreleg. He leaned back, hauling the animal up hard against his legs then stretched across to reclaim the shears with his right hand.

Aussie looked up at Briar and nodded. 'Great! Now, keep them shears against the sheep. Just use your knees and crunch down hard. He's a big bugger but you've got him.'

One of the watching boys cheered and others whistled.

'Yeah, go CityBoy, show him who's boss!' called Red.

Briar glanced up and couldn't help smiling at the encouragement. He hauled back on the ram and set back to work with a look of fierce determination on his face.

Dennis reappeared, holding the closed flick blade out. Victor swiped the knife from Dennis' hand, glaring at the sound of the boys across the shed cheering Briar on.

'Those damn shits think they're smart,' spat Victor. 'Here, gimme a hand.' He crouched down and used his fingers to bend up the end of the loose floorboard then wrapped both hands around it. Dennis squatted down beside him and grabbed hold of the timber. Without letting go of the floorboard, Victor stretched up to peer over the railings at Briar.

'Wait... wait...' he muttered to Dennis, gauging the right moment. 'Okay, now!' They both hauled back on the board. For a second it resisted then with a loud squeal it moved a fraction of an inch. The three boys on the fence looked over to see what Victor and Dennis were up to.

Dennis hunched down and whispered. 'They heard us.'

'Who cares,' Victor growled. 'Now pull!' They both hauled on the board and this time it slipped six inches backwards.

Briar had almost finished clipping the ram's belly when everything went wrong. His boot slipped sideways and his leg was suddenly unsupported. He tumbled forwards across the ram and his hands shot out to stop his fall. He watched in slow motion as the razor sharp shears in his right hand sliced straight through the ram's groin. Blood arced from the wound, spraying Briar's face and as he slammed to the ground, the iron tang of blood filled his nostrils. The animal twisted and thrashed and pulled itself free. Briar opened his eyes to see the bleeding ram stumbling and slipping on its own blood, its hind legs kicking in terror as it tried to flee from the station. Suddenly everyone was yelling.

Tane appeared, summoned by the commotion. His eyes flicked from Briar to the bleeding animal and then back again. He reached down and helped Briar to his knees. Satisfied the boy wasn't seriously hurt, Tane threw himself at the ram, grasping its horns and wrestling it to the ground. Once he had subdued the struggling animal, he lifted its leg to survey the damage.

Before he could say a word, the side door slammed open and Major Dwyte appeared. The frown on the Major's face hardened into anger as he surveyed the scene in front of him. His voice boomed, 'What the hell is going on here?' Silence fell as the boys shrunk back, fear on their faces.

The Major stormed over to check out the ram. He shook his head in disgust, a grim look setting on his face.

'Stay here the lot of you. Someone's going to answer for this!' He stomped to the cupboard above the tool bench, slid open the latch and pulled out a rifle. With practiced military precision, he grabbed a round from a box and loaded the gun as he strode back towards Tane. Shoving his boot on the ram's neck, he pulled the trigger without a second's hesitation. Everybody flinched. The shot ripped through the animal's brain leaving a gory mess on the floor.

Briar took a second to register the carnage. His back arched as he retched onto the floor of Aussie's station.

Major Dwyte shouted, 'That was a bloody expensive breeding ram, damn you! Who caused that damage and why the hell was a breeding ram being shorn by hand!'

The three boys who had been watching the lesson turned and looked at Victor. Tane frowned, noting their reaction.

Briar stumbled to his feet. 'It was me. I was shearing him, Sir. I tripped and...' His eyes darted to the dead ram and he retched again.

Major Dwyte turned on Tane. 'The new boy? What the hell was he doing with a ram? Goddamn it, man, where the hell were you?'

Tane picked up the blood covered shears and stood up. 'I'm sorry, Major, it's my fault. The boy was meant to be training on a ewe. I should have been here.'

Major Dwyte looked exasperated, unsure where to aim his anger. 'Damn it! This is not acceptable.' Shaking his head, he turned to the boys. 'I don't know exactly what was going on here, but you should all know better than to let a new boy train on a ram.' He glowered at them. 'Sunday outings are cancelled until I say otherwise!'

A round of groans escaped the boys and Briar shrank back with guilt.

Still bristling, Major Dwyte turned back to Tane. 'Get that animal butchered, I won't have it wasted.' He stormed back to the work bench and returned the gun to the cupboard. Then he exited the shed, the door slamming behind him.

All eyes turned warily towards Tane whose face was creased in anger.

'What's wrong with you?' He hissed at them, 'This is a work place, not a playground! Why do I bother?' He growled in frustration and threw the shears towards the work bench where they clattered on the floor. 'Damn the lot of you!' His fists clenched at his sides and he sucked in a deep breath to calm himself. He looked down at the dead ram. 'We'll deal with this later,' he said without looking at the boys. 'Get out of here. Go! All of you.' After a second he changed his mind. 'Not Victor. You stay, boy. We need to talk.'

A minute later, the woolshed was empty except for Tane and Victor who glared at each other in silence.

'You don't fool me, boy. You might not have been holding the blade but I know you were involved.'

'It's that stupid kid, Briar. He's a weakling. Can't even hold a ram!'

'What was he doing with a ram in the first place! When I left, there was a ewe in that pen.'

Victor shook his head defiantly. 'Nah. It was a ram.'

Tane's anger flared. 'Don't lie! I know what I saw.' His eyes narrowed and his fists clenched again. 'You gotta stop pushing the other boys around.' He shook his head and sighed. 'You want their respect but that's not how you get it. You've got to earn it.' He waited for some response but Victor just glared his resentment. '*You* should be setting an example. Being a brother to the younger boys. Bullying is a coward's way.'

'Don't you call me a coward!' Victor spat through gritted teeth, 'You're the coward! You're... You...'

'Spit it out, boy.'

'I'm the best shearer here. Better than you. And better than bloody Aussie! Mrs Dwyte says I'm old enough to be doing *your* job.'

'This is real life. Not some competition.'

Victor was no longer listening. He squared his shoulders. 'Mrs Dwyte says I'm from *good* blood.'

'Your blood's the same as anyone else.'

'I'm gonna run this farm one day.'

'Someone's been filling your head with dreams...'

'It's not a dream, you stupid shit! Mrs Dwyte told me.'

'Mrs Dwyte doesn't make the decisions around here.'

'*You* can't stop me. Even Rosemary says I should be in charge.'

Tane scoffed at Victor's admission. 'You should be careful of what Rosemary says. She likes to toy with you.'

'Don't you dare talk about Rosemary!' Victor punched his fist into his palm. 'She's gonna be mine one day. You don't know shit. You're … you're …' His face reddened as he stammered. 'You're just a dumb hori.'

Tane's eyes narrowed and suddenly his voice was cold. 'I fought a war to win respect. And I *will* have respect from you.'

'You didn't win nothing,' yelled Victor.

Tane's left fist slammed into Victor's jaw. Victor flew sideways, hitting a divider then sliding to the floor. For a moment Tane stood over him, fists clenched. Then, shaking his head he backed away.

Victor struggled up, hand cupping his face. He glared his hatred at Tane, spat a gob of blood on the floor then turned and ran out of the shed.

For a long time Tane stared at the door then he slumped against a wall and looked at the dead ram. He pulled out the silver chain from under his shirt. It had a cufflink hanging from it, an enamel horse head in a silver setting. It had been white once. Decades had weathered and chipped its face to a golden ivory. He rubbed his thumb over the enamel then whispered to it.

'Why am I here? Why did I come back?'

The blood around the ram was starting to congeal and flies were gathering, drawn to the smell. Tane slipped the chain and pendant back beneath his shirt and collected his knives from the locker. He found a wheelbarrow then hauled the dead body into the tray. The ram's blood covered his hands and left sticky red streaks running down his legs where the sodden wool had smeared his thighs. Trundling across the dusty yard with every rut vibrating through his tired joints, all he could think about was what it felt like to dive into the clean crystal waters of the Caribbean surrounded by the laughter of friends.

CHAPTER 24

ATLANTIC OCEAN · 1914

TANE LEANED ON THE BULWARK AND GAZED down into the green waters of the Caribbean. They were still anchored in Christobel harbour. Creighton's guess about the captain's intentions had been right on target. Now that they were through the Panama Canal, they were going to steam across the Atlantic in convoy. As the sun rose and fingers of warm light danced across the waves, the *HMS Antebellum* set a heading along with two other ships bound for ports in northern Europe. The town of Colón and the huge American battleship slipped away astern; the ship's bell sounded and all hands returned to duty.

'I heard it from the third engineer,' Creighton confided to them as they swabbed the gantry ways a couple of hours later. 'German u-boats have been seen in the Atlantic. They've already taken out a dozen ships.'

'But we're not a navy ship,' said Tane.

'They don't care. The Germans just want to stop any supplies going to England. We're fair game as far as they're concerned.'

Wiremu looked worried. 'Surely the British navy will protect us.'

'Well, you didn't hear it from me but I heard we're making for Lisbon.'

'Where?' asked Wiremu.

'Portugal.' Tane had unloaded many barrels of port wine as a boy on the Auckland docks.

'That's right,' said Creighton. 'The Poms are using it as a navy base. We should be able to join a flotilla for the passage to England.'

'But what about from here to Portugal?' Wiremu still looked worried.

Creighton patted him on the shoulder. 'Don't lose any sleep. It's a huge ocean, bigger than you can imagine. We're a needle in a haystack. We ain't gonna see no German u-boats.'

Staying in convoy meant running at fourteen knots, a lot slower than their maximum cruising speed. Eleven days later, as they steamed through the night, the middle watch sighted the lighthouse of Cape Saint Vincent, the south-western tip of the Portuguese coast. They turned to port and by daybreak they were passing the fortified lighthouse of Torre do Bugio and entering Lisbon Harbour.

The inlet was busier than anything Tane had ever seen. Wharves jutted from land on all sides into the natural lagoon created by the river Tagus. Dozens of sidings held ships of all shapes and sizes, many of which flew unfamiliar colours. The most striking thing was the number of warships. The imposing shape of turrets and gun decks could be seen spread amongst the merchant shipping. Most of the grey painted military vessels flew the green and red Portuguese ensign or the blue, white and red of the French navy. Anchored in the middle of the harbour lay a Dreadnaught class British battleship, its wide hull topped by a bristling array of huge gun barrels.

The *HMS Antebellum* was allotted a berth on a south-facing pier but nobody was allowed ashore until an inspection had been carried out of the ship and its holds. All hands were instructed to gather on the rear deck and shortly thereafter, a Portuguese customs officer boarded the boat accompanied by four armed soldiers. For almost four hours, they inspected the boat, stem to stern, even going through the bunkrooms. Rumours circulated amongst the crewmen about what they might be looking for or what they might find. As the search ground on, the men began to grumble their annoyance. Eventually emotions boiled over.

'The second engineer's got a head full of blonde hair. I hear tell he's Austrian,' said Finlay, a wiry deckhand who usually kept to himself. There were a few mumbles from the gathered crew.

'Don't you be spreading any of your rubbish,' replied one of the stokers. 'Our second is a good man and he ain't German.' He stepped up to Finlay, his muscled body towering over the deckhand. 'If there's any traitors on this boat, they'll be deck rats.' Suddenly men were taking sides, accusations and denials ringing out. Within moments, the crew were separated by a line, deck workers on one side and engine crew on the other.

Before things could escalate, the third mate stepped between Finlay and the stoker. 'Stow it, both of you,' he looked around the entire crew who had fallen to silence. 'We all know each other. I'm telling you once and for all... there aren't any traitors on this boat.'

The cook stepped in to back up the third mate. 'Too right. I feed every damn one of you and if I hear any more stupid accusations like that, the lot of you can go hungry.'

'You're shipmates,' the third mate continued. 'This boat needs you all working together and I won't hesitate to put off any man who stirs up trouble.' The stoker stepped back and the tension melted away as quickly as it had appeared.

'What *do* you think they are looking for?' Tane asked Creighton.

'Can't say that I know,' replied the big man. 'I was as surprised as anyone when they boarded.' He scratched his beard which had thickened considerably during the voyage. 'I guess it makes sense though. The powers of Europe are at war. Any ship here could be carrying supplies for the Huns.'

Another man spoke up. Tane couldn't remember his name but he knew that he worked in the boiler room. 'My sister-in-law has family in Portugal. Before we left she told me they were still a neutral country. She reckons they won't get involved in the war.'

'They might be neutral at the moment,' said Creighton, 'but there's been trouble between them and the Germans in Africa. The Captain reckons they're gonna declare for the Allies, mainly because they need the French and the Brits to protect their shipping.'

The Captain appeared, accompanied by the customs officer. They made their way to the gangplank and after talking for several minutes, the customs man and armed guards left the ship. The Captain climbed up to the bridge castle deck where he looked down at the waiting crew.

'I know that in the past, we haven't had to put up with this sort of search but we're going to need to get used to it. In the month we've been at sea, things have been escalating quickly in Europe. Realities have changed. The North Sea is being contested and any ship making for Britain is in real danger. Tomorrow, this boat will join a flotilla bound for England. I can't give you our exact destination but it will no longer be London. Given the circumstances, I've decided to grant you a few hours shore leave.' There was a cheer. He raised a hand. 'Wait, I'm not finished.' He paused and looked slowly over the crew, 'I will not order anyone to sail into a war zone. Every man must decide for himself.' He stopped, removed his hat and leaned forwards on the rail. 'I'll be in my quarters for the rest of the day. If any man wants to resign his position, he can report to me and I will release him from his duties and arrange passage back to New Zealand. There's no shame in making this choice. I know many of you have families to consider.' The Captain stood straight again. 'You're dismissed until eighteen hundred hours. Any man who wishes to remain a crewman on this vessel should report for duty at that time.' Without waiting for any sort of response, the Captain turned crisply and disappeared.

The men burst into a hundred different conversations until the third mate raised his hands for quiet. He had to yell several times to get their full attention.

'Okay. Listen up!' He looked around at them all. 'You heard the captain. You all have a decision to make. I want you to return to quarters and get them shipshape. Then, after mess, you can report starboard side to disembark.'

The moment they were dismissed, Tane grabbed Wiremu and pulled him out of earshot.

'You're gonna stay, aren't you?'

Wiremu glanced across the quarterdeck at the rest of the men. Most of them were deep in conversation with fellow crewmates. 'Well, the old man said they're going in a flotilla, so I guess they'll have protection.' He folded his arms. 'What about you?'

'I'm staying. This boat is...' Tane shrugged, 'I guess it's my home now.'

Wiremu cocked his head. 'I dunno about that. Home is back in New Zealand.' He chuckled. 'Well, it will be as soon as Mere and I find somewhere to live.'

'But you've gotta stay. We won't be in the war zone for long and you need the money. I mean, we both need the money.'

Wiremu put his hand on Tane's shoulder. 'Don't worry, I'm gonna stay. I already thought about it. The Germans are just another storm.'

Tane broke into a relieved smile. 'Anyway it's like Creighton said. We're just a needle in a haystack.'

Tane and Wiremu spent the whole day exploring Lisbon. As they walked through the city they discovered cobbled streets, ancient monuments and narrow lanes lined with tall white buildings, each capped by a red tiled roof. From almost everywhere, they could look up and see the square walls of the castle on top of the hill and they slowly climbed towards it. By early afternoon they reached the outer part of the ancient fortifications;

a low wall encircling the castle beyond. Following it around the hill, they came to an imposing gated entranceway surmounted by the coat of arms of Portugal. A market occupied the small square in front of the gate and, as they mingled with the bustling throng, the sounds and smells made Tane's thoughts rush back to Sailors Alley. The language was different but the energy was the same; the reality of humans trading and sharing and making a living.

Passing through the gate, they found themselves in the Praça d'Armas, the main square of the fortified castle. Old cannons stood at intervals around the edge and in the centre, a bronze statue rose on a plinth; an armoured king, sword raised over his shield.

'Imagine being a soldier back then,' said Tane. 'No shooting people with guns. You had to get up close and look your enemy in the eye.'

'He was a king. He probably just told everyone else who to fight,' said Wiremu.

Tane stepped up to peer more closely at the inscription on the plinth. Alongside the king's name was the year 1147. He shook his head. 'It's amazing. So long ago.' He looked around at the castellated stone parapets. 'It's like being in history.'

'We got plenty of history back home.'

'Not like this.'

Wiremu scoffed. 'You really need to learn about your tupuna.' Tane looked confused. 'Your ancestors,' explained Wiremu.

'I guess,' Tane shrugged, 'but there ain't no statues of them.'

'What do you think the koruru are?' Again Tane looked lost. Wiremu shook his head. 'Never mind. Anyway I reckon deeds are what really matters and as long as we remember what our tupuna did, that's just as good as any statue.'

They explored the castle for several hours, poking through its complex web of side rooms and tunnels until Wiremu realised it was almost five o'clock. 'Hell, we better get going.' They found the nearest exit. At first they walked back towards the harbour but as time dwindled they ran.

Finally, with minutes to spare, they neared the dock and Tane turned to Wiremu. 'Do you think many will have resigned?' he panted.

Wiremu thought for a second. 'I reckon Finlay will be gone and Dodson, he's got a big family back home, always talking about his kids.' He screwed up his face. 'Hope we haven't lost too many though.'

'Yeah, me too. I've gotten to really like some of them.'

It was almost six o'clock when they stepped onto the gangplank. They hurried aft to the quarterdeck and, as they passed the bridge castle, they found the entire crew assembled on the rear deck.

The boatswain was standing with a clipboard. He checked their names then called up to the Captain, 'That's all of them.'

They tucked themselves in beside Creighton who gave them a nod and a smile. Tane looked around. He saw Finlay standing near the back, and Dodson leaning on the portside rail, tapping tobacco into his pipe. In fact, there didn't seem to be a single absentee. Tane's chest expanded with pride. It looked like his new family was going to stay together.

CHAPTER 25

LISBON · 1914

THE CREWMEN WERE TOLD THEY'D BE LEAVING the following day, a late evening sailing to run north under the cover of darkness. They were dismissed and Creighton told Tane and Wiremu to turn in early as their detail had drawn the early watch.

When they reported at 4 am, it was still dark. Creighton gave them a list of light duties, primarily oiling the deck strap swivels and retightening all the deck lashings. He then disappeared aft to rig new lights that would be used to signal other ships in the flotilla.

With only the docking boiler running, the electric bulbs gave out a wan light so they had to carry a lantern for extra illumination as they worked. Tane and Wiremu started at the bow, oiling and checking each cleat and hitch, one of them holding the light, the other checking the tension with a crowbar. Work was slow and often awkward as they had to squeeze between rows of wool bales and unhitch the edge of heavy tarpaulins just to get to the deck lashings. As they worked their way across the deck from starboard to port, the faintest hint of red crept into the sky. Dawn was approaching.

At the end of the second row, Tane stopped and took a moment to stretch his back. He slowly twisted his neck left and right and sighed as the bones in his neck clicked. 'I like this boat. It really is home,' he chuckled, 'but I'd give half my pay for a night in a decent bed.'

'I hear ya,' said Wiremu. 'Don't know if I'll ever get used to my hammock.'

'Do you think we'll still get time onshore in England? My mum used to talk about it sometimes. I can't wait to see it.'

'Sure we will. Davies reckons we'll be in port for a few days at least.'

'I hope so. Lisbon was great. I can't wait to see more places.' Tane yawned and looked across the water. Squinting into the semi darkness, he could just make out the menacing bulk of the Dreadnaught class warship anchored in the middle of the harbour. He froze as the sound of a man yelling drifted across the water, piercing the still morning. Another yell followed then a chorus of panicked shouts. Wiremu, who had been fiddling with the last tarpaulin, sprung up beside Tane and they both rushed forwards to the bulwark, staring in the direction of the clamour.

The world burst with bright yellow light centred on the warship. For a fraction of a second, its outline was burned into Tane's retinas before the deafening noise of an explosion washed over him and his brain made sense of what he was seeing. The noise made him stagger backwards and his eyes grew round with horror as the warship rolled towards them, a blast of seawater and torn metal thrust into the air on the far side of the boat.

'It's blown up!' he screamed, throwing himself back to the rail, visions of injured and drowning sailors filling his mind. Noise was suddenly coming from all directions and his eyes flicked left and right where he could see men appearing at the rails of other boats. He noticed one man pointing, furiously waving his arm at the water. Tane frowned at an unfamiliar buzzing sound and looked down to see a white line in the water, a trace just beneath the surface running from a point near the bow of the stricken warship and growing in size as it approached the stern of the

Antebellum. His brain made the connection too late to react. Before he could scream "torpedo," his whole world erupted. An ear splitting explosion sucked the air from his head, sending a searing pain through his eardrums. At the same time it felt like sledge hammers hit the soles of his feet, his knees and hips screamed in protest as he was thrown into the air, flying backwards into the wool bales. For a second he lay; his face crumpled against the taut surface of the tarpaulin then his whole body jerked and his eyes popped open. The hot pain of his torn left cheek and the disorienting ringing in his ears filled his head. Movement registered in his mind... his shoulders were being shaken. He rolled over to find Wiremu standing over him. Wiremu's shirt was torn and blood was dripping from a long laceration on his arm. Tane squinted at Wiremu's face; he could see his friend's lips moving. He strained forwards trying to stand, but the boat suddenly listed to port and his feet slipped away from him and he collapsed to the deck. Again Wiremu hauled at him and this time Tane managed to stagger upright. Wiremu was still speaking and, concentrating hard, Tane could just make out his words, muffled as though he was hearing them through a wall.

'We're sinking. We need to get the others.' Wiremu took a step towards the nearest hatchway but before he could get to it, the door swung outward and a crewman fell through the opening onto the deck. Two others dived out behind him. The collapsed man didn't get up, just lay on the deck where he had fallen and Wiremu rushed to help him. Thick grey smoke poured from the open hatchway.

Tane coughed and, with a painful pop, sound came rushing back into his ears. It was like being dunked into cold water. His muscles tensed and his mind cleared. He suddenly remembered Creighton. He had last seen him heading aft. He yelled to Wiremu, 'I'm getting Creighton.'

'Wait!' said Wiremu who was struggling to lift the unconscious sailor. 'I'll come with you.'

'You help here. I'll see you on the dock,' Tane yelled as he dashed into the cloud of black smoke.

The boat was listing more drastically now, rolling to port away from the wharf and the stern was sitting lower in the water. Tane found himself skidding, half sliding towards the quarterdeck. As he passed the derrick, he was stopped by the hulk of the bridge castle. The two-storey steel structure had partially collapsed and now blocked his way. Tane looked for a route around the obstruction. He scrambled across the base of the derrick, pushing his way through the truss supporting the body of the crane. Something behind him gave way with the sound of tearing metal and the girders above him creaked.

He extracted himself from the side of the steel frame to find the starboard deck bulging. The metal plating was pushed up at an irregular angle. Climbing around to the rear deck he was confronted by an alien landscape. The shape of the ship's stern was almost unrecognisable. The entire port side was missing, torn and twisted bulkheads framing a gaping hole in the side of the ship much of which lay beneath the water. The rear bulwark was almost at sea level and, as he stared in shock at the massive damage, the deck beneath him moved again. With a reverberating slosh water was sucked into another internal cavity. An array of flotsam was ejected from inside the hull, splintered timber shelves, a mattress, pieces of cloth. And a body. It emerged feet first slipping slowly from under the half submerged deck until the head scraped its way free.

Tane instantly recognised the shock of red hair. He released his grip on the steam vent and scrambled down to Creighton, lunging out with both arms to seize the huge man's shoulders. Bracing his feet on a torn deck plate, he twisted with all of his strength to turn Creighton over to allow him to breathe. The body turned sluggishly, head flipping over first. Creighton's face was as white as a sheet, his eyes staring. Tane felt bile rising in his throat as he remembered Billy. With a growl of exertion, he finally rolled the body over. Tane had to blink twice to make sense of the dark shape that broke the water. A section of steel ladder was buried in the man's chest and where his sternum should have been blood poured from a gaping wound, mixing with the sea water. The sloshing sound shook the ship again and seawater rose higher sliding up Tane's legs. For long seconds he just stared, not wanting to admit his friend was dead but the current pulled at Tane's legs and he had to let go to stop himself from being pulled into the hull. He turned and scrambled back up the slanting deck, stopping to look back as soon as he was clear of the water. Creighton was gone, his body sucked back beneath the sea.

A series of dull explosions made Tane look out towards the middle of the harbour. He could see glimpses of flames through the roiling black smoke pouring from the warship and the air was full of men's screams. His lower lip quivered and a sob escaped from his throat before his features hardened into a grimace of anger.

'You German bastards,' he hissed. 'I'm gonna pay you back.' He grabbed the nearest loose object and with a roar of anger he hurled it at his unseen enemy. 'Do you hear me!'

Tane and Wiremu were reunited on the dock as they helped pull injured and dead crewmen from the sinking Antebellum. Less than half of the crew survived and the casualties included the Captain and all the officers. Water covering their wrecked ship was only a few fathoms deep and, along with several others, Tane spent a good portion of the morning diving down to the wreck to find more survivors. Their efforts came to nothing and after several hours they hauled themselves out of the water, exhausted and frustrated.

Eventually, the surviving crew of the *Antebellum* were rounded up by local port authorities and taken to join the British dreadnaught survivors. They were delivered to an empty cargo shed that had been hastily converted into temporary accommodation. One end of the shed was sectioned off for triage and they spent the day listening to the moans of wounded or dying men behind the curtains, sounds that hardened Tane's anger towards the Germans. Every hour he grew more determined to avenge his shipmates.

By the time night fell, the *Antebellum* men had heard nothing from their shipping company nor had they recieved any further instructions from port authorities. Many were mumbling about plans to find their own way back to New Zealand. Tane tried to sleep but each time he dozed off, Creighton's face appeared, or Billy's, and his eyes would spring open and his heart would pound. He gave up on the idea of rest. He paced around the warehouse and eventually found himself talking with a young man from the British crew.

'You one of the New Zealand blokes are you?'

'Yeah. Chapman's the name,' Tane shook the man's hand.

'Rotten luck you caught the torpedo that missed us.'

'The *Antebellum* was a merchantman. We weren't meant to be fighting.'

'Well, I'm glad that some of you made it off.'

'Dunno what we're gonna do now. The officers are dead. Haven't heard from our company. They don't even know we've been sunk.'

'One of *our* guys was a New Zealander.'

'Really. Did he make it?'

The seaman shook his head. 'No. Bloody shame. He was a hell of a decent chap. He'd been working in Blackwall as a shipbuilder. Joined up as soon as war was declared.'

Tane nodded slowly, a plan forming in his mind, 'So your navy takes New Zealanders then?'

'Well, I guess. You thinking of fighting?'

'Maybe. I wanna pay those German scum back.'

'That's the spirit but you better hurry up.'

'Why?'

'I've been told they're hiding in u-boats because their navy is second rate. The admiralty thinks we'll have them beaten in a few months.'

'That's good to know.'

An hour later Tane stood outside with a blanket draped over his shoulders watching a second dawn break over Lisbon harbour. He had asked the naval rating everything he could about the Royal Navy and now he was determined to join. Behind him the warehouse door opened.

'There you are,' said Wiremu. 'I been looking for you.'

'I couldn't sleep. I've been thinking things over.'

'While you've been gone the crew have been talking. They want to get to England. They don't want to wait for the Shipping Company.'

'What are they planning?'

'Dobson wanted to go overland. The Portuguese say France is full of Germans so the only way is by sea but no captain will even talk to you without papers and ours are on the boat.'

'I don't care about the company. I wanna fight. I wanna pay those bastards back.'

'I do too,' said Wiremu, 'but how can we do that? First we need to...'

Tane cut him off pointing at the waters of the harbour. His voice was angry 'Our friends are down there. Dead on the ocean floor. All because some cowardly Huns murdered them without even showing their face. They were like family to us!'

'I'm angry too,' snapped Wiremu, 'but how the hell we gonna fight? We're in Portugal. Or have you forgotten?'

'I talked to one of the British guys. I'm gonna try to join up with the British navy.'

Wiremu stared at him for a moment. 'Can we do that?'

'I think so. There was a New Zealander on *their* ship.'

'I didn't know that.' Wiremu thought for a moment, struggling with something. 'I want to join too but it might mean we're away from New Zealand for a long time.'

'The British sailor said the war would be over in a few months.' Tane stepped out of the way as two men carried a stretcher out of the warehouse. 'Wiremu, I can't just let them kill Creighton and the others. I'd feel like a coward if I didn't do something.'

'Yeah, I know what you mean. I can't get their faces out of my head.'

Tane grabbed Wiremu's wrist. 'Lets join together! We can fight side by side, look out for each other.' He let go of Wiremu and turned away his voice dropping. 'But you don't have to do it on account of me.'

'We're best friends, Tane. Besides, I want to pay those Germans back for what they did.'

Tane nodded slowly. 'Do you think Mere will mind?'

'I wish I could talk to her. I miss her so much. She wouldn't want me to be a coward,' he shrugged, 'besides, I'm here for her and the baby. I've gotta provide for them one way or another. I hear the navy pays better than merchant.' He placed a hand on Tane's shoulder. 'Lets go fight.'

Later that morning they stood inside a small dock house that had the Royal Navy ensign hanging over its door. In the full daylight they both looked strung out.

Tane was frowning at a junior officer. 'What do you mean we aren't qualified? We just sailed from New Zealand on the *HMS Antebellum*.'

'And got blown out of the water by a torpedo that was aimed at *your* ship,' added Wiremu.

'Do either of you have your ticket?' asked the Royal Navy ensign.

'No. But...'

The ensign raised his hand stopping Tane before he could finish. 'You haven't even qualified as able seamen.'

'We know our way around a ship.'

The ensign shook his head. 'I appreciate your passion. I know you lost a lot of men.'

'Good men,' said Wiremu.

'It makes no difference. If you had your ticket you could apply to enlist as foreign nationals. Given you're from a Commonwealth nation, the C.O. might have approved it but you have no qualifications and almost no experience.' He straightened up. 'I'm sure your shipping company will organise transport home for you eventually.'

It was Tane's turn to interrupt. 'That could take months.'

'Then perhaps one of the merchant companies will offer you work. Scores of them use this port.'

Tane balled his fists in frustration. 'We want to fight. We want to fight *now*. We're gonna make those damn Germans pay.'

'Look, I can't help you. The Royal Navy has strict guidelines. You should get home and join your own forces.'

The wind went out of Tane's sails. His shoulders sagged with the exhaustion of the last two days. 'Forget it.' He elbowed Wiremu. 'Come on, we ain't welcome here.'

The young officer removed his cap. 'Wait,' he looked around to check nobody else in the office was paying attention. 'If you're determined to fight, you might want to try the *HMS Forthright*. She's an ex-passenger ferry that's just returned from Africa. They've been taking on recruits for the army.' He pulled out a pencil and notebook and scribbled down an address. 'Talk to a chap named Vale. Tell him I sent you. I hear they've been recruiting from all over. So you might get lucky.'

CHAPTER 26

Hunua · 1954

VICTOR RAN OUT OF THE WOOLSHED, his eyes narrowed in anger. He rubbed his jaw where Tane had punched him and licked the blood from his lip. Muttering to himself, he stormed up the hill to the dorms. As he walked through the front door, several of the farm boys looked up from around the common room.

'What happened?' asked Dennis. 'Why did Tane make you stay?'

'Nothing happened,' growled Victor.

Dennis leaned forward and peered at Victor's face. His eyes widened seeing the dried blood at the corner of his mouth. 'Did Tane hit you?'

'Piss off! Tane's a damn coward. He would *never* fight.' Victor wiped the blood away. 'This was a ricochet. Something flew up and hit me when the Major shot the ram.'

The back door opened and Tony came in followed by Red. He stopped at the end of the hallway when he saw Victor. 'Thanks a bloody lot,' Tony said to him. 'Now we've got no Sunday outings.'

'Yeah, it sucks,' agreed Red.

'What the hell do you mean?' said Victor.

'I dunno what you did but I know you were involved in killing that ram.'

'Stuff you! I had nothing to do with it,' Victor looked around the common room. 'None of you like that CityGirl. I've seen you all laughing at him.'

Red looked down, scared by Victor's glare.

Dennis stepped up to Victor's side. 'We didn't do nothing.'

Victor pointed a finger at Tony. 'Briar cut the ram, not me. It's his fault, not mine!'

'I'm getting sick of you, Victor.'

Victor bared his teeth but didn't reply. Instead he turned and stormed back out the front door. Dennis followed him.

Victor stepped out onto the porch with Dennis following him. He kicked at the line of boots sitting on the edge of the wooden decking. The footwear scattered, several pairs flipping off the porch onto the dirt. Dennis watched him but said nothing. Eventually Victor motioned for Dennis to follow and he ducked around the left hand side of the building, behind the water tanks. He stopped and pulled a small tin from his pocket and extracted a half smoked cigarette. Lighting the blackened end, he threw the spent match into the dirt. Dennis stood with his hands in his pockets and watched a line of smoke rising from the match.

'Are we gonna get into trouble about the ram?'

'Don't be stupid. I kicked the board back into place. Nobody can prove anything.' Victor's eyes narrowed at Dennis. 'Not unless you tell.'

'Nah. Of course not.'

Victor stepped forward and looked down at him, 'You better bloody not. I'll hurt you so bad.'

Dennis raised both hands and shook his head furiously. 'I wouldn't tell on you. Not ever.'

'Hope not. For your sake.' Victor took a deep drag on his smoke, 'Loyalty. You gotta be loyal no matter what.'

'I'm loyal.' Dennis slipped his hands back into his pockets. 'One hundred percent.'

They stood in silence for a while.

'That little CityGirl has had his last damn chance!' said Victor without removing the cigarette from his mouth.

'What about Aussie?'

'The two of them are working together. Briar and Aussie. Always trying to make me look bad.'

'Aussie used to be cool. He always gave me gum.'

Victor's fag was down to half an inch and he pinched it between his thumb and forefinger and sucked a last long drag. He squinted at Dennis. 'Forget Aussie. I'm getting rid of him. Mrs Dwyte said I'm the only one they need to run the farm. So he can't stay.' He threw the butt into the dirt then stomped it with the heel of his boot. 'Right now we need to teach Briar a lesson.'

Dennis' eyes lit up. 'Yeah, let CityGirl know who's boss.'

'Exactly.' Victor leaned back against the concrete tank. It had been painted a dirty white but the paint had long failed and flakes fell away where his shoulders scuffed the rough curve. He frowned in concentration as he formed a plan. 'Tane'll be hours butchering that ram. I've got an idea that'll sort Briar out once and for all.' He narrowed his eyes at Dennis. 'You in? Or you gonna be a pussy?'

'Of course I'm in. What we gonna do?'

Victor walked back to the front of the dormitory. 'Go get Nate. I need you both.' Dennis jumped to obey and as he ran off Victor hissed one last instruction. 'And don't talk to anyone. We gotta keep this real quiet.'

Victor pulled out his tin again but before he could shake out another fag, the door opened and Red appeared.

'Oi, Red. Come here.'

The young boy looked scared but trotted obediently over to Victor. 'Sorry for what I said in the dorms, I just...'

Victor cut him off. 'You better be bloody sorry.' He grabbed Red by the collar and lifted him until the boy was choking. 'Are you sure you're sorry?'

Red's hands gripped Victor's wrists and, unable to speak, he nodded desperately.

'Good, because now you can make it up to me.' He dropped Red and the boy's mouth opened as he gulped a lung-full of air.

'Sure. I'll do anything you want,' Red gasped.

'First you can go find out where Briar is.'

'He'll be at the stables. He always goes there at this time of day.'

'Perfect, I want you to wait quarter of an hour then go take a message to him.' Victor leaned down at the boy. 'Now listen carefully. You gotta say these exact words to him...'

All Briar could think about was the ram. The image of the shears slicing into the ram's body filled his head. He could still smell the blood. After Tane had dismissed them, Aussie had run off. Briar knew exactly where Aussie was heading—the same place he always went when he was angry; up to the ridge paddock to hurl stones into the ravine. Briar desperately wanted to be up there with him throwing his own frustration at the world but he knew Aussie needed to be alone. Instead he went to find Wairua hoping that being with the horse could somehow lessen his guilt.

He led her into the stables, tied her up with a length of twine then gave her a good hard brush. When he finished, he leaned forwards and pressed his face into Wairua's neck, the soft warm cleft just behind the jaw. Briar could feel the animal's pulse throbbing against his cheek, slow and powerful, and he felt his heart rate slowing to match. For a while he just leaned there and breathed in the familiar scent.

'Hey Briar, I got a message for you.'

Wairua and Briar flinched in unison. He turned to see Red standing on the slats of the round-pen gate.

'What?'

'I got a message for you.'

'What message? From who?'

'From Aussie. Yeah, it's a message from Aussie.'

Briar stared at Red, his brain still catching up.

Red frowned. 'Aussie is looking for you. Um, he needs your help and he's waiting for you in the wool shed.'

'He's in the wool shed?'

'Yep. That's the message. He's waiting in the wool shed.'

'Oh, did he...' Before Briar could finish, Red was gone.

Briar straightened up. Aussie needed him. He turned back to Wairua, 'I'm going to put you in a stall girl, but only for a while. I'll be back soon. I promise.'

Briar ran to the woolshed and let himself in. Motes drifted through shafts of fading light and the building was silent. There was no sign of Aussie.

Briar frowned, 'Aussie? Hey Aussie, are you here?' He walked into the middle of the work area and turned full circle, 'Aussie! It's me, Briar.'

Three shapes leapt out of the shadows. Before Briar could utter a word, Victor shoved him in the chest, slamming him back against a post. Dennis and Nate grabbed his arms, hauling them back and locking him in place.

Victor leaned forward and pushed his nose into Briar's face. 'Looking for Aussie are ya?' He sneered, 'He gonna protect you, is he?' Dennis and Nate pulled Briar's arms back even further and his spine complained with a popping sound.

Briar tried to reply, 'I don't...' The pressure on his arms meant his head was pushed back and he couldn't see Victor's fist but he registered the twist of the older boy's shoulders and knew the gut punch was coming a split second before his stomach exploded with pain. A muffled gasp was erupted his throat with the escaping air.

'I didn't say you could talk,' spat Victor. Unable to double over, Briar's body convulsed heaving for breath. Victor laughed, 'Where are your clever words now?' He nodded to his henchmen to let go of Briar's arms. Briar collapsed to his knees, his head hitting the floor and his hands clenched across his stomach.

'Now we're gonna do some shearing,' Victor announced.

Briar tried to look up but couldn't. The pain in his belly was like a red hot spring and any movement just stretched it unbearably.

'Take his clothes off,' Victor said and Dennis and Nate jumped to obey. They grasped Briar's shoulders and shoved him onto his back. The pain from his stomach lanced through his body and at last he uttered a muffled cry. Nate kneeled over Briar's head and unbuttoned his shirt then, grabbing it by the tails, he peeled it up over Briar's shoulders, hauling the arms up in the process. Nate twisted the shirt several times, tying Briar's wrists together with it. Dennis started at the opposite end. He pulled Briar's boots off and without a pause he grasped the bottom of Briar's shorts and hauled them down and over his ankles. With a cheer he held them up like a trophy, waving them in Briar's face.

Briar felt a desperate sense of vulnerability. Beyond everything else; the physical pain, the fear of serious injury, he couldn't bear to be naked. Somehow his clothes felt like one last shield, one last vestige of self respect. Briar tried to scream but only a strangled hiss left his throat. He twisted and strained and managed to unravel the shirt binding his wrists. His hands flicked down and grasped the waistband of his underwear just as Dennis tried to pull it down. Briar clung on and for a second they performed a tug-o-war. Victor laughed at the struggle.

'Get his hand,' said Victor and Nate pried Briar's fingers off the fabric. At the same time Dennis pulled with both hands and the underpants slipped off leaving Briar naked. His body went completely limp, the entire struggle stripped away and his eyes looked up in resignation as Victor's shadow towered over him.

Victor stepped over Briar's limp body and pulled a length of twine from his pocket. He crouched down and grabbed both of Briar's wrists then flicked two loops around them. He rolled Briar onto his side, folded his ankles behind his knees and tied them with the other end of the rope. The position he was left in was unnatural and almost immediately Briar felt the muscles in his shoulders and lower back beginning to cramp. It was a human version of the process Victor liked to call "hog-tying" and all the boys had witnessed him using it on animals that were to have surgical procedures. Victor hooked his forearm under Briar's armpit and dragged him across the wool shed and into his station. He smiled down at Briar.

'Now let's complete your training.' He seized a pair of hand shears and squeezed the blades slowly together in front of Briar's eyes. 'Just like this, see. Squeeze them nice and tight.' He grabbed a fistful of Briar's hair and hauled him up, clamping him against his knees as though he were a sheep.

'You should feel honoured. Now you get a lesson from a champion,' said Victor.

Aussie's head hung as he walked back towards the dorms. He had thrown rocks until his arm was sore but he still felt guilty. 'It was an accident,' he muttered.

Ten minutes later he reached the dorms. On the porch outside, Red was sitting on the step poking at the heel of his boot with a stick.

'So did Briar find you?' asked Red.

Aussie looked at him, confused. 'What do you mean? Was he looking for me?'

'Nah. You was looking for him,' said Red.

'What are you talking about?'

'You wanted Briar to come find you. In the wool shed. That's what Victor told me.'

'Huh?' Aussie stared quizzically at him as his brain stitched things together. His expression turned to alarm. 'Damn!'

Red jumped out of the way as Aussie dived off the porch, sprinting for the wool shed.

Victor pressed the cold blades against Briar's neck then slid them up onto his head.

'Gonna say goodbye to your CityGirl fleece?' He slowly dug the tips through Briar's hair then pushed the open blades downwards so they were sitting either side of Briar's left ear. Briar whimpered.

'Accidents happen, eh CityGirl? Just like today with the ram.' Victor squeezed the shears slightly and the cold blades touched Briar's skin. Briar winced and the tiny movement brought a sharp pain as one of the blades cut behind his ear. He stopped breathing, terrified to move again.

'I should slice this off,' hissed Victor, 'but you'd go running to Tane wouldn't you, you little coward.' He sniggered. 'Anyway I got a better idea.' He shoved Briar with his right leg.

Briar instinctively tried to move his arms as he was pushed over but the bindings were firm and he slammed to the floor, his head whacking the floorboards. Victor rolled him onto his back then dropped a knee onto his chest. Briar's hog-tied limbs were crushed awkwardly beneath him and he couldn't help crying out.

Victor's left hand reached between Briar's legs and grabbed his testicles. 'You ain't no breeding ram. Maybe we should castrate you,' said Victor. Dennis and Nate sniggered as Victor opened the blades and slid them around Briar's scrotum. 'Shall I do it? Then you'll be a real CityGirl.'

Briar's neck was strained forwards as he stared in terror at the sharp blades. 'Please,' he whimpered. 'I'm sorry. I'm sorry.'

'You'd make a great wether,' said Victor. He leaned down and put his face up to Briar's. 'Do you know what mountain oysters are? They're testicles. If we cut yours off, maybe we can cook them up. Serve them for breakfast.'

Briar's shoulders were shaking. 'Don't,' he pleaded.

Victor smirked at Denis. 'Hear that? He doesn't want to be a girl after all.' He pulled the clippers away from Briar's scrotum. 'His balls are tiny. They wouldn't make much of a meal. So I'll just crutch and dag him.' In one swift stroke he grabbed a handful of Briar's pubic hair and sliced through it. He followed up with a few more brutal cuts and in a matter of seconds he had sheared Briar's pubic area to a stubble.

Dennis pointed and laughed, 'Ha. Check out his baldy.'

'Just like a baby,' Nate chipped in.

Victor looked down at Briar with a triumphant smile but his expression slowly turned into a snarl. 'I know about your precious little horse. If you mention this to anyone, I'll gut her just like you gutted that ram! Do you understand?'

'No. Not Wairua,' gasped Briar. 'Don't hurt her.'

Victor leaned down again, his mouth almost touching Briar's ear. 'Now I'm gonna give you a little reminder,' he whispered. 'A scar so you'll always remember this lesson.' Victor opened the shears wide and pressed one blade against the inside of Briar's leg, high up in his groin. 'Just up here where no one else can see. I'll make it a V. Then you're branded and you belong to me.'

The door crashed open and Aussie's voice yelled out.

'Briar! Briar!'

Victor leapt up.

Briar let out a panicked wail, 'Aussie!' He thrashed desperately, straining at the rope and the bindings around his feet slipped. He flicked out with his legs and managed to push himself half way out of Victor's station. Aussie gasped when he saw him. He rushed forwards to help but was stopped in his tracks as Victor stepped out to confront him.

'Yeah come on,' Victor smirked. 'Come rescue your little CityGirl.'

'Leave him alone,' said Aussie.

'You can't tell me what to do,' growled Victor. 'I'm the one in charge here.' He threw a quick glance over his shoulder at Dennis and Nate. 'Let's get him,' he hissed and the two younger boys stepped up to flank him raising their fists.

Aussie moved like lightening. He leapt sideways into the

nearest station and reappeared a fraction of a second later brandishing a pair of hand-shears. 'Get outta my way,' he yelled.

Nate's eyes widened when he saw the weapon in Aussie's hand. He stepped backwards. 'Stuff this,' he mumbled then with a brief glance at Victor he turned and fled.

'Come back here, you coward,' yelled Victor. The only answer was Nate's receding footfalls.

On the other side of Victor, Dennis also looked unsure. He swallowed. 'We taught him a lesson, let's just go.'

Victor turned on Dennis. 'No! We're gonna finish this. You said you're loyal. Now you gotta stay.'

Aussie pointed his shears at Dennis. 'I'm gonna get *you* first. Cut your bloody head off.'

'Don't listen to him,' Victor growled. 'There's two of us, he hasn't got a chance.' The damage was done. Dennis backed away and a moment later he turned and ran after Nate.

'Pussy,' Victor yelled. He turned back to Aussie. 'I'm not scared of you.'

'Really?' Aussie started moving forward closing the gap between him and Victor.

Victor moved back keeping the distance between them. 'You'll never be better than me,' he hissed at Aussie, 'and you'll never run this farm'.

Aussie finally reached Briar. 'You can have the farm but I'm not gonna let you hurt anyone.'

'You couldn't stop me if you tried,' Victor spat as hard as he could but the gob only made it half way to Aussie. 'You're not worth it. I'll leave you to your sissy girlfriend.' He smiled down at Briar and made a show of running his thumb along the blade of the shears. 'The girl with the pretty horse.' He threw the shears on the ground in front of him then disappeared in the same direction as Dennis and Nate.

Aussie's shoulders slumped and his skin paled. His shears clattered to the floor. Briar started blabbering in relief.

'If you hadn't come. He was going to...' he stopped as his body was wracked by sobs.

Aussie rushed to him. His breath caught as he realised Briar was completely naked, lying on his side, legs hunched up into a foetal position with his wrists tied behind him. Aussie knelt down and helped him into a sitting position, then spun him around to untie his hands. 'Are you okay? What did they do to you?' He struggled with the knot.

'I'm fine,' breathed Briar. He sniffed back his tears. 'Now that you're here, I'll be fine.'

'Did they hurt you?'

'No, not really. He was going to but you came.'

'What did he mean about your horse?'

Briar's tone grew defensive. 'Nothing. He didn't mean anything.'

The knot wouldn't undo so Aussie pushed his fingers between the rope and Briar's wrist worrying the twine loose. 'When I saw you, I thought they'd done something to you. Something serious.' Finally the rope loosened and Aussie prised the knots apart releasing his wrists. Briar groaned at the freedom. He rolled his neck and shoulders then wrapped his arms around his knees.

'Are you sure you're alright? Victor had hand shears, did he cut you?'

Briar lifted his head and looked nervously at Aussie. Then he slowly leaned back to expose his cut pubic hair. 'He did this,' he whispered. Amongst the light brown stubble there were a few bloody lines where the blades had nicked the skin.

Aussie glanced down at Briar's nakedness and the damage Victor inflicted. His breath caught in his throat. 'I wish I'd been here. I should have been with you.'

'You can't be with me all the time.'

'But I want to be. I think about you all the time.' He sat back on his ankles, 'You've made me realise something.'

Briar arched his back to release the cramped muscles along his spine. 'What?'

'You've made me realise that I should be honest to myself.'

'What are you talking about?'

Aussie was silent for a moment. 'Nothing important. I just thought you should know that I care about you and I'm never gonna let anyone hurt you again.' Aussie frowned and leaned forward to peer more closely at Briar's face. He reached a finger out and touched the drop of blood that was running from behind Briar's ear. 'You *are* hurt,' he said.

Briar cupped his hand over his ear. 'It's nothing. Victor was just trying to scare me.'

'Bloody Victor. He's going down for this! Once we show Tane what he did to you...'

'You can't tell anyone,' blurted Briar.

'What do you mean?' Aussie frowned. 'We have to.'

'No. It's too embarrassing.'

'He was gonna hurt you. He might try again.'

Briar grabbed Aussie's arm. 'You can't tell anyone. You've gotta promise me.'

'Why?'

Briar thought for a second. 'Because I need to stand up to him. Just like you said.'

'This is different.'

Briar's voice cracked. 'Please.' He looked away from Aussie. His eyes screwed up and his lip quivered slightly.

'Hey, don't cry.'

'I'm not.' Briar clenched his jaw but he couldn't stop a tear from rolling down his cheek. He drew up his knees and wrapped his arms around them, 'Where's my clothes?'

Aussie reached out to touch Briar's shoulder.

'Don't,' said Briar.

Aussie flinched and pulled his hand away. He stood up, retrieved Briar's clothes and handed them over.

Briar dressed in an awkward rush. 'I better get back to Wairua,' he pulled his shirt on.

'I'll come with you down to the stables.'

'I'll be alright. Victor's not gonna try anything now.'

'Please. I'll feel bad if I don't.'

After a moment Briar shrugged. 'Yeah sure. It's about time you met Wairua.'

CHAPTER 27

—————

HUNUA · 1954

THE AIR IN THE HUNUA VILLAGE CHAPEL stank of sweat, perfume and musty prayer books. It was Sunday morning and the wooden pews were full of worshippers; farmers from Hunua and Ararimu who made the pilgrimage.

On one side of the aisle the Dwyte family sat in the front pew along with Aussie, Victor and Tane. The rest of the farm boys were crammed into three rows immediately behind. On the other side of the chapel several nuns perched before a flock of convent girls. Boys flashed hopeful smiles across the chapel only to be met with feigned indifference. This was a weekly ritual. As soon as the service was finished the boys would rush outside and circle the girls, bragging and vying for attention until the nuns emerged and gathered up their charges. The girls would board a bus which would deliver them back to the convent, a luxury the boys didn't share. Instead they walked an hour each way over Ponga Hill and across the valley to fulfil their religious obligation.

Father Patrick stood in the pulpit half way through delivering his homily. His words were impassioned today, angry and direct; an old fashioned fire-and-brimstone sermon.

'And finally I will speak to the young people in our congregation.' He looked at the boys and then the girls. 'Many of you are on the cusp of adulthood and it is at this age that the devil's voice becomes strongest.' He gripped the lectern with both fists and leaned forward. 'Satan knows you are struggling with change. He knows you are easily tempted. So he will try to fill your heads with evil. With thoughts of disobedience and carnality and gluttony. You must resist these urges! If you do not, the Lord will punish you just as he punished Sodom and Gomorrah.' Father Patrick lifted his right hand and waved a finger at the congregation. 'God sent angels to those towns in the form of men. Instead of bowing to the angels, the men of Sodom wished to "know" them through unnatural sex and the women spoke to the angels as they would to their husbands. These are sins that God will never abide. Arrogance. Homosexuality. Disobedience. They are the gifts of Satan.' He brought down his fist and the lectern shook. 'But God offers us something different. He offers the only *true* gift. The gift of love.' His voice softened and he leaned forward again, 'One day each of you will be offered the gift of love from the man or woman who God has destined for you. Until that day each of you should be keeping yourself pure. When the time comes, when that true, godly love is offered to you—you must never spurn it. Because it is the greatest gift anyone can give.'

There was a quiet grunt of agreement from Victor who was leaning forward and looking along the row at Rosemary. The priest opened the Bible that lay on the lectern in front of him and finished his sermon with a reading.

The man who knows not his place in front of the Lord shall be nameless. He will not prosper in his days nor have any sons. And so with women who disobey their fathers and their husbands and heed not the teachings of the Lord. God will abandon them to their shameful desires and their lives will be empty.

When the service finished and the congregation filed out of the church, Aussie excused himself and waited by the sacristy door. Eventually Father Patrick emerged buttoning up his black shirt and slipping his white clerical collar into place.

'Oh, hello Aussie. It's nice to see you.'

'Father, I need to talk to someone.'

'Of course, my boy. Come, have a seat.' He led him to the nearest pew and both sat down. 'How can I help you?'

'If I tell you something, will you keep it secret?'

Father Patrick patted his wrist. 'Of course.'

Aussie couldn't hold the priest's gaze. He looked at the floor. 'Father, I'm so confused. Because of your sermon. I can't...' His voice cracked.

'What is it, Aussie?'

'It's... I didn't want to be this way.' Words stuck in Aussie's throat.

'I can't help you if you won't tell me what it is.'

Aussie began wringing his hands. 'It's hard to say it. Sometimes I feel ashamed but when I'm with him it seems right.'

'What are you talking about?'

Aussie took a deep breath. 'I'm having feelings for another boy.' His words were little more than a whisper. He looked up, searching the priest's face.

For a second Father Patrick looked shocked. He opened his mouth to reply then closed it again.

'I'm disgusting, aren't I?' said Aussie. 'Just like the Bible says.' He hung his head. 'I tried to stop it. Tried to make it go away. But I can't. I just can't.'

'Slow down, Aussie,' the priest thought for a moment, 'it's good you came to me. Have you told anyone else? Said anything to this boy?'

Aussie shook his head.

'Good. Let's keep it that way.' Father Patrick put his hand on Aussie's shoulder. 'This is a very important thing for you to understand. You're confused. What you are feeling is a brotherly love. It's God's way of showing you that you have love in your heart for everyone. Men, women, young, old.'

'You don't understand! Whenever he comes near, my heart beats faster! I want to put my arms around him and protect him.'

'Enough! I won't let you taint God's house with words like that.' Father Patrick let go of Aussie's shoulder. 'These feelings you're having aren't real love. That can only be between a man and a woman. Now put it out of your mind.' The priest stood up and turned to leave. 'You need to distance yourself from this boy and spend more time praying.'

Aussie exited the chapel, his stride carrying him so quickly he was almost running. Briar was waiting for him at the bottom of the steps.

'Hey, are you okay?' Briar saw the confused look on Aussie's face.

Aussie stopped mid-stride and stared at Briar. 'I'm fine but...' Aussie looked away, 'I need to be alone.'

'Why? What's wrong?'

'Nothing's wrong. I just can't spend time with you.'

'What do you mean?'

Aussie's head flicked back to Briar and his face was angry. 'I need to be alone!' Briar frowned and took a step backwards. Aussie dashed past and disappeared towards the farm.

Just as Major Dwyte had ordered, that afternoon there was no free-time. As soon as they returned from church, the boys changed into their work clothes and reported to the woolshed. It was stifling hot and the heat in the air made the inside of the shed dance. As the boys worked, sweat dripped into their eyes. Briar was dagging at the bottom end of the stations and from his vantage point he kept looking up the shed at Aussie but the older boy was avoiding his gaze.

The side door opened and a swish of bright blue entered the wool shed. It was Rosemary. She was carrying a feathered sun hat which covered her nose to mask the smell. She wandered up the shed, straight past the shearers, most of whom had their heads down working. She stopped by a stacked pile of hay bales and absentmindedly poked a finger into a couple of them but her eyes were looking elsewhere. She lifted her hat to fan herself, turning for a better view of Aussie's shirtless body. He was bent over a sheep and unaware of her presence.

Victor straightened up and saw Rosemary only ten yards away. Noticing the direction of her gaze, his eyes narrowed. He hastily discarded his handset and stepped towards her. 'Hi Rosemary. Would you like a hand with something?'

'No thank you, Victor.' Rosemary flicked her hat dismissively at him. 'I'm just checking that we have enough hay bales for the garden party.' She glanced back at Aussie, running her eye over his muscled back.

Victor frowned his disapproval. 'Most of the hay is in the loft above the stables. I'd be happy to collect some for you.' He flexed his arm muscles. 'I can lift four bales at a time.'

'Actually, I was going to ask Aussie to bring a couple up to the garden.'

At that moment Aussie stood up and released his sheep into the chute. He saw Rosemary standing nearby. 'Hello Miss Dwyte,' he gave her a polite smile, 'never seen you in here before. Is there something we can help you with?'

'Yes. I was wondering if...'

Victor pushed his way past her, planting himself between them. 'I wouldn't bother asking Aussie to help you,' he said loudly. 'He's too busy with his girlfriend, Briar.'

Aussie scowled. 'You watch your mouth.'

'Aww, how sweet. Protecting your little CityGirl.'

Aussie flipped a finger at him. 'At least I have the courage to fight my own battles. I don't need three-on-one.'

Rosemary broke into a smile. She pushed herself between them, rubbing her hand across Aussie's chest. 'Boys, boys! Don't fight over me.' Clutching her hat to her breast she turned one way then the other looking each of them in the eye. 'It's really not that important.' She leaned and whispered something in Victor's ear and his face broke into a victorious smile. Rosemary turned and walked off leaving the two boys facing one another.

'You see! She likes me. She doesn't bloody well like you!' Victor sauntered back to his station and pulled a new sheep from his side pen.

'Bloody dunce,' muttered Aussie, shaking his head and stepping back to his work.

From the bottom of the line, Briar watched Aussie return to his station. He felt relieved. A fight between Aussie and Victor could put Wairua at risk. Red came past dragging a sheep up the line. Briar put down his shears. 'I'll deliver this one to Aussie.' He took the prone sheep off Red.

When he got to Aussie's station, Briar leaned his shoulder against the side pillar.

'What the hell's wrong? What'd I do?'

'You didn't do anything,' said Aussie without looking up.

'How can we be friends when you won't even talk to me?'

Aussie shoved his shorn ewe into the chute and turned to Briar. 'My pen's empty. Just gimme the sheep. We don't need to talk.'

Briar felt the hurt rising in him but he swallowed it down, determined to never again become emotional or show weakness in front of the farm boys. He slid his leg around and shoved the ewe's butt into Aussie's stall.

Aussie reached out and grabbed the animal, pulling it from Briar's hands. Without a word he set straight to work.

'Why are you ignoring me?'

Aussie didn't respond, he just crunched down harder and set to working faster. Briar stared in frustration. He glanced around to check nobody else was watching then knelt down in front of Aussie's sheep and reached out and took hold of its back legs. 'Please tell me what's wrong. You're my friend. I want to help.'

Aussie flicked the handset off. 'I can't be your friend anymore.'

'Why? Is this about Victor?'

Suddenly Aussie was glaring. 'No! Of course it's not about Victor.' He glanced nervously down the shed then realising nobody was paying them any attention his face softened a little. 'Look. I've been told some important things. Given some solid advice. We need to stop being friends, you and me. Just workmates. That's all.'

'But I feel something special between us, and I know you feel it too.'

Aussie looked away. He pulled the ewe up and flicked the handset back on. He had to speak up to be heard over the clatter. 'I don't feel anything!'

Briar knelt up and leaned forward so Aussie could hear him. 'But the other night when Victor was gonna hurt me...'

'Just leave me alone!' Aussie lashed out with his handset to wave Briar away but the shears caught him square on the chin, the impact jarring Briar's head back and throwing him to the floor.

Briar blinked. He could taste the tang of blood trickling down his throat. He sat up clutching his chin and spat blood from his mouth where he had bitten his tongue. His hand reached up to cup his jaw and he winced as he touched the graze the handset had left.

Aussie's eyes widened and his jaw dropped open. He abandoned the ewe and reached for Briar with his left hand. 'Shit, I'm so sorry. I didn't want to hurt you.'

From across the shed Tane appeared. 'What's wrong here? What happened?'

'It's nothing.' Briar tried to hide his face. Fresh blood was seeping from a line of nicks where the shears cut him.

'It was an accident,' stammered Aussie.

'This boy is bleeding.' Tane waved his hand at Briar's face. 'What's going on between the two of you?'

Aussie leapt up. 'Nothing's going on. Nothing! We're not even friends.' He threw down the handset and took off.

Aussie ran into the bathroom, threw himself into a toilet-stall and chained the door. He buried his head in his hands.

A curse escaped through his clenched teeth, 'Shit! Shit!' A minute later the sound of footsteps made him look up.

'Aussie, we need to have a talk,' came Tane's voice through the wooden door.

'I didn't hurt him on purpose. It was just an accident.'

'We need to talk about you. Not Briar.'

'I don't want to talk.'

'There's a boy bleeding in there. You can't tell me it's nothing.'

'I just need him to stay away from me.'

'You know very well we all have to work together. If you can't do your job, I will move you on.' Tane crossed his arms. 'Is that what you want? If you're not happy here, I can probably get you a job at the mill.'

'No! I wanna stay.'

There was silence between them. Tane sat down on a shower step, pulled out his tobacco pouch and rolled a cigarette. 'Aussie, I've watched you grow into a decent young man but you've changed in the last couple of months. Something's bothering you. What is it, boy?'

'It's nothing.'

'Is "nothing" the reason you're constantly fighting with Victor?'

'Victor keeps telling lies about me. Lies about me and Briar.'

'I know you and Briar are friends. Good friends.'

In the cubicle, Aussie leaned his forehead against the door and said nothing.

'Aussie, I know more than you think. If there's anything else, you can talk to me. Even if it's… hard to talk about.'

Aussie slid down until he was sitting on the cubicle floor. 'I already talked to Father Patrick.'

Tane lit his cigarette. He inhaled then blew a long coil of smoke from the corner of his mouth. 'Maybe you should listen to his advice.'

'What if I don't want to?'

'You have to make your own choices, boy. Same as all of us,' Tane stubbed out the cigarette and stood up, 'but sometimes fighting for something costs you more than you expect.' He turned to leave. 'Don't be too long. You have responsibilities in the woolshed.'

For several minutes Aussie was motionless, his head still resting on his knees. All of a sudden his fist shot out and punched the wall, cracking one of the boards. He stared at his bleeding knuckles, trying to connect them with the pain he was feeling.

CHAPTER 28

Hunua · 1954

THAT EVENING BROUGHT THE FIRST grey clouds in weeks. George and Tane were drinking in the stables and they'd been at it for a while. George looked ruddy and his words were slightly slurred. He gazed out the open doors where the setting sun was painting the clouds on the horizon in endless shades of crimson and gold.

'Red at night, shepherd's delight,' he muttered.

Tane looked around at George. 'What was that, Major?'

'Nothing important. Believe it or not, I'm hoping for a bit more sunshine.'

'Why? The ground is parched.'

'Rosemary's party on Saturday. Edna will be so disappointed if it rains.'

Tane nodded. 'Of course. The party is all the boys are talking about. Wish they were half as focused on their work.'

George chortled and raised his glass. 'I hope you're going to be there.'

Tane cleared his throat. 'I'm afraid I'm busy on Saturday.'

'It's her eighteenth birthday, Tane. It's a big deal.'

Tane lifted his hand. 'My daughter is leaving to go away. She's having a do. It's the last chance for me to see her before she goes.'

'Oh, I see. Pity. Would've been nice to have you there.' George drained his glass and refilled it from the whisky bottle. 'Here I was thinking you had a date? Some lucky lady you'd been keeping hidden?'

Tane studied the dirt floor. 'There's things I have to tell my daughter. Things I should have said to her a long time ago.'

'She seems a nice woman, that daughter of yours. Is she going far?'

'To the Wairarapa. I'll miss her, that's for sure.'

'You know, I never did meet her mother.'

Tane took a swig from his glass. 'It's complicated.'

George eyed Tane sympathetically. 'I always wonder if you're lonely. Living here on your own. Always thought you'd find yourself a missus. Edna and I might have our differences but at least we're a family.'

'I'm not lonely,' said Tane a little too quickly.

'Don't you want someone to share your life with?'

Tane looked at the distant clouds which were losing the last of their colour. 'I had someone once.'

George waited for him to elaborate but there was just the sound of crickets. 'Damn it man, I've known you thirty-five years. You don't need to hide things from me.'

'What would you know about hiding things?'

'Don't you presume with me. You know what I did in the last war. I've kept my share of secrets.'

'Other people's secrets.'

'Ugly secrets. Things *nobody* wants to know.'

'Do they make you feel ashamed?'

George frowned at Tane's question. He took a swig before answering, 'You learn to live with them.'

'Yes. You do.'

Both men looked out into the dusk at the sound of a morepork.

'Well, whatever you're hiding I'm glad you had a sweetheart.' George raised his glass. 'Here's to love. May every man find it once in his life.' He sealed the toast by draining his glass, picked up the bottle and held it out.

Tane shook his head. 'I've had enough, Major.'

George poured himself another measure then threw it back in a single gulp. They sat in silence for a while.

'I've got a bit of a confession myself,' George's voice was slurred. More silence.

George let out a long frustrated sigh. 'I might have lost the farm.'

Tane was still focussed on the horizon. He didn't look around at George's admission but his brow creased.

'I made some bad wagers,' George continued, 'and I borrowed against the farm. I'm in debt, Tane. Bad debt. If I had some time, just a few more months to fatten the lambs...' He drank again. 'If I don't pay up, they're going to sell the farm.' George looked up at the corrugated iron roof with its faded British Iron stamping. 'I don't know how I'm going to tell Edna.' He got up uncertainly, stepped into the stable doorway and looked out at the sky. 'What is it that horses do to us, eh Tane? They can lead us to risk everything.' He stumbled three steps backwards and sat heavily on the hay bale. He looked startled then sprawled back, sighed and closed his eyes. A moment later he was snoring.

Tane pushed himself to his feet and looked down at George. He shook his head. 'You're glad I had a sweetheart, are you? I don't need your pity.' Turning away Tane pulled the cufflink out and held it up in the fading light. The silver outline of the horse-head glinted, the last of the daylight reflecting off a surface that had been polished for decades by the shirt that hid it. He let the cuf-flink drop to his chest but for once he didn't tuck the chain away. He drained the last of the whisky from his glass, grimacing as it burned his throat then looked back down at George.

'You think you've had it hard?' he muttered at the sleeping figure. 'We might have fought in the same war, but we were never the same. You came back a hero. I didn't even earn the right to be myself.' He leaned down, picked up the bottle and stood over the

Major's prone figure. His eyes narrowed. 'It would be so bloody easy, wouldn't it? Your life.' He stared at George for a long time.

Then he straightened up and took a deep gulp from the bottle. Outside the light had drained from the sky allowing the naked eye to see the stars. Tane held the whisky up to toast the emerging lights of the Milky Way. 'You're always there, aren't you? But nobody sees you in the daylight. You don't exist in this world until it's dark.' He turned and disappeared inside the stables to stash the glassware away.

When he returned, he reached down and hauled George to his feet. Slipping the man's arm over his shoulder he half dragged him through the door and off towards the farmhouse. Tane's limp was more evident under the extra weight.

A little later as Tane returned from delivering George home, a rusty old car rattled up the driveway. Its lights cut through the twilight and it stopped outside the woolshed. The door opened and Tane's daughter climbed from the driver's seat.

Tane called across the driveway, 'Hi my girl,'

'Hi Dad,' she threw herself around his neck hugging him, 'I hoped I'd find you here.'

'Come into my office. I'll brew some tea.'

'I can't stop, I've gotta take the car back. I brought the stuff I told you about. I don't need it and I thought maybe the boys might want it.'

'Sure.'

They walked around and extracted two cartons from the boot and took them into Tane's office. 'It's good you're here. There's something I wanted to talk to you about.' Tane put down the box he was carrying. 'I got some money. Some money I didn't expect. I want you to have it.' He took the carton from his daughter and stacked it with the other.

She shook her head. 'Dad, That's silly. I don't need your money. You should keep it.'

'Of course you should have it. You're my girl. I want to provide for you.'

She took his hands in her own and smiled at him. 'I'm not taking your money. Paul has everything we need. Our own house. Our own land.'

'But.. '

'No. And that's final.' She lifted his hands to her mouth and kissed them. 'I love you, Dad. You keep the money. Do something nice. Something for yourself.'

Tane frowned at the floor.

She released his hands. 'Are you still coming to my farewell party on Saturday?'

He nodded.

'I'm gonna cook pork. Just the way you like it.'

He looked up. 'Well, for pork I guess I'll drag myself along.'

She scoffed and mock-punched his arm. 'Thanks a lot.'

Tane smiled. 'Of course I'm coming. Already told the Major. I'm gonna miss you, my girl.'

'Me too. I'm sure you can visit. It's not *so* far.' There was a pause and her words echoed off the timber walls.

Tane frowned. 'You know what. There's something I need to do before you go.' He opened his desk drawer and pulled out a small package wrapped in a strip of khaki. 'I've been meaning to give this to you.' He unwrapped the cloth to unveil a piece of jewellery; a black cufflink matching the one around his neck. 'Was gonna give this to you on Saturday but since you're here,' he looked reverently at the cufflink, 'it's important that you have it.' He reached up to touch his daughter's face and his hand was suddenly shaking. 'No matter how far away you are, they'll keep us together. Remind us of each other.'

'Dad, it's beautiful. It matches your one. I didn't know there were two.' She took the cufflink from his hand. 'Where did you get them?'

'In France.'

'During the Great War?'

'They were given to me by someone, someone special.' He choked on the last word and she reached out and touched his arm.

'It's okay, Dad. You don't need to say anything.' She held the jewel against her chest. 'I'll put it on a chain. Just like yours.' She hugged him tightly. Tane's shoulders quietly shook and tears rolled down his face.

'Are you okay?'

'I'm fine, my girl.' He stepped away from her and wiped his eyes. 'It's because I've been drinking. You go. Take the car back.'

'Are you sure? You look upset.'

'Just an old fella being sentimental.'

'Alright.' She gave him a last peck on the cheek. 'Thanks Dad. See you on Saturday.' As she slipped out the door she waved the cufflink at him. 'And you can tell me the story of how you got this.'

The door closed. Tane reached up and touched his own pendant. 'I'll tell you it all, my girl. I remember it like it was yesterday.'

CHAPTER 29

FRANCE · 1915

TANE AND WIREMU FOUND THEMSELVES IN FRANCE. They had followed the British officer's suggestion and spoken to the captain of the *HMS Forthright*. He needed some convincing but eventually they were both given passage from Lisbon on the converted passenger ferry. Now, along with several hundred new recruits they were assembled on the edge of a wet field. The English were taking the war to the Germans, and Tane felt proud to be part of it. It was a new year, 1915 had rolled around with barely an acknowledgement on their short voyage from Portugal.

Tane looked across the field. Beyond the expanse of grass lay a training camp. They had been told it was one of several which stretched along the Channel. This one doubled as a supply station for the Territorial Force. It sprawled for several acres in each direction but boasted few permanent buildings. Until the outbreak of war it had been a farm owned by a retired French colonel. The quiet Limousin cattle were gone and the imposing manor house and its out buildings were now surrounded by a complex of Bellhouse huts, their corrugated iron cladding joined panel to panel to produce an ever growing hub where officers and clerks administered the despatch of machines, munitions and men. Beyond the huts, lines of tents expanded outwards in orderly ranks of canvas. On all sides, the farm's remaining fields were crisscrossed by roads worn into the mud by the wheels of wagons and the boots of soldiers.

Tane breathed deeply, taking it all in. The winter sun was up and while it offered little warmth, its light was coaxing tendrils of mist from the wet grass and the smell reminded him of New Zealand. He watched as lines of soldiers in olive uniforms marched through the rows of tents, bending like snakes as they turned each ninety-degree corner. The sound of sergeants keeping the men in formation echoed across the field competing with the clatter of horse drawn artillery and the revving engines of motor trucks as they hauled the ingredients of war.

The men surrounding Tane and Wiremu were mostly young and they looked like a *Who's Who* of the Commonwealth; a mixing bowl of skin tones and clothing. Tane could sense the growing excitement around him. Despite the sadness and anger that had driven him here, he too felt a sense of adventure.

'So where are you from?' came a voice from over Tane's shoulder. The English was heavily accented. Tane and Wiremu both turned to find a short man smiling at them. He wore a dun coloured shirt that hung almost to his knees and down the front and around the sleeves, an intricate crosshatch pattern had been embroidered with a dark thread.

Tane held out his hand. 'I'm from New Zealand and from your accent, you're from India I guess.'

'Oh yes. Right you are.' The man beamed and shook Tane's hand. He nodded at Wiremu. 'Goodness, you are tall. Are you from New Zealand also?'

'Yep. Best country in the world,' said Wiremu. 'What's your name?'

'Neerav. Neerav Patel.'

'I'm Wiremu Toa,' he nodded at Tane, 'and this is Johnny Chapman.'

'So here we all are, joining the British army,' said Neerav. 'Have you been living in England then?'

'Nah. We sailed directly from Lisbon to France. We docked at Étaples yesterday and then we marched here overnight,' said Wiremu.

'A German u-boat torpedoed our ship in Lisbon harbour,' explained Tane.

Neerav scowled. 'That's terrible.'

'They killed our friends and we weren't even a navy ship.'

'Well, you are amongst friends here.' Neerav patted Tane's arm. 'We are all in this together.'

Tane smiled at Neerav. 'Thanks mate.' He looked southwards, in the direction he knew they were headed. 'I owe those German bastards.'

Wiremu clapped Tane on the shoulder. 'Don't worry buddy. We're gonna pay them back.'

Another man who had been listening spoke up. His skin was ebony and his accent was more difficult to comprehend although Tane guessed it was from somewhere in Africa. 'My brother's family is in Portugal,' said the man. 'They are still neutral, yes?' The man was thin and tall, even taller than Wiremu.

'Yes, still staying out of the conflict,' said Wiremu, 'but our captain reckoned they were gonna declare for the Allies.' He held out his hand to the tall man. 'I'm Wiremu. From New Zealand. Pleased to meet ya, mate.'

'Mosi Tinibu. I'm from Kenya.' They all shook hands, introducing themselves. Before they could continue their conversation, there was a series of shouts and suddenly they were being hustled into line formations under the barked commands of a burly sergeant. They were marched through the camp and onto a long narrow parade ground that stretched between the Bellhouse huts and tents. A few minutes later they stood in a dozen rows, an arm's length from the man either side of them.

Facing the rows of men stood several officers. A middle aged captain decked in military formals and sporting a long bar of ribbons on his chest leaned to his side and spoke quietly to the young lieutenant standing beside him.

'Good to see you back on the right side of the globe, George. Never could fathom why anyone would take themselves off to Australia. Nothing down there but rats and trouble if you ask me.'

George looked a little awkward. 'Thank you Captain Faulks. Ah, but it's New Zealand, Sir. I've been living in New Zealand.'

'Right you are. Can't imagine it's much different.'

'Actually it's a bit like the Midlands, Sir.'

Captain Faulks frowned. 'Is that so? Well, both your older brothers seem to be doing just fine for themselves in England.'

George raised one hand. 'Don't misunderstand, Captain. I love England, of course but I needed a challenge. Something new.' George smiled proudly. 'I've got a holding of my own now.'

The older man raised an eyebrow. 'Well, land is important. It's the foundation a good name is built on but I'm not sure I'd punt on the antipodes.'

'New Zealand is such a new country. I can really make something of myself there,' George replied.

'Ah, to be young and adventurous.' Faulks managed a stiff smile. 'Well, in any case it's nice to know the officers under me are of good breeding.' He looked at the men assembling in front of them. 'I can't imagine this lot will be much use on the field of battle. Mostly coloureds. Half of them barely speak English.'

'Why put them all together?' asked George. 'Wouldn't it be better to spread them around?'

'Damn War Office have got it into their heads that we need the manpower. They've given me a bunch of Corporals who speak various languages and a Warrant who's served in India.' The Captain frowned. 'Personally, I think it's putting all the trouble in one basket.'

'They look quite undisciplined,' said George.

'That's why the Lieutenant Colonel has brought in extra junior officers. Second-lieutenants from his old cavalry unit. They'll be staying attached when we move to the front.'

George straightened up, sensing an opportunity. 'Well, Captain, I've worked with plenty of Māori back home. They're hard working although they are not always respectful.'

'No doubt your experience will come in handy.'

'How long do you think we'll be training them?'

'Too damn long,' Faulks snorted. 'This whole charade is a waste of decent officers. They should have spread these men throughout the division and let *us* focus on halting the German advance.'

A barrel-chested sergeant bellowed and the soldiers came to attention. The commanding officer appeared, an elderly lieutenant colonel. He marched crisply onto the parade ground and stepped up onto a shell box that had been set in front of the troops.

'I am Lieutenant Colonel Goldman, your commanding officer,' he announced to the assembled men. 'I will be overseeing all aspects of your training and deployment. You will drill until I deem you are fit to be called soldiers because, I assure you, you are not yet fit to be wearing his Majesty's uniform.'

Tane and Wiremu, along with their new friends Neerav and Mosi, stood to attention in the second row. As the Lieutenant Colonel's address droned on, Tane glanced surreptitiously down the row at Wiremu. They shared a twitch of a smile buoyed by the excitement of their changing lives.

The commanding officer's voice took on a darker tone, refocussing Tane's attention.

'Serious insubordination will earn you imprisonment or penal servitude. I will say this *once* and *only once*. The punishment for desertion is death,' he swept his eyes across the soldiers, 'a sentence I will not hesitate to carry out.' Lieutenant Colonel Goldman let his words hang until he was satisfied his audience was suitably intimidated. 'Now, in case any of you thought this was to be some sort of holiday, let me introduce your second-lieu-tenants.' He blew a whistle and six mounted officers cantered onto the parade ground, sabres in hand. They formed their horses into a line and advanced on the assembled men, stopping inches from the front row. Several recruits shuffled backwards.

'Hold your line!' hollered Goldman. He pointed to the horse-men. 'These junior officers are my eyes and ears. They will be watching you day and night and they will brook no insubordi-nation.' He watched as the front line scurried back into place. 'I *will* have discipline in this company even if I have to drill you twenty-four hours a day. Rest assured I will forge each and every one of you into a soldier; a soldier who will serve his army, serve his Commonwealth and serve his King.' He nodded to Captain Faulks. 'Now I will turn you over to your senior captain who will supervise the issue of your uniform and kit.' He abruptly turned and stepped from the box, muttering to Faulks as he did so, 'They're all yours. They're going to need an iron fist.'

In contrast to Lieutenant Colonel Goldman, Captain Faulks' address was brief and to the point. They were dismissed twenty at a time with instructions to report to the quartermaster. Tane and Wiremu were almost the last to leave the field. As they hastened down a pathway, Wiremu pulled a scrap of paper from his jacket.

'I drew this picture last night. I wanted to have something to remind me of Mere.' He showed Tane the sketch. It depicted a pregnant woman standing with her hand on her belly. 'You saw the photo. Do you think it looks like her?'

Tane peered at the picture. It was a charcoal rendition of the girl he had seen in Wiremu's photograph which was now at the bottom of Lisbon harbour. 'That's really good, Wiremu. You didn't tell me you were an artist.'

Wiremu beamed proudly, 'I'm no artist. Just like to draw stuff. Animals mostly. But sometimes people.'

Tane nodded. 'She looks much more pregnant than she did in the photo.'

'I've been trying to imagine how big she's getting.'

'When is the baby coming?'

'Mere thought the end of March or maybe April.'

'Don't you wanna be there? When it's born I mean.'

'Of course, but getting enough money so we have somewhere to live is the most important. Besides, Mere and I already talked about that before I signed on for the shipping job. She knew that I could be away for a year, depending on the ship I got assigned to.'

'Well, the pay here is better than the Shipping Company,' said Tane. 'A shilling and pence a day. That's almost twenty pounds a year.'

'I ain't gonna spend any of it. Gonna take it all home.'

Tane patted Wiremu's shoulder. 'You're a good father, doing this.'

Wiremu scoffed. 'Mere doesn't need to worry. The war'll be over in a few months. I'll see my boy soon.'

Tane gave Wiremu a lopsided grin. 'How do you know the baby's a boy?'

Wiremu frowned. He thought for a moment, 'Dunno, I just sorta... Yeah, he'll be a boy.' He flexed his biceps. 'Strong like his father, eh!'

They both laughed then Wiremu grew silent. For a moment he was lost in thought then he placed both hands on Tane's shoulders and looked into his eyes. 'If anything happens to me, someone's gotta take care of them.'

'Nothing's gonna happen to us.' Tane waved the idea away with a flick of his hand. 'We're gonna show the Germans how New Zealand boys fight and get this war won.'

Wiremu shook his head. 'Seriously, Tane. I gotta think of Mere and the baby. You and me's like brothers. So I guess that make's you my boy's uncle.'

A smile spread across Tane's face. 'Yeah. Guess it does.'

'You gotta promise me to look after them.'

'What do you mean?'

Wiremu's eyes lit with a thought. 'Swear an oath, a ki taurangi! If anything happens, you'll take care of my family.'

'Wow. Nobody's ever asked me anything serious like that before.' Tane hesitated for a second then stood up as straight as he could. 'I swear it. If anything happens to you, I'll take care of them.'

Wiremu pulled him into a bear hug. 'Thanks brother.' Eventually they stepped back and Wiremu frowned in thought. 'So can you write?'

'Yep, my mother taught me when I was little. But I'm not very tidy.'

'Good enough,' laughed Wiremu. 'I wanna send Mere a letter. Tell her all about you.' He spun them around in the direction of the other new recruits. 'Come on, we better catch up or that officer's gonna roast us.'

They started running, heading towards the quartermaster's tent. They ducked across an intersection where two rutted roads met and without warning, a young mounted officer appeared from behind a line of tents. He looked up from fiddling with the cuff of his jacket and his startled horse snorted and side stepped. 'Whoa!' The officer twisted lithely in the saddle to regain his seat. His hands lunged forwards and grabbed the reins and the cufflink he had been adjusting fell to the ground embedding itself in the churned mud.

Tane and Wiremu froze, wondering if they were in trouble. The man's uniform bore a single bath star on the epaulettes; he was one of the second lieutenants who confronted them earlier.

Tane was the first to move. He dropped to one knee and retrieved the cufflink, rubbing it on his trouser to remove the dirt. It was fashioned from silver and depicted a horse's head enamelled in white. He reached up and held out the piece of jewellery to the second-lieutenant. 'Sorry, Sir. Didn't see y...' His voice stopped dead as he made eye contact dumbstruck by the man's face. The young Second Lieutenant looked just like Billy;

blond hair, similar features, the same piercing blue eyes. Tane was overcome by a sudden feeling of loss and longing. It squeezed Tane's chest leaving him speechless. He stood there staring open-mouthed, his arm still outstretched.

The Second Lieutenant reached out to take back the cufflink but the look on Tane's face stopped him. He stared for a second, his expression hovering between a frown and a smile. 'Do I know you?'

Wiremu piped in, 'So sorry, Sir. We was just going for our kit.'

The young officer didn't take his eyes off Tane. He took the cufflink from his hand. 'Thank you,' he raised an eyebrow, 'much appreciated, Private...?'

Tane snapped out of his reverie. 'Tane. Oh, I mean Johnny Chapman, Sir.' He snapped to attention and saluted.

'Well, thank you Tane or Chapman or whatever your name is.' He looked at the cufflink then sat upright in the saddle, a formal note creeping into his voice. 'Alright, get a move on.' He flicked his heels and his horse walked off.

Wiremu mumbled, 'That was close. Don't need no trouble on the first day. Come on.' He tried to pull his friend forward but Tane was staring after the junior officer.

He waved Wiremu to go on without him. 'You go. I'll be right behind you.'

As he rode away Second Lieutenant Zach Coe slipped the cufflink into his buttonhole. He could still feel the presence of the young private behind him. Gathering the reins, he leaned to turn the horse towards the stabling area but he couldn't help glancing back over his shoulder. The private was standing in the same spot, alone now, watching him ride away. Zach flicked his head forward and turned his horse onto the crossroad. His heart beat a little faster and a smile played on his lips.

CHAPTER 30

France · 1915

'**YOUR PERFORMANCE WAS PATHETIC!**' yelled the Sergeant. 'You're a disgrace to your uniforms!'

The sun had not risen but in the cold predawn light, the platoon of trainees covered in mud and scratches marched through the camp. Tane and Wiremu were amongst them and Tane felt uncomfortable, pin-stepping with his legs pressed together. Finally the unit was told to halt near the shower block, a long flat-board shed with a doorway at each end. Naked shivering men emerged from the far door to have clean uniforms shoved into their hands. Tane's unit joined a long waiting line of muddy soldiers.

'You will take your turn in the shower then report for trenching duty!' The Sergeant shook his head then stormed off.

At the front of the line, fifty yards from Tane and Wiremu, a dozen men were ordered to wash by a bored lance corporal. The men stripped naked, threw their uniforms into large baskets beside the building then ran inside. Tane grimaced and bit his lip.

Wiremu frowned at him. 'What the hell's wrong, Tane?'

'I'm busting to take a crap. It's painful!'

'You shoulda done it when we was crawling in the mud. It

smelt like shit anyway,' laughed Wiremu. 'Just go use the latrine.'

Tane shook his head. 'Turner got into trouble for that last week. They said he was attempting to desert his post.' He squirmed, 'I'm gonna crap my pants soon.'

'Well, go ask the lance jack then.' Wiremu nodded towards the lance corporal seated in front of the shower block.

Tane nodded. 'Alright.' He walked up the line and saluted the non-commissioned officer. 'Sir, permission to use the latrine?'

The Lance Corporal sneered, 'Get back in line, Private. If I see you out of place again, you'll be punished.'

'But we can usually go when we've finished drill.'

'That's someone else's rule, not mine. Now get back in line,' he looked towards Tane's section, 'and if I see you trying to relieve yourself, I'll punish the lot of you. Learn some self control. Discipline is what the Lieutenant Colonel wants and discipline is what the Lieutenant Colonel will get.'

Tane shuffled back to his friends. 'He won't let me out of line.'

'Just find somewhere else to do it,' said Wiremu.

Tane glanced around. 'There's nowhere. It's all open. Besides, he's watching me like a hawk now.'

'He's a bastard.' Wiremu lowered his voice, 'I've heard things about that lancie. Lester. That's his name. He's always sucking up to the commissioned officers.' He brightened with an idea. 'Hey, I still got that paper I found in the mud. I can make a diversion so you can go.'

Tane glanced toward Lester. 'Dunno. If it doesn't work he'll punish you too.'

'We're brothers. We look after each other, thick and thin. Just make sure he doesn't see you.' Tane nodded, desperate enough not to argue.

Wiremu walked up the line, approached Lester and saluted. 'Sir, I found a paper in the mud. Thought it might be important.'

The Lance Corporal looked annoyed. 'Well? What is it?'

'Dunno, Sir. I don't read, Sir.'

The officer shook his head in disgust and muttered something to himself. He held a hand out to Wiremu. 'Well come on, hand it over.'

Wiremu took his time digging through his muddy uniform, patting every pocket, searching through every piece of kit. 'Hang on, I tucked it away. It's here somewhere.'

While this exchange was taking place, Tane snuck along the fence line, passing behind the Lance Corporal. He ducked behind the shower block to find a narrow embankment covered in weedy shrubs. He used his hands to scrape a shallow depression in the dirt then unbuttoned his trousers and squatted over the makeshift latrine trench. He had barely finished his business when a voice behind him made him freeze. He spun around hauling up his trousers. Two junior officers were climbing over the fence into camp. Tane threw himself flat in the low vegetation then lifted his head just enough to watch the officers. His breath caught as he recognised the younger of the two; it was the blond Second Lieutenant who had dropped his cufflink. Tane peered at the other man. He looked a bit older, maybe mid-twenties, and from his insignia Tane could see he was a full lieutenant. The older man was carrying a bottle and both looked a little drunk. With their heads down, the officers dashed down the embankment and pressed themselves against the shower block only ten yards from Tane.

'Here, Zach, you take this,' said the Lieutenant. He held the bottle out but he slipped sideways and onto one knee before the Second Lieutenant could grab it.

Tane hunkered down further, desperate not to be seen but he kept his head just high enough to stare at the blond junior officer. 'Zach,' he whispered and he couldn't help smiling to himself.

Zach frowned at the Lieutenant. 'Come on George, sober up would you. We could get into serious trouble.'

George tried to push himself back up but his leg slipped on the wet ground and he ended up on both knees. 'Ooops. Damn it all,' he muttered. He took a long breath and, trying again, he climbed unsteadily to his feet. When he lifted his head, he found himself looking straight at Tane. For a second, he froze then hastily swung the bottle behind him to hide it. It banged loudly against the shower block wall then fell to the ground causing a cry from the showers.

'Oi, who's out there?'

Zach flicked around to see what George was staring at. His eyes widened in recognition when he saw Tane. 'Chapman?'

A second cry arose from the showers followed by a stiff banging on the wall. A moment later, they could hear Lester's voice approaching from beyond the building. 'Who the hell is back there?'

Zach's eyes widened. He grabbed George by the sleeve and hauled him towards the opposite end of the shower block.

Tane threw one quick look over his shoulder then dashed after them buttoning his trousers as he ran. He rounded the corner to find himself in lines of pegged laundry, hundreds of drying uniforms. He stopped, unsure which way to go. To his right he watched Zach and George diving over an embankment that would lead them down to the stables. Behind him he heard a shout.

'Sir! I found a bottle.'

Tane dived between the lines of laundry, zigzagging his way towards the munitions store and the firing range beyond. His heart was racing at his narrow escape.

Ten minutes later, muddy and breathing hard, Tane reappeared at the back of the shower line. He looked cautiously down the queue but there was no sign of Lester. He headed along to rejoin his section.

Tane's respite was short-lived. Half an hour later he found himself standing to attention between Wiremu and Neerav. The whole training battalion was lined up on the parade ground in various states of dress. Lieutenant Colonel Goldman stood in front of them, brandishing the port bottle in one hand and a leather-wrapped riding crop in the other.

'If the culprit doesn't come forward, I will punish the whole lot of you!' Goldman's words hung in the air and he looked more irritable with every passing second. The silence stretched. Men glanced left and right, willing the guilty party to own up.

Facing the assembled trainees, Zach and George stood at either end of a line of junior officers. They were both pale and sweating. They cast glances across the parade ground at Tane, wondering if the young private was going to expose them.

'Right. That's it! You can all march the perimeter until the guilty man comes forward!' yelled Goldman.

'Wait.' Tane's voice cut into the tense air. He stepped forward. All eyes turned to him.

Across the square Zach's knees began shaking.

Goldman barked at Tane, 'Name, soldier!'

'Chapman, Sir!'

'What have you got to say, Chapman?'

Tane straightened his back. 'It was me Sir. I was behind the shower block.' His eyes flicked briefly up at Zach.

'And what do you think you were doing there?' snapped the Lieutenant Colonel.

Tane looked Goldman in the face. 'I was relieving myself, Sir.'

The senior officer looked incensed. 'Relieving yourself! Do you think I am an idiot, boy?' He shoved the bottle at Tane. 'Where did this come from?'

'No idea, Sir. I was just taking a shit.'

'No idea! Just got there by itself, did it?' He pointed at Tane's feet. 'Mud was also found on the fence, boy. Did you leave camp?'

Tane swallowed. 'No, Sir. I just snuck around there to relieve myself, Sir.'

'Aha, snuck around there, did you?' His voice lowered to a growl. 'Leaving your unit without permission is insubordination at the very least and if you left the confines of this camp, it could be construed as desertion.' The Lieutenant Colonel flicked his riding crop under his arm and advanced on Tane until they were nose-to-nose. 'Either way, I will make a fine example of you.' He stepped back and raised his voice so all could hear his proclamation, 'This soldier will be held under guard while I have this matter investigated. If this was an attempt to desert, he will be shot as an example of how we deal with cowards.' A shocked murmur rippled through the assembled men. Across the parade ground Zach's jaw dropped open.

The soldiers of Tane's section looked at one another then Wiremu stepped forward.

Goldman glared at him. 'Do you have something to add, Private?'

'Sir, he did go for a crap, Sir.' Wiremu nodded at Lester. 'Cos the Lance Corporal wouldn't let him use the latrine, Sir.'

Goldman turned to Lester. 'Is this true? Were you involved in this?'

Lester's reply was inaudible.

'What was that? Stop mumbling and speak up, man.'

Lester looked up, avoiding Tane's eyes. 'Didn't happen Lieutenant Colonel! Nobody asked for the latrine.'

Goldman bellowed at Wiremu. 'I will hear no deceit! I should have *you* arrested for conspiring! Get back in line. Your sergeant will deal with you.'

Zach wiped the sweat from his forehead with his sleeve. Registering the movement, Tane glanced in his direction. For a second they held each other's gaze then Zach marched forward and presented the Lieutenant Colonel with a sharp salute. 'Sir, I saw that man relieving himself behind the shower block.'

Momentarily fazed Goldman lowered his voice and leaned forward. 'What? How in the hell did you see that?'

'I dropped my whistle when I was patrolling the perimeter yesterday. I was searching the fence line when I saw that private.' He pointed to Tane. 'He *was* relieving himself.'

The Lieutenant Colonel looked irked; his victory snatched from him. 'And you just remembered this now?'

'I'm sorry, Sir. It took me a minute to make the connection.'

A repressed curse escaped from Goldman. He glared at Zach. 'This is highly irregular. I'll speak to you later.'

Goldman turned back to Tane. The parade ground was silent. 'You have no idea how lucky you are, Chapman. A better man has spoken for you,' he sneered, 'and you can wipe that smug look off your face. You still have your insubordination to answer for!' He turned to an NCO. 'Sergeant, this man is to receive field punishment. It will continue until I tell you otherwise.' He dismissed the men then left the parade ground.

As the Sergeant marched Tane away, they strode straight past Zach. Tane gave the Second Lieutenant a conspiratorial wink. Zach's face reddened and he lowered his eyes in shame. A moment later, Lieutenant George Dwyte stepped forward and stopped the Sergeant. 'One second. I need a word with this miscreant.' He leaned forward so only Tane could hear his muttered words, 'I owe you. You just saved my commission. I'll make this up to you.'

CHAPTER 31

Hunua, New Zealand · 1954

AUSSIE SAT ALONE IN THE DORMITORY. It was lunchtime but he didn't want to eat. Earlier in the day Major Dwyte had taken Tane into town to see the dentist. Everyone else was given the day off. The boys had split into two groups. Some went to start a game of cricket but most went down to the waterhole where they could swim and get away from the stifling heat. But not Aussie. He had found somewhere to be alone. Somewhere he could wrestle with the confusion in his head. The day before, he had struck out at Briar with the shears, cutting Briar's face. And ever since he had been morose.

Aussie sat on his bed and examined his grazed fist, picking at small spots of dried blood between his knuckles. At the sound of the door he looked up. Rosemary's head poked through. She smiled at Aussie, glanced around to check nobody else was in the dorms then slipped inside.

Instinctively Aussie stood up. 'Miss Dwyte.'

'Hello Aussie. I looked for you in the dining hall but you didn't go to lunch.'

'I don't wanna be around the other guys,' his shoulders slumped a little, 'I just feel...' He stopped. There was a moment of silence before he cleared his throat and straightened his back. 'Um... I'm resting because I hurt my hand yesterday while I was shearing.' He half-heartedly presented his grazed fist before slipping it into his pocket.

'Aussie, you don't have to call me Miss Dwyte.' Rosemary smiled expectantly waiting for a reply. Aussie frowned. There was an awkward pause so she spelled it out, '*You* can call me Rosemary.'

Aussie glanced around the dormitory. 'I'm sorry about the mess. I... I didn't know you were allowed in here.'

Rosemary shuffled a little closer to him. 'Rules are made to be broken. I won't tell if you won't.'

'Yes Ma'am.' He noticed Rosemary's frown and hastily corrected himself. 'I mean yes, *Rosemary.*' He looked down at his feet. 'Um, is there something I can help you with?'

'I just wanted to tell you how wonderful it made me feel. When you stood up for me the other day. With Victor.'

'Oh. Well, I was just angry with him because he was acting like an idiot.'

'That Victor is such a pleb,' Rosemary continued, 'he does get above his station.' She shuffled still closer to Aussie then clutched her chest. 'He scares me sometimes, you know.'

Aussie didn't respond. Eyes downcast, he was lost in his own thoughts.

A look of annoyance crossed Rosemary's face. She waved a hand at him, trying to get his attention. 'Um, you seem distracted.' She leaned forward to peer more closely at his cheeks. 'Have you been crying?'

Aussie leaned his head back away from her gaze. 'Nah. I don't cry.'

'There's tear marks on your cheeks.'

'That's from hurting my hand.'

'You said that was yesterday.'

'Well I...' Aussie sucked in a breath to deny her but an involuntary sob escaped his throat. His eyes filled with tears and he quickly covered his face with his hands.

'Oh my goodness. What is it?'

'It's nothing. Nothing.' He sniffed. 'I can't talk about it.'

'What can't you talk about?'

'I just can't. It's wrong.'

'Wrong?'

He drew in a long faltering breath. 'I mean it's wrong for me to… to lay my problems on you.'

Rosemary's face brightened. She pushed her chest out and surged forward. 'Oh Aussie, you can lay all your problems on me.' She pulled his hands away from his face so she could look into his eyes. His jaw was clenched and his lips were forced into a tight smile. Tears kept welling in his eyes. Rosemary reached up and touched his cheek. 'You poor thing. Why don't you sit down?' She pushed him towards the bed. For a moment, he resisted then his shoulders slumped and he sat down. Rosemary crouched on one knee in front of him. 'I'm here for you, Aussie. Tell me everything.'

He exhaled. 'Well. You see, I have these…' He looked down, unable to look her in the eye. 'These *feelings* for someone.'

Rosemary's face burst into a smile, 'Oh, Aussie! I knew it.' Her shoulders wiggled in delight.

Aussie's voice wavered with confusion, 'But these feelings… It's *wrong.* I'm not meant to love this person.'

She grasped both of his hands again and pulled them into her chest. 'We both know it's right. Didn't you hear Father Patrick's sermon, "never spurn love".'

'But it was Father Patrick who told me it was wrong.'

'Don't believe that priest. He doesn't know what he's talking about.' She reached up, cupped his chin in her hand and lifted his head so they were looking into one another's eyes. 'Aussie, I know exactly how you feel. You're worried people won't accept our choice. That society says it's inappropriate.'

Aussie's mouth dropped open and he just stared at Rosemary. 'Yeah! That's exactly it. I know what other people will say. They won't understand. They'll say it's sick.' He shook his head. 'I didn't think *anyone* would understand.'

'Of course I understand. Can't you see? If both people love one other, then it can't be wrong.'

Aussie pulled his hands from her grip and rubbed his eyes dry. 'You're right.' He nodded his head slowly and his voice grew firmer, "Thank you. Thank you so much.'

Rosemary popped herself on the bed beside him. 'Oh Aussie, it's going to be wonderful.' She leaned her face towards his just as the front door banged open. Aussie and Rosemary leapt up, a look of guilt on their faces. Footsteps and voices approached.

Rosemary dashed for the back door just as Col appeared beside Aussie's partition. Before she slipped out the door, Rosemary looked back at Aussie. 'You know, really the *man* should make the first move.' Aussie nodded.

Col ducked back behind the partition and his voice could be heard calling excitedly to the other lads, 'Guys! Guys! It's Miss Dwyte.'

Rosemary whispered one last message to Aussie. 'Don't waste any time.'

'I won't.' He nodded in almost disbelief. He had never expected anyone to be so understanding, least of all Rosemary.

With a wink, Rosemary disappeared out the door.

A moment later several boys crashed into Aussie's cubicle, all talking at once. 'Wow, Rosemary was in your room,' said Roy.

'How come she was in here?' asked Col.

Aussie waved his hands, trying to brush their questions aside but they wouldn't be dissuaded.

'What were you two talking about?'

Aussie shrugged. 'She was just telling me something I needed to hear.'

Col piped up again, 'What was she saying about making the first move? Is she your girlfriend?'

Aussie was startled. Had he misunderstood Rosemary? He grimaced. 'Don't be stupid.'

Col became animated, his voice growing louder, 'You have a girlfriend, eh? That's what she was talking about.'

All the boys pressed forward, throwing questions.

'Who is it?'

'Who's your girlfriend?'

'Is she pretty?'

'Have you kissed her?'

Aussie held up his hand to stop them but Col wouldn't be stopped. 'Tell us Aussie! Tell us! Are you in love?' The boys fell silent, hanging on his response.

'No!' Aussie's reply was instinctive. Then hearing himself he paused, his brow knitting slightly. 'I don't know.'

The boys leaned closer willing him to spill the beans and Aussie couldn't help breaking into a grin. 'Maybe.'

The word was like a signal to the boys. They whooped and cheered, jumping around him.

'Leave off.' He pushed a couple of them away, the smile still on his face. 'Don't some of you have chores?'

'Come on. Tell us more,' said Col.

'Sod off. All of you. It's nobody's business.' He shooed them away out of his cubicle. As they exited, he grabbed Col. 'Was Briar at lunch?'

'Yeah, then he went to the stables I think...'

'Thanks.' Aussie was out the door before Col could say anything more.

At the stables there was no sign of Briar. Aussie stood on the rails of the round pen and scanned the lower fields, looking for horses. In the distance he spotted movement, a rider dismounting from beside the river. With a smile Aussie climbed over the railing and headed across the parched paddocks and down the hill.

As Aussie drew closer, the figure resolved into Briar. A second horse and rider moved into view. Aussie stopped dead. He shielded his eyes from the sun and peered at the figure. It was a young man. Very slim. Wearing a cap and waistcoat. For a moment Aussie stood in indecision. Then with a shrug he continued towards the river. Towards Briar.

As he reached the bottom paddock, Aussie saw the stranger remove his hat and waistcoat. He blinked in recognition and mumbled, 'Diana Colton?' He shook his head, a smile of bemusement on his face, and continued walking towards them.

Dee removed her hat and unbuttoned her waistcoat. She ran her hands through her flattened hair.

'You know, it's good having someone to ride with. It was boring on my own.'

'I'll *never* get bored of riding!' Briar glanced at the horses which were nibbling at the weeds by the riverbank. 'Now I can't imagine life without Wairua.'

Dee plonked herself down on the grass and Briar sat down beside her.

'I guess I should be happy that I'm a crap rider,' he said.

'Huh?'

'If I hadn't fallen off, we probably wouldn't have become friends.'

She laughed. 'I guess that's true but you're not a crap rider anymore.'

'Thanks to you.'

Dee put her head on Briar's shoulder. 'You know, I'm growing really fond of you.'

'Yeah, me too.' Briar touched her hair, twirling a lock of it between his fingers. 'I think you're officially my *best* friend.'

Dee lifted her head and looked him in the eye. 'Maybe we could be more than best friends.'

'Huh?'

'Don't you like me?'

'Of course I do.'

'Then why don't you do something about it?'

He looked quizzically at her. Their faces were only inches apart and he could see the playful look in her eyes, 'What do you mean? I *am* doing something about it. I'm riding with you every chance I get.'

'I'm not talking about riding.'

'Well, what then?'

Before he knew what was happening, Dee's lips were on his, pressing into him. He froze, caught utterly by surprise. His breath stuck in his throat and his ears filled with the sound of his blood pulsating. He felt her lips part slightly and her smell filled his nostrils; moist breath and makeup and a cloying undercurrent of sweat.

Aussie jumped over the last fence. The area near the river was usually swampy but the long hot summer had dried out the ground and left the river low. The toitoi clumps and blackberry, however, seemed unaffected and Aussie had to pick his way around the cutty grass and thorns to get down to the river. Finally he pushed between two manuka bushes just in time to see Dee and Briar kissing.

The sight stopped him in his tracks. He dropped to a crouch and ducked back behind the toitoi, desperate not to be seen. His breath stuck in his throat as though he'd been punched in the stomach. Testing every footstep to avoid making a sound, he slunk away.

Briar felt a rising panic. He pulled away from Dee's kiss with a thousand thoughts clamouring in his head. They stared at each other and for a long time neither of them said a word.

It was Dee who finally broke the silence. 'Did I shock you?'

'Ah, yeah. Sort of.' Briar could still feel his heart pounding. He scratched in the grass, scared of saying the wrong thing.

He wanted to tell her the truth but he knew what happened when people found out about his true feelings and he desperately wanted this friendship with Dee. He picked up a pebble and threw it in the river. 'Why did you do that? I mean…' His words petered out.

'I dunno. I thought it was what you wanted.' She fiddled with her cap, rolling the seam in her fingers. 'I mean, you're a boy.' She placed the cap on her head and pulled it down tight, shading her eyes. 'That's why boys make friends with girls, isn't it?'

'I suppose most boys want that.'

Dee pulled her knees up to her chin. 'I'm sorry.'

'No. Don't be sorry. You're really pretty. And…' Briar searched for the right words, 'and any boy would want you as a girlfriend.'

'But not you, huh?' She looked him in the eyes and his face reddened.

There was a snicker and they both looked around to find the two horses grooming one another, Wairua nibbling at Star's mane.

Briar took a deep breath. 'Dee, I need to tell you something. Something important.'

She just looked at him.

'But I'm scared you won't like me anymore.'

'You're my friend. Why would I stop liking you?' asked Dee.

He swallowed and could feel his Adam's apple bounce in his throat. 'Because I'm not like other boys. I'm different.'

'Briar, we're all different.'

He tipped his head back and looked up at the sky. 'I've fallen in love with someone.'

'Oh, I see,' she looked a little peeved. Her eyes narrowed as she became lost in thought. Eventually she gave up and shrugged. 'Who?'

Briar opened his mouth to reply and, overcome by panic, he tried to force the words out of his mouth but they wouldn't come. His lower lip quivered. He grunted in frustration and rocked forward to bury his face between his legs.

Dee put a hand on his shoulder. 'Well, I guess we know it's not me.'

Briar's back shook as he began to sob.

'What's the matter?' whispered Dee. She slipped an arm over his shoulders. 'It can't be that bad.'

With his head buried in his legs his sobbing slowed into a series of sniffs. Dee patted his back. 'Whoever it is, I'm happy for you. You don't need to tell me if you don't want.'

'Dee... It's not a girl,' he murmured. He looked up, searching for her reaction.

Her face slowly changed from concern to confusion to surprise. Her brow creased as she put the pieces together. 'Aussie.'

Briar just looked at her.

Dee was silent for several seconds. Then she grunted, 'Well, I guess I don't really care. You're still my friend.'

Briar felt a lightness rising through him from his toes all the way up to his head, a huge weight lifted off his shoulders. He sighed and the sound seemed to drift away down the river.

She shook her head slowly. 'I should have known. He's all you talk about when we're riding.' Suddenly she had questions, 'How do you know? Have you...? I mean, are you sure...?'

He tilted his head and raised an eyebrow. 'Trust me. I know. Actually, it's the reason I'm on the farm.'

'Oh, right.' She shrugged. 'Well, you're a pretty good rider for a shirt lifter.' A smile slowly spread across their faces.

Briar lay back on the grass and Dee followed suit. The river babbled its gentle rhythms and the horses grazed at the river edge.

'What about Aussie? Is he... you know. The same as you?'

Briar sighed. 'I thought he liked me. I was going to tell him how I feel. Then last Sunday he just changed.'

'Maybe he's scared.'

There was another silence then Briar spoke, 'You won't tell anyone will you?'

Dee sat up and pointed to the men's clothing she was wearing, 'You're keeping my secret. It's only fair I keep yours.' She ripped a handful of grass and threw it playfully at Briar. 'I suppose I should teach you to ride side-saddle now?'

He snorted and sat up. 'Tell you what. I'll ride side-saddle if you stop galloping and jumping.' Briar pushed her and she rolled several yards down the hill, laughing as she turned over and over in the grass. When she stopped, they both leapt up and gathered in their horses.

Dee looked up towards the stables. She frowned at something in the distance. 'Who's that?'

'What?' Briar tried to follow the line of her eyes but toitoi and blackberry blocked his view.

'I thought I saw someone running up to the stables. Just my eyes playing tricks.' She tightened her horse's girth-strap, unknotted the reins and pulled herself up into the saddle. 'Wanna ride on Tuesday night?'

'Yeah sure.'

'Great. See you then.' She turned her horse and walked along the river edge. As Star stepped out, wading into the water, Dee turned back with a cheeky grin on her face. 'If you need to borrow a dress, just let me know,' she laughed, 'though I don't think I have a bra in your size.'

Briar poked his tongue out at her. 'Look who's talking, moustache lady!' He kicked Wairua to a trot and ducked as he passed through the manuka trees.

CHAPTER 32

HUNUA · 1954

AUSSIE SKIRTED THE ROUND PEN AND HEADED up the driveway. His heart was thumping in his chest and even though he had only come from the river, his cheeks were flushed as though he'd run for miles. The sound of boys throwing a ball further up the driveway made him duck off the path behind a line of flax bushes. He stood there for a moment peering between the long green stems then turned and headed for the woolshed.

He knocked on the door of Tane's office but there was no reply. Peeping through the door he slipped inside. As soon as he was away from prying eyes, he slumped back against the wall. His legs began to shake. He leaned forward, hands on his knees and sobs wracked his body. After a moment, he breathed deeply, stood upright and focussed on a picture on the opposite wall that looked straight back at him—a sketch of a soldier on a horse, head tilted so the shadow of his Tommy helmet obscured his features. Aussie nodded slowly at the figure then slipped back outside and headed for the farmhouse.

Climbing the stairs to the porch Aussie knocked on the farmhouse door. There was a long wait and as he turned to walk away, the door finally opened.

Edna peered at him. 'Oh, it's you.' She looked him up and

down. 'If you're looking for Major Dwyte, he's out.' She began to close the door.

Aussie put his hand out. 'Um, I'm sorry to bother you, Mrs Dwyte but it's important. I need to talk to Tane. Can you tell me when he'll be back?'

'I don't know precisely. Sometime soon I would imagine.'

'Um, would it be alright if I waited here for him?' Aussie glanced over his shoulder. 'I don't really want to be around the other boys.'

Edna's eyes narrowed. 'Tane won't be stopping in when he gets back.' She was about to close the door when she seemed to have second thoughts. 'You know, it's time someone had a talk with you.'

'What about?'

Edna stepped out onto the porch. 'Look, it shouldn't be me having to tell you this but quite frankly, you're a bit of a fifth wheel around here.' Aussie frowned in confusion. Edna gave an exasperated sigh. 'There comes a time when someone wears out their welcome. You came here as a boy to learn a trade. Now you're a man and you should be out earning a living.'

Aussie stammered, 'But... I help with the training.'

'We don't need two helpers. Victor is perfectly capable.'

'Tane never said anything. I thought he needed me.'

'It's not his place to make those decisions. Frankly, my husband should have had a word to you but he's been very busy lately.'

'I see. I didn't realise. I um... I...'

Edna glanced into the house then pulled the door closed and stepped a little closer to Aussie. 'I don't mean to be insensitive. This is an awkward situation.' She reached out to pat his arm but stopped short. 'That's one of the problems with you boys. You never had a mother. Perhaps if you had, she would have taught you to be more sensitive to what is going on around you. It's high time you moved on. I hear you're a passable shearer, no doubt you'll find somewhere you're wanted.'

'Yes ma'am. I'll talk to Tane about...'

She cut him off with a scowl. 'You don't need that man's permission. He's just an employee. You need to grow up and make the decision for yourself. I've given you the truth of the matter. I'll leave it to you to make the right choice.' She opened the door and stepped into the house. 'If you want to wait on the porch that's fine. Just don't touch anything.' Before he could respond, she closed the door.

Aussie sat himself at the end of the porch, his feet dangling over a line of lavender bushes. His head hung dejectedly and when George's truck pulled up an hour later, he hadn't moved. George and Tane got out of the vehicle and headed for the house. As they walked across the driveway, Tane poked at his teeth where a molar had been extracted, winced and pulled his finger out of his mouth.

'Are you sure about this?' he asked George. 'Edna doesn't appreciate me around. Don't wanna be a thorn between you and your wife.'

'Bah, too late for that. She's the queen of thorns most days,' said George. 'Just ignore her and her meddling. It's *my* house and you're my guest. Besides, nothing cures a pulled tooth like a shot of rum. You're not getting away until you've had a couple of medicinal shots.'

As they climbed the steps to the porch Aussie stood up. 'Excuse me Tane, could I talk to you?'

For a second, Tane was startled then he turned and mumbled to George, 'This is a private matter between me and the boy. Won't take long. I'll be in shortly.'

George nodded and disappeared into the house.

Tane walked over to Aussie, indicating for him to sit, then he sat down beside him. 'Mrs Dwyte doesn't like the boys to come up to the house, you know,' he said.

'I was looking for you. I need to talk to someone.'

'What is it?'

Aussie fidgeted with the hem of his shorts. He opened his mouth to speak but his lower lip quivered and he clamped his jaw shut.

Tane frowned, 'Take your time, boy.'

Aussie buried his face in his hands. A moment later he was sobbing. 'You know, don't you?' he said through his tears.

'Only *you* know what's in your head. It's nobody else's business.'

'The other day, after I cut Briar. You said that you knew.'

'I know you like Briar. That the two of you are... close.'

'It's more than that.' He cleared his throat then swallowed, 'It's hard to say it.'

Tane waited.

'I think... I thought... I was falling in love with him.' The admission made Aussie hunch forward, sobs racking his body.

Tane's expression remained unchanged. 'Have you said anything to Briar?'

'I was going to but...' Aussie sniffed hard as his nose dripped. 'He was kissing her. He was kissing Diana. I almost made an idiot of myself.'

Tane looked at his boots where they hung over the edge of the porch. 'I understand what you're going through.'

'No you don't. You all think I'm disgusting.'

'Priests will tell you that,' Tane scowled, 'they never damn well change.'

'He said I'm confused. That it's not real love.'

'I know your feelings for Briar are real.'

'How could you?'

Tane was silent as he considered his response. 'I knew two men once. Men who were... who wanted to be together.'

'What happened to them?'

'Aussie, some things just aren't possible. It's not the way the world works.'

'But it's not fair.'

'Who told you life should be fair?' snapped Tane. He shook his head. 'Look, we have to fit into society. We can't expect society to fit around us.'

Aussie's voice was ragged, 'I've tried to make my feelings go away but they keep coming back.'

Tane slapped his hand on the porch. 'You need to be firm with yourself.'

'What if I can't change?'

'It sounds like Briar has come to his senses. You need to do the same.'

The front door opened and George emerged waving a glass. Tane leaned forward and lowered his voice. 'You asked for my advice, so listen. I'm telling you this for your own good. You have to bury these feelings deep down. That path leads to a lonely life.' Tane glanced beyond the garden at the distant hills. 'It's not worth it.' He got up and headed inside.

In a daze, Aussie watched the door close. For a while he just sat alone slumped on the porch. Eventually he set off down the farm driveway towards Hunua Road.

Aussie clambered the last few yards to the top of the path and edged out to stand on the precipice of Hunua Falls. Thundering spray pummelled the air, shrapnel flung from the endless battle between water and land a hundred feet below. The noise was deafening.

His face had dried on the long walk from the farm and dust clung like war paint to the tear tracks on his cheeks. His glazed eyes stared down at the churning water. With a grimace on his face he inched forward until he stood on the edge of the cliff.

'I tried,' he said to the water. He looked up at the sky and yelled, 'I can't change!'

Screwing his eyes shut, he stepped forward into nothing. A fraction of a second later his scream sounded over the barrage of the water, echoing off the walls of wet stone as he plummeted through the air.

He plunged into the dark water head first. Pain shot through his neck, shock exploded through his body and his consciousness faded.

His whole body was screaming for oxygen but there was only water. A cold sucking in and flooding lungs and panic. His limbs flailed but there was no direction. No up. No down. No air. Just terror. He thrashed with each failed attempt to breathe; the water filling his chest felt like lead. Cold spread through him and his thrashing slowed and finally ceased. His eyes were open. Everything turned grey. Everything grew quiet. Fragments of memory fired through his brain.

Briar and Dee leaned forward and kissed one another.
Edna, *'You've worn out your welcome.'*
Victor, *'He's too busy with his little CityGirl.'*
Father Patrick, *'The sin God will never abide. '*
Tane, *'It's not worth it.'*
Briar, *'If you hadn't come. They were gonna...'*

A spasm shot through Aussie. His arms and legs contracted and his body shot forward, away from the no man's land beneath the falls. In three panicked strokes, he broke the surface fighting between the need to spew water and suck air.

Gasping, he dragged himself back onto land. Hunched into a ball, head between his legs he puked water until his throat was raw and his stomach was cramping.

When his breathing slowly returned to normal, he threw his head back and howled at the sky, 'Damn you!' The ceaseless detonation of the falls drowned his words. 'Damn you,' he muttered.

He felt empty. He lay back on the wet rock and watched the sun climb down the sky. Time seemed meaningless. Darkness came and with it, shivers began to wrack his chilled body but his heart kept beating. With a groan he gathered his defeat and started back to the farm.

Two hours later Aussie stood in the night and looked at the dormitory. Light and noise spilled from the windows and he could hear the boys cheering as they listened to the radio. Looking down at his damp clothes, he made a half-hearted effort to straighten them. Then climbing the four steps to the door he let himself in. The boys were crowded around the radio, tense at the close game.

> *...and the New Zealand Captain, Bob Stuart, scoops up the loose ball. This will be the All Blacks last chance to save the match. Stuart fakes a pass. And he's off up the left wing. The Welsh aren't giving him any ground. He's tackled at twenty yards. It's Keith Davis. But Stuart gets the ball away...*

Aussie slipped into his cubicle unnoticed. He closed the curtain, picked up a penknife and a small wooden figure then lay down on his bed and started whittling. Out in the common room, the boys' volume increased as the match drew near to full time.

Briar slipped through the back door of the dorms. He was filled with the warm after-burn of sharing his secret with Dee. Seeing the boys cheering together around the radio, he smiled and headed up the corridor to join them. As he passed Aussie's cubicle, he noticed the drawn curtain. Peeping through he saw Aussie lying on his bed. The older boy looked dishevelled and there were scratches on his face. Briar stepped into Aussie's room. 'Hey, I didn't see you at dinner.'

Aussie's eyes flicked up then quickly down again. 'Didn't feel hungry,' he mumbled.

Briar frowned at Aussie's clothes, stepping closer to get a better look. 'Are you wet?'

Aussie pulled himself into a sitting position, knees up to his chest, pressing back against the wall.

Briar wasn't deterred. He crouched beside Aussie's bed. 'I dunno what I did wrong but whatever it was, I'm sorry. Can't we be friends again?'

Aussie's knuckles had gone white from gripping the whittled

figure. He relaxed his fingers then slowly pushed the blade into the wood. A curl of timber landed on the floor in front of Briar. 'Why would you want to be *my* friend?' he said.

'Please, Aussie, you're the only real friend I've got here on the farm. If you hadn't been here when I arrived I would have...' Briar shrugged. 'You're the only one who stood up for me.'

Aussie stopped whittling but didn't look up. 'You're doing just fine without me around. You've got your riding and now you've got a girlfriend. You should be spending your time with her.'

'What? What girlfriend?'

Aussie shook his head. 'Don't lie. I saw you two kissing by the river.'

Briar's mouth dropped open. 'No you don't understand.' He leaned forward and put a hand on Aussie's shin. 'Look, Dee's not my girlfriend.'

Aussie flinched at his touch. 'Don't be ashamed! Most guys would love to get a girl like that.'

'But she's just a friend...'

'You don't need to lie,' Aussie dropped his piece of wood and climbed off the bed, 'you should have a girlfriend. It's what we're meant to do.' He pushed past Briar and out into the hallway.

'I'm *not* lying...' Briar began. But Aussie was gone and a moment later the back door slammed closed after him.

A collective groan from the boys around the radio sounded like the end of the world. Briar poked his head around the divider. The boys were silently glued to the wireless and the crackling voice of the announcer filled the room.

Wales have done it. They've beaten the All Blacks by thirteen to eight in the first international test. Bleddyn Williams runs forward...

Briar shook his head. He looked at the unfinished carving on Aussie's bed and considered chasing after him but as boys drifted down the hallway, he thought better of it. Instead, he went to his cubicle and rifled through his collection of books but he couldn't

settle on one title. His mind was distracted, replaying his conversation with Dee and he couldn't help smiling at how she accepted
his secret. Briar chose a comic, something Aussie had given him.
He sprawled back on the bed to read.

At the other end of the dorms, Victor entered the common room.
'I got it,' he announced, holding up a box.

Dennis and Nate rushed up to him, along with a few younger
boys. Dennis held up his hand and gave Victor a thumbs up.
'You're the man.'

'Can we see it? Come on, show us,' Nate demanded.

Victor opened the package and lifted out a small red jeweller's
box. He cupped it in his hand and slowly opened it, drawing out
the suspense for the boys who were gathered around him.

There was a collective murmur of appreciation as the contents
were revealed.

'Man, it looks expensive,' said one of the younger boys.

'Of course it's expensive. The necklace is real silver,' Victor
puffed himself up. 'I spent all my savings but Rosemary's worth it.'

Nate craned forward and peered into the box. 'What's that on
the pendant? Is it a horse?'

Victor rolled his eyes. 'You're so stupid. It's Pegasus. It's from
the olden days. He has wings and people could fly away on him.'

'She'll love that,' said Dennis.

'It's what she wants. She told me.'

'When you gonna give it to her?'

'At her party.' Victor closed the box and headed for his cubicle.
Dennis followed him. 'I was thinking about it, When you give it
to her, you should kneel down like a prince.'

'Huh. Why?'

'It's in that book the teacher made us read,' said Dennis.

'Books are shite.' Victor replied, 'Just cos people read stuff they
think they're smart. You can't learn anything *real* from a book.
You gotta do it with your hands.'

'I don't mean the book is right. I'm just saying that rich girls like that stuff.'

Victor thought for a moment. 'Yeah, maybe.' He glanced out the door of his cubicle to be sure the other boys were out of earshot. 'Do you think she'll like the necklace?'

'Of course she will,' said Dennis.

Victor nodded slowly. 'Yeah, she will.' He straightened up. 'Yeah, she will,' he repeated more confidently.

CHAPTER 33

Hunua · 1954

SUNSHINE FLOODED THE BACK LAWN of the farm house where it seemed the whole of Hunua was in attendance for Rosemary's eighteenth birthday. A huge white tent shaded a long table full of garnished plates; scones, cheese rolls and angle-cut sandwiches all decorated with summer flowers. The centrepiece was a leg of roasted ham presented on a silver platter surrounded by bowls of pickles and mustard and jars of relish brought by women who smiled and assured Edna they prepared it, "just for the occasion." On the lawn beside the tent, gaily dressed couples played croquet accompanied by a jazzed-up version of the *Tennessee Waltz*. The music flowed from the back porch where a plump woman in a floral dress was banging away at a pedal-organ. At the far end of the porch by the kitchen door Edna was glaring at George.

'How could you not tell me!' she spat. The music stopped briefly as the organist flipped the page of her songbook. Edna grabbed George by the wrist and dragged him inside, closing the door behind them. 'Do you have any idea how humiliating it was to find out from the neighbour?'

'I didn't want to worry you. I was going to sort it out.'

'I can't believe you. How could you have got us into this mess?'

'Edna, it's not for certain. There's still a chance I can hold off the bank.'

She looked around as someone walked along the porch. 'How the hell am I meant to go out there and enjoy our daughter's birthday when we're about to lose our home?'

'I'll borrow some more. Sort something out.'

'You're a dead loss.'

'Calm yourself down,' said George. 'Now is not the time. We'll talk about it tomorrow.' He pulled opened the kitchen door. 'We both need to put a smile on our faces for Rosemary's sake.'

Edna picked up a plate of pastries and pushed past him. 'We'll talk if you still have a wife tomorrow.'

Half an hour later, George was on the lower lawn organising races. The cricket wickets were gone and around the edge of the grass field families sprawled on picnic blankets drinking lemonade. Wide-brimmed sunhats and fedoras could be seen wandering through the garden. The farm boys were in their Sunday best; button shirts and long pants, and young ladies wore knee-length skirts. A few military uniforms were evident, including George who, despite the hot weather, was wearing old parade formals.

He shot a starting gun into the air and a line of children sprinted across the lower lawn. At the far end, they rounded a tree and raced back towards him. Moments later, to a chorus of cheers, a tall young lad dived across a white line painted on the grass. A dozen puffing boys and girls followed. George rounded up the winner and presented him to the crowd of mums and dads.

He lifted the boy's arm in the air. 'Our kids' champion! Young Master Wilson.' There was a round of applause and George handed a paper-wrapped box to the boy. 'Congratulations, lad,' he leaned forward and spoke into the boy's ear, 'and don't go flying it in the house or your parents will blame me.'

The boy disappeared into the cluster of excited children and George raised his hands to the crowd. 'Okay. It's the one you've been waiting for! Time for the young men to battle it out.'

At the announcement, the farm boys rushed forward to crowd behind the start line. A few local youths also stepped up.

George addressed the young men. 'I'm not going to make this easy for you. Life is competitive so let's make this a real competition. You'll run four laps.' He pointed to the far end of the field. 'Around the lower hedge, up past the rose garden and back across the line.' The boys grew serious. Some of them stripped off their shirts and a few dropped into a starting crouch. Without further preamble George raised the pistol above his head. 'On your marks. Get set.' He fired the starting gun and they were off.

The line of runners stretched like an uncoiling spring and the fastest runners quickly formed a bunch at the lead. Three times they dashed across the white line, puffing harder at each pass. As they began the fourth lap, two figures emerged at the head of the pack, Aussie and Victor. They jostled one another as they rounded the hedge and sprinted towards the finish. The noise of the crowd swelled as they dived across the line, Aussie just a fraction ahead.

George waved Aussie and Victor over. 'That was a close race. Both of you did the farm proud,' he lowered his voice, 'but I have to call it as I saw it.' He winked at Victor. 'Sorry, lad, don't take it personally.' He reached for Aussie's wrist to declare him the winner when Edna appeared and pushed herself between them.

She smiled at her husband, grabbed Victor's arm and raised it up high. The crowd applauded and the farm boys erupted in cheers.

George stammered at his wife, 'What on earth. Why would you...'

She slipped her arm through George's and guided him towards the garden with a smile on her face. Once they were out of sight she turned on him. 'You can't let Victor lose.'

'But he did lose!'

'That doesn't matter. People need to see he's the best.' She waved a finger at him and staggered a little.

George frowned. 'You're drunk.'

'I am not! It's just a little champagne. We're celebrating our daughter or have you forgotten?'

'You can't just storm down here and change the outcome of things. That was a fair competition.'

'Don't talk to me about fair. You've been hiding everything from me and I'm sick of it! I'm your wife. This is my farm too. If I say Victor wins, Victor wins.'

'Why the hell do you molly-coddle that boy? You're always pushing his case. It's created all sorts of friction between me and Tane.'

'You and that bloody Māori. You're more interested in spending time with him than me. Is that who you've spent our money on?'

George's face reddened in anger. 'I won't hear that sort of talk from anyone. Especially not my wife!'

'You're a dead loss as a husband. Maybe you should be married to him.'

George's hand shot out and slapped her across the face.

Edna took a step backwards and cupped her cheek. 'What a brave soldier you are attacking a defenceless woman,' her eyes narrowed, 'you were my biggest mistake. You're a waste as a father. I'll tell you exactly why I protect Victor. It's because he's my son, and *I* know what it means to be a parent.'

George's mouth fell open. 'What do you mean? He's not your son. He's an orphan.'

'Oh, he's from the orphanage alright. That's where I suffered in labour for forty hours delivering him. That's where the poor child had to spend the first ten years of his life.' Edna stared defiantly at George while he processed what he had just heard. A vein in his forehead pulsated and he spoke in a cold and measured voice. 'That's why I have no son.'

'Well, I guess you've got a choice to make then. I'll be seeing to it that he stays here. That he's given the opportunities he deserves. You can be a man and treat him like a son. Or you can fight me and I'll see to it that everyone's talking about you and that Māori and the unnatural connection you have.'

George glared at her. 'You know very well he and I are just friends. How did I ever love you? You're a snake.'

'I'm a mother and I will protect my child.' She whipped around and walked off.

From the upper lawn Rosemary watched as Victor leapt in jubilation and dozens of boys rushed to congratulate him. She rolled her eyes and turned back to the group of convent girls who stood around her.

'My mother is so ridiculous. Anyone could see that Aussie won.' The convent girls nodded their agreement.

Dee appeared through a gate in the hedge, wearing a long skirt. She waved to Rosemary. 'Happy birthday.'

Rosemary looked Dee up and down and frowned when she noticed trousers poking beneath the skirt. She grabbed Dee's arm and marched her a few steps away from the convent girls. 'What are you wearing?' She looked down at Dee's legs. 'Are you trying to embarrass me?'

Dee lifted the front of her skirt and looked down. She giggled, 'Oh yeah. Looks a little ridiculous doesn't it. Sorry, I ran out of time.'

'Time for what?'

'I was riding with a friend and the morning just sort of disappeared.' She bobbed down and rolled up the hems of the trousers, leaving her legs bare.

'That's much better.' Rosemary turned back to the convent girls, 'I suppose you all want to meet my golden boy.' There were giggles and nods. Rosemary beckoned for them to follow and she led them down to the lower lawn.

A few minutes later they emerged beside the rose garden. The races were over and families were conversing in small groups. Aussie was standing across the lawn with his back turned. He was shirtless, talking to an elderly couple.

Rosemary raised a hand to halt her friends. She pointed at Aussie. 'That's him. From here you can see him at his best.'

'Look at those muscles,' sighed one of the girls.

Dee turned to Rosemary. 'Aussie looks like he's busy. Maybe we should go play croquet.'

'Don't be silly. It's my birthday and I want to have some real fun.' The elderly couple walked off and Rosemary led the girls straight across the lawn.

'Hi Aussie. How's my man?'

Aussie turned to see Rosemary smiling at him with a dozen girls standing behind her. 'Oh, hi Miss Dwyte,' there was a brief pause and he hastily corrected himself, 'Rosemary. Hi, Rosemary.'

She nodded her approval. 'So what are you giving me for my birthday?'

Aussie froze and a look of embarrassment crept onto his face. 'I'm sorry. I didn't really get anything, um...'

Rosemary ran the tip of her finger from his chest slowly down to his navel. 'Oh yes you did,' she purred. There were giggles from the girls. Dee rolled her eyes.

Aussie looked perplexed. 'I did?'

Rosemary leaned forward close enough to whisper in Aussie's ear but she didn't lower her voice, 'Be a darling and get me another lemonade.' She handed him a half-empty glass. 'That one seems to have gotten rather *hot*.' This raised more mirth from the girls. Rosemary turned, waving for her retinue to follow. She called over her shoulder, 'I'll be waiting for you by the fountain. It's a bit less public up there.' She winked at Aussie then walked off.

Dee peeled off from the group of girls and walked back to Aussie. She nodded at the glass in his hands. 'I suppose you're going to run around after her just like all the other boys.'

Aussie looked at the glass as though he'd just noticed it for the first time. 'Well, I suppose I should do what she tells me. It is her birthday.'

Dee looked him up and down.

Aussie frowned and reached for the shirt tucked through his belt. 'You shouldn't be looking at me like that.'

'What do you mean "like that"?'

Aussie put on a smug look and lowered his voice a little, 'I know. Okay.'

'Know what?'

Aussie shook his head. 'There's no point denying it. I know about you and Briar.'

'Me and Briar?' She shrugged. 'We're friends. So what?'

'You don't have to lie. I know you're more than friends.' He folded his arms. 'I know you two are going together.'

Dee looked perplexed. 'Oh trust me, we aren't together.'

'I saw you. The two of you.'

She thought for a moment then snapped her fingers. 'That must have been you I saw running up to the stables. Look, you've got it wrong. Me and Briar aren't together.'

'I saw him kissing you.'

'Actually, I kissed him.'

'You were kissing. What's the point in you both denying it.'

'Listen, Aussie. We're just friends. Riding buddies. I'm not with him. And he's definitely not interested in being with me.'

'He can be with whoever he wants,' Aussie's reply was a little too loud. 'I don't care.'

Dee's eyes widened in surprise. 'Oh my gosh, you do. You do care.'

'No, I don't. We weren't real friends anyway.' He turned to walk away.

'Wait!' Dee blurted. 'He's not my boyfriend.'

Aussie flicked around. 'Don't keep denying it. I saw you two together.'

'You don't get it. That was just... A dare!'

'What do you mean?'

'You know, a dare. One of my friends dared me to do it.'

Aussie looked at her with incomprehension.

'Yes, I kissed him,' she said, 'but he didn't kiss me back. He's not interested in me.' She raised her eyebrows and her voice softened, 'Briar's not interested in any of the girls here. He likes someone else.' She nodded meaningfully. 'Someone right here.'

'But how could he have met anyone else? He hasn't left the farm since he got here.'

Dee grunted in exasperation. 'You're not listening to me. He's not interested in any of the *girls*.' She pointed to the ground beneath them. 'He's in love with someone standing right here.'

Aussie, still refused to understand.

Dee rolled her eyes. 'I give up. I'm going to find a grown-up to talk to.' She pushed past him muttering, 'I can't imagine why he's in love with an idiot like you.'

It finally registered with Aussie. He was motionless for a moment then his lungs filled with air and his eyes darted around looking for Briar.

Dee called over her shoulder, 'He's in the stables.' She hurried off, all innocence, a smile playing at her lips.

He turned and ran down the driveway.

Wairua flinched at the sound of the stable door bursting open. Her large head turned slightly eyeing the intruder and Briar followed her gaze. Silhouetted in the open doorway, Aussie stood holding his shirt in one hand and a glass in the other. Briar patted Wairua on the back.

'I thought everyone was at the party,' said Briar.

'Yeah they are.'

'Then how come you're here?'

Aussie took one step inside. 'I wanna say sorry. I acted like a dork.' He looked embarrassed. 'In my room. When you said you wanted to be friends again.'

The frustration Briar had felt the night before rushed back to him. 'You took off before I could explain. Look, Dee's not my girlfriend.'

'I know. At least, I know that now.'

For a moment, Briar looked confused then nodded. 'You must have talked with Dee.'

'Well, she talked to me really.' Aussie took a deep breath. 'Dee told me you're in love.' His eyes narrowed a fraction, searching Briar's face for a reaction.

Briar swallowed. He glanced sideways at Wairua, searching for courage. 'Aussie, I don't like girls... Well, not like that anyway.' Briar held his breath and his confession hung in the air between them.

Aussie took another step forward, out of the doorway and into the light. 'I know. Me too.'

Briar could breathe again.

'So, can we be friends?' asked Aussie.

Briar put the brush down. There was a look of resignation on his face. 'I can't keep lying, Aussie. It's more than that. Ever since you saved me...'

'What?' prompted Aussie.

'Don't you know? Isn't it obvious?'

'What's obvious?'

'Aussie, I've fallen in love with you.'

Aussie's eyes opened wide and he covered the distance between them in three giant strides. He wrapped his arms around Briar almost lifting him off the ground and a second later, their mouths were locked together in a kiss. Briar's lips parted, his heart pounded and he felt his whole body collapsing into Aussie's arms. The glass in Aussie's hand dropped to the ground and shattered.

CHAPTER 34

—————

Fʀᴀɴᴄᴇ · 1915

ZACH STEPPED OUT OF THE OFFICERS' MESS AND surveyed the sprawling camp around him. The training facility was growing as more recruits arrived. Rows of tents stretched across the valley and extended up the slope to the west. He turned to head for the stables but was stopped by Captain Faulks exiting the mess tent.

Zach snapped to attention. 'Sir!'

Faulks nodded in recognition. 'Second Lieutenant, I checked the horses this morning and I see you've taken that troublemaker, Chapman, under your wing.'

'Yes, Sir. After his field punishment, I felt it was best to keep an eye on him. So I made him a junior groom. Keeps him nearby.'

'Quite. Sterling idea,' said Faulks.

'It's been two weeks and he's been following orders. I think it was just a one-off incident.'

'I'll take your word for it. The important thing to remember is that we must have utter submission from these men.'

'I understand, Sir.'

Faulks tapped Zach on the chest. 'Don't be scared to use an iron fist. Discipline is the best tool.'

'I will, Sir.'

Faulks crossed his arms. 'It's good to see you taking initiative, Coe. You're just like your father.'

'Thank you Sir.'

'Right. Jump to it then.'

Zach saluted and hurried off.

Zach entered the stables, a long structure comprised of a series of partitioned stalls covered by a large canvas roof. Most of the structure housed draught horses and their burdensome equipment but at one end, a wall of sand bags formed a separate partition to house the cavalry mounts. A doorway between the two areas was covered with a heavy canvas sheet. Several men were tending horses and Tane was dragging a sack of oats down the central race.

Zach tapped one man on the shoulder. 'Parker, relieve Chapman,' then he beckoned to Tane. 'Chapman, I need you to prepare my horse.' He turned and strode into the cavalry stables, pushing through the canvas doorway. Tane passed the oat sack to Parker then followed.

As soon as the canvas flap fell back across the doorway, Zach's military formality melted. He removed his cap.

'It's so hard to find an opportunity to talk to you alone. I owe you so much and I just want to...'

Tane interrupted him, 'You need to stop saying that. It was nothing.'

'Soldiers have gotten serious illnesses from field punishment.'

'Huh, not likely,' Tane shrugged. 'I was only up for two days. The worst part was the way some of the other blokes treated me after.'

'I still feel guilty. I could have said something. Owned up.'

Tane looked down at the ground. 'It was worth it because now I get to be a groom. That means I get to spend time with you.'

'I feel the same. I love spending time with you.' Zach smiled. 'I never thought I'd make such a close friend with an enlisted man.'

'Well, I never thought an officer would even want to talk to me.' Tane raised both eyebrows. 'In fact, I thought officers could only yell.'

Zach laughed and threw a friendly punch at Tane's shoulder. 'We are actually human despite what the Lieutenant Colonel might want you to think.' They smiled at one another and Zach stepped closer to Tane. 'I can't get you out of my mind,' he said. 'Whenever I'm off doing anything else, I just can't wait to get back here and talk to you.'

'Same here,' said Tane. 'I have some good friends in my unit. Even someone I think of as a brother. They're real important to me but even when I'm with them, I'm thinking of you all the time.'

The sound of a horse snorting came from the draft stables and Zach glanced nervously at the door flap. He motioned for Tane to follow him to a more discreet corner. Hidden by the warm bulk of Zach's horse, the two young men stood facing one another. Zach reached tentatively for Tane's hand. Tane's breath stopped in his throat but he didn't pull away.

'It's alright,' whispered Zach as his fingers closed gently around Tane's. 'I just want to hold your hand.' For almost a minute they stood saying nothing, looking into one another's eyes.

'Are you scared,' whispered Tane, 'of going to the front?'

Zach took his time answering, 'I guess everyone is. I've seen the wounded. Hundreds of them were waiting on the dock when we unloaded the horses at Boulogne-sur-Mer.'

'Most of my section can't wait to see action.'

'I think men use that bluster to cover their fear.'

'Maybe.'

A loud voice from the draught stables startled them and they stepped away from each other. Zach pushed himself up on tiptoe and glanced nervously over his horse but the door flap was still closed.

'We have to be careful. If anyone saw us together...' Zach shrugged. 'Well, they wouldn't understand.' He reached out and took Tane's hand again. 'It seems like the Lieutenant Colonel is desperate to make an example of someone. So if anyone's around, we have to keep our distance. Act our ranks.' He brightened as an idea came to him. 'I'll put you in charge of the spare mounts. After detail, you can graze them by the river.' He patted his horse's neck. 'I'll ride out to exercise Cinder and meet you there. That way we can spend time together without anyone else around.'

'That's a great idea,' said Tane. His eye sparkled with a cheeky smile. 'Sir.'

Behind them the flap door opened and Lance Corporal Lester pushed through. Cinder snorted and Zach and Tane froze hastily pulling their hands apart. Lester walked further inside, looking around.

Zach stepped out from behind Cinder, 'What do you want in here, Lance Corporal?' He puffed himself up. 'You're not cavalry.' Behind him Tane tried to look busy bending over and gathering straw.

'Faulks wants ya. Wants all the lieutenants,' said Lester.

'You will address your commanding officer using his proper rank.' Zach stepped closer to Lester in an effort to block his view. Lester's eyes narrowed and he leaned sideways to look at Tane working in the corner.

'Well, *Captain* Faulks wants ya on the double,' said Lester.

Without a backwards glance, Zach took a firm grip of Lester's shoulder and guided him back through the flap. 'Let's not keep him waiting then.'

Two weeks later, Tane was leading three horses along a river path away from the noise and clutter of the training camp. He walked half a mile then tethered each horse with a long rope to a ring spike he hammered into the ground. The animals put their heads down and grazed on the fresh grass.

Tane looked across the slow moving river at the tawny fields of winter wheat that stretched to the horizon. Over the last two weeks this had become the favourite part of his day. To his surprise he discovered that he enjoyed working with horses. Somehow they calmed him. As he spent more time around them, he found that like people they each had their own character.

He heard the sound of hooves. Zach was approaching at a canter. The horse turned towards Tane and in a single fluid movement Zach reined the horse to a halt, vaulted from the saddle and landed on his feet.

Tane laughed out loud. 'Wow! That's amazing. Wish I could do that.'

'You could, I suppose. I could teach you to ride.'

'Really?'

'Why not,' Zach shrugged, 'it can be our secret. Just like your real name.'

'Wow. That'd be great.'

'Alright. Let's do it. Should be fun watching you fall off and make an arse of yourself.'

The smile disappeared from Tane's face. 'What if someone sees me riding? You could get into trouble. We both could.'

'Nobody will find out. Not if we do it out here.' Zach took Tane's hand and placed it on Cinder's neck. 'Let's start by getting to know how a horse is built. Where its strengths are.'

'What? Right now?'

Zach laughed. 'There's no time like the present. Or that's what my father always says.'

Half an hour later, Tane's head was full of the anatomy of horses and the bewildering names of various pieces of tack.

Zach smiled at Tane's expression. 'It's a lot to learn, I know,' he bent under Cinder's belly and unbuckled the girth strap, 'but don't panic, it doesn't really matter whether you know all the theory. The real learning begins when you start communicating with the horse, and Cinder is a great teacher.' He pulled the saddle off then leapt on to Cinder's back. With a wink he reached down and offered Tane his hand. 'Come on then.'

'Are you sure?'

'Of course. Got to get on the horse sometime.'

Tane grabbed Zach's arm and started to swing himself up.

'Not behind me.' said Zach, 'You won't learn anything back there.' He pulled Tane up to sit in front of him. Tane's eyes lit with excitement and Zach laughed as he felt his exhilaration.

Zach slid his arms around Tane and gathered up the reins. 'Here, hold these. Put your hands by mine.'

Tane followed instructions. 'It's amazing. So high. Makes me feel... powerful.'

'Welcome to my world.' Zach adjusted his position and swung his legs back a little. 'Now, sit up straight, keep your heels down and just feel the movement of the horse under you.' With a squeeze of Zach's feet, the horse moved forward. Tane rocked uncertainly. He laughed and rebalanced himself.

'That's good,' Zach said. 'Try to feel how the horse moves. How her stride rolls her shoulders and her back flexes. Once you can feel that, you can move with it. Anticipate it.' He kicked Cinder into a slow trot.

Every evening, Zach gave Tane a lesson passing on his passion for horses. Riding came quickly to Tane. He had always been athletic and fit and clambering around ships from a young age had given him an excellent sense of balance.

'You're a natural,' Zach told him a few weeks later. 'Took me months to really understand the rhythm of the rising trot.'

'It's because you're a good teacher.' Tane tapped his heels to put Cinder through her paces.

'I don't think teaching's my forte,' Zach called after him, 'I've no patience.'

Tane got the horse to ride in circles, changing the pace from time to time. Then he repeated the process in large figure-eights, pushing Cinder to pick up speed.

Zach watched Tane ride, nodding his approval and calling instructions. When Tane cantered through a particularly tight turn, he flicked the rein to ask the horse to change its lead leg. 'Hey, I didn't teach you that,' Zach called.

Tane pulled the horse up. 'Teach me what?'

'The flying change. What you did when you pulled out of the turn. Getting her to change her lead leg.'

'Oh that. Well, you said I should feel the way the horse moves. She felt like she wanted to lean the other way.'

'That's impressive, Tane.'

Tane rubbed Cinder's neck. 'I think it's just her making up for my bad riding.'

'The flying change is an advanced technique. Not for beginners. You're learning at breakneck pace.'

'That sounds painful.'

Zach laughed. 'Yes maybe that was a bad choice of words. One thing I am not going to let you do is break any necks.'

'Riding is so much fun. It must be amazing being rich.'

For a moment Zach looked uncomfortable. He frowned then shrugged, 'I never really thought of it that way. I mean, my family has land but we're not rich. Not like some of our neighbours.'

'Well, I'm glad you got to have horses because otherwise you wouldn't have taught me to ride.'

'Don't go thinking you're finished. There's a lot of fine-tuning to do and points of horsemanship I still need to teach you,' Zach cocked his head, 'but you've got your basic paces. I'll give you that! Twenty days and you can damn well ride.'

'I never want to stop. I want to ride for the rest of my life.'

Zach took hold of Cinder's headstall. 'Yes, horses can get under your skin like that.' A smile spread over his face. 'We could try something more serious.'

'I'll try anything.'

'It's one of the first tests of a cavalry officer.'

'What is?'

'Jumping.' Zach scratched Cinder's muzzle. 'It's really fun. But I don't know if you're ready. You'll probably fall.'

'I fell plenty when I started, remember?'

'This is different. Cinder gets quite excited when she's jumping.'

'I don't mind.' Tane lay forward onto Cinder's neck and put his face close to Zach's. 'Please,' he whispered.

Zach reached up and traced Tane's forehead with the tip of his finger, following the line of his fringe. 'Alright,' he whispered back.

They set up a jump. For poles Tane climbed into a tree and bounced on branches until they snapped and fell to the ground. Then they stripped the leaves and twigs away until they had clean lengths. They fashioned uprights from smaller branches and pushed them into the ground, reinforcing them with piles of river stones.

'I guess jumping is important for cavalry,' said Tane.

'Well, it's an important part of cross-country riding.'

'No, I mean for fighting. Like if you were charging at the Germans.'

Zach smiled. 'Nobody charges a horse into battle anymore, Tane. You've been listening to too many Wild West stories.'

'Then why do we have cavalry?'

'The horse is still the most reliable form of transport. Command personnel can move quickly, orders can be dispatched, ground reconnoitred. Wheeled vehicles are hopeless on rough terrain.'

Zach pulled out a knife and cut a couple of notches in the uprights he was making. The result was a pole jump that could be set at two different heights.

'That should do it.' He set the pole in the higher position. 'Let me show you how it works.' He gathered up Cinder and led her over to the jump so she could inspect it. She sniffed at the branches then shook her neck. Zach mounted and rode back thirty yards. 'Now watch me closely,' he called to Tane. He set

Cinder into a collected canter. 'You've got to soften your seat, be in the stirrups, weight on your heels.' He accelerated towards the pole. Cinder shortened her stride, lining up for the jump. 'Let her rotate underneath you.' Cinder leapt into the air, stretching her forelegs up and out. Her whole body rolled forwards and her hind legs sailed over the pole, clearing it by a wide margin. Zach was like a spring rocking against the horse's motion to keep his body steady. As Cinder landed he bent forwards a little then popped upright in the saddle. He reined in the horse and trotted over to Tane. 'Got to make sure she doesn't throw you as you go over. You should bend at the waist but don't move your weight forward until you land.'

'It looks like flying.' Tane had a huge smile on his face.

'That's what it feels like. Come on then, you give it a try but I better lower that jump first.'

Between them, they adjusted the jump then Tane climbed onto the horse. He followed the same procedure as Zach, riding the horse at the jump, kicking her into a trot then transitioning quickly into a canter. Cinder would not hold her line. Half a dozen times she refused to go over the pole, pulling up short of the jump or stepping sideways and going around it.

'You've got to be positive, Tane. She needs to know you're ready to do it.'

Tane lined up again, this time relaxing down into the saddle before moving. As the horse went from walk to trot to canter, Tane focused only on the jump. He rose into the stirrups willing Cinder to stay on target.

And she jumped.

He felt her stretch beneath him and he pushed himself forward, his body flying over the obstacle with her. Then the front of the horse disappeared and as Tane tried to lean back he kept rotating forwards. Before he could do anything to reorient himself, Cinder's front hooves hit the ground and he found himself smacking into the back of her neck and bouncing off at forty-five degrees. He hit the ground on his side and rolled to a stop as the horse whinnied and cantered off.

He sat upright to see Zach sprinting over to him.

'Are you alright? Are you alright?'

Tane touched his ribs and winced at the painful bruise. 'Yeah, I'm fine. Nothing broken. Might have a sore chest for a while though.' He grimaced at Zach who crouched in front of him. 'I see what you mean about staying upright though.'

'I shouldn't have let you do that. I should have known better.'

Tane cut him off. 'Of course I should have done it. That's how ya learn. With a few bruises.' He lifted his arm above his head and stretched his ribcage, 'It's nothing serious.' He looked towards Cinder who was standing twenty yards off eyeing them warily. 'I wanna try again.'

'Tane, I'm not sure if you should. You really could get hurt.'

'We're going to the front soon. Then we're gonna get shot at.'

'Well, when you put it like that.' Zach mussed Tane's hair. 'Tell you what, I'll put her over a couple of times first, just to calm her back down. Then we'll see.'

Zach rounded up Cinder and worked her out for a few minutes, riding her over the jump three times. He trotted back to Tane. 'You sure you want to try again?'

'Damn right I do.'

They swapped places and Tane rode Cinder through her paces before he lined her up for the jump. Then he tried again. Deep in the saddle. Focussed on his line. Transitioning through the gaits, he lifted himself into the stirrups, freeing the contact with the horse. This time he kept his eyes up looking straight ahead, not at the jump. He felt the horse rock, first backwards then forwards, but he kept the weight through his shoulders and knees vertical and his legs bent. The horse landed and he was so overwhelmed with excitement that he almost forgot to flex forwards. The slam of gravity bent him down anyway causing Cinder to stagger at the unexpected weight.

He held on. And he couldn't stop the elation escaping from his throat, 'Yeehaa!'

'You did it!' Zach yelled, his fist pumping the air.

Without stopping, Tane cantered over to Zach, skidded to a halt and dismounted.

'You're amazing,' Zach laughed and threw his arms around him.

Tane wrapped his arms around Zach and pulled him in tight. They clung together, breathless, neither willing to be the one to break the moment. Behind them the horse shook at the confines of its tack then lowered its head.

'I think I'm falling in love with you,' Zach whispered.

Tane hugged him harder. For seconds he said nothing then he whispered, 'Me too.'

'Tane, I'm scared.'

Tane sighed. 'I don't wanna let you go. Ever.'

Zach gently pushed Tane to arm's length and looked into his eyes. 'I was so scared to tell you. I thought you were like me but I wasn't sure.'

'I am. Of course I am.'

Zach touched Tane's face, running a finger across his cheek. 'When did you know?'

'About you?'

'No. About yourself. When did you know you were different?'

'Dunno. I never felt this way about any girls. I guess in a way I always knew.' He kissed Zach's finger as it touched his lips, 'There was this fella, Billy. I thought he was like me. Like us.' Tane looked down. 'But he wasn't.'

'It's alright.' Zach cupped Tane's chin and tilted his head. 'We found each other.'

Tane nodded. 'So what about you?'

'I had a chum at school. We were... together. We did things but then he decided he didn't want to be like this.' He pulled Tane back into a hug. 'I'm never gonna let you go.'

For several minutes they just clung together until Zach broke into a broad smile. 'You jumped.'

Tane pushed back to look in his eyes. 'I jumped.'

Suddenly they were laughing, arms across one another's shoulders, foreheads together, bodies shaking with the release. Cinder lifted her head and looked at them.

'Let's ride together.' Zach disengaged from Tane and gathered in one of the grazing horses, 'I'll ride Merlin, you bring Cinder.'

First they followed the river, tracing the ribbon of verdant grass then they plunged into the golden ocean of planted fields. Zach and Tane yelled, the freedom blowing in their faces. Their galloping horses left trails that coiled like gun smoke rippling through the burnished wheat.

Fifteen minutes later, two lathered horses grazed unattended outside a crumbling stone shed, their reins tied off to their saddles. The sun was low in the sky and the lengthening shadows made it seem like each spike of wheat was leaning towards the light.

Inside the ruin, Zach and Tane stood holding hands, shafts of light illuminating their faces. Zach reached into his pocket and pulled out a small package wrapped in a kerchief. He opened it to expose the inlaid silver cufflinks. One was black engraved with a white horse emblem, the other white engraved with black.

'These were my father's. He used to tell me their story when I was very young. He touched each cufflink in turn, 'Xanthos and Ballios. Achilles' horses. They were immortal so long as they fought together.' He looked up at Tane. 'It's how we first met. Remember?'

Tane touched the cufflinks. 'You dropped one.'

'I looked back at you as I rode away. Couldn't help it. You were… you are so beautiful.' Zach picked up the white cufflink and held it out to Tane. 'I want you to have this. I'll keep the other one. Then we'll always be together.'

Tane took the cufflink and peered at the engraved image. When he looked back up, his face was contorted, an inch from tears. He stepped forward and kissed Zach on the lips.

For a second Zach was surprised, then his body responded and he hauled Tane into him, chest pressing chest, mouth on mouth.

Time slowed down as they kissed, their tongues probing and their breaths growing short and desperate. Their arms slipped around one another and they slowly collapsed onto the straw; first floating to their knees then their sides, arms and legs entwined and never, not for one second, letting go. Surrounded by the light falling through the crumbling roof, they felt a giddy lightness rising through them, months of suppressed feelings and years of quiet denial melting away and laying bare their raw need to give and receive love.

An hour later, they were still sprawled on the floor, on their backs, Tane's head on Zach's chest. As they talked, their fingers subconsciously wove together.

'After the war, I want to travel,' said Zach. 'I want to go everywhere. See everything.' He kissed Tane's fingers. 'Let's go together.'

'That would be amazing,' Tane replied. 'When I was a boy I'd see all the ships come into the wharves. I always dreamed I'd see the world on one.' He let out a long contented sigh. 'Yes, I'll go see the world with you. I want to do everything with you.'

'We can visit Greece.' Zach held up his cufflink. 'See the statue of Xanthos and Balios.'

Tane propped himself up on his arm. 'And the Suez Canal! We should sail through the Suez Canal. I heard it's even more amazing than Panama.'

'Yes! And we should see the pyramids.'

'And the sphinx.'

'We can ride camels!' said Zach and they laughed at the thought. 'I'll take you to England. To the estate. You'll like my parents.'

'How could we? I mean we can't tell anybody.'

'But ...' Zach looked a little confounded. 'Well, we can stay in different rooms. Just for a few days. I'll tell the family you're my groom.'

Tane stared up at the dust motes that glinted in the last of the sunlight. 'My mum wouldn't understand either.'

There was a pause as they were lost in thought.

'What's it like in New Zealand? You know... for men like us?'

Tane shrugged. 'You have to be careful, I guess.'

'Thought it might be different.'

'It's not something to talk to other men about.'

Zach sat up and pulled Tane into an embrace.

Tane sighed and closed his eyes. 'I want to stay here forever.'

'Me too.'

The light around them faded. Tane eventually pulled away. 'We better get cracking. We're gonna be late for mess call.'

Zach broke into a cheeky smile. 'I'd rather have a private meal.' He nipped Tane's ear with his teeth. Laughing at his own joke, he leapt up pulling Tane up with him.

Trailing clothes and dressing as they ran, they gathered their horses and headed back to the camp.

They rode into the stables twenty minutes later and hastily untacked the mounts. They doled out a small bucket of hard feed to each horse and whenever they glanced at one another they couldn't resist smiling.

Zach rubbed his tunic with his hands, brushing away the last vestiges of straw from the stone shed. He glanced over to check Tane's uniform.

'Damn, you're covered. Come here.' He grabbed Tane and started brushing him down. He spun him around, wiping his back then dropped to one knee to brush the trousers. His movements slowed as his hands reached Tane's crotch.

'Yeah. That's definitely the dirty bit,' Tane giggled.

Zach laughed, 'I'm sure there's a regulation somewhere that assigns this particular duty to second lieutenants.' He straightened Tane's trousers then stood up. 'If I can finish the reports early, let's go to that shed again tomorrow.'

Tane's smile was all the answer he needed. With a quick glance over his shoulder, Zach grabbed Tane for one last kiss. At the same second, the door flap lifted.

'Well, look at that would ya,' Lance Corporal Lester sniggered, 'I figured you two for a couple of poofs.'

Zach and Tane leapt apart, Tane stumbling over backwards and falling to the ground.

'I suppose you two's been off buggering.'

Zach stepped towards Lester. 'Now you listen here, Lance Corporal. You saw nothing.'

'I know exactly what I saw.'

'You will shut your damn mouth. That's an order!'

'You can't get away with that. What you's done is field punishment,' Lester sneered, 'at the very least.'

'I'm giving you an order...'

'I'll take me to the Lieutenant Colonel then. See if his orders are the same as yours.' He glanced at Tane who was still sprawled on the floor with a shocked look on his face. 'Goldman hates you. You'll cop it, you will.'

Zach advanced on Lester, raising his fists. 'You little turd.'

Lester lifted the door flap fully open stopping Zach mid-stride. In the distance two grooms were stacking equipment. Lester nodded at the grooms. 'Yeah, that's right. They could easily hear our little chat,' he raised his voice, 'if we just talked a bit louder.' The men next door looked around at the sound of Lester's voice and Zach jumped back, out of view. Lester slowly lowered the door flap again. 'I've heard you talking with the other officers, I know you come from Daventry and I know your toff family's loaded.' He jabbed a finger at Zach. 'I'll be coming to see you when we get back to England. Let's see how much your little secret's worth. I'm guessing you'll pay better than a newspaper.' He dashed through the flap and disappeared.

CHAPTER 35

Hunua · 1954

BACK AT THE PARTY, THE GAMES had started again. On the lower lawn, a rowdy tug-of-war was under way between the men and the farm boys. Victor was leading the boys' team with a rhythmic chant, 'And pull, and pull, and pull.'

Even Father Patrick was participating, hauling on the heavy rope and blustering at the top of his lungs, 'Come on men! We can't let these rapscallions beat us!'

The two teams heaved. The rope teetered, inching one way and then the other but the farm boys had the numbers and finally, the rope leapt in one direction as the younger team won out. The men toppled, some letting go and others falling forwards as their grip was snatched away. A huge cheer went up from the boys and Victor found himself surrounded by jubilant lads.

'You're the best captain ever!' said Nate.

Red pumped his fist in the air. 'Let's challenge them again.'

Victor shook his head. He pulled the jeweller's box from his pocket and smiled. 'I have a more important job.'

Nate patted him on the back. 'You're gonna win everything today, Victor.'

'Yep, I'm on a winning streak.' He gave the boys a thumbs-up then headed for the upper lawn.

Victor stepped through the gate and found Rosemary and her flock waiting by the garden fountain. Rosemary noticed him immediately. She scowled and quickly turned to chat with her friends. Victor didn't notice the snub. He strode directly up to her and cleared his throat. The convent girls fell silent. Rosemary kept talking. Victor cleared his throat again, louder this time. Rosemary still wouldn't stop talking. For a moment he looked unsure of himself. Then he straightened his shoulders and addressed her in a loud voice, 'Excuse me, Rosemary, I have something to tell you.'

Rosemary turned around, feigning surprise. 'Oh goodness. Victor. What are you doing up here?'

'I need to talk to you.'

'Some other time. I'm waiting for someone.' She waved him away.

Victor wouldn't be put off, 'I'd like to talk to you alone. It's important, Rosemary.'

Her voice took on a haughty tone, 'Really Victor, you should address me as Miss Dwyte.'

He frowned. 'Ah, I'm sorry but that's not what you said at the shearing competition.'

Rosemary's eyes flashed. 'I'm telling you now! Using my first name is taking liberties.'

'I just want to talk to you,' Victor glanced at the girls around the fountain, 'alone.'

'Whatever you have to say, this isn't the time,' she nodded at the girls surrounding her, 'my friends and I have more important things to do.' The convent girls whispered to one another.

'Of course. Mrs Dwyte always says that a lady's friends are important.'

Rosemary rolled her eyes. 'And of course we must always listen to Mrs Dwyte.'

Victor nodded. 'She wants us to be a family.'

'I already told you, I don't...'

Before she could finish, Victor pulled out the jewellers' box and went down on one knee. He opened the box, held it up to Rosemary and he repeated a rehearsed speech, 'Happy birthday Rosemary, this is a token of our feelings for each other. It's Pegasus because I want to give you a new life.' His eyes were full of pride and hope.

Rosemary looked startled. She threw a hasty glance towards the gate. 'But I don't have any feelings for you, Victor.'

Victor looked confused. He didn't get up, he just stammered, 'But... in the woolshed. You whispered to me. You said you liked me.'

'I said I liked *one* of you. I didn't mean you.'

He stared at her for a second, mouth half-open as he made the connection. 'But that means... no... no, you can't like Aussie.'

'I can like whoever I want!'

'But you can't like him. He's a loser!'

'I love Aussie and he loves me! Go away, you're ruining everything.'

Victor staggered to his feet. He looked down at the box in his hand. 'But... I got this, 'specially.'

Rosemary eyeballed the necklace with disdain. 'Well, perhaps you should wear it yourself so it makes you special.' One of the girls giggled.

Victor's face screwed up. He held out the box again. 'Please...'

Rosemary finally lost her cool. She raised her voice, a waver beneath her commanding tone, 'Victor, go away! I don't love you and I don't want your silly Pegasus.'

Victor's face grew angry. He threw the necklace on the ground at her feet and sprinted off. The girls huddled around Rosemary, tutting and condoling.

Rosemary took a deep breath. 'Goodness. Some boys are so silly,' she forced a smile onto her face, 'and now my makeup must be ruined.' She pulled a handkerchief from her purse and covered her face, surreptitiously wiping the wetness from the corners of her eyes. She forced a smile onto her face and turned back to the girls. 'It's frustrating to have so many admirers.'

A tall girl pointed to the jewellers box lying on the lawn. 'Aren't you going to take the necklace?'

Rosemary rolled her eyes and clutched her pearls. 'Yuck. It's *so* tacky,' she sniffed, 'besides, you should never settle for silver when you can have gold.' Instinctively, the girls moved to the other side of the fountain like a flock of sheep distancing themselves from the scent of blood.

By the time Victor reached the lower lawn, he had rage in his eyes. The farm boys came rushing over.

'How did it go?' called Dennis, 'What did she say?'

'Did she like the necklace?' asked Nate, 'Are you two going together now?'

Victor silenced them, 'Where the hell can I find Aussie?'

The boys looked at one another but none seemed to have an answer.

Finally Tony spoke up, 'I saw him running towards the stables but that was a while ago.'

Without another word, Victor sprinted off. Five minutes later, he stepped through the stables doorway with fists clenched. He scanned the inside of the building, searching for his rival. Apart from a single horse it seemed deserted. He turned to leave but as he did, he heard something. He stepped back inside. The noise came again, a murmur of voices. Victor walked past the horse and peered around the low divider into the stall. Lying on a pile of hay Briar and Aussie were entwined in an embrace. They kissed and whispered and their hands grasped one another.

Victor stared in shock. His mouth dropped open.

Aussie's lips kissed Briar's neck, Briar's head arched backwards, a passionate sigh escaping his throat.

Victor recoiled, stumbling back and almost colliding with the horse. He spun around and staggered out into the round pen. He squeezed his temples with his hands and muttered, 'Rosemary.' He dragged himself over the rail and back to the party.

Aussie smiled at Briar. 'I want to do this forever.'

Briar snuggled his head into Aussie's chest. 'So do I, but we should be careful, someone could walk in.'

'Don't worry, everyone's at the party.' Aussie threw his leg over Briar's and rolled on top of him pressing him into the hay. His eyes sparkled with an idea. 'I want you to leave with me.'

'Leave? What do you mean, leave?'

Aussie grew excited as he thought out loud, 'The Dwytes don't want me here anymore and Tane said he could get me a job in Onehunga. At the wool mills.' He sat up and clasped Briar's hands in his. 'Come with me. We can live together in town.' He kissed Briar's hands. 'Just the two of us.'

'Do you want to leave?'

'I just wanna be with you.'

A warm smile spread over Briar's face but a moment later he frowned. 'What about Wairua? And Dee. She's my friend.'

'We can visit, I'll save up for a car and we can come every weekend.'

Briar smiled again. He nodded eagerly. 'That's perfect.'

'Let's do it. I'll tell Tane tomorrow.' And with that, Aussie was lying on top of Briar again kissing him like it was the end of the world.

By the time Victor got back to the party, the shock on his face had turned to anger. The farm boys were on the upper lawn, gathered near the tent, scoffing snacks. He marched straight into their midst.

'Aussie's a fuckin' homo!' he announced to them, 'I just saw him with Briar. They were kissing. They were damn well kissing each other.' Silence spread around him as the boys stopped what they were doing to tune in. Victor shook his head as though still trying to convince himself. 'I can't fuckin' believe it. That's so disgusting.'

'What the hell? Are you serious?' Dennis cried out.

'It's true. The two of them were kissing each other.'

A low buzz of shock ran through the boys.

Tony looked sceptical. 'I don't believe you.'

'Then come see for yourself. They're in the stables. Doing it.'

'You hate them. You're just making it up.'

Victor grabbed a handful of Tony's shirt. 'Don't you dare take their side! They're nellies!'

Other boys added their voices to Victor's.

'Man. That's disgusting,' growled Nate.

'Those dirty bastards!' said another.

Victor grimaced in satisfaction. He raised his voice to make sure all the boys could hear him, 'Just think about it! Those dirty homos have been showering with us. Looking at us.'

The buzz grew louder. Victor thrust his fist in the air. 'Are we gonna let them get away with it?'

The mob responded. 'No!'

'Dirty queers.'

'Teach 'em a lesson!'

'Let's deal to them.'

'Come on,' yelled Victor. 'This way.' He led them to the stables.

Aussie slipped his hands under Briar's shirt. The feel of fingers on his bare skin sent a wave through Briar's body and he gasped as Aussie fumbled at the buttons. A moment later Aussie was peeling Briar's shirt off, sliding it over his shoulders and down his back.

Briar wriggled his arms free of the sleeves and their naked chests pressed together. In the back of his mind Briar heard a voice but it barely registered through the passion throbbing in his head. Then there were many voices, a noise rose like a swarm of bees.

Aussie and Briar froze. They rolled off the hay, grabbed their shirts and stood up to find Victor storming into the stables with the farm boys pouring into the round pen behind him.

'See, there they are. They're a couple of faggots,' Victor yelled pointing his arm at Aussie and Briar. The boys rushed into the open doorway, spreading into the stables and cutting off the exits. There were mutters and a few gasps as they saw Aussie and Briar standing together shirtless.

Victor spat his accusations, 'They're perverts. And they've been living with us. Looking at us.'

'Perverts!'

'Poofters!' spat Nate.

'Yeah. Bloody girls!'

Aussie ignored the mob and focussed on Victor. 'What the hell are you on about? We were just mucking around.'

'Don't you bullshit. I saw you kissing.' Victor scowled in disgust. 'All naked together.'

'We weren't naked,' Briar intervened.

Several boys jeered disbelief. More called out and Aussie's eyes darted around trying to make out whose voices he heard.

'Listen to the little fairy.'

'Nancy boys!'

'Let's smack 'em over!'

Aussie winced at the last comment and stepped forward, shielding Briar. He tried addressing the boys, all of whom he had known for years.

'Don't listen to Victor. He's just angry at me because I stopped him hurting Briar.' The crowd seemed less sure. Their noise subsided as they listened to Aussie. 'Briar and me are mates. So what? You've all got mates. What's wrong with two mates having a wrestle?'

'You weren't wrestling!' yelled Victor.

Aussie focussed on particular boys, 'Tony, why are you listening to him? You and me are friends aren't we?' He pointed to another. 'Lucas, come on man, Briar helps you with your schoolwork.'

Victor turned to the boys. 'They *were* kissing! Of course they gonna lie about it.'

Tony pushed to the front of the crowd. 'I don't believe you. They've done nothing. Let's just leave them alone.' Some of the boys nodded their support.

Victor looked incensed. He waved a fist in Tony's face. 'Are you calling me a liar?'

'Yeah. That's exactly what you are,' Tony shoved Victor's chest.

'You fucking sissy lover!' sneered Victor. He threw a fist at Tony's head and the crowd erupted, boys yelling and taking sides.

Aussie lurched forwards to help Tony but Briar grabbed his arm. 'Let's get out of here,' he hissed. He dragged Aussie deeper into the stables and over to a ladder. He clambered up the rungs and Aussie followed him into the loft which was filled with bales of hay. 'The hay doors are over there.' Briar pointed to a wall of stacked bales.

'Oh, right,' said Aussie. They threw themselves at the hay, hauling the bales aside, desperately digging for the exit.

CHAPTER 36

HUNUA · 1954

TANE WALKED UP THE FARM DRIVEWAY from Hunua road but instead of stopping at his office, he continued to the farm house. He knocked quietly on the front door, waited for a moment then let himself in and went straight to George's study. Reaching into his jacket pocket, he pulled out the letter addressed to Johnny Chapman. He removed the cheque from the envelope and examined it. It now had an endorsement on the reverse that read *Pay to Mr George Dwyte* and an official stamp. Tane picked up a pencil and scrawled a note beside the endorsement. *Keep the farm. It's my home too.* He propped the cheque in a prominent position on the desk then exited.

Rosemary and the convent girls walked into the food tent. They did a lap of the table, nodding politely at people who were helping themselves to food. All the time Rosemary's eyes were searching for Aussie but there was no sign of him.

'I told him I'd be waiting for him by the fountain,' she turned to the girl beside her, 'maybe he didn't hear me.'

The girl shrugged. 'Well, the farm boys were in here a few minutes ago. Aussie must have been with them.'

Rosemary approached the elderly man serving wine and beer

from a trestle table. He smiled convivially as he recognised the birthday girl, hailing her in a strong Scottish accent, 'Happy birthday, young lass.'

She smiled her thanks. 'Tell me, do you know where all the farm boys went?'

He pointed down the driveway towards the stables in the distance. 'You just missed them. They headed off that way a wee while back.' He crossed his arms and leaned back against a tent pole. 'Rowdy bunch. Reminds me of me own youth. I was such a troublemaker at that age.' He took a breath ready to launch into a story but before he could start, Rosemary turned on her heel and hurried off. She gathered her girls and headed for the stables.

From the other side of the tent, George approached the bar, brandishing an empty glass. He stopped and frowned at the sight of the girls disappearing down the driveway but was quickly distracted as the barman handed him a full glass.

'Quite the shindig you've organised here.'

'Nothing but the best for that girl of mine.' George took a swig of his beer. 'Her mother wouldn't have it any other way.'

'Women, eh? Expensive habit. But worth every penny.'

'Well, you got the expensive bit right.' George glanced out of the tent and caught sight of Tane walking down the driveway from the house.

'You're back.' George stepped out the tent. 'Some of the other chaps are asking where you were.'

'Just got back a few minutes ago, Major.'

'Did you see your daughter, then?'

'Yes. Saw my girl. And we talked.' Tane trailed off.

'Talked about what?'

'Things I should have told her years ago,' Tane pulled out his tobacco pouch. 'She's an amazing young woman. I'm going to miss her.'

George raised his glass. 'To family. Because blood is thicker than water, eh?'

Tane glanced up at the farm house. 'Family isn't always about blood.'

'I guess that's true.'

Tane scanned the lawn. 'Have you seen Aussie?'

'Not for some time. Why?'

'I need to talk to him. There's something I need to put right.'

'Don't be silly, the boys can wait. Come share a glass with us men.'

Tane thought for a moment. 'Tell you what, I've got a couple of things to do but I'll come up shortly and have that drink.'

'Good man,' George winked, 'don't be too long or we might have drunk the lot. I've already paid for it and I'll be damned if I'm going to let it go to waste.'

Aussie and Briar removed the last hay bale that was covering the door. Aussie pulled the slide bolt and the door swung open. Both boys flinched as rusty hinges screeched but the noise from the mob below didn't stop.

They looked through the hay-door. The drop to the ground outside was several yards. 'Come on, let's jump,' said Aussie.

Briar's face turned pale. 'I didn't realise it was this high. I don't think I can.'

Aussie glanced around the loft. 'What if we make a landing pad? Quick, gimme a hand.' He dragged a bale towards the opening. Briar caught on immediately and, between them, they pushed three bales out of the open door. They poked their heads out to look down at their improvised cushion.

'I really hate heights,' Briar mumbled.

Aussie grabbed his shoulders and looked into his eyes. 'I'll lower you so you won't have far to jump. As soon as you land, get up to the party and find Tane.' He glanced back across the loft towards the ladder. 'I'll go calm them down.'

'No. You won't be able to calm them down.' Briar grabbed Aussie's wrist. 'I'm not leaving you. Whatever happens.'

From below, the sound of timber breaking was followed by Victor's yelling, 'And don't come back ya sissy lover.'

Aussie and Briar shared a panicked glance.

'Come on. We'll both jump,' said Aussie.

'You go first. Then catch me.' Aussie nodded as he leapt onto the bales below. He held his arms up to Briar, coaxing him to jump. Briar inched forwards and hung his legs over the edge then froze.

Another voice called from the stables, 'They went up here!' The sound of someone climbing the ladder pushed Briar to act. He leaned out then launched himself. The ground flew up at Briar and as he landed one foot slipped straight between the hay bales. He yelped as his ankle was twisted sideways.

'Come on.' Aussie grabbed Briar's wrist and pulled him off the bales. The moment Briar put weight on his foot, he let out a stifled scream and fell to his knees.

'My ankle,' grimaced Briar, 'I think I sprained it.' Above them, a face appeared in the open door. It was Red. Briar shook his head at the boy, begging him to stay silent.

Red yelled over his shoulder, 'They jumped outside! Quick, go round!'

Aussie hauled Briar up and slipped an arm under his shoulders. Before they managed a dozen steps, Victor flew around the corner.

'Gotcha!' Victor launched himself at Aussie and the three of them went down in a heap, Briar screaming in pain as his ankle twisted again. Victor grabbed at Aussie's neck. Aussie seized Victor's wrists before they could find purchase. Locked together the two of them rolled on the ground thrashing at one another, legs and elbows swinging. Briar climbed to his knees and grabbed the back of Victor's shirt. He hauled backwards and Victor slid sideways. The momentary distraction gave Aussie the chance to push himself away. He let go of Victor, leapt to his feet and grabbed Briar just as the rest of the mob came running around the building. The farm boys surrounded them in a semicircle of jeering faces. Aussie and Briar backed away until they found themselves up against the wall of the stables.

Victor was on his feet again. 'You faggots! Running like cowards. We're gonna show you what we do to nancy boys.'

The crowd's jeering turned into a chant, 'Faggots, faggots, faggots.'

'Just leave us alone. We did nothing,' said Aussie.

'Nothing! You turned Rosemary against me,' spat Victor.

'You idiot. I don't like Rosemary.'

'Let's get them!' Victor turned to rouse the mob then froze, staring past them. The crowd turned to find Rosemary and the convent girls standing by the corner of the stables. She pushed her way through the farm boys and stopped in front of Aussie.

'I've been waiting for you,' she said reprovingly. She turned to Victor who was standing with his fists clenched. 'What on earth is going on here?'

Victor spat on the ground. 'Your boyfriend here's a faggot! We caught him doing it with his sissy friend.' The mob buzzed assent.

Rosemary sneered at Victor, 'Don't be disgusting! You're just jealous. Making things up won't turn me against Aussie.'

Victor sniggered and shoved his nose in Rosemary's face. 'It's true. You're in love with a queer!'

Rosemary swung a hand out to slap Victor but he rocked back easily avoiding her. She turned to Aussie for his support. 'You tell him. Tell him about us.' Aussie pressed back against the wall. Rosemary slid her eyes down to notice Aussie's hand on Briar's wrist. She looked at their open shirts and uncertainty flickered across her face. The mob started to buzz again, a growing chorus of growls and hissed accusations with the whispers of the convent girls adding a new note.

Rosemary rounded on the crowd. 'Don't be so filthy, all of you!' She turned to Aussie. 'Tell them it's not true!'

Aussie looked defiantly at her. He slowly let go of Briar's wrist and instead took his hand, pulling Briar closer so their shoulders pressed hard together. 'Damn you all! Our feelings are nobody's business. Leave us alone!'

There was a collective gasp. Victor smirked triumphantly. A look of horror crossed Rosemary's face. Her voice rose, 'No, it can't be true! You're lying! You said you wanted to be with me. That you didn't care what society thought...' Her hand covered her mouth as she realised her misunderstanding. For a second she stared then with an enraged howl, she lunged forward and pummelled Aussie with her satin-gloved fists. 'You filthy liar! You led me on. You pretended you were in love with me.'

Victor yelled to the mob again, 'Let's get 'em!' A stone flew from the crowd hitting Aussie on the forehead and blood dripped down over his eye. Then chaos erupted.

As Tane crossed the driveway to his office, he noticed a commotion further down the hill. A group of girls was walking towards the stables. He stopped and watched as they disappeared around the corner of the building. His eyes narrowed and he grunted to himself then turned down the driveway to follow them. A few moments later noise erupted from behind the stables, a crowd yelling. Tane broke into a run.

A dozen farm boys surged forward with raised fists. Others, along with many of the convent girls, grabbed at them, yelling for them to stop. Scuffles broke out as people took sides. Dennis and Nate emerged from the crowd to flank Victor. Screaming through her gritted teeth, Rosemary was still swinging her fists at Aussie who fended off her blows.

Briar stepped forward and pushed her away. 'Leave him alone!' Rosemary turned on Briar, her eyes ablaze with anger. She landed a few blows on his shoulders and chest before two girls grabbed her elbows and dragged her back.

Aussie swung around and grabbed Briar by the shirt. 'Stay

down.' Victor threw a punch at the back of Aussie's head. Briar's eye's widened as he saw the attack coming. He reached out with both arms trying to stop Victor's fist. They connected but too late to stop the momentum of the blow. Instead the punch was deflected, grazing Aussies ear and slamming into the wall of the stables.

Victor grunted in pain then spat at Briar, 'You little queer!' He grabbed Briar by the hair and drove a fist into the side of his head. Briar collapsed to the ground, moaning incoherently.

'No!' Aussie shrieked. He punched out at Victor but Victor was ready. He ducked under the blow and came up to deliver a punch to Aussie's jaw. Aussie staggered backwards into the wall. He flicked both arms up just in time to deflect Victor's follow-up. Unbalanced, Victor stepped forwards, almost tripping. With a grunt Aussie twisted his body sideways swinging his knee up and into Victor's ribs. Victor doubled over and fell to his knees, a roar of pain forced from his throat. Dennis dropped down to help Victor. 'Get him proper.' He reached into his pocket and passed Victor a flick-knife.

Briar opened his eyes and saw Victor climbing to his feet with a knife in his hand. He tried yelling a warning to Aussie. Dennis dived on Briar and shoved him against the wall. 'Too late,' he sneered pushing his nose right into Briar's face, 'Victor's gonna fix Aussie.'

Straightening up, Victor held out the knife, pointing it at Aussie's face. 'I'm gonna cut you open!' He pulled back, gathering momentum to deliver a thrust.

'Stop! All of you!' Tane's voice clapped like thunder. The crowd stilled, turning towards the adult voice. Tane pushed through, planting himself between Victor and Aussie. 'Stop this right now!'

Victor growled, 'Get out of my way you fucking Māori! I'm gonna get that queer bastard.'

Tane held out a hand. 'You're not gonna *get* anyone. Give me the knife, Victor. Let's start acting like men.'

'Aussie's not a man,' Victor screamed and he pointed the knife at Tane. 'Get outa my way.'

Tane spat a gob of tobacco-stained saliva on the ground. 'You don't scare me, boy.'

Around the corner of the stables, Tony appeared and a second later George followed, red-faced and puffing. 'What the hell is going on here?'

Tane glanced around at George. Victor saw his opportunity and ducking sideways, he lunged at Aussie with the knife.

Tane reacted like lightening. His arms shot sideways, clasping Victor's wrists and halting the blade's thrust. Victor was spun around until he and Tane were locked with the knife between them, each straining to pull the weapon from the other's grasp.

Aussie's eyes widened in horror. 'No,' he gasped but before he could intervene, George grabbed him and yanked him out of harm's way. Victor howled with rage as his target disappeared. The muscles of Tane's arms were bulging as he strained to hold Victor's wrists but somehow his voice was calm, 'You can't win.'

'You faggot lover!' Victor threw his body forwards and redirected his thrust, no longer trying to break free, but driving towards Tane with all his hatred.

Still sprawled on his back, Briar watched the two figures above him come together. They seemed to move in slow motion. Victor's head dropped like a charging bull and his shoulders rolled forwards as he lunged. Tane leaned to his left sweeping Victor's arms down. But there wasn't time to deflect the knife. The tip of the blade pierced Tane's skin quivering for the barest second before sliding into his body, the cross guard impacting with a dull wet thud. A convent girl screamed. George rushed forwards and Tane collapsed into his arms.

Victor stood rooted to the spot, staring open-mouthed at the protruding knife. A guttural sound escaped from his throat, half gasp half growl, and he backed slowly away, the crowd parting as though he was tainted. Eventually he stumbled, turned and ran, leaping over the dropped hay bales and disappearing down the drive to Hunua Road.

Tane's hand reached up to clutch at the knife in his abdomen and he drew in a pained breath. His lips moved and George leaned closer, straining to make out his words.

'Protect them,' whispered Tane.

'Hold on, man, we'll get help.' George lay Tane on the ground, cradling his head and Tane's wound began to bleed. The blood seeped into the fabric of his shirt, a red stain opening outward from the dark hilt like the petals of a flower. George peeled off his own jacket and pressed it around the base of the knife then looking up at the horrified onlookers he bellowed, 'Someone get up to the party and get Doctor Bowles.'

Tony flinched as though he'd been woken from a nightmare. 'Doctor... yes... of course.' Then he turned and sprinted off.

George leaned down to Tane. 'Hang in there. Medic's on the way.'

CHAPTER 37

FRANCE · 1915

THE ARMY TENT WAS DARK, ONLY A THIN STRIP of dim starlight leaking in where the flap hung. Tane's eyes could barely make out the shape of snoring soldiers in the cots around him. He couldn't sleep. Instead he had spent the night fuming about Lester's threat. Despite Zach's superior rank, Tane felt driven to protect him, to protect their feelings for one another, and his mind raced searching for a way silence Lester. He lay on his cot and as night wore on his thoughts grew darker.

When Tane finally drifted off to sleep, his dreams were turbulent, full of threats and angry faces. They coalesced into a nightmare where Tane watched himself strangle Lester, and he and Zach were chased into the future hiding for all eternity. The trumpeting of reveille sliced into his dream and he woke with his heart filled with a sense of foreboding.

An hour later, it seemed his dreams were a harbinger. It was raining as he and Wiremu headed for the mess, a cold wind-driven drizzle froze their faces. Before they got as far as breakfast, the bugle signalled a quarter call. They returned to their tent to be told they should pack full kit and assemble on the parade ground.

As the company formed up, Tane watched a column of lorries rolling into camp. Half an hour later the Lieutenant Colonel announced they would be leaving immediately for the front to help repel an impending attack. The war was coming for them at full tilt. As he stood to attention in the rain, Tane felt a great weight on his shoulders. In the disciplined rows of tents surrounding him, he'd found family, he'd found friendship and at last he'd found love. The thought of losing all this was a greater burden than the heavy pack and weapons weighing him down and pressing his boots into the muddy fields of France.

He looked left and right at the lines of assembled soldiers and for the first time he understood the sacrifice these men were making. They had abandoned everything. Left behind sweethearts, wives, family and all that defined their lives. He was humbled by their commitment and wondered if his service was as worthy. They about-faced and marched towards the waiting transports and he saw that the imprint his footfalls left behind was as deep as any.

They were herded onto the vehicles, packed together like farm animals. Tane desperately searched faces for any sign of Zach but didn't see him until the truck he was on joined the convoy of vehicles crawling out of camp. As they rolled past the stables Tane recognised Zach and the other cavalry officers loading horses up a steep ramp onto a cattle truck. Tane pressed himself to the side of the lorry, hoping to catch Zach's attention. He didn't want to call out for fear of giving their connection away. Aching with frustration Tane willed Zach to look in his direction. At the last minute as the lorry was pulling away, Zach turned around and the two of them made eye contact. Fear and desperate longing passed in their glances before tents and equipment blocked their view.

Tane staggered back to his friends and they spent hours pressed together, with no room to sit, swaying around in the lorry as they were driven almost a hundred and fifty miles southeast. As the trucks ground their way across France, the Tommies smothered their fears, bragging about the fight they would give the Hun and the ground they would win. When the vehicles finally stopped, they climbed out to stretch their cramped muscles and were given a brief rest and some hard rations before they were lined up again to march the last ten miles. They struggled back into their heavy packs, formed a column and filed down muddy lanes until eventually they struck directly east across farmland towards the trenches of the western front.

Their war lasted seventy-two hours, a short and brutal reality that made a mockery of their months of training. They arrived in the reserve trenches in time for a hell-storm. Before they had unburdened themselves of their kit, the Germans started shelling their fortifications.

Tane and Wiremu were ordered to carry medical supplies to a forward supply bunker. They loaded up with crates which they carried two at a time, and followed other men along traverses that changed direction every few yards. The ground shook from exploding shells and they staggered along the timber duckboards trying to keep their heads low. When they reached the first-aid bunker to deliver their loads, they saw the first casualties from their unit. Dead men they recognised were being dragged or carried back up the supply trench. They had died before reaching the front lines. Tane and Wiremu returned for more crates but had to hastily step aside, off the duckboards and into the foul smelling mud as wounded were rushed past on stretchers, some moaning, some screaming, others deathly quiet.

As soon as the trucks were unloaded, Tane and Wiremu's unit were deployed along the front line trench to reinforce soldiers exhausted by weeks of fighting. The whole battalion was at permanent "stand-to", a level of readiness reserved for the hour before dawn or when an attack was deemed imminent. Where sentries would normally stand at the corners of various traverses, men were spread along the entire trench, perched on the fire-step, glancing from time to time over the parapets, ready to repel enemy troops.

'Get yourselves spread along the wall,' yelled a sergeant who Tane didn't recognise. 'Pair up and find yourself a gap. You're up on the half hour.'

The buddy system was familiar to Tane from his training—soldiers would pair up so each could spend a half hour on the fire-step while the other rested. He nodded to Wiremu and they threw themselves into a gap at the trench wall. Either side of them soldiers waited, seated or hunched against sandbags. They looked exhausted, despondent, barely reacting to the arrival of the new men. Every single one of them had a dirty unshaven face, red eyes and a torn, mud covered uniform. It was a far cry from the picture of clean, victorious Tommies that adorned many recruitment posters.

Tane leaned towards Wiremu. 'It's not what I expected.'

Wiremu nodded. 'You think the smell ever goes away?' Tane shrugged. Since arriving in the reserve trenches his sense of smell was overwhelmed by the odour of open latrines, the sharp stench of rancid mud and the drifts of acrid smoke that made his eyes water. In the frontline trench he could also smell the stink of filthy men.

'The medic told me they haven't had reserve time for almost a month.'

'What happened to the sixteen-day rotation?'

The Sergeant appeared again. Around them, the men started rousing and checking their rifles.

'I'll go first,' Tane said.

'You sure?'

'They already got some of our blokes with their damn shells. I hope they come soon so I can shoot the bloody lot of them.'

The Sergeant raised his arm and looked at his fob watch. 'Change,' he called and dropped his arm. The Tommies on the fire-step jumped down and the men in the trench scrambled up to take their place. Tane used the sandbags to pull himself up onto the fire-step. He watched the experienced men and followed their lead, pushing his rifle onto the top of the parapet before lifting his head just enough to peer over. Between the top of the fortification and the rim of his tin-hat, Tane surveyed a thin strip of no mans land. The ground was muddy and little green was visible. Stands of wooden pickets held entangled barbed wire. German lines were lost in the distance beyond drifts of grey smoke. The sound of a bullet and a gout of flying mud reminded Tane that he was in a precarious position with his eyes above the parapet. He pulled his head down and waited. The rules of sentry duty had been etched into his head by the training sergeants—*Short glances only. Stay still when your head's up. Shoot at anything that moves. Report movement.*

After half an hour Tane's legs were burning and his nerves were frayed, not just from the German sniper fire but because the artillery barrage did not abate. Twice during his first fire-step, mud rained down on him from nearby explosions and he started listening for the tell-tale whistle of falling rounds. The Sergeant called change and Tane jumped down with a feeling of relief. Wiremu was already scrambling up to take his place and 'keep your head down' was all Tane had time to say to him.

For two days and nights they stayed at their stations as German artillery pounded them. Each hour was torture. Thirty minutes of noise and smoke and terror followed by thirty minutes of breathless waiting. In the first twenty-four hours the casualties reduced their men by half. Wounded men, often screaming, would get stretchered away. The dead commanded less attention. Their bodies were lifted to the rear of the trench or placed into dug-outs until bearers could remove them. And there was a third sort of casualty that Tane quickly learned to recognise, men whose faces wore a haunted, empty look, men who had seen too much carnage to comprehend.

The surviving soldiers kept their vigil, climbing up to the parapet and shooting at the enemy. They felt like they were spitting into a storm. The crackle of their rifle fire was met by the crash of exploding shells. The prelude to each detonation was a shrill descending whistle and the blasts were often followed by a coda of human screams. It was the music of defeat.

On the morning of the third day, the pounding stopped and enemy biplanes appeared in the sky, buzzing backwards and forwards over their positions. Tane had only managed the briefest moments of sleep as the bombing and shooting raged continuously around him. As he looked around at the smoking craters and the endless stream of wounded on stretchers, his exhaustion made everything surreal—as though he too was flying above, looking down on himself from a great distance.

Immediately behind the lines, dozens of officers converged on a command bunker. Many of them carried scars from the days of heavy bombardment; bandages covering serious wounds or dried blood marking cuts and lacerations they had deemed too minor to treat. They assembled outside the bunker and Lieutenant Colonel Goldman stepped up to brief them, delivering his orders in rushed staccato bursts.

'The Germans have three times the artillery that was reported. They've broken through at Villefranche. If we stay here, we'll be facing them on two sides. We must retreat. A small section of our own artillery will arrive within the hour to cover our withdrawal.' He nodded at his Aide. 'Norton has my orders for each unit. We will abandon any damaged equipment. Speed is of the essence.' He faced Captain Faulks and stiffened. 'Captain, your company will not be retreating. They will provide a diversion to cover our withdrawal. Spread them along the front line and prepare them to go over the top.' He nodded to the assembled officers. 'Dismissed! Faulks, you stay.' The various officers rushed away to their respective units, several with a sympathetic glance at Faulks.

Goldman waved Faulks into the bunker. 'Our command structure is already desperately thin. I won't lose good officers in what amounts to a suicide charge.' He raised his eyebrows and tapped his sidearm. 'Get the men over the top by whatever means necessary! Then bring the officers and re-join us. You will be redeployed north.'

'Yes, Sir!' With a nod and a crisp salute Captain Faulks exited.

An hour later, the fortifications were bedlam. Piles of equipment lay everywhere and men, loaded like pack animals, struggled their way along supply trenches away from the front. In the front-line the remaining men of Tane's company were equipped only with rifles.

Tane leaned against the fire step wedged between Wiremu and Neerav. They were demoralised. The fighting they had imagined had turned out to be nothing but slaughter delivered by a faceless enemy. Tane stared at the line of corpses piled haphazardly against the far side of the trench. Casualties had mounted too fast for the stretcher bearers to keep up and now, if two men needed to pass in the cramped space, one had to step on the dangling limbs of his deceased comrades. Tane's chest tightened as he realised the distorted grey face staring back at him belonged to Mosi. A deep sadness seeped through him and he knew that, despite everything, he had been clinging to the idea that he and his friends would make it out together.

Zach appeared from the far end of the trench. He stopped on the duckboards to address the soldiers under his command; a small platoon formed of Tane's section and one other. Tane looked longingly at Zach. Since arriving to the front, Zach had been overseeing the clearing and reinforcing of a section of front line trenches and there had been neither time nor place for them to be together or even speak to one another. All they had managed was the occasional glance. Tane's heart ached to have the man he loved so close yet so far away. For a second, they looked at one another and Tane could see his own feelings reflected in Zach's eyes. It cut through his despair and gave him hope.

Zach addressed the men, 'When I give the order, we will be advancing across no mans land,' he said. 'I want one section lined up beneath each ladder. The fastest man from each section will be at the top and will be issued with wire cutters. We will be relying on you to clear the way.'

As they listened to orders, the Tommies looked around at one another. Some faces hardened for the coming ordeal, others looked nervous.

Zach straightened his back and pulled down on the front of his jacket. 'Right, lads, our time has come to show the brass we're the best company in the goddam army.' A strained cheer erupted. He pointed to two men in turn. 'Glaznee, you're the fastest in your outfit so you'll lead on ladder one. Toa, you'll lead on ladder two.'

Annoyance flashed across Tane's face. He stepped forward. 'But I'm the fastest, Sir.'

Zach kept his expression neutral. 'Yes, Chapman. I'm aware of that. You will be with me leading the charge.' Some of the men nodded taking courage from Zach's words. Tane allowed himself the briefest smile, a secret message of thanks to Zach.

Zach issued a command, 'Form lines and fix bayonets!' As the men leapt to obey, another second lieutenant entered the trench and approached Zach.

'I have new orders.' He glanced at the men then leaned forward and whispered in Zach's ear. Zach's face grew dark. 'Wait! That *can't* be right...'

But before Zach could finish, Captain Faulks appeared, carrying a revolver. He nodded to the messenger and said, 'This is the most central position. I'll give the signal from here. Inform the other lieutenants.'

'Yes, Sir!' The messenger saluted and rushed off.

Zach couldn't hold his indignation at the new orders. 'Sir, I just got told we won't be...'

'Stow it, Coe. You have your orders. Now step over here and draw your sidearm.' Zach moved to Faulks' side but he didn't draw his gun. Behind them an aide appeared carrying two saddlebags. The soldiers grew angry mutters as they began to realise what was happening.

Lowering his voice Zach pleaded with Faulks, 'This isn't right, Sir. The men need leadership. We can't abandon them.'

The Captain glared at Zach. 'We are all expendable, Second Lieutenant. You, me, all of us. These men have a job to do. We will all follow orders!'

The messenger reappeared at the southern end of the trench. He marched briskly down the duckboards glancing nervously at the grumbling soldiers. He saluted Faulks. 'All sections ready, Sir.'

Faulks nodded at the man. 'Get to your post.' As the messenger rushed off, Faulks turned and addressed the aide behind him, 'Go to the command tent and tell the sergeant to signal the artillery.' He nodded at the saddlebags the man was carrying. 'Leave those.' The Aide handed them to Zach and disappeared back into the supply trench.

Faulks checked his watch and started counting to himself. He pulled out a whistle.

A look of desperation crept onto Zach's face. He turned away from Faulks and hastily beckoned Tane over. As Tane approached him, Zach held out the bags. 'Take these, Private.'

Tane frowned. He glanced back to where Wiremu was staring nervously at the ladder then replied in a forced whisper, 'I can't desert them. They're my brothers.'

Zach responded through clenched teeth, almost in tears, 'Put down your rifle and take the damn saddles. That's an order.'

Tane hung his head. 'I... I can't.'

'Faulks looked up and noticed what was going on. He bellowed at Tane, 'Get back in line, Private!'

Zach spun around and stammered, 'Sir, we can't go without a groom. What about the horses?'

The Captain lost his cool. He yelled at Zach, 'Step back here and draw your sidearm!' There were gasps from several of the men. Faulks raised his pistol sweeping the muzzle over the two lines of soldiers. 'At the signal, you will charge!' He put his whistle in his mouth.

At that moment, the Aide returned and whispered something to Faulks who turned to the man in fustration then pulled out a pencil and notebook and began jotting words down.

Zach's face contorted with grief as Tane walked away. He dropped the saddlebags and stepped forwards, grabbed Tane and turned him around. 'I can't live without you.'

For a moment Tane was rigid. Then he opened one side of his jacket to show Zach the cufflink pinned like a medal over his heart. 'I have you with me.'

Zach choked, 'I'd rather die than leave you.'

Tane grasped Zach's forearm. 'You have to follow orders.' He smiled tenderly. 'Don't worry, I'll make it.'

Zach threw his arms out and pulled Tane into a tight, desperate hug. The two lines of soldiers stared in shock, not at two soldiers hugging on the cusp of battle but at the blatant familiarity between an officer and enlisted man.

Lester's voice spat from the far end of the trench, 'They're homos!'

Captain Faulks' howl cut through everything, 'What in heaven's name?' Faulks stepped forwards and grabbed Zach's collar, dragging him away. Tane darted back, scrambling through the men to take his place by the ladder.

Faulks gave Zach a look of pure disgust. 'You will explain that breach of discipline to a court martial.'

Lester rushed forwards. 'Captain, I saw the whole thing. I know what they been doin' for weeks. You'll need me at the court martial.'

Faulks stepped back from Lester. 'Shut up you snivelling animal!'

But Lester pressed his case, 'I saw them at it. I'm a witness.' He stepped closer to Faulks. 'You gonna need me.'

Faulks' pistol fired and Lester crumpled. There was shocked silence and the Captain turned his gun at the assembled men. 'You will follow orders. You will go out there and fight to protect your fellow soldiers.'

The sound of allied artillery fire bellowed from behind them, accompanied by the shriek of shells flying overhead.

Faulks glanced at his watch, paused for a second then blew three long blasts on his whistle.

The sound was echoed almost instantly by a whistle further along the trenches. Then another and another followed by the distant cries of charging soldiers.

The men in Faulks' trench didn't move. They stared at Zach and at Faulks with Lester's unmoving body at his feet.

Until Tane's voice rang through the trench, 'Come on! Let's get those murdering bastards.' He looked across into Zach's tearful eyes. 'Lets make our fathers proud!' With a yell he scrambled up the ladder and threw himself over the top. His action ignited the soldiers. The rest of the section followed him, their bellows uniting into a battle-cry. Zach's hand reached forwards, clutching at the shadow of his disappearing lover.

The last soldier up the ladder stopped on the parapet to unsling his rifle. His helmet jerked upwards and his body fell back into the trench with a heavy thud, head torn open. The sound of German artillery started up again, countering the sound of the allied bombardment. Captain Faulks holstered his revolver and commanded Zach to grab the saddle-bags. They turned their back on the front lines leaving the rhythms of war and death beating behind them.

Ten minutes later, mounted officers converged on the open ground behind the supply trenches. To the west, rising dust marked columns of troops marching away from the front lines. The officers wheeled their horses then galloped towards the retreating troops.

As he rode, Zach twisted in his saddle to look back at the

smoky curtain of the front, searching hopelessly for any sign of Tane. Tears streamed down his face. Cinder, confused by Zach's posture, slowed to a trot. Other horsemen thundered past them and when Zach looked forwards again he found himself at the rear of the retreating officers.

A German shell flew over no man's land. Over the charging soldiers. Over the allied trenches. It finally plunged to earth exploding in the middle of the galloping officers. Horses screamed as the ground was torn around them.

Smoke cleared to reveal carnage: half of the officers and their horses were dead or dying. Zach, at the rear of the line, had been thrown from Cinder's back. His ears rang and his vision was blurred. He dragged himself up, somehow managed to catch his scrambling horse and pulled himself back into the saddle.

Lying amongst the slaughter with his leg torn apart, Captain Faulks watched Zach mount. His hand reached out to clutch at his junior officer. 'Second Lieutenant! Assistance here!'

Zach focussed on the Captain's voice until his vision cleared. When the world swam back into focus, he retched at the carnage of horses and men. With a deep breath he steadied himself and started forwards to peform his duty to his commanding officer. As Cinder paced forwards, his hearing returned, bringing the sounds of battle from behind him. He turned and looked back.

'Over here!' Faulks' voice called again.

A sound like rolling thunder drifted from the front and Zach made his decision. Whipping his horse around he galloped back towards the lines.

He zigzagged his way around the supply trenches then spurred Cinder harder as he reached the front line trench. With a wild jump he cleared the fortification and plunged into no mans land, racing after Tane and the men of his company.

Tane, flanked by three of his section, dashed blindly into the maelstrom. Bullets tore mud from the ground and blinding light flashed through rolling grey smoke. Bent double, soldiers wove their way around craters, mud and entanglements of barbed wire. As he ran, Tane's helmet bounced awkwardly and he held it against his head with one hand, lowering it towards the oncoming gunfire. Without warning a shell exploded behind them, shaking the ground. Tane dived into a crater and two of his companions followed him. Kneeling up to peer over the crater's rim, Tane looked back to find the fourth man. He lay on the ground twenty yards away spattered in mud. As Tane watched, the soldier's shoulders moved and he levered himself up. It was Neerav. His face was all shock and confusion.

'I'm going back for him,' yelled Tane. He dropped his rifle and scrambled out of the crater. Before he could cover the thirty yards to his stricken friend, he was blown flat by another blast. Mud spattered down on him. Tane shook his head to clear his vision and looked up again. Where Neerav had been there was now a smoking hole. Crawling back to his crater, all Tane could hear was the sound of large-calibre shells whistling past in both directions, high overhead.

A moment later there was a lull. Tane and his two fellow soldiers crawled from the crater. They scrambled forwards through the mud, searching in all directions for signs of their company. The barrage suddenly began again and through the rolling smoke Tane saw men pinned down, forced flat by the constant stream of gunfire. As he watched, a lone soldier struggled to his knees only to be caught by a bullet. The man was twisted sideways and thrown onto his back where he lay unmoving, an arm protruding awkwardly into the air. Tane knew they had to move. If they stayed where they were, enemy fire or indiscriminate shells would eventually pick them off. He tried to rise but a bullet instantly tore a gout of mud from the ground beside him. A rain of shots followed, tearing the ground around them. They were pinned.

Zach burst from the murk, emerging from a drifting cloud to

leave wings of smoke roiling behind him. A cry went up. A voice of defiance and hope followed by others.

'Sir! Here, Sir!'

'The officers are coming!'

'The cavalry!'

The German guns changed targets, firing at the rapidly moving cavalry officer. Tane rose to his knees to see Zach flying through the grey blizzard, magnificent. For a fraction of a second their eyes met and Tane leapt to his feet filled with his lover's courage.

Tane screamed at the top of his lungs, 'Charge!' The remaining men rallied. Yells rose from a dozen directions and fifty soldiers stormed forwards with a renewed focus. They sprinted through hell. A machine gun spat from the German trench and the crush of mortar blasts sucked the air from their lungs. Shrapnel clawed at flesh and each yard was paid for in blood.

As he threw himself past a German listening post, Tane felt a bullet tear into his leg. Pain and shock bit into him and he fell, a scream wrung from his throat as others rushed past. Gasping at the pain, Tane dragged himself out of the slime just in time to witness a miracle. Zach galloped into a hail of bullets and launched Cinder in a reckless leap.

For a second he was flying; a moment of beautiful suspension amidst the slaughter.

Gravity returned and horse and rider crashed earthwards disappearing from sight into the German trench. Men followed, pouring through the breach into enemy lines.

Tane dragged himself up. His leg was agony and he lurched twenty paces, every step forcing a scream from his throat until he dived blindly into the trench calling Zach's name.

Tumbling down the German embankment, he splashed into a pool of muddy water every bit as toxic as the allied trench. He rolled over and dragged himself to his knees to be confronted by carnage. To his left and right, dead German soldiers lay at all angles and Tommies could still be seen fighting their way further

into German defences. Tane pushed himself to his feet and staggered over the twisted hulk of Cinder's body. Zach lay sprawled
beside his dead horse, blood oozing from a bullet wound in his
chest. Tane slumped down beside him.

'Zach! Zach! Can you hear me?'

Zach drew a wet breath, coughing bubbles of blood. His lips
moved as he tried to speak but no sound came from his throat.
With the last of his strength he moved his hand in small shivering jerks beneath his jacket then held out the black cufflink.
Tane clutched Zach's hand, enclosing the cufflink and drawing
Zach's fingers to his lips. Zach's hand relaxed in Tane's grip and
his eyes glazed.

Tane grasped his lover, holding on with all his strength. He
sobbed. He raged. Eventually he just cradled Zach's head, his lips
brushing his lover's blond hair.

CHAPTER 38

Hunua · 1954

THE AMBULANCE SPED ALONG THE Hunua Gorge Road, weaving its way through the hills. The journey was not being kind to Tane. His shoulder thumped against the wall with every turn the ambulance took. As he lay rocking and bouncing on the bed, a nurse struggled to hold a bandage in place where the knife protruded from his stomach.

George sat beside the nurse, still cradling Tane's head. He grimaced as each bend in the road sent pain through Tane body. 'Just hang in there, soldier,' said George, 'we're almost there.'

Tane coughed, a laboured wet hiss that finished in a series of short gulps. 'It's cold.' He looked up at George.

'You'll survive, Tane. Just don't think about it.' George glanced at the bandage the nurse was holding, it was soaked through with blood. 'Shouldn't be long now and we'll be out of the hills. Then it's just flat road.'

Tane coughed and the movement made him cry out in pain.

'Damn it, can't you do something?' George asked the nurse.

'I'm sorry, Sir. I've already given him morphine. Any more and he'll stop breathing.'

Tane's hand gripped George's arm. 'It doesn't matter.' His eyes rolled deliriously and for a moment he looked like he would lose consciousness. Then he focussed on George again. 'I don't think I'm going to...'

George wouldn't let him finish. 'You're going to make it. You hear me!'

'You need to look after them.'

'Who are you talking about, man?'

'Briar. Aussie.'

'Forget about the farm. It's not important.'

'Is important,' Tane struggled to speak, 'they're like me. They love each other.'

George glanced awkwardly at the nurse beside him. 'This isn't the time, Tane. Don't talk. Just save your strength.'

'You knew didn't you? About me. Me and Zach.' Tane groaned as a particularly hard bump jarred his body. The movement forced the breath from his lungs and with it came a string of bloodstained saliva.

'You're having morphine dreams, Tane.'

Tane opened his lips to respond but nothing came out except a long whimper. His eyes lost focus then closed.

George leaned down and whispered, 'Just hold on, alright. I need you.'

There were several seconds of silence then Tane's eyes popped opened again. This time his pupils were glazed, focussed on an impossibly distant point. His hand let go of George's arm and dropped to clutch the shape of the cufflink beneath his shirt. His lips moved slowly forming words, 'You wore your uniform.'

'Of course I did. A man will do anything for his daughter.'

Tane muttered again and George had to crane forward to hear him, 'I followed you. But I was too late.'

'Don't say that. It's not too late.' George gently rocked Tane's head and his voice began to crack, 'Don't go. I don't want to lose you. You're family.'

'It was worth it.'

'What are you talking about? Just save your energy.'

The barest shadow of a smile Tane's face. His eyes closed and his hands slipped from his chest, falling onto the cot beside him. Only his lips moved. George crouched even closer until his ear was touching Tane's lips.

'You ride Cinder,' breathed Tane, 'I'll follow.'

CHAPTER 39

HUNUA · 1954

BRIAR LOOKED OUT OVER THE MIST. It clung to the trees and filled the valleys in the distance like a shroud wrapping the peaks of the Hunua ranges. He had to squint as the morning sun reflected off it.

Aussie, Briar and Dee stood at the edge of the chapel courtyard, watching people arrive. Apart from the farm boys not many had come to attend the funeral. Two nuns appeared with a few convent girls. Half a dozen local farmers stood conferring with George. Edna was at the top of the chapel steps, flanked by two well-dressed ladies.

'Where's Victor?' Dee asked in a hushed tone.

'The police came last night,' said Aussie.

'Oh, right. Well, I guess it would be inappropriate if he were here.'

Tyres crunching on gravel announced the arrival of the hearse. Eyes turned to watch it glide to a halt. The driver emerged, cueing George and the farmers to lift out Tane's coffin and carry it into the chapel. An organ played a slow, reedy rendition of *Abide With Me*. The crowd filed in after the pallbearers; adults first, then the convent girls and finally the farm boys.

Dee nodded to Aussie and Briar. 'I'll see you inside.' She followed the other mourners into the church.

As her figure disappeared through the open door, Briar looked up at Aussie. 'Shall we go in?'

Aussie's eyes were puffed and he looked exhausted. 'I guess.'

Briar squeezed his hand. 'Hey, it will be okay.'

They climbed the chapel steps. As they were about to enter the church, Edna appeared blocking the doorway.

'You are *not* coming into this funeral. You caused all this,' she stepped closer and her voice dropped, 'and if I see you anywhere near my farm, I'll have the police arrest you.'

'You can't stop us paying our respects,' said Briar. 'Tane saved our lives.'

Edna's eyes flashed with anger. 'Don't you try and spread your lies,' she hissed, 'I've already explained things to the police. Victor is the victim in this.' She pointed into the chapel where Tane's coffin was resting before the altar. 'A week ago, that Māori attacked Victor in the woolshed. Punched him! Victor was just protecting himself.'

Her words cut Briar like a knife and he stepped forward in anger. 'You can't lie like that! Tane was a good man…'

'Shut your trap! I won't have Victor going to prison because of perverts like you.'

Briar tried to push past her. 'It's Tane's funeral, not yours.'

Edna shoved him back. 'That's where you're wrong. I'm paying for this funeral. I'll decide who attends. And what gets said.'

Briar stifled a scream. His hand flew up to slap her but Aussie grabbed his wrist. 'Come on. We're leaving. It's not worth it.' He dragged Briar out the doorway.

At the bottom of the stairs they were confronted by a tall Māori woman. Aussie frowned in recognition. 'I know you. I've seen you visiting the farm. You're Tane's daughter, aren't you?'

The woman nodded, 'You must be Aussie and Briar.'

'How do you know that?' asked Briar.

'Major Dwyte came and told me about my dad. He also mentioned you. Both of you. Said you might…' she tilted her head to one side contemplating them, 'that you might need some family.' She nodded towards the chapel. 'Aren't you going in?'

'We aren't welcome,' said Aussie.

The woman's eyes narrowed. 'Come with me.'

She strode purposefully up the stairs and Aussie and Briar followed her through the door and up the aisle of the church. The casket was now open and they could see Tane's reposed face.

Edna leapt up from the front pew and intercepted them, blocking the aisle, but the woman raised her arm and Edna shrank back as they walked past her.

Tane's daughter stopped beside the casket and looked down at him. He had been dressed in plain black clothes and lay on a bed of black cloth. The only decoration was the pendant that lay in the centre of his chest like a medal. The organ wavered then stopped playing and a hush descended in the church. The woman dropped to one knee and wept. The silence was filled with her grief. Briar's eyes filled with tears. He felt Aussie's arm slip around his shoulders and he leaned into him and sobbed.

Eventually the woman stopped crying. She reached into her pocket and pulled out the black cuff-link. She gently placed it beside the matching one on Tane's chest. 'Go to him, Dad. Be together.'

The woman stood up then turned and looked directly at George. He gave her a nod. She headed for the door and Aussie and Briar followed her.

As the three of them stood on the porch, Edna emerged followed closely by Father Patrick. Edna pointed at Aussie and Briar. 'They aren't welcome here,' she growled at the priest.

Father Patrick gave the boys an apologetic smile. 'This is the Lord's house. Everybody is welcome.' Edna grunted but before she could object Father Patrick addressed Tane's daughter, 'You clearly knew the deceased?'

'I'm Zac,' she said, 'Tane is my father.'

Edna snorted, 'What sort of name is Zac for a girl?'

Zac straightened to her full height. 'One I will always be proud of.' She strode past them. At the bottom of the steps she turned and placed her hands on Briar and Aussie's shoulders. 'We'll go to the cemetry together. I've arranged a tohunga.' She looked from Briar to Aussie then back again, 'I've got another suggestion but you might need time to think about it. I want you both to come with me to Wairarapa. You can live with us until you find your own way.'

For a moment Briar stared at her then with a single sob tears began running down his face. He looked at Aussie who nodded slowly.

In the chapel, the uncertain strains of the hymn started up again. Without a backward glance, the three of them walked across the gravel.

EPILOGUE

Ellerslie · 1962

'OVER THERE,' SAID BRIAR, POINTING TO A SIGN that read *1962
National Showjumping Championships.* Aussie turned the steering
wheel and they drove down a line of parked cars that stretched
forever. At the end beside the railway tracks, Aussie pulled into
the last empty space and Briar twisted around in his seat and
fished in the back to find the gift they had packed.

'I hope we're in time to see her ride,' said Briar.

'Quit worrying. She said she was competing in the afternoon.
It's barely midday.'

Briar found the parcel. He smoothed the wrapping with the
palm of his hand and adjusted the yellow bow, plucking at the
ribbon to make it stand up. 'It's squashed.'

'She won't even notice.'

'I wanted it to be perfect.'

'I reckon she'll just be glad you're here.'

They climbed out of their little Morris panel-van and headed for
the entrance, a pair of painted timber gate houses connected by a
high arch of wrought iron bearing the name Ellerslie Race Course.
Aussie glanced back at the van. 'Do you think we should lock it?'

Briar surveyed the row of fancy cars. Their van stood out, not
only for its age but because it had dents and dirt on almost every

panel. The only clean spot was the sign he had painstakingly hand-painted on the side; long narrow letters that read *A&B Wool Grading* surrounded by an emblem depicting two entwined horses' heads, one black, one white. He winked. 'I wouldn't worry.'

They passed through the gates and found themselves surrounded by a crowd of people. The air was thick with the smells of wet sawdust, candyfloss and hot pastry.

'Wait here a sec. I'm starving.' Aussie pushed his way through the crowd to a pie-van.

Briar watched people drifting past. Many of the women were in elegant pencil skirts with pillbox hats, a fashion he had only seen in shop windows in Wairarapa. Men wore turtlenecks under jackets and a few were even sporting 'mod' hairstyles. He smiled at how modern Auckland had become.

The public address system crackled and a voice blurted from speakers mounted on poles. *'Next up, Ladies and Gentlemen, we have Diana Colton competing for Auckland Pony Club.'*

Briar looked back towards the food stalls where Aussie was being handed his change. 'Come on, it's Dee. She's starting.'

Aussie wove his way back through the throng and handed Briar a hot meat pie in a paper bag. With a grin he held up two bottles of beer. 'Now we're sorted.'

They hurried towards the arena and got to the rail just in time to watch Dee canter in. She stopped for a moment to acknowledge the crowd's applause then with a flick of the rein she rode at the first jump, sailing gracefully over it. The course was long and convoluted, weaving back on itself to take in jumps that looked like hedges or piles of logs. The final hurdle was a row of cut-out timber sunflowers that would have looked equally at home as the backdrop in a theatre. They cleared every obstacle without a single fault. The crowd applauded again and as she cantered away from the last jump, Dee tipped her riding helmet in acknowledgement. Trotting out of the arena she saw Briar waving and steered her horse over to the fence.

'Well, well,' she smiled at Briar and Aussie, 'Look at you two with your matching moustaches.' She leaned down from the saddle and pecked Briar on the cheek. 'You made it. All the way from Wellington.'

'Wairarapa, actually,' he corrected her.

Dee rolled her eyes, 'Close enough. Once you're south of the Waikato, it's all wilderness.' She ruffled his hair. 'Thanks so much for coming.'

'We wouldn't have missed it for the world.'

Aussie spoke up, 'He wanted to bring his new horse so you could meet her but no matter how hard we tried, we couldn't fit her in the van.'

As they laughed a young Māori man in a bright floral shirt pressed through the crowd to join them. He was carrying a baby.

Dee made the introductions. 'Boys, this is Tom. Tom, this is Briar and Aussie.'

'We finally meet,' Tom said, as they all shook hands. 'Dee's told me so much about you.' He turned the baby in his arms to face them. 'And this,' he smiled and brushed a lock of hair from the boy's face. 'This is Michael.'

Briar leaned forwards and smiled at the child. 'Hi Michael, I'm so glad your parents finally agreed on a name for you.'

There was an exasperated sigh from Dee. 'It didn't take us that long.'

'Um, six months is definitely a long time.'

'Oh, it's easy for you to joke about it. It's not that simple. You want to get it right. To make sure it fits,' she smiled at Tom. 'I liked all the Māori names and Tom liked all the European ones.'

'So Tom won then.' Aussie raised his beer bottle in salute to Tom. 'Grab your victories where you can, mate.'

Dee's voice grew softer. 'Actually we agreed on a middle name too.' She looked at Briar. 'Tane.'

Briar stiffened, the smile disappearing from his face.

'It's for Tom's grandfather,' Dee continued, 'we both like it, but

I know you...'

Briar lifted his hand to stop her. 'No, it's perfect. I just...' his face took on a sad smile. 'Actually, it's perfect.'

Aussie put his hand on Briar's shoulder.

The crowd around them burst into applause as another competitor entered the arena. 'You boys go find some mischief to get up to,' said Dee. 'I'm competing again in forty minutes.' Her boot tapped her horse's flank and she trotted off.

Tom balanced the baby on his hip. 'I'm glad you're staying at our place.' He winked. 'Gives me an excuse to have a few beers.'

'We've been wanting to come for ages.' Briar held a hand out and the baby wrapped his little fist around Briar's finger. 'Especially since Michael Tane was born.'

'Well, looks like he's happy to meet you too,' said Tom. 'Oh, and speaking of meeting people, I want to introduce you to the guys living next door to us. They've just joined a group called the "Dorian Society" and they're looking for more members.'

They headed towards the grandstand where spectators were pouring down the stairs, leaving empty seats beckoning. They marched forwards, three men pushing against the current, carrying the past and the future with them.

Acknowledgements

Tane's War was far too long in the making. I owe so many so much. This book examines the complex and often crucial role of mentors in our life. I thank my own mentors; Dave O'Brien with his keen eye for history, his late partner Clarry Slade who provided the kernel of this story from real life, Peter Wells for opening my mind to the power of words, Ian Watt for giving honest guidance, James George for his wisdom and sensitivity to Tane's journey, Richard Galloway for offering inspiration whenever it was needed and Mike Johnson for believing in me and carrying me the first mile.

Thank you to my confidants Matt and Anna as well as my sister Gillian who struggled through my unwieldy first draft. Thanks also to my friends Nicola and Daniela, Lynn and Alison, Jordan, Calum, Sidney, Danny, Steven, Elle, Belinda, Linus, Julie, Kirsten and Tanya, all of whom gave constructive feedback, offered support or helped me believe in this story.

To my creative cohort; Katie, Maxine, Mark, Annabelle, Susan, Panisa, Lisa and all the MCWs. This would have been a blunt club without your sharpening.

My dearest thanks go to my partner Fred for keeping me focussed and honest, providing support and loving me unconditionally.

www.ingramcontent.com/pod-product-compliance
Lightning Source LLC
Chambersburg PA
CBHW030834110726
47900CB00006B/1882